Soheir Khashoggi ... .pt. A member of one of Saudi's most prominent families, she has used her influence to highlight the plight of women across the Arab world. She has participated in conferences worldwide and was a speaker at the international Women's World Forum Against Violence, an organization founded by Queen Sofia of Spain. Her acclaimed first novel, *Mirage*, was published in 1996 and was followed by *Nadia's Song* in 1999. She has four daughters and lives in New York City.

Critical acclaim for
Mirage

'One of those rare books on Middle Eastern women that is lively, provocative and thought-provoking'
Jean Sasson, author of *Princess*

'Like a modern Scheherazade, Khashoggi spins an irresistible tale of romance and heart-pounding drama in that rarest of fictions – an intelligent page-turner'
Kirkus Reviews

'Breathless, larger than life . . . Khashoggi paints in glamorous and startling colours . . . Her depiction of the rarefied, claustrophobic lives of many privileged Arab women, as well as of the jet-set world of their families, adds depth and sparkle'
Publishers Weekly

Nadia's Song

'Soheir Khashoggi has smoothly combined meticulous historical accuracy with intense insight into the human heart to peel away layers of nationality in this fascinating story of divided loyalties, forbidden love, and tender camaraderie caught up in the clash between British imperialism and Egyptian patriotism'
Jean Sasson, author of *Desert Royal*

'Utterly enthralling . . . Khashoggi grips the imagination' *Daily Mail*

Also by Soheir Khashoggi

MIRAGE
NADIA'S SONG

and published by Bantam Books

MOSAIC

Soheir Khashoggi

BANTAM BOOKS

LONDON · NEW YORK · TORONTO · SYDNEY · AUCKLAND

MOSAIC
A BANTAM BOOK : 0 553 81410 9

First publication in Great Britain

PRINTING HISTORY
Bantam edition published 2003

3 5 7 9 10 8 6 4 2

Set in 10.5/12pt Sabon by
Phoenix Typesetting, Burley-in-Wharfedale, West Yorkshire

Bantam Books are published by Transworld Publishers,
61–63 Uxbridge Road, London W5 5SA,
a division of The Random House Group Ltd,
in Australia by Random House Australia (Pty) Ltd,
20 Alfred Street, Milsons Point, Sydney, NSW 2061, Australia,
in New Zealand by Random House New Zealand Ltd,
18 Poland Road, Glenfield, Auckland 10, New Zealand
and in South Africa by Random House (Pty) Ltd,
Endulini, 5a Jubilee Road, Parktown 2193, South Africa.

Printed and bound in Great Britain by
Cox & Wyman Ltd, Reading, Berkshire.

Papers used by Transworld Publishers are natural, recyclable products
made from wood grown in sustainable forests. The manufacturing
processes conform to the environmental regulations of the country
of origin.

Dedication

This book is dedicated to the memory of my dear friend Michele Heidenberger who died on September 11th. Her affection and friendship and the mutual admiration we shared will live forever in my heart.

Acknowledgements

To Lillian Africano, I owe special gratitude for her devotion and dedication in making this book possible. It has been a fun project; we did it again. Thank you, Lillian for all your help – as always it's great working with you.

To my children, Samiha, Naela, Farida and Hana: my heart is tied to a cord which can never be broken. You have been my inspiration and my strength; you have made it possible for me to write yet another book.

To the memory of my beloved mother, for all the love and confidence she instilled in me.

To my family, I am grateful for your love, support and belief in me, without which I could not continue writing.

To all my wonderful friends who stood by me through the ups and downs and listened and cheered me up supporting me every step of the way. I love you all.

Special thanks to my very fine agent, Liv Blumer, who made it all possible.

PROLOGUE

Gone.

The twins. Gone. Taken.

Dina couldn't grasp it, couldn't make it seem real, despite the dead silence of the townhouse, the clothes missing from the children's closets, despite even the note from her husband. It had to be his idea of a joke. A punishment. In the kitchen she glanced expectantly at the big refectory table, as if, this time, if she could only get it right, Suzanne and Ali would be in their chairs, eagerly awaiting the treats she had for them.

CHAPTER ONE

It was a beautiful spring day in New York, the kind of day that made it possible to believe that the terrible events of 2001 would not hold the city forever in their grip.

Dina awakened early. She looked down on her sleeping husband, her body remembering their love-making the night before. It had been a long time since Karim had approached her with such passion, such hunger. She had responded in kind, and for a time all was as it had been during the early days of their marriage, when love was new and sex all-consuming. 'I love you, Dina,' he'd murmured over and over. 'Know that I love you, no matter what.'

How handsome he is, she thought, as she lightly stroked his face. His skin, under the morning bristle, was the color of cafe au lait, his dark wavy hair was lightly silvered, his mouth generous and quick to laugh. The lashes were as thick as a movie star's, his cheekbones high, and his patrician nose more Roman than Arab. He'd laughed when she told him that. 'For you, I'll be a Roman,' he said, 'or a Greek or whatever you want.' He was certainly joking, for during the years of their marriage, Karim had only become more

11

and more Arab. More traditional. More – whatever she was not.

She slipped into her robe and slippers, made the Kenya coffee Karim liked and brought it to him in bed, something she hadn't done for a long time. He opened his eyes slowly and gazed at her with such longing that she almost gave up the idea of going to work. Almost. But it was to be an important day at *Mosaic*, the floral design business that she'd created and nurtured for so many years. There was an important order to fill for Daniel Bouloud's new bistro and a meeting with the owner of a new boutique hotel. Dina – and *Mosaic* – hadn't become regular items in *New York* magazine and the *New York Post* gossip columns by taking days off. Not when there were so many others who would gladly take over what she had so painstakingly built for *Mosaic*: a reputation as Manhattan's premier floral design boutique.

Still, she lingered, sipping coffee with her husband, then nestling into his arms for a few delicious moments. It felt so warm, so cozy, that she had to force herself out of bed. She dressed quickly but carefully. In New York's highly competitive atmosphere, keeping herself attractive was good business, not simply personal vanity. Dina was a perfect size six, even after three children and twenty years of marriage; her luxuriant chestnut-brown hair, unmarred by gray, was cut in a soft chin-length bob that framed and flattered her oval face. Her hazel eyes were clear and bright, her fair skin almost unlined, thanks to heredity and occasional visits to a top dermatologist.

After a quick shower and a light application of make-up, Dina slipped into one of the designer suits that were her work uniform. By the time she went back downstairs, Fatma, the children's nanny, was already bustling about in the kitchen. A spinster cousin of Karim's, Fatma was as punctual in her ways as an old-time railroader. According to the household's usual schedule, breakfast should already have been prepared for the eight-year-old Ahmad twins, Suzanne and Ali. Since Dina had not been present to do the cooking, Fatma had taken over, and the meal was now underway, but under protest.

'Mommy, you're supposed to give us breakfast,' brown-eyed Suzy complained, 'but you were still sleeping.' And Ali, a carbon copy of his sister, but with shorter curly brown hair, agreed loudly.

'All right, all right,' Dina said, accepting the guilt that was constantly thrown her way, simply because she was trying, not always successfully, to be three people: wife, mother, career woman. 'Well, since I goofed on breakfast, how about lunch? What if I have Fatma bring you to meet me in the park? We'll have hot dogs and a nice visit. Would you like that?'

A loud 'yay' signaled that the twins would indeed like that – and Dina thanked God that children were so quick to forgive and forget. Would that adults were so easy.

She glanced at Fatma and repeated her wish to have the children picked up from school and brought to the park. The older woman grunted an assent. Fatma had lived with the family for some fifteen years, yet Dina still hadn't figured out how to deal with her in a way that was mutually satisfactory. Dina always had the sense that Fatma disapproved of her; for her part, Dina found the woman dour and unlikeable. Ah, well, in spite of Fatma's difficult personality, those of

13

Dina's acquaintances who were constantly hiring and firing nannies envied her a nanny who stayed – and stayed.

When Dina arrived at work, her assistant, Eileen, was already looking frazzled. After a quick conversation, Dina understood why: Bouloud had asked for orchids to be prominently featured in his arrangements, but the morning delivery had brought no orchids. It would mean indignant phone calls to the supplier, who would insist the mistake had been Dina's, followed by begging phone calls to other shops, and pleas for enough blooms to fill her order.

The morning brought other problems as well. A well-known editor of a shelter magazine wanted Dina to style the dinner setting on an antique table that was to be featured on an upcoming cover. Another coup for *Mosaic* – except that the job had to be done within three days.

She was tempted to call off the lunch with her children, but something stopped her. Perhaps it was the thought of letting them down twice in one day. The meeting with the hotel owner was not until after lunch, and the prospect of an hour in the park, of putting aside the pressures of constantly marketing herself, suddenly had great appeal.

In spite of being so busy, Dina arrived early in the designated area. She staked out a bench and waited, closing her eyes for a moment and allowing the April sun to warm her face. The weather was unseasonably mild, and Dina enjoyed the pleasures of spring after a hard winter.

When she opened her eyes, she saw them approaching: Dark, heavy-set Fatma in her long dress and headscarf, and her two curly-haired angels, twin bundles of energy, bounding towards her. She rushed towards them, wrapped them in her arms and inhaled their fragrance. No longer babies – they were growing quickly now, a constant reminder to Dina that she spent all too many hours away from them.

As she had promised, Dina threw out her rule about eating only good food at mealtimes and bought hot dogs and cream sodas, which the children devoured enthusiastically. Fatma declined the treat, unwrapping the pita sandwich she'd brought and consuming it slowly and methodically and without any visible pleasure.

'This is so nice, Mommy, can we do it again tomorrow? Can we, can we?' Suzy begged, and again guilt tore at Dina. Such a small thing was being asked of her: just to give a bit more of herself to the children she loved more than life itself. She ruffled Suzy's hair, patted her dimpled cheek, and looked into the enormous dark eyes that reminded Dina of her mother-in-law, Maha. While there was no denying that Maha must have been very attractive in her youth, Dina was glad the resemblance ended with the eyes – she had found it very hard to like the woman who had never really accepted her.

'Not tomorrow,' Dina said, 'but soon. I promise. Very soon.' The children seemed content with that.

Fatma got up from the nearby bench and prepared to take them back to school. 'Kiss Mother goodbye,' she instructed in her heavily accented English. Strange, Dina thought, Fatma had never before cared about displays of affection. Oh, well, maybe the beautiful day had affected her, too. The twins kissed her, loudly and with gusto, and Dina kissed back, laughing, and wishing suddenly that she could take the afternoon off, tell her babies that they could have the afternoon off, too. How pleasant it would be to stay here in the park, enjoying the sunshine and the lush green surroundings. But there was still too much to do at *Mosaic*.

She sighed and turned away, walking quickly back to work with the children's farewell tucked away in her heart.

The meeting with Henry Charenton, the hotelier, went well. He'd seen some of her trademark floral arrangements in a Chelsea boutique hotel and wanted to know if Dina could provide his hotel with arrangements that were 'beautiful, but sophisticated'. She could. *Mosaic* specialized in arrangements that were as unique as they were beautiful, and Dina spent the next half-hour showing Charenton the many books of photographs that backed up her reputation. Yes, Charenton said, yes, contracts would be drawn up immediately, with the first arrangements to be delivered early next month.

Shortly after the meeting concluded, Eileen signaled to Dina that there was a phone call for her.

'Take a message.'

'It's your mother.'

'I'll take it in my office.' Ever since Dina's father had undergone surgery for colon cancer, she had been on the alert for every bit of news her mother could give.

'Mom,' she said breathlessly. 'Is something wrong?'

'No, sweetheart, no, nothing's wrong. I just want to thank you for the thoughtful gift you and Karim sent over this morning.'

'Gift?'

'Yes, sweetheart, the dried fruit. Karim said he picked it up in Brooklyn – on Atlantic Avenue. He said he knew how much your father loved the apricots and figs. He hoped they might restore his appetite.'

'Oh. Yes.' Dina hadn't known that Karim had been to the Arab shops on Atlantic Avenue – or that he'd sent a gift to her father. Why hadn't he mentioned such a lovely gesture? she wondered. Joseph Hilmi hadn't been doing well lately, and the latest round of chemo had left him nauseous and without much appetite. How sweet of Karim to try to help. She knew that he had been very busy, too, these past few weeks.

When she hung up the telephone, Eileen was standing in her doorway, signaling again, but Dina just shook her head and dialed Karim's office.

He picked up on the first ring, though his secretary, Helen, usually answered the phone.

'Dina,' he said, 'what a surprise.' That was true enough. She rarely called his office these days. When they were first married, they talked on the phone at least once a day.

'Thank you,' she said. 'Thank you for sending the fruit to my father.'

'It was nothing, Dina, you know I'm very fond of your father. And I'm sorry he's been so ill. I thought if there was something to tempt his appetite . . .'

'Thank you anyway. And Karim . . .'

'Yes?'

'Why don't I try to get away a little early today? It's been crazy around here, but if I whirl and spin for the next couple of hours, Eileen can finish up. I could defrost those grape leaves I made last month – and I can pick up some fresh pita and a special dessert. We'll have a nice evening together,' she finished, thinking how good it would be to build on the warm feelings of last night and this morning.

'Ah, well, I—'

'What's wrong? Will you have to work late tonight?'

'No, Dina, I won't be working late tonight.'

'Great. I know I've been preoccupied with the business lately, but I really do want to spend more time with you and the children.'

There was a long silence, and for a moment, Dina thought the connection had been broken. 'Karim?'

'Yes, Dina, I'm still here.'

'Well, then, I'll see you later. Bye now.'

'Goodbye, Dina.'

True to her word, Dina stepped up her pace to finish work that could not wait. Then she left instructions on what remained to be done and headed out the door, leaving a puzzled Eileen in her wake.

She hurried to Grace's, picked up a package of pita, some yogurt and cucumbers for a salad to accompany the grape leaves. She chose a raspberry tart for Ali, cannoli for Suzy and herself, and chocolate mousse cakes for Karim and Fatma. Dina always bought enough for Fatma, though the older woman often refused the treats she brought home.

Fatma had been difficult lately. Was sullen the word? But that seemed to suggest that she had once been cheerful, which was not the case – at least not in the fifteen years since Karim had brought her over from his native Jordan, more as a kinship responsibility to her, it seemed, than as a help to Dina.

Possibly the woman was missing the old country,

the old ways, Dina thought as she fumbled with the keys. Or entering menopause. Or maybe it had something to do with September Eleventh and its aftermath. Whatever it was, it made her presence an uncomfortable one.

Dina had debated speaking with Karim about it. But with the other points of dispute between herself and her husband – mainly centered around the cultural differences that seemed to have grown over the years – she didn't want to raise another. She had lived with Fatma and her moods for so many years, she would just put up with her a while longer. And then maybe she'd say something to Karim.

Dina called out as she entered the house. No answer. She shouted upstairs – there were three full floors and a basement, a vast space by New York standards. Nobody was home. But there was nothing unusual in that. Perhaps Fatma had taken the twins back to the park after school. If so, they would be back any minute, before the first hint of twilight. After all these years in the city, Fatma still held the outsider's belief that to be on the streets when darkness fell was madness.

The first hint of something wrong was the absence of a note. Difficult or not, Fatma was meticulous in every duty that related to the children. She could not write in English herself, but always had one of them scribble a message as to their whereabouts and placed it solidly under the wooden peppermill on the kitchen table (for some reason she disliked the refrigerator-door magnets that Dina had purchased for this specific purpose).

Dina felt uneasy, but told herself there was no

reason. If the twins were excited enough, they could distract an invading army, and Fatma might simply have forgotten the note. Or maybe Suzanne and Ali had neglected to write it, or had stuck it in his or her pocket in the rush. Or whatever.

On an impulse she checked the answering machine. No messages.

She took a glass from the cupboard and filled it with filtered water from her state-of-the-art refrigerator.

The light outside was distinctly falling.

Had Karim come home early and taken them all out somewhere? For ice cream, say? It seemed unlikely. After all, she'd made it clear that she was planning a special family dinner. She called his office.

The call gave her the first chill of real fear.

'Mr Ahmad is unavailable,' the woman who answered the phone informed her. Dina didn't recognize her voice. She certainly wasn't Karim's secretary, Helen.

'This is his wife. Do you know if he left for home?'

'He's not in the office. That's all I can tell you.' Coldly remote, as if Dina were some kind of crank.

'Is Helen there? May I speak with her?'

'Helen is not available.'

'What do you mean not available?'

'She's not here. Neither is Mr Ahmad. Do you wish to leave a message?'

'Have him call me. As soon as he can. It's . . . it's important.'

It made no sense. But surely there was a reasonable, very ordinary explanation: some emergency meeting, something that required not only Karim's personal attention, but also Helen's.

Oh, God, what if Suzanne or Ali had been hurt at

school? Could Helen have driven Karim to the hospital?

Surely not. That was far-fetched.

She told herself to be calm. No need to get into a silly panic. Wait a bit. Take a deep breath. Fifteen minutes. Then call – who? Her mother? No. She would not worry her mother. Maybe check with neighbors. Andy, the newspaper vendor on the corner? He saw everything that happened on the block.

Dina went into the bedroom to change from the charcoal silk suit she had worn at work into her favorite sweats. It was as if their comfortable familiarity could restore routine, allay fear.

When she turned towards the bed she saw the note – the letter, actually.

Dear Dina, it began, and continued in what she recognized as Karim's formal mode, *I wish you to know that I have reached this decision only after long consideration. I have concluded what I think is best.*

As you know, we have discussed, many times and in detail, my concerns about the influences to which Ali and Suzanne are subject . . .

Oh God, oh God, what was this about? Her heart began to hammer in her chest and her breath caught in her throat. She forced herself to continue reading.

. . . and especially, as you know, I am concerned for Ali, that he will not be influenced like his brother. But for Suzanne, too, I am concerned . . .

Dina read more words, words she'd heard before about the shortcomings of American society. But then:

For these reasons, and so that they know their other heritage, I have decided to take Ali and Suzanne with me, home, to my home, Jordan.

'No!' she sobbed. 'No! No! No!' Her voice sounded

distant and far away, and the room began to tilt. She tried to breathe deeply, to steady herself so that she could finish reading.

There were some sentences about money. There were funds in the joint account, she would want for nothing. She hardly read them.

The children will be well, you should not fear for them. You know that my family, as well as I, will care for them. I have found work in Jordan also, an important job already arranged for . . .

A job? Karim had taken a job in Jordan? He had planned for God only knew how long to take her children? The same Karim who said he loved her? It didn't make sense.

By the time you read this, we will be on our way. I will call to let you know we've arrived safely, but please understand that you will not change my mind. This is my decision. It is not what I would have wished for, years ago, but I think it is the best for our children. It is not my intention to hurt you, though I know you will think so . . .

She set the letter on the comforter and stared, as if it had fallen from space. She couldn't believe it. It wasn't real.

Like a sleepwalker, she staggered into the children's room. Some clothes were gone. Favorite books and toys.

Fatma's room was cleared out. Of course she would have gone with them.

Jordan. It had to be a mistake, she told herself, Karim's idea of teaching her a lesson.

Years ago she had read a magazine article on foreign husbands who left their American wives and took the children back to Germany or Greece or Saudi Arabia or wherever. She had not imagined it might be relevant to her life. It was simply not something that could happen between Karim and her, no matter what their disagreements, their difficulties.

She went back to the bedroom and buttoned the blouse she had started to take off. She went down to the kitchen and leaned the letter against the peppermill where a note from one of the twins should have been.

This doesn't feel real, she thought, none of it feels real. It was like some horrible nightmare, but she knew she would not be waking up. She had to do something. Call someone. Her mother? No. Not yet. The news would crush her. And her father . . . in his fragile state, it might kill him. No. Maybe something would happen. Maybe Karim would change his mind. Hadn't he said he loved her? Maybe they were all in a cab driving from the airport at this moment.

But they weren't. She could feel it. She could hear it in the unnatural silence of the apartment.

'Please God,' she whimpered, 'please, please, please . . .'

Suddenly she thought of her older son. She was going to have to tell him about this. How would he handle it? Blame himself? She would have to protect him from such a feeling.

But that would be hard, especially since her son – his name was Jordan, too, after his father's homeland – *was* clearly part of what had set Karim on this course. She could put off telling Jordy for a while – he was some two hundred miles away. He didn't have to know that their family had been shattered, that just the two of them remained.

What to do *now*? that was the question.

She had friends. People from work. Couples with

whom she and Karim socialized. Acquaintances, she realized, was a better word. There were really only two people she could lean on in this greatest crisis of her life.

She picked up the phone.

CHAPTER TWO

'Jeez,' said Arnie Stern. 'Frick and Frack.'

'You sure these guys aren't married?' said Tom Wu.

'But it works, doesn't it?' said Emmeline LeBlanc, who was, after all, the star of the *Em–New York* show – not to mention the producer. 'I mean, *doesn't* it?'

Arnie was the show's director; Tom, the editor. The show they were now viewing on Tom's computer had been recorded that afternoon. It was about home security, an evergreen topic in New York, where it generally meant apartment security. The two guest experts were Mary Ann Cangelosi of the NYPD, burglary detail, and Morty Mortenson, a career burglar, supposedly 'retired' after dozens of jobs and three sojourns upstate, courtesy of the Department of Corrections. For some reason Mary Ann and Morty, who looked like everybody's favorite uncle, had hit it off from the very first, playing off each other like a dance team.

They had covered locks, alarms and dogs, and were now winding down with a cautionary discussion of guns. Mary Ann's take was simple: guns were in many cases illegal – and in all cases more dangerous to the owners than to potential intruders. Morty grinned and nodded. 'I always hated it when I came across a gun in one of the homes I visited,' he said and waited like a veteran member of the Screen Actors Guild for the audience laugh, which came as if on cue. 'Not because I was worried about *them*. Seriously, folks, I never carried a gun in my life, but there are some *bad guys* out there. They'll take your gun away and use it on you before you can blink. Get a dog. The worst they do is pee on the rug.'

'Oh yea,' Arnie reassured Emmeline. 'It works.' Tom nodded emphatically, or as emphatically as he ever did anything. Both men, in fact, had crushes on their boss. Arnie, fifty-something and on his third marriage, saw her as the exotic younger woman he'd love to parade at cocktail parties and in the East Side watering holes he frequented. After a few drinks he had once described her to a colleague as 'a Louisiana Masai princess'. He had never seen a Masai princess in person and had been to Louisiana only once, for Mardi Gras, but that was beside the point.

To Tom, fresh out of NYU, she was simply a very exciting woman. The fact that she was a dozen years older than he was – and six inches taller – did not affect his fantasies. There were times when he had almost physically to restrain his hand from reaching out to touch her arm or cheek, just to see if her chocolate skin felt as soft as it looked.

'I'll just switch that spot where Mary Ann's looking at camera two,' he said.

'Anything else?'

Arnie shrugged. 'Not by me.' They both looked at Emmeline.

'Me either,' she said. 'Except that I look like I'm

26

running a dating service or something – just along for the ride.'

'The great ones make it look so easy,' said Arnie. 'Good to go, Thomas.'

Emmeline stood. 'All right, then,' she said and mimicked Vivian Leigh's Scarlett. 'Tomorrow is anothah da-yay.' Tomorrow they had only one show – about the art of getting and riding a taxi in New York. Not exactly an earthshaking issue, but like everything else Em dealt with on her lifestyle show, *Em* – the poor, Creole Martha Stewart, as she jokingly called herself – it would be as lively and engaging as she could make it. That was why *Em–New York* had a good – for cable – and steadily growing audience share. Even now, Emmeline's agent was pitching in to the networks.

She felt pleasantly drained. A good day's work. It might be only a cable show, but it was her baby and she loved it. And even if *Em–New York* never made it into the golden land inhabited by Oprah and Oprah wannabes, it was still a long, long way from cooking jambalaya in Grosse Tête, Pointe Coupée Parish, Louisiana.

'Early night,' Arnie commented. It was. Often the three of them sat diddling the tapes into the wee hours. 'Anyone for a libation?'

Emmeline was about to decline politely – she wanted to get home at a civilized hour for once, before her son Michael and her boyfriend Sean forgot who she was – when her assistant Celia poked her head in the door and said, 'Call for you, Em. Dina Ahmad. Says it's important.'

Emmeline went to the semi-private cubicle that served as her office to take the call. 'Hey, girl,' she said easily. The ease quickly left her manner. 'What? Slow down. Tell me again. He what?' She listened intently. 'All right, you hang in there, kiddo. I'm on my way. Yes, I'll call her. Hang in there.'

She hung up and glared at the phone. 'That *couillon!*' she said. She had not used the word in a decade. It literally meant 'fool, imbecile', but in its fullest sense it referred to the trashiest kind of person or behavior. She was applying it now to Karim Ahmad.

CHAPTER THREE

Sarah Gelman heard the chirp of her pager but ignored it. At the moment a little girl named LaKwinta Thomas was more important than some pain-in-the-ass call from the office. At age five, LaKwinta had acquired a case of penicillin-resistant gonorrhea. Others were dealing with the *how* of that depressing fact. Sarah's job was the *what*: the physical illness. Curing it.

She made a note on the chart to change the girl's medication to rocephinol. Maybe it would do the trick. Even if it did, in another year or two the disease would show up in a resistant strain. There were millions of people who gobbled antibiotics every time they sneezed, and it had only gotten worse since the goddam terrorists started doing their bit and threatening the city with all manner of biological horrors. And of course a big part of the problem was the thousands of her colleagues who would write a scrip just to get some twitching hypochondriac out the door and off their backs. The result was that the lab wonks were in a perpetual race with micro-organisms exercising their God-given right to survival of the fittest.

Sarah talked with the duty nurse to make sure the

medication change was understood. Only then did she check the beeper.

To her surprise, the call was from Emmeline. What could that be about? Em knew that this was her day at Lenox Hill. Some kind of emergency? Nah. More likely an impromptu Girls' Night Out. Good. It was overdue. It would be good to let her hair down, have a few drinks, dish acquaintances, co-workers and ghosts of husbands past (her own ex, Ari), present (Dina's Karim), and possibly future (Em's Sean, although in Sarah's book that one was beginning to look like a long shot).

She made a mental note that, wherever the gossip and confidences led, this time she would *not* mention the goddam *get*. It was boring to everyone but her. No one else understood it. Or if they understood it, they did not consider it terribly important.

She and Ari had divorced three years earlier, relatively amicably except for one thing: Although they were divorced in the civil, legal sense, Ari would not grant her a *get*, a divorce in the eyes of her Jewish religion. Why, she didn't know. Maybe because he knew it mattered to her. Though she didn't think of herself as zealously religious, her faith was important to her. She did want the damn thing. She wanted a fresh start, recognized by the State of New York and sanctified by her faith. If she were to meet someone, if it were to become serious . . . well, the chances of *that* were looking fairly slim, too. Seeing that she had no social life beyond the occasional Girls' Night Out and even-more-occasional so-called dates with other doctors that invariably ended up with both of them playing beeper tag.

She walked to the doctors' break room and picked

up a phone. Em's assistant – Stella? – Sarah couldn't remember – sounded as if she had spent her middle-school years at the Royal Academy of Dramatic Arts. She also sounded harassed. She said that Ms LeBlanc was on another line. Sarah gave her name and said that she was returning Ms LeBlanc's call.

'Oh, it's you, Dr Gelman,' the thespian said. 'She's expecting you. Hold on, I'll put you right through.'

Five minutes later she hung up in shock. What kind of *mishegoss* was this? Had Karim Ahmad gone completely crazy?

She dialed Dina's number. It rang several times before her friend answered and said, 'I'll call you right back, I'm on the phone with the police.'

'Don't call back, I'm on my way,' Sarah told her, with no idea if Dina had waited long enough to hear her. The miracle of call waiting.

She quickly slipped out of her whites and into street clothes. For half a second she thought of keeping the whites on for this crisis. Emmeline had hatched some wild idea that Karim and the kids might still be on the ground and that it might be necessary for them all to go to the airport. Sarah briefly envisioned herself striding into the control tower. Stop that plane. I'm a doctor.

That was the trouble with standing five-two in heels and still wearing a size six: people didn't take you seriously. She noticed that Emmeline, at six-one, got taken seriously just by walking into the room. On the other hand, Em complained that she had spent her whole life being treated like a giraffe.

As her car cleared the hospital garage, Sarah was thinking that her immediate role in this crisis was going to be that of the voice of reason: to give whatever support was needed, to counsel a little calm. After all, one of the first lessons you learned in medicine was that no matter what you saw on TV, heroic measures were the exception rather than the rule. Most things got better in the morning.

She checked to make sure the 'Physician on Call' placard was in place atop the dash. Parking was a bitch in Dina's neighborhood. In which respect, Sarah reflected, Dina's neighborhood was a lot like life.

CHAPTER FOUR

Calling the police had been a stupid idea. Or at least naïve. Dina understood that now, as she tried to make Officer Frances Malone understand what had happened. No, this was not about domestic violence. And no, it was not about a dangerous situation in the home. It was about her husband snatching her children and taking them out of the country.

'Let me make sure I understand, Mrs Ahmad,' the officer repeated slowly, as if speaking to someone who was not familiar with the English language. 'You say the children are with their father?'

'Yes.'

'And you have no reason to believe they're in any danger?'

'No, but—'

'And their father is your husband, is that right, ma'am?'

'Yes.'

'Not divorced? No custody judgment outstanding, anything like that?'

'No.'

'And there's been no violence? No threat, nothing of that kind?'

'No. He just took them out of their school. I called the principal before I called you. She said he and the nanny picked them up. And now he's on his way to Jordan. That's in the—'

'I know where that is, Mrs Ahmad,' Officer Malone said, a bit sharply.

'I'm sorry, but you don't seem to understand,' she said, desperation growing. 'He's taken my children and he doesn't intend to bring them back.'

The officer's tone softened. 'I do understand, Mrs Ahmad – we've had a couple of cases like yours – and I wish I could help, believe me, but it's out of my hands. This isn't a police matter. Your husband hasn't broken any laws, so there's nothing I can do.'

'But—'

'Mrs Ahmad, with all respect, ma'am, what you need is a lawyer.'

Dina stared at the telephone. A lawyer? Could a lawyer bring her children back? Karim used a lawyer, Carlton Harris – was that his name? – for a few things. Dina had met him when they signed papers for the house. Should she call him? Some instinct told her not to. Not yet. He was really Karim's lawyer, not hers. But she had to do something or she'd lose her mind. Hell must be like this: waiting, knowing nothing, fearing everything.

Once again she grasped at the possibility that it wasn't really happening at all. At least not in the way it seemed. Maybe Karim was just bluffing, trying to gain some advantage over her. Any minute now . . .

But she knew better.

Once again she longed to call her mother. And once again decided to postpone it as long as possible.

Tonight, she told herself. Or tomorrow. If nothing happens.

She poured herself another glass of water. Karim's letter was still there on the table. She sat with her drink and read it slowly now, as if the words themselves might somehow lead her to a solution. He didn't want the twins subjected to the prejudice he'd faced himself. Didn't she remember how they'd suffered after the World Trade Center tragedy? How they came home crying that they didn't want to have an Arab name because Arabs were bad? Surely she could see why he didn't want them growing up in New York? But Dina couldn't see.

After all, her own father had been born in Lebanon. Even though he'd emigrated to America when he was sixteen, he'd brought many of his customs – and his native cuisine – into his marriage to her Irish-American mother. In spite of their cultural differences – and on occasion because of them – Joseph and Charlotte Hilmi had built a rich and strong marriage.

Dina, though she loved her Lebanese relatives, the country, the warmth, and the food, had never thought of herself as anything but American. The Arab part of her was like a warm and loving aunt who lived far away, someone Dina could visit and embrace from time to time, bask in affection and memory – and then return home, to her American self.

Yes, Dina had heard her share of cruel remarks since September Eleventh, but for the most part people didn't make assumptions about her because of her last name. And what was the prejudice Karim had encountered? A deal that didn't happen? A rude cabbie? You didn't run away from things like that, you got past them.

35

Yes, Dina had felt terrible when the twins came home crying. She had spoken to them, explained that some people behaved badly when they were scared. She had promised the taunting would stop – and it had. After she'd spoken to the twins' teacher and their principal – and after the class (and later, the entire school) had been lectured on the subject of prejudice. Dina had taken action to protect her children; didn't that show she loved them as much as Karim did? More, really – for had he even asked himself how they were going to fit in Jordan? A culture that was, for the most part, foreign to them?

. . . and especially, as you know, I am concerned for Ali, that he will not be influenced like his brother.

That was it, she thought bitterly. That was the crux of the problem, the real reason that this had happened.

The doorbell sounded. Dina had a vivid image of a policeman come to tell her something about the children. But it was Sarah's voice on the intercom.

Into each other's arms, a long hard hug. Then Sarah stepped back. Dina recognized the Doctor Gelman look: what does this child have and what can I do about it?

It was incredibly comforting.

Dina burst into tears.

CHAPTER FIVE

At 38,000 feet there was still light in the sky, though the earth below was in darkness. Soon there would be a meal and then a movie. Meanwhile, the screen at the front of the first-class cabin showed the aircraft's altitude, ground speed and progress. Karim did not need it to know that they were passing the eastern tip of Newfoundland: he had flown this route many times, and from his portside window seat he recognized the lights of the little landfall town of Gander. Ahead lay the black of the open North Atlantic. The arc of a great circle would swing them near the coast of Ireland before the last leg to France.

As familiar as it was to him, this flight was like none Karim had ever taken. For the past hour, with each mile more distant from New York, from America, he had felt tension draining from him, as if it were some fluid whose drop could be observed and measured.

It was all right now, he told himself. He had done it.

The long wait in the airport had been hell: two long hours worrying that something might go wrong, that simply because of their ethnicity he – or perhaps Fatma – might be stopped, pulled out of line, detained. He knew people to whom it had happened in the months since September Eleventh. It could happen to anyone with a name and features like his.

But there had been only the now-routine heightened security: the tedious searches and questions.

Even after they were airborne, he had fretted that the plane might turn back – mechanical trouble, even some ploy by Dina, who knew? It was clear now that nothing like that would happen. They were home free, as the saying went. By this time tomorrow they would be in Jordan.

With relief came weariness. He felt as if he had run a marathon.

He also felt like a thief.

He had expected this. Indeed he had experienced guilt almost from the moment he had conceived his idea, and throughout the planning and execution of it. He had analyzed this feeling as he would any difficult business problem, and had concluded that it was inevitable in any decent person in similar circumstances. It was an unavoidable side effect that he had to suffer in order to achieve the desired result. What was necessary was simply to go forward despite the personal discomfort.

He did not think of himself as any sort of paragon, but he did consider that he was a man of honor and reasonable integrity, values instilled in him by his own father. He would have preferred to have done all of this openly, to talk it out with Dina and persuade her that his way was the correct one – the best for Suzanne and Ali, the best even for Karim and Dina. But clearly that was impossible. Their world views had diverged too greatly and for too long. He still loved the young woman he'd married, but it seemed to him that years had passed since they had agreed on anything really substantial. She would never have acceded to moving to Jordan. How many times, in the heat of one argument or another – over proper discipline of the children for instance – had she insisted that they were Americans, not Jordanians? Period. End of discussion. End of reasoning.

No. He had taken the only way open to him. But still . . .

Twenty years of his life were sliding away behind the great aircraft in the growing night – a marriage, the dreams of a younger Karim Ahmad.

And of course he knew what he was doing to Dina as well. He had promised himself that he would never prevent her from seeing them. But still . . .

He had not the slightest doubt how he would feel if the situation were reversed. He would be prepared to – to what? Kill? Well, maybe not that. But anything short of it. Dina would feel the same. She would hate him for ever.

It was the only way, he told himself for the thousandth time.

Was it possible to do the right thing for wrong reasons? The wrong thing for right reasons?

'Do you have a headache, Daddy?'

Suzanne looked up at him with concern in her eyes. He had suffered almost nightly from headaches ever since – when? Since he had found out about his oldest son? Earlier, perhaps? In any case, his little daughter took his pain as her special concern. At home it was her cue to play nurse, ceremoniously bringing him water to take with his aspirin.

'No, darling girl,' he said, although he did in fact feel the familiar throbbing beginning behind his eyes. 'Just a little tired. But thank you for asking.'

She sat beside him, small in the outsized first-class seat. Directly behind them were Ali and Fatma. The children exchanged places from time to time.

'Will we be there soon?' It was the second time Suzanne had asked. Ali had asked twice as well. Twins.

'Soon, precious. You'll go to sleep, and when you wake up we'll be there.' He hoped that the children would sleep shortly. And Fatma. He himself did not expect to rest well that night.

'And will Mommy be there too?'

'I told you in the cab, precious. On the way to the airport. Remember? Mommy won't be there right away. Later. Right now it's just the three of us. And Fatma, of course. But when we get there you'll see your *Jiddo* and *Tayta*, grandfather and grandmother. And your Uncle Samir and Aunt Soraya. And your cousins, do you remember them?'

Surprisingly, given that she and Ali had only visited their relatives in Jordan once a year or so, they had vivid memories of their cousins, and for this Karim was glad. As long as there were laughing stories about Samir and Soraya's children, there would be no more questions about Mommy.

Dinner came as a further welcome distraction. On Air France, at least in first class, the phrase 'airline food' held no horror. The handsome young flight attendant pampered them, especially the children, and charmed even cranky old Fatma into a grudging smile or two.

There was a selection of movies on their personal TV screens. Karim chose the last Harry Potter movie for the twins; even though they'd seen it, the film would keep them entertained. They held out against sleep for a while but eventually succumbed. Another

40

flight attendant, this one a brisk, chic young woman, wrapped them in blankets, fluffed pillows.

The last thing Suzanne said before closing her eyes was, 'I wish Mommy would be there when we wake up.'

'Later, darling girl. Soon. Sleep tight.'

Before long Karim heard Fatma's soft, weary snores as well. He had drunk wine with his meal and now he ordered another glass from the attendant. He was not much of a drinker and expected to be even less of one in Jordan, but there were times when a glass of wine brought comfort. If nothing else it eased the headache that had now taken firm hold.

Burning bridges, he thought. The words echoed from ancient military campaigns: an invading army would burn the bridges over which it had crossed so that there would be no temptation to retreat from the battles ahead. But Karim felt as if he *were* in retreat. Running. Running from an enemy that he could hardly define, burning bridges so that the enemy could not pursue.

It was only in the past few years that he had begun to recognize the nature of the enemy, to understand that it was something in American culture itself, including even parts of it that he himself had, as a younger man, enjoyed and praised. That, it seemed to him now, was precisely what made it so insidious: a certain maturity was required to see where freedom degenerated to license and irresponsibility – and maturity was the last thing America valued.

It was hard to put it all in one piece, like a diagram. His thoughts were muddled by the wine and by weariness. But certain images welled up. The teenaged singers Suzanne already worshiped: girls who seemed

41

consciously to compete as to who could look the most like a prostitute. And the athletes Ali idolized: selfish, thoughtless young men with pierced ears and bleached hair and tattoos disfiguring their skin. In such a place, and if Dina had her way, Ali would come to believe that the life his brother had chosen was not unnatural but normal, even commendable.

It was too late for Jordy, and Karim blamed himself, at least in part, for this failure. And it would soon have been too late for Ali and Suzanne. Another year or two, and they would have been caught up irrevocably in the anarchic moral relativism that was the result and reality of the much-vaunted 'American way'.

And to top it all off, they would never be truly accepted even into this rootless society. He had learned that in the aftermath of September Eleventh, and it had been a hard lesson. Until then he'd enjoyed a certain prestige and autonomy in the investment bank where he'd worked for a dozen years. He was, unofficially, the 'Arab department', the one who handled deals with important companies and institutions in the Middle East. But after the attack on the World Trade Center, he found himself – and his clients – held to microscopic scrutiny, examined for possible ties to terrorist organizations.

The atmosphere at the bank changed considerably: hidden glances, words overheard just before the speaker knew that he was listening, the realization that he was not as trusted as he once had been.

And it was just as bad for the children: remarks from their classmates, things they saw on television.

No. America might corrupt them but it would never accept them. Better he should give them a new home, his own home, before it was too late. As for Dina, well, that would be worked out, in some way. Things did work out – eventually they did. He would see that they did.

He woke to early sunlight in the window and a shift in the sound of the engines as the descent to Paris began.

CHAPTER SIX

The idea hit Emmeline while she was on the phone with Sarah. She knew it was a long shot, but what was there to lose? While grabbing her coat and bag and doing a quick make-up fix she laid the plan out for her assistant.

'Write this down. Your name is Dina Ahmad. A–h–m–a–d. Your husband, Karim – K–a–r–i–m – Ahmad, is flying to Jordan with your two children. Their names are Ali and Suzanne. Ali has serious asthma. He has to take medication – it's very important. And they've gone off to the airport without it. Kennedy. Customer service, whatever they have out there. You don't know what flight or even what airline. You've lost the information, forgotten, whatever. All you want to know is whether they're still on the ground so you can get the medication to them. Start with direct flights to Jordan, whatever airlines go there. Then try flights to Paris and, I don't know, London. Use that Brit accent, play Ophelia or whatever, you don't want to throw up any red flags after you give them an Arab name. Call me on the cell the minute you have something, whether the flight's left or not.'

Celia was an uncommonly quick study, even for an aspiring actress. Especially for an aspiring actress. She was already dialing as Emmeline swept out the door.

Em put on her sunglasses in the elevator – just in case some autograph hound with a thing for cable TV semi-celebrities was lurking downstairs – and hit the street waving for a cab. It was dinner-before-theater time and they were scarce, but one wheeled right around a desperately signaling, briefcase-wielding suit to stop for her. Friend in trouble or not, you had to love New York. She gave the anguished Gen Y-er her best butter-wouldn't-melt smile and climbed in.

The driver looked and sounded as if he'd spent his life up till a week ago on some island in the Caribbean, but at least he didn't ask how to get to Dina's Upper West Side address. In a minute Em saw that he was giving her the I-know-I've-seen-you-somewhere look in the mirror. She returned a pleasant little nod – no need to alienate the fans – and ended it there by taking out her cell phone. The things were a godsend for all sorts of reasons, one being that Em hated doing nothing, and a cab ride was the very definition of doing nothing.

First she called home. Sean answered. Though they didn't live together – Em was far from ready to go that route with Sean – these days he spent more time in her splendid loft than he did in his own tiny shared apartment. She couldn't blame him, really – her place was much nicer and her refrigerator was always well stocked. She explained the situation briefly, promising to fill in the details later – maybe much later, no telling when she'd be home.

Sean said, 'No worries, mite,' in the phony Aussie

45

accent that probably meant he'd had a couple of beers. He and a couple of the guys were going to the Rangers game. Michael had a party with some of his Stuyvesant High classmates. So no worries, mite.

But Em detected a faint undertone. Of what? Hard to say. Maybe she was imagining it. But maybe not. They had been together for three years – monogamous but not totally committed was how Em saw it – and the first bloom was wearing off. Maybe it was Sean's acting career. It was tough to be thirty-seven and still waiting for that one big break. It could happen any day. Or never. Maybe that was all. She said goodbye with that small undefined something still hanging between them.

It often happened that Emmeline reacted to events before their reality actually hit home. Maybe because she had just been talking about her own son, it was at this moment that the realization fully struck her: Dina's children – *Ali and Suzanne*, for God's sake – were gone. Dina might not see them again for years, till they were teenagers, or even grown-ups.

It was a terrifying thought. She tried to get her mind around it by imagining how she would have felt if Michael's father had spirited him away like that. She couldn't do it. Along with his faults, Gabriel LeBlanc had a fair assortment of good qualities, though a sense of responsibility was not among them. A few phone calls, some checks, a few postcards, that was about his limit. And even if for some reason he decided to burden his freewheeling life with a growing boy, where could he have gone with Michael that she couldn't get at him? True, Gabe had fallen into something of an international career. The zydeco that he'd played for a few dollars and free beer in every backroad dance joint in south Louisiana was now popular enough to get him gigs in Montreal, Paris – places he'd hardly known the names of when she and he were young and happily making Michael. But he'd never live in those places. No, the farthest she'd ever have to go to find him would be to some trailer park or bar in Bayou Grosse Tête.

Jordan. Where the devil was it, besides in the Middle East? She couldn't pick it out on a map if the February sweeps depended on it. It was an Islamic country, that she knew. Like everyone else, she'd learned more about Islam over the past year or so than in her whole prior life, but it was still largely *terra incognita* to her. What, for example, were their laws about child custody?

Manny Schoenfeld. Her lawyer. Why hadn't she thought of him before? Not that he'd know any more than she did about Jordan, but he might have some ideas on what could be done right here and now. And otherwise she'd just be sitting in a cab. Doing nothing.

She punched his number, 8 on the speed dial. The man was a strict, devout, observant workaholic – certain to still be in his office.

He was.

'Emmeline! The rising superstar! What a lovely surprise.'

'Save it for the chorus line, Manny, I've got a situation here.' She outlined Dina's problem.

Manny obviously had no immediate solution. 'I'm a show-business lawyer, Em. I know contracts, some copyright stuff, a little about tax law. Negotiations with some Hollywood hotshot, I'm your guy. But I don't do divorce work, child custody. Not even in this country, much less off in Muslim territory. You're talking international law here. And local law in – what is it, Jordan? – if that's tied up in any way with religious law, it's not the kind I can ask my *rebbe* about.'

'What if they're still here?'

'What, sitting out at the airport or something? Doesn't seem probable, not like they're your luggage or something, and you're on your way to Miami without it.'

'OK, but what if?'

'Well, maybe some kind of restraining order. I'd have to look into it, but I've got to tell you that it doesn't—'

The phone beeped to indicate incoming voice mail. The display showed her office number. 'Can I get right back to you, Manny?'

'I live to serve, Em.'

The message was from Celia. Karim Ahmad and the two children had boarded an Air France flight that had departed at 6:15 p.m. Emmeline glanced at her watch. Suzanne and Ali were now over the Atlantic. She called Manny back.

'I was saying, about a restraining order,' he began.

'Forget it, Manny. The birds have flown. Unless the pilot forgot his lunch or something, they're gone.'

There was a pause before Manny said, 'Look, I don't know what to tell you here. Your friend has a serious problem.'

'I think she's aware of that. The question is, what can we do about it? You're the lawyer. What's the next step? What do I tell Dina when I see her about five minutes from now?'

'Like I said, Em. I'm an entertainment lawyer. You need somebody who specializes in this kind of thing.'

'Give me a name.'

'What? Are you serious, Em? Half a million lawyers in New York and you think I can say, "Oh yeah, you want so-and-so"?'

'But you can find somebody?'

'I can ask around.'

'Tonight?'

'Tonight, I don't think so. I've got this cast party I'm locked into with iron chains.'

'Cast parties don't start till the show's over, Manny. Please?'

'All right, all right. I'll make a few calls. No guarantees, but—'

'You're a prince. I'm gonna put you on TV, make you a star.'

'Promises. Always promises.'

'Later, Manny. Thanks again.'

'What "again"?' he said.

She clicked the phone off. And for the next few minutes there was truly nothing further she could think of to do except talk with the cab driver, who, it turned out, thought she might be Whitney Houston.

She was still laughing when they pulled up in front of Dina's brownstone. Sarah's car was already there, parked in front of a fire hydrant.

Dina and Sarah had settled in the kitchen, where the letter was. Sarah had read it once quickly and said, 'What a jerk.' She had made herself and Dina a pot of tea and read the thing again slowly. 'What a total, consummate jerk.'

'I was thinking along those lines myself,' Dina had said, trying to smile. 'But it's always good to get a second opinion, Doctor.'

Sarah laughed, regarding it as a good sign that Dina could even attempt to joke at a time like this.

That was as far as they had gotten when the doorbell sounded and Em came sweeping in like a troop of cavalry. Another big hug. 'Now look, darlin', don't worry. I mean I know you can't help but worry, but we're gonna get on this case. It's gonna be all right. Gonna work out. We're gonna *make* it work out all right.'

Sarah said 'Read this' and Dina said 'Get you something?' at the same time.

Em wasn't much of a tea drinker. Actually she was thinking that this was the kind of thing that called for a big pot of strong boiled dark-roast coffee, real paint remover, at least back in Grosse Tete. But considering the situation, she decided that a cup of tea wouldn't hurt and might help.

Sarah handed her the letter, she read it in one quick take and set it down. The three friends exchanged glances.

'OK,' said Em. 'The first thing we need is a lawyer. I've got Manny on it. He doesn't know jack about this kind of thing, but he's looking for someone. I'm hoping to hear from him tonight.'

'We definitely need a lawyer,' Sarah agreed. 'That's step one. But there are other things we may need to think about too. Other avenues.'

'Like what?' said Dina.

'All suggestions gratefully considered,' said Em.

'Well, for instance,' Sarah said, 'I'm thinking State Department. Karim is connected back home, isn't he?'

Dina thought for a moment. She recalled the members of the royal family and the public officials who had attended her wedding in Amman. 'Yes, his family has some connections. And family is everything there.'

Sarah pointed at the letter. 'Something about an appointment with the king.'

Dina nodded. 'That's how connections work. It's a small country, certain people know each other . . .'

'Right,' said Sarah. 'So maybe that's a way to get at him. Somehow I don't see important people wanting an international incident.'

'What, you mean like Elian?' asked Em, and Dina had a sudden vision of reporters and camera crews camped on her doorstep, helicopters overhead.

'No, no,' said Sarah. 'There are quieter ways. Back channels.'

Em and Dina knew that Sarah, through Ari, had socialized with a heavily international and diplomatic set at one time. If she knew about quieter ways, back alleys, that would certainly be handy at this moment.

'I'll make some calls tomorrow,' Sarah said, making it sound clandestine.

'And there's your dad, too, Dina.'

Dina's father had been involved as a respected go-between, an honest broker, during the conflict in his native Lebanon. But that had been a long time ago.

'No,' she said. 'I don't want him in this. He's been through a lot and he's not very strong yet.' Joseph Hilmi had been a vital, energetic man, but the grueling course of chemotherapy had weakened him terribly, and to say that he wasn't strong enough *yet* was a statement of desire rather than of optimism.

'OK,' said Em. 'What about your mom?'

'I haven't called her yet. She's got so much to deal with, with my father being so sick.'

'They're gonna have to know sooner or later.'

'Later, then. And maybe it will work out sooner.'

'Knock wood,' said Sarah, and did. So did Em and Dina.

'What about Jordan?' asked Sarah, indicating the letter. 'Jordy,' she added to make it clear she meant Dina's son, not the country. 'Have you told him yet?'

'No. Not yet.'

'No point in it till we know a little more,' said Em. 'Tomorrow's soon enough. The jerk' – meaning Karim – 'says he'll call. Maybe he will.'

Sarah nodded. She and Em knew all about the trouble between Jordan and his father, and this was no time to go into it. 'You talked to the police?' she said. 'What did they say?'

'They said "good luck",' Dina replied bitterly. She told them about her exchange with the policewoman. The conversation moved on from there.

By ten o'clock they had exhausted every possible idea for remedying the problem. When the conversation slowed, Dina looked from Em to Sarah and began to weep.

Sarah's arm went around her quickly, and she began to murmur: 'There, there, Dina, it's going to be all right. One way or another, we'll figure out a way to make it right.' She might have been talking to one of her patients, soothing, reassuring, even when she wasn't sure of the outcome. She tried to imagine how she would feel in Dina's place, but she didn't even want to contemplate that possibility. What could be worse than losing your children?

They were trying to figure out when Karim and the twins might reach Amman – when a purring sound animated Em's purse. She pulled out the cell phone and said 'Uh-huh' three times while motioning urgently for a paper and pencil. 'Say it again, I'm getting interference, this damn building.' She scribbled down a couple of lines. 'And he's *experienced*, right? Like a specialist?' She listened again. 'OK. Sounds good. Thanks, Manny. I mean it. Undying gratitude.'

She clicked off the phone and turned to Dina and Sarah. 'Looks like we've got ourselves a lawyer.'

CHAPTER SEVEN

The call came exactly at seven in the morning, almost as if Karim had been waiting for a decent hour to phone. His greeting was calm, perhaps a little wary. 'Dina.'

'Karim!' It was a cry from the heart more than a greeting. 'My God, what have you done?' she sobbed into the phone. 'How could you, Karim? How could you do this to me?'

A sigh on the other end. 'This isn't about you, Dina – or about me, for that matter. I did this for our children. I tried to explain—'

'Explain?' she cried. 'How do you explain taking children from their mother?'

Another sigh.

'Dina, please . . . I can't discuss this with you now. I just wanted to assure you that the children are well, and that—'

'I want to talk to them,' she pleaded. 'I want—'

'Not now, Dina. They're tired and Fatma has put them to bed. I promise to call again soon. And then you can talk to them.'

Sensing he was about to end the conversation, she pleaded. 'Karim, don't hang up! Please don't hang up!

You can't just pretend this is a normal trip. I've been going crazy with worry.'

'I understand,' he said, 'and that's why I called. To assure you that Suzy and Ali are well.'

'You can't do this,' she sobbed, 'I won't let you, Karim, I won't—'

'Dina, please . . . it's done,' he said. And then: 'Goodbye.'

She held the phone in her hand for a long time, stared at the instrument as if it were a lifeline to her children. Which in a way it was. Then she made up her mind. She dialed the number of her in-laws' home. She heard ring after ring after ring. But no one answered. She put her head down on her pillow, feeling the dampness of the tears she'd shed against her cheek.

Chapter Eight

He looks like a nice man, was Dina's first thought, as David Kallas, Esquire, came out of his office to the tiny ante room that served as his reception area. He was a slender man, conservatively dressed in a vaguely stylish navy suit. The lines around his eyes suggested that he was in his forties, but his manner was boyish. 'Mrs Ahmad?' he said in a soft voice, glancing at each of the three women who were looking intently at him.

'I'm Dina Ahmad.'

'And . . .'

'And these are my friends, Sarah Gelman and Emmeline LeBlanc.'

'Shall we go into my office?'

Sarah and Emmeline rose from their chairs, right along with Dina, as if they had choreographed the movement in advance.

David shot an inquiring glance at Dina, then at the women. She nodded. 'It's all right,' she said. 'I want them to hear whatever we discuss.'

David nodded. 'That isn't usual, but if that's what you wish, welcome to my office. All of you.'

The office was scarcely bigger than the reception

area, but it had a comfortable, even somewhat elegant look. Piles of legal documents were neatly stacked on walnut file cabinets. The lawyer's desk, an antique, was also made of walnut and had a lovely patina that came from years of care. The client chairs were thickly cushioned and designed as much for comfort as for style.

'Would you like something to drink?' he asked. 'Coffee? Tea? Mineral water?'

Dina asked for water; her friends did the same.

David stepped into the doorway and spoke to the young woman who sat at a small desk in the reception area. 'Rebecca, could we please have three bottles of Pellegrino?'

Rebecca apparently made some protest because David stepped out into the reception area and returned with the waters on a small tray. He caught the questioning looks and smiled sheepishly. 'Rebecca is in law school and works for me part-time. She often seems to feel that the things I ask her to do are not part of her job description.'

'Then why don't you fire her?' Sarah asked.

Again the sheepish smile. 'My aunt would complain to my mother, who would then have something to say to me. Rebecca is my cousin, so I'm stuck with her until she graduates. I'm glad to say that will be in just two months.'

The explanation made Dina like him more.

Emmeline spoke up. 'My friend Manny says you know the Middle East pretty well.'

David thought for a moment. 'Actually, you could say I know something about Arab culture. My parents were born in Syria. Aleppo. Like most of Syria's Jews, they emigrated about forty years ago. To Brooklyn. I

57

speak Arabic, and I studied Middle Eastern affairs at Columbia. So I think it's fair to say that I have some understanding of the region.'

'And divorce,' Emmeline pressed. 'You're an expert on divorce law?'

David smiled and shook his head. 'I don't call myself an expert on anything. But at least half of my practice relates to divorce, so I do know the laws of this state and the laws of some neighboring states as well. Does that answer your question?'

'I guess . . .' Emmeline replied in a way that was uncharacteristically tentative.

Kallas tented his fingers and said, 'Maybe it would be best if you just tell me what brings you here, Mrs Ahmad. Manny mentioned only that your husband had taken your children and gone to Jordan. Without your knowledge. I'd like to hear the rest from you.'

Dina gulped some water, then took a deep breath. She told the story, stopping once or twice when she felt she might cry, Sarah and Emmeline gripping her hands, as if to give her strength.

David waited until she was finished. When he spoke, his expression was solemn and the smile had disappeared. 'I'm afraid I can't offer much encouragement, Mrs Ahmad. Since you and Mr Ahmad aren't divorced, there's no question of kidnapping here. Or of custody. If you were to press the matter in Jordan, I doubt you'd make much headway because there, you would be a foreigner, and your husband would surely prevail. Furthermore, if it's true that his family has powerful connections, then . . .' He spread out his hands as if to convey the futility of it all.

'Please,' Dina said. 'Isn't there anything you can do?'

He looked as if he wanted to say no, studied the three women for a moment. 'I'll look into the matter, talk to some people who have some experience with similar situations. Beyond that . . .'

'Dina's family has some connections in the Middle East,' Sarah spoke up. 'Her father worked with the State Department during the war in Lebanon. Do you think that could make a difference?'

David considered the question. 'I don't know,' he replied. 'But it certainly couldn't hurt to make some inquiries. They're a conservative bunch at State, so if they actually get involved, that would mean something.'

'All right,' Dina said. 'I'll do that. I'll make some calls right away.'

She opened her purse and took out her checkbook. 'How much do I owe you?' she asked. 'Should I give you a retainer, or—'

David shook his head. 'Let's not discuss a fee just yet. Let's wait to see if I can do anything for you. Meanwhile, I've had the pleasure of the company of three lovely women. How often does that happen to an old bachelor like me?'

Dina was charmed by the gesture and the gallantry. 'What a nice man,' she said after they'd left the office, voicing the thought that had struck her when she first saw the lawyer.

'Hmph,' commented Emmeline, who was never one to make positive judgments in a hurry.

'Yes, he is,' Sarah agreed, the phrase 'old bachelor' triggering her mother's voice in her head: A nice Jewish boy. One who listens to his mother. And he's single. She smiled to herself. She had no interest whatever in starting a new relationship, but try as she might, she couldn't seem to outrun Esther Pearlstein's advice, admonitions, and general instructions on how to live her life. Instructions that would certainly include what to do when you met a nice, single Jewish boy.

Chapter Nine

She couldn't put it off any longer. Dina would have to tell her mother that the twins were gone.

Now, as she entered the ornate lobby of the turn-of-the-century building that had been home to her parents for almost fifty years, she murmured a greeting to the elderly doorman who had, as far back as she could recall, always seemed old. She walked to the bank of elevators, stepped into the gilded car and pressed '10'. She waited patiently as it lumbered upward. She had grown up in this building, could remember running up and down the marble service stairs, to avoid the ancient Otis's eccentric ways.

She had been happy growing up in this splendid old building, and it usually warmed her to return to the scene of childhood memories: winter mornings watching the snow gather on the Juliet balcony outside her window, snuggling under the warm quilts made by her Lebanese grandmother; lazy summers in Spring Lake, idyllic beach days ending with her father grilling kababs on the back porch of their seashore Victorian; family holidays rich with good food and the booming laughter of relatives, both Irish-American and Lebanese. Today was different.

When she reached the tenth floor, she rang the bell to 10A. There were only two apartments on this level, a throwback to the days when middle-class families could comfortably raise children and even keep a servant or two in a Manhattan apartment.

A moment later, Charlotte Hilmi opened the door. Her smile, when she saw Dina, illuminated her face. At sixty-eight, Charlotte was still a beautiful woman, her complexion creamy and smooth, green eyes clear and bright, her once-golden hair lightly streaked with silver. Charlotte often joked that her blond hair was the principal reason her dark-haired Arab husband had fallen in love with her. And Joseph teased back, saying yes, indeed, to an Arab man, a blonde was irresistible. Laughter always followed. Dina reflected bitterly on how Karim had once loved her thick chestnut hair, as he had apparently loved so many things about her. All gone now, it seemed, along with her children.

'Mom.'

Charlotte held out her arms and enveloped her daughter in a warm hug, and Dina wished for a moment that she could stay there, protected and safe.

'Dina, sweetheart, it's good to see you.' Charlotte took her daughter's hand and led her into an enormous living room that was furnished very much to her husband's taste, with overstuffed damask couches and tables inlaid with mother-of-pearl that had belonged to his parents.

'What's wrong?' Charlotte asked as soon as they were seated.

Dina hedged. 'What makes you think something's wrong?' she asked, forcing a smile.

'Dina.' The word was a reproach.

'Mom, you have to promise me you won't say a word to Daddy about what I'm going to tell you.'

Charlotte's expression froze. 'Is it so bad?' she asked.

Dina nodded.

'The children? Has something happened to the children?' Charlotte's hand flew to her throat.

'The children are fine, Mom. But . . . they're in Jordan. Karim has taken them and he's not coming back. Jordy's still here. Karim doesn't want him,' she added bitterly.

Charlotte looked stunned. 'But how? What . . . ?'

Dina told her story, much as she had told it to David Kallas.

'I still don't understand,' Charlotte said. 'How could this happen? I didn't know you were having problems . . . not that kind.'

'I don't really understand either,' Dina said. 'I thought we were like most married couples: solid, in spite of whatever problems we had, which never seemed so big to me.' She paused. 'But Karim obviously saw our marriage in a different light. He seems to feel he's saving the children from getting corrupted. Like Jordy was.' A harsh laugh to make her point.

Charlotte was silent, as if trying to absorb what she had just heard.

Dina sighed. 'It's going to sound so simplistic, but for Karim, the problem seems to be the American way of life versus the Arab way of life.'

'Ah.'

'Ah – what? Does that actually make sense to you?'

'Not sense, necessarily. But it's something I might understand.'

Dina looked at her mother as if she had begun speaking in tongues.

'Don't look at me like that, sweetheart. Have you forgotten? Your father and I have the same cultural mix as you and Karim.'

'No, I didn't forget. But you and Daddy were always so great together, the differences didn't seem to matter. To me, they seemed like a plus. I mean, we had the best St Patrick's Day parties, with corned beef and music and singing. I still remember Uncle Terry singing "Danny Boy" so beautifully that everyone cried. And for Christmas and Daddy's birthday, we danced the *debka* and had all the Lebanese dishes he loved. Daddy said your cooking was even better than his mother's. I learned from you, Mom. That's why I was so confident that Karim and I would always be able to work things out.'

'And you imagined we never had any problems?'

'You did? I mean, I know you argued sometimes, but your marriage always seemed . . . so right.'

Charlotte smiled. 'It is right – and we are great together. But things weren't always rosy. If you didn't notice, it's because children don't pay much attention to their parents' problems unless they're forced to.'

'So you're saying you and Daddy had . . . serious difficulties.'

Charlotte shook her head. 'What I'm trying to say is that adjustments always have to be made in every marriage. And when they come from different cultures, the adjustments are even harder.'

'Yes, but Daddy's family is crazy about you.'

'Not in the beginning,' Charlotte said with a smile. 'They were always polite . . . they didn't know how to be otherwise. But when we got married, Joseph's sister made it clear I was . . . on probation, so to speak. Of course, that all changed over time, and now . . . well, now, we couldn't be closer.'

Dina couldn't imagine anyone not loving her mother. All she'd ever seen at home was love. Maybe that's why she expected it to last in her own marriage. The evening she'd first seen Karim at one of the Arab-American social events her parents attended, she had been attracted by his movie-star looks. The attraction was obviously mutual, for Karim made his way over to her like a homing pigeon. And after they talked, she had been impressed by his intelligence. He could talk with such clarity about so many subjects, from history to literature to politics.

'Do you remember when Karim and I first started seeing each other?' Dina asked. 'Remember how he used to say he was part of a new, forward-looking generation? How people like him would integrate the best that the West had to offer with traditional Arab values?'

'I remember,' Charlotte said. 'I think that's what impressed your father and me. Your father liked Karim's passion and sincerity, although . . .' Charlotte paused, reaching back into her memory.

'Although what?'

'Well, your father felt that one of the reasons we were a good match was that he became an American: Arab in his roots and traditions, but a real melting-pot American. He felt that even if Karim lived here for the rest of his life, he might well remain a Jordanian through and through.' She paused. 'Not that there's anything wrong with that,' she added. 'It's just that we weren't sure how that would match up with the way you'd been brought up.'

'But you never said anything.'

Charlotte smiled and squeezed her daughter's arm. 'But we did, sweetheart, don't you remember? I spoke to you about the freedom you'd been accustomed to all your life. The fact that you'd never been made to feel you were less important because you were a woman.'

Dina tried to remember the conversation. She couldn't. 'What did I say?' she asked finally.

'You made a face. And you said that Karim was a modern man, just as you were a modern woman.'

Yes, Dina thought, she'd once believed that with all her heart. But over time, Karim seemed to have forgotten about 'integrating' the best of the West with his own traditions.

'But why are we talking about the past now?' Charlotte asked, interrupting Dina's reverie.

'Maybe because it's easier than dealing with the present.' Dina's tone was flat, harsh.

'I understand. But we need to do something, sweetheart. Maybe your father—'

'No, Mom, I told you, we're not telling Daddy about this. As far as he's concerned, Karim has taken the kids to see his family. We'll say we didn't want to take Jordy out of school, so I stayed behind. We'll tell him that I just got a contract to do the flowers for the new Folk Art Museum, so I couldn't leave if I wanted to. He'll believe all of that for a while. Then . . .' Dina trailed off, not wanting to contemplate 'then'.

Charlotte nodded. 'All right, Dina. I hate to lie to your father, but you're right. He tries to pretend he's all right, but he isn't.' She thought for a moment. 'What can I do to help?'

'I don't know, Mom. I've been trying to figure out what can be done. I've seen a lawyer. He isn't optimistic, what with Karim's connections in Jordan and the fact that we aren't divorced. I thought maybe you might have the names of the State Department people who know Daddy. If any of them are still around, I want to ask if they can do anything to help.'

'Yes,' Charlotte said, 'that's a good idea. Most of your father's old friends are gone. But you can try Danielle Egan. She and your father spoke not long ago. She told him that America owed him a debt for all his good work during the trouble in Lebanon. He was so pleased to be remembered.'

'He should be remembered,' Dina said staunchly. Her father's family connections – prominent Lebanese Christians – had enabled him to undertake discreet behind-the-scenes assignments during the civil war that had all but destroyed his native country. And after the war had ended, her father had used his banking connections to steer investment money into the re-building of the hotels and tourist attractions that would bring Lebanon back to life.

Her father had done a great deal of good for a great many people. So perhaps someone would be willing to help her now.

'I'll get you Danielle Egan's number,' Charlotte said. She rose and headed towards the adjoining study, then paused. 'Do you want to spend the night here, Dina? I don't like the idea of you being alone.'

'Thanks, Mom, but if I do that, Daddy is bound to ask questions. Besides, I want to be home in case Karim calls.'

Karim did not phone again. Dina sat on her bed, waiting. Not reading. Not watching television. Just ruminating. Replaying scenes from the past. With the benefit of hindsight, perhaps she should have seen potential problems in her marriage from the start.

Karim was devoted to his family, and his family had not been welcoming to her. Her father-in-law, Hassan, a dignified *pater familias*, hadn't said much, but her mother-in-law, Maha, openly questioned the suitability of a Christian bride, the daughter of an American mother, for their Muslim son – the son of a prominent and well-to-do family, at that. Maha had gone so far as to suggest that she had in mind several more suitable candidates for her son's hand.

At first, Dina tried to take Maha's attitude in her stride; a woman in love overlooks so much. And Karim used to joke about it, saying that in his mother's eyes, no woman would be good enough. Over time, the jokes ended and Dina found herself overlooking very little.

At first, she had tried to adopt her own mother's example in blending two cultures. She had faithfully prepared Middle Eastern dishes several times a week (and served them to the accompaniment of Middle Eastern music), had enthusiastically entertained Karim's visiting relatives, had respected his religion and made an effort to learn about it. To her children, she had spoken warmly of their Jordanian grandparents, regardless of her own feelings.

If she hadn't gone the whole way – Karim's way – with her children, it was because she had discovered over time that although Jordan was one of the more progressive countries in the Arab world, there were still elements of the culture that remained both foreign and unacceptable to her. Like the fact that arranged marriages – and multiple marriages – were still common. Or the fact that while a man alone might dine anywhere he pleased, a woman alone could not. But most abhorrent of all to Dina were the so-called 'honor' killings, which constituted about a third of Jordan's homicides each year. These were perpetrated by fathers, husbands and brothers against women who supposedly had brought dishonor to a family, either by actual sexual misconduct or by the appearance of it. Men who claimed they killed for honor received little punishment (a jail term of six months or so) or no punishment at all.

When Dina once raised this issue at her in-laws' home, saying that the law should be more severe with killers, no matter their purported motive, her brother-in-law Samir piously declared that it would be wrong to change the existing law. If honor killings were not allowed, or at least sanctioned, he said, morals at home would become as loose as they were in America.

Dina had looked around the room, waiting for someone to disagree, but her father-in-law was nodding – and so was her mother-in-law, Maha. Karim said nothing. Had she begun to suspect then that her husband was not the man she fell in love with? One thing she did remember: it was at that point that she began to question the frequent visits to Karim's family.

At first, Dina had made no objections to the trips; after all, wasn't it a good sign when a man had strong ties to his family? But over time, she observed that Karim always seemed more Arab afterward. He became more critical of some of her 'American' ways – her edgy Manhattan style of dress, skirts too short, the fact that she was 'too friendly' with both men and women. Dina had no doubt that his intolerance was stoked by his family, particularly his mother and his brother, who bullied and dominated his own wife, Soraya – and who seemed to feel that Karim was not being given the respect – meaning obedience – he was due at home.

When Dina gave birth to their first son, all that seemed to recede into the background. Jordan Jamal – a nice compromise between Karim's wish that his son have an Arab name and Dina's desire that the boy be comfortable with his American identity, too. A son. Karim was thrilled. Even his family sent good wishes and lavish gifts.

Yes, there had been some arguments when she wanted to return to her floral design business a few months later. Karim had wanted her to sell *Mosaic* – or at least hire a full-time manager to run the business. They didn't need the money, so why on earth wouldn't Dina see reason and stay at home? She'd tried to explain that *Mosaic* was her creation, something she did not simply for money, but because she needed to be something – something other than a housewife. Karim had not understood. And that was when they'd brought in Fatma, Karim's older cousin from back home. A spinster. It was a real opportunity for her and seemed at the time a godsend to Dina. But what a mistake it looked like now!

Then, just months ago, came the trouble with Jordan.

It had started with a call from the counselor at Jordy's school, Jessica something. Dina had met her only once, at a typical parent 'conference'. A young woman who somehow seemed both petite and a little chubby, both buoyantly optimistic and vaguely guarded in her words.

'Ms Ahmad, there's a problem with Jordan.

70

Nothing serious, he's fine, we're not talking an injury. But it's an issue of school policy.' Jessica something sounded firm yet apologetic. 'We're sending him home. A three-day suspension.'

'Suspension? For what?'

'That's what I'm calling about, Ms Ahmad. We can talk about it by phone or, of course, you or Mr Ahmad or both of you can meet with me here. And with the principal.'

Dina naturally had wanted to know immediately what it was about.

It seemed that Jordy had been caught 'engaging in a display of physical affection beyond what we consider appropriate' with another student.

A male student.

Both of them were being suspended.

The first impulse was to say that there must be a mistake. But Dina didn't say it. She said nothing at all for a moment. Had she known? Had she suspected? All the times she'd told herself that Jordy was a late bloomer, or more interested in his studies, or that this was just the way kids were nowadays, teenaged boys didn't moon over teenaged girls like they used to.

She'd never mentioned it to Karim. It was bad enough that he was continually blaming her for making the boy 'soft' by pampering him.

When she finally spoke, what she said surprised even her. 'Do you suspend students for "displays of public affection" if they happen to be of the opposite sex?'

Jessica something managed to sound both sympathetic and primly correct. 'Ms Ahmad, I assure you that's not an issue here. We have a firm policy of non-discrimination. It's just that the . . . *level* of physical affection was beyond what we would allow for any student, regardless of orientation.'

'Orientation,' said Dina. It seemed the strangest word she had ever spoken. She took a deep breath and somehow managed to end the conversation.

Oh God, she thought, could it really be true? She had heard of things like this; they happened to other families. But Jordy? Her beautiful, intelligent, sensitive boy. Was she now to believe that he was like the flamboyant designers and models and actors who flitted around the city? Who were still dying in alarming numbers? No, not her Jordy. She certainly wouldn't believe it on the word of some inexperienced, underpaid functionary. She had to find out for herself what was going on.

She left the office and went home, where she more or less ordered Fatma to stay in her room until further notice. She picked up the twins at school herself and, back at the house, told them to do their homework and watch TV upstairs.

Jordan came in at his usual time. Dina wondered if he hoped to carry the suspension off without her and Karim knowing. But one look between them was enough.

'I guess the school called,' he said quietly. 'Mom, I- I just—'

'Just tell me what it's about, Jordy.'

He had seemed on the verge of tears. But now his face flushed with anger. 'What it's *about*, Mom? Tell you I'm a fag? A queer? A homo? Because that's what it's about!'

'Jordy, this is all . . . I mean, are you sure?'

He erupted again. 'Am I *sure*? Give me a break,

Mom. You really *don't* know anything, do you? Not a thing.' And again he quieted, shrugged. 'I've been sure since I was maybe eleven. Twelve. I just didn't . . . I couldn't . . . It's really hard to explain, you know? It's like, when did you know that you liked, you know, guys? Well, I guess it's the same with me.' He gave a little laugh. The bitterness in it broke Dina's heart.

'OK.' It was all she could say.

'OK what?'

'OK,' she said, swallowing hard, praying the words she said were the right words. 'OK, we go from here. You think I'm going to stop loving my son because he's . . .'

'Gay, Mom. The word is "gay".'

'Jordy.' She went to her son and held him. All this time he had been holding his backpack in one hand. Now he let it fall to the floor and put his arms around her. They held each other in silence for a long minute. Dina absolutely willed herself not to cry.

'I'll bet you could use a drink, Mom.'

She smiled ruefully. 'You'd win that bet. What would you like?'

'Whatever you're having.'

Dina decided against the brandy she'd first thought of and instead made a pot of tea. She took it into the living room, and they sat together as the city outside eased into twilight.

'I can't pretend I'm not upset,' she said slowly. 'It's just . . . it's just that I always wanted only the best for you, and—'

'And gay people can't have the "best" – is that it, Mom?' Again there was a hint of tears.

'Jordy, sweetheart, I'm sorry if I'm saying the wrong thing. I just meant that life will be harder. And different.'

'Yeah,' Jordy said. 'Tell me about it. Different.'

Again she searched her heart for the words that might somehow ease his pain instead of making it worse. 'Look at me,' she said finally. She held his gaze. 'I love you. I'll love you until the day I die, no matter what you do. No matter who you love. Do you understand what I'm saying?'

'Yeah.' He rubbed at his eyes, attempted a smile. 'I guess we have to tell Dad.'

Dina had been wondering about that ever since the phone call from school, feeling apprehensive about his reaction. 'Maybe he doesn't have to know,' she said slowly. 'Not right away.'

Jordy stared at her and she knew she had said the wrong thing again. 'I'm not going to be ashamed of who I am,' he said defiantly, 'not any more.' He looked like the ten-year-old boy he'd once been.

'It's up to you, sweetheart,' she said quickly. 'I was just thinking out loud about what would be easier for you.'

'I know.' He forgave her with a smile. 'Poor Dad,' he said softly, and now he sounded like a mature man.

A short time later, as if on cue, there was the sound of keys in the door and Karim's voice, his typical greeting, 'Hello, the house.'

'We're in here,' Dina called.

He came in looking a little worn – a difficult day in the office, obviously. He seemed surprised to see the two of them sitting so formally. 'What's wrong?'

'Something happened at school,' Dina said. And in a few words she told him what it was.

As she spoke, Karim's mouth slowly opened in astonishment. When she finished, he looked at his son as if seeking confirmation of the obvious fact that Dina was talking nonsense.

'It's true, Dad,' Jordy said simply. 'I'm gay.'

Karim looked quickly back and forth at the two of them. 'This is some kind of mistake. It has to be.'

'No,' said Jordy.

'It's no mistake, Karim,' said Dina.

She watched the realization dawn on her husband. His face crumpled, and at first it seemed he might cry, but then she saw the anger rising in him. She knew instantly that it was going to be bad.

He turned on Jordy. 'If this is true, I do not want you in my house,' he said fiercely. 'This is against God. It's against nature. It's filth, do you hear me? I will not have it around me.'

His voice had risen to a shout. 'Karim,' said Dina, pointing to the ceiling, 'the twins.'

He stared at her. 'Oh, yes, the twins,' he snarled. 'Do you think I want them exposed to this . . . this perversion?' He turned back to Jordy. 'I want you out of here. Now.'

Dina could not believe it. Even in the worst of her imaginings she hadn't foreseen this kind of primitive anger. This was their firstborn, the apple of his father's eye.

'He's not going anywhere, Karim. He's our son. And he's still a minor. You can't put him out even if you want to act this way.'

He focused now on her. 'You! This is your fault. Didn't I tell you, warn you, all those years ago? But no, you just had to spoil him. Turn him into a woman! Now look at your work!'

75

Jordy had stood. 'No, Dad. It's not Mom. It's not you. It's me.'

'You!' Karim moved towards him aggressively and actually drew back his fist as if to strike.

'Karim! No!' Dina shouted.

Jordy stood his ground, hands clenched at his side.

Karim stopped, dropped his hand. 'The two of you disgust me,' he said. He turned toward the door. 'I'm going out. I can't stand to look at you. Either of you.' But then he halted, a look of hard concentration on his face, as if he were contemplating a business problem.

'There are people who deal with these matters,' he said to both of them. 'Specialists. Jordy will go to one of them tomorrow.'

'Dad, I'm not going to some loopy shrink. I'm not crazy. Just gay.'

Karim was adamant. 'You're going. Or you're going away from here. I'll put you in a military school somewhere, how do you think you'd like that?'

Even Dina knew that the threat was empty. Jordy was simply too old for military school.

'You think I'm joking?' said Karim, although no one was smiling. 'Tomorrow I find a specialist. You go to him. Or you're out of here, one way or another.' He turned to Dina. 'I don't want to see him while I'm here. Morning or night. Let him eat in his room.'

'Karim, you—'

'Don't argue with me, damn you! Haven't you done enough already?'

With that he stalked from the room. They heard the front door slam.

Dina and Jordy looked at each other helplessly.

An exhausted sigh, almost a sob, escaped Jordy's

lips. 'Well, I guess I know what my father thinks of me.'

Dina put her arms around him. 'He'll calm down,' she said. 'It'll just take a while, that's all.'

She had almost believed that. Dina knew that it would be hard for Karim to accept his son's homosexuality. In most cultures, there was some stigma; in some of the stricter Islamic cultures, it was punishable by death. But Karim was light years more enlightened than people in those societies, and eventually love would prevail – wouldn't it?

There had been a therapist for Jordan – quickly abandoned when he brought them in and said there was really nothing wrong with the boy, he was simply gay. After that came the prep school – Karim wanted the failure out of sight. And of course he continued to blame it all on Dina: if she had raised the boy as a mother is supposed to do, if she hadn't been so intent on her important liberated-American-woman career . . . et cetera, et cetera. She felt the injustice of his anger, but she understood his hurt. And still she loved him, still she thought that they could work things out, given a little time and effort. Only a month ago she had suggested that he go to counseling with her. He had said he would think about it.

And all along he had been planning this.

Now she realized that she had let her son down by not fighting harder for him – and all for nothing. She had let herself down, too, by allowing Karim to believe he could do anything he wished with regard to his family, and without consequence to himself.

The following morning Dina made her call to the State Department. Danielle Egan was polite, even cordial when she heard Joseph Hilmi's name. But when Dina explained her problem, the woman's tone grew cautious, tentative. She made sympathetic noises but offered nothing.

'I was hoping you . . . the Department . . . could help me get my children back,' Dina finally said. 'Maybe someone could get in touch with my husband, put some pressure on him to bring the twins back.'

Egan was silent.

'Can you do anything?'

'It's not that simple, Mrs Ahmad. How would it look if the State Department attempted to interfere with a Jordanian national who hasn't broken any laws? Especially a Jordanian national with powerful connections?'

'So you're saying you won't help me.'

Another silence. 'What I'm saying Mrs Ahmad is that these things sometimes work themselves out. Your children have only been gone a short time. There's always the possibility that your husband will return to your home in a while, after he's had a chance to get passed whatever the two of you quarreled about. Married people argue, but then—'

'It's not like that,' Dina cut in. 'We didn't argue. And he won't be back. I know my husband.' And then she thought, How stupid. Of course, I don't know my husband. The man I thought I knew would not have done this.

More silence. 'What I'm saying is that there's no need to panic and assume the worst. People don't always do what they say.'

Dina snapped. 'No, I suppose they don't. What I seem to remember is that your colleagues told my dad they were grateful for his help in Lebanon – and that the door was always open to him, should he ever call upon them.'

'We are grateful, Mrs Ahmad,' Egan said, with the kind of exaggerated patience she might use with a child. 'And if there was anything I could do personally, without putting the Department in an awkward position, I would.'

'I'm sorry,' Dina said. 'I shouldn't have said that.' It was not her place to alienate her father's old colleagues.

Egan's tone softened immediately. 'Look, Mrs Ahmad, I have two children of my own. Believe me, if something like this happened to me, I'd be upset, too.' A pause. 'And maybe I'd be doing exactly what you're doing, trying to get help wherever I could.'

Strangely enough, Dina felt a little better. At least this woman was admitting reality instead of trying to sugarcoat it.

'I'll make some inquiries,' Egan said. 'Maybe there's someone over there who's in a position to check things out. Unofficially, of course. Meanwhile, keep in touch.'

'Of course,' Dina said, wondering what the point would be.

CHAPTER TEN

Once again the telephone rang at seven in the morning. Dina picked it up on the first ring; she'd been up since three, unable to get back to sleep.

'Dina . . .' Karim's voice was soft, almost tender.

'Karim!' was her anguished response. 'For God's sake, please bring my babies back! How could you take them from me? What have I done that was so terrible . . . ?'

'Dina, Dina,' he cut in, 'please believe that it wasn't my intention to hurt you. The children are here because I know in my heart they'll have a better life in Jordan. They'll be surrounded by family, with people who love them, not paid babysitters who see them only as a job.' It was a reference, Dina knew, to the succession of babysitters she'd employed before Fatma came to their household. 'They'll learn solid values,' he continued, 'and they'll grow up to be decent adults—'

'Not perverts like their brother, you mean,' she cut in bitterly.

Karim sighed. 'Dina, I blame myself, too, for this thing with . . .' apparently he couldn't even bring himself to say his firstborn son's name. 'It wouldn't have happened if he'd been raised here, in the proper way. I won't let something like that happen to Ali. This isn't easy for me either, you know. But it's the only way.'

'The only way,' she repeated. 'To deprive my babies of their mother, that's the only way.'

'I'm not trying to do that, Dina. You can spend as much time with them as you want. As often as you want. But here – in Jordan.'

'In other words, if I'm not going to be cut off from my children entirely, I'm entirely at your mercy.'

He sighed again. 'Dina, this isn't about me, it's about Suzanne and Ali.'

'No, it isn't, Karim. It's about having your way. You couldn't get me to share your way of thinking, so you've taken my children away to . . . to brainwash them.'

Karim was silent. Then he asked quietly, 'Would you like to speak to Suzanne and Ali? They're eager to talk with you.'

'And what exactly did you tell them about me?' she asked coldly. 'That you've kidnapped them for their own good? To protect them from their mother? Because she refused to bring them up in what you call the "right way"?'

Again the silence. 'I haven't told them anything . . . definitive yet. I just said that we were going to see their grandparents and cousins. I thought it would be best to introduce them gradually to . . .'

'. . . to their new home,' she finished.

'Yes.'

'And what do you expect me to say when I speak to them? That I'm going along with this . . . this horror you've inflicted on me?'

'Dina . . . I leave it to you to say what you think best – for their sake.'

'You bastard,' she muttered. 'You know I won't say anything to hurt or frighten them. You're forcing me to be your accomplice.'

He sighed again. 'Let me put Suzanne on the phone. She's been very anxious to tell you all about her plane ride.'

'Mommy, Mommy,' Suzy shouted into the phone, 'wait till you see the pony *Jiddo* bought me!'

'Bought us!' Ali shouted in the background. 'He said it was for both of us!'

Suzy ignored her brother. 'It's so fun here, Mommy. When are you coming?'

Dina felt her throat close up. Clearly her children were having a good time at their grandparents' home, too good to miss her yet. It was all she could do not to weep, but somehow she managed to speak. 'I'm glad you're having fun, Suze.'

'I am, I am. And Aunt Soraya said I could help her make *baklawa* today. And then we're going to read the new Harry Potter book – Uncle Samir bought it in London. And tomorrow . . .'

Dina managed to choke out an appropriate response, as she exchanged a few more heartbreaking words with Suzy and then with Ali.

As loath as she was to do it, Dina felt compelled to support Karim in the fiction that all was well and that they were still a family. By the time she hung up she was almost choking with pain and rage. How she hated Karim! She hated his entire family, not to mention Fatma, the traitorous caregiver. But stronger than hate was the longing to hold her children, to smell their hair and embrace their sweet bodies.

The house seemed colder than it had before the phone call. She turned up the heat, put on a pot of coffee. She showered and got dressed, as she did every morning. Prepared to go to work. But suddenly that prospect seemed absurd. Her career, her work at *Mosaic*, that seemed absurd, too, in the face of her overwhelming feeling of loss. Why had it seemed so important? Yes, she got pleasure from creating the stunning floral sculptures that adorned tables in fine French restaurants, graced some of Manhattan's grandest homes and apartments, enhanced gala events at museums and corporate headquarters. The work gave her a great deal of satisfaction, as did her celebrity client list, the repeated mention of her name in *New York* magazine's annual 'Best of New York' issue. All right, maybe it was all a bit shallow, but was it so terrible? Clearly Karim thought their life together *was* terrible or he wouldn't have stolen away like a thief in the night.

Today it didn't seem to matter whether or not she showed up at *Mosaic*. It probably wouldn't matter tomorrow either. Dina picked the phone and called her assistant, Eileen. 'I won't be coming in for a while,' she said. 'I'll keep in touch by phone and fax. Please contact that Barnard student who worked for us part-time last year. Ask her if she can give you a hand while I'm out.'

'Is something wrong?' Eileen asked.

'Family problems,' Dina replied tersely, cutting off any further discussion. Eileen got the message, and after a few questions about current clients, she hung up.

Dina couldn't help but remember the times Karim had asked her to take time off – and how important it had seemed not to. But why? Had it been so important to make her point? And what had her point been? She was not passionate about her work, though it did give her pleasure. If she had been passionate about anything, it was the need not to be like the women in Karim's family: placid, boring, homebound. But it was those women who had her children now, and Dina thought, Yes, if I had to, I would gladly trade places with them.

CHAPTER ELEVEN

'*Ahlan wa sahlan, ya Karim, ahlan wa sahlan,*' Karim's uncle, Farid, boomed as he entered the Ahmad home. It was always like this when Karim came to Jordan. Relatives streaming in and out of the big house, welcome upon welcome, hugs and kisses upon kisses and hugs. Karim never tired of it; this was the way a family should be – close and strong and ever-present. Dina had sometimes complained of a lack of privacy when his family monopolized all their time in Jordan. She had never understood that the concept of privacy was alien here. Even as a boy, he had heard the old proverb: 'Where there are no people, there is hell.'

'How long will you be in Jordan this time?' Farid asked.

'A while,' Karim replied, hoping that would satisfy his uncle. He was not ready to explain the full circumstances of his return to one and all.

The old man sniffed the air, inhaling the fragrance of succulent lamb, butter-laden rice, and other delectables. Karim took the hint. '*Itfuddal*, Uncle, *itfuddal*, we were just about to have lunch. Let's see what my dear mother has for us today.'

Ever since his arrival, Karim's mother had been

running what amounted to a continuous open house, preparing one lavish meal after another for the friends and relatives who were constantly dropping in to see Karim and his children. Karim realized just how much he had missed this way of life.

He led his uncle towards the sounds of conversation and laughter in the dining room. 'Please, Uncle,' Karim said, 'you must sit down to have a bite with us.'

'*W'Allah*, I did not come to dine, *ya* Karim – in fact I finished a meal at home not more than one hour ago.'

'*Ma'lesh, ma'lesh*, come and join us anyway.'

Karim's father, Hassan, rose to embrace his younger brother; then he pulled out an empty chair at the massive carved dining table that had been in the house for as long as Karim could remember.

Farid sat down. Samir's two children, Nasser and Lina, after a pointed look from their father, rose obediently, went to their great-uncle and kissed his hand. Farid patted the children benevolently, rewarded the gesture of respect with a blessing – and a few coins plucked from his pocket. Karim's children looked at their father and then followed suit. Karim smiled approvingly. Traditions like this were out of fashion in some households, but he was raised to revere his elders and he wanted the twins to learn the old ways, too.

The formalities out of the way, eating resumed. The meal was a traditional one for festive occasions, and to Karim the foods were themselves like old friends. Trays of *mezze* – *hummus* and *baba ganoush* and *tabbouleh*, not to mention assorted cheeses and olives – preceded a main course of *mansaf*, the national dish: lamb seasoned with aromatic spices and cooked in a yogurt sauce, piled atop a mountain of rice and flat bread, the whole further enlivened with pine nuts. A *rashoof* soup of lentils, yogurt and onions served as an accompaniment. Karim's mother and sister-in-law, with the assistance of Fatma and the family servant, had labored for hours to put it all together.

For tradition's sake as well – Karim's father Hassan suggested it – the *mansaf* was being eaten in the old manner, by hand, each person reaching into the communal dish for the morsels he or she wanted. The technique of rolling the food into a ball and pushing it into one's mouth with the thumb proved especially difficult for Suzanne. Her older cousin, Nasser, stepped in. 'Like this,' he said, adopting a grown-up tone. 'You have to hold the food firmly.'

Suzy tried to follow his direction, but the rice kept slipping through her fingers. Ali began to laugh. 'Suzy doesn't know how to eat,' he chanted, 'Suzy doesn't know how to eat.'

Suzy's brown eyes began to fill with tears. She turned to her father, who came to her rescue. 'Of course Suzy knows how to eat, Ali. She just needs a bit of practice eating this way. And until she gets it down, I'm going to help. Come here, Princess,' he said, holding out his arms. Suzy rushed to her father, who boosted her onto his lap and proceeded to feed her from his plate. She turned to her brother and smiled. Ali scowled. Although the twins shared a deep and abiding bond, they sometimes behaved as if they couldn't stand each other. Ali wasn't doing particularly well eating with his fingers either, but he would rather starve than admit he needed help. Quietly and without fanfare, Soraya brought Ali a plate and a fork.

Samir edged closer to Karim. 'Raised a couple of

regular little Americans there, haven't you, brother?'

Karim laughed. 'Looks that way, doesn't it?'

'They'll get the hang of it, once they're here for a while.' Samir reached into the *mansaf* and expertly withdrew a healthy portion.

'*You've* got the hang of it at any rate, little brother,' Karim told him. It had become something of a running joke between them. His little brother was not so little any more, a substantial middle-age belly bulging his Polo golf shirt over the beltless waist of his double-knit slacks.

'Ah, well, hazards of the business,' said Samir. It was his standard defense. He owned a travel agency, quite successful to all appearances, and maintained that heavy meals with clients were unavoidable burdens of the profession. 'At least,' he added, 'I'm not some gray-headed old man still dreaming of winning the Olympics.'

This was a dig at both the silver that was creeping into Karim's black hair and his devotion to physical fitness; he had already found a Western-style health club in Amman and went three times a week, just like in New York.

Before Karim could formulate a suitably withering reply, a light touch on his arm signaled Soraya's presence. 'Did you eat, brother?' She seemed a little breathless with her work as *de facto* co-hostess of the party. 'Do you think there's enough?' she asked her husband.

'It will have to do,' Samir answered with gruff authority. He could have easily said, Karim thought, that there was enough for an army and a navy besides.

'See if my brother needs anything,' Hassan instructed his daughter-in-law.

'Uncle?' Soraya asked. 'Would you like some cheese and bread?'

Farid considered the prospect of yet another course, appeared to savor it with some pleasure. Then he sighed. 'No,' he said finally and with regret, 'my doctor says I must cut down on everything I enjoy.' He began to regale Hassan with the details of his latest medical exam.

While the two older men were chatting animatedly, comparing ailments, Soraya spoke once again to Karim. 'Have you told the children yet about Marwan?' she asked, speaking softly so as not to be overheard. She understood that Karim wasn't yet ready to broadcast his intention to stay.

He looked at her blankly, having no idea what she meant. Was it some localism he had forgotten?

'The tutor,' she said.

Samir was waving a hand. 'I didn't tell him. Just slipped my mind. I talked to a young man about tutoring Ali,' he explained to Karim. 'And Suzanne as well, of course.'

'Ah.' Karim had sought Samir and Soraya's help in finding someone to teach the children Arabic. It was something he had always wanted to do but somehow had never got around to in New York. Dina had opposed it on the grounds that they were too young to spend long, extra hours in study – even though he had pointed out to her that childhood was precisely when it was easiest to learn another language. Whatever the case, now it was important, if the twins were to attend school and mix easily with their peers. He could teach them himself – and would, to some degree – but he wanted a deeper knowledge for them than he could impart in the odd hour here and there.

'Marwan Tawil,' Samir was saying. 'Son of a friend of mine. He's a good boy, smart, third year at the University. Speaks English better than you do. I talked with him yesterday and he agreed to do it. I'll arrange it, if you tell me what hours you want.'

'Well, that's great,' said Karim. 'Let me talk with the children, come up with a schedule.' He saw his brother and sister-in-law exchange a quick amused glance. What was it about America, that adults let their children decide such things? 'How much does he want?' he asked in an attempt to cover up. And was immediately aware that he had mis-stepped again.

'Next to nothing,' said Samir. 'He's a hungry student, after all. But,' he added with a smug twinkle, 'if there's a problem, brother, I can certainly help . . .'

'No problem, little brother,' Karim said quickly. 'Just wondering. I . . .' He had started to say he was an American. 'I've been in New York too long. They have to know the cost of everything.'

'And the value of nothing?' Soraya smiled. She was very pretty when she smiled. Karim wondered where on earth she had heard the Oscar Wilde aphorism. But of course she was a college graduate herself. It was easy, somehow, to forget that fact when she was in the role of Jordanian housewife. For some reason he thought of Suzanne. When she had found out that Soraya covered her head to go out into the city, Suzanne had thought it was fun. Now that she was beginning to understand that the headscarf was more than a fashion statement, that it was emblematic of a way of life, she didn't find it quite so entertaining.

'In any case,' said Samir, 'he's a good boy. I can vouch for him myself. And he can teach more than just the language. For instance, he can give them a little religious instruction, if that's something you're interested in.'

It was another area that Karim had neglected. Dina had not opposed the children's learning *about* Islam, but it was her belief that children should not be indoctrinated in any religion, but be left to decide what they believed when they were older. And in truth, at least until lately, Karim was only mildly observant himself. As a result, the twins had only a superficial awareness of the faith of their forefathers. At Ramadan they did one day – not the full month – of dawn-to-dark fasting. And once or twice they had engaged in prayer three times a day – not the five times that constituted one of the Pillars of Islam, because they were too young for it. As for Jordan, well he had seemed interested in his father's faith – in his own actually, for according to Islamic law, if the father is a Muslim, so are his children. Karim recalled how he and Jordan had traveled uptown to the lavish mosque on 96th Street, how close he had felt to his son when they prayed together. He shook his head as if to shake away the pain of that memory.

'Sure,' he said to his brother. 'I wouldn't mind that. What's his orientation?'

Samir lifted an ironic eyebrow. 'His *orientation*, brother? Don't worry, he's not one of the fundamentalists. He's not related to any of the old Muslim Brotherhood, the Taliban, or the Al-Qaeda people.'

Karim laughed. 'OK, OK. Have him call me at the office.' It would make a welcome break, he thought, something to do. He had been on the new job a week. It amounted to consultant work on all things to do with aircraft procurement, as far as he could tell. But to a much greater degree than in New York, it also appeared to be about politics, both office and otherwise. Until he learned exactly whose buttons to push when, he would not be doing much more than pushing papers and looking at the kind of diagrams and spreadsheets he had all but memorized five years ago.

'That's good,' Soraya brightened. 'Let me tell the twins. I'll make it sound like more fun than you two grim old soldiers will.' She was ten years younger than Samir, fifteen younger than Karim.

Karim made a gesture of acquiescence and Samir nodded with evident satisfaction at having resolved this difficulty for his naïve Americanized older brother.

'Dessert,' said Soraya. 'Sweets to the sweet.' And hurried off to help the other women set out plates of *baklawa* and fruit.

Just as the desserts were being brought into the dining room, Karim's cousin, Hamid, arrived and took a place at the table. The cousins hadn't seen each other for almost ten years – Hamid had been working in the Gulf for that long. Between mouthfuls of pastry, Hamid asked Karim: 'So what is life in America like these days?'

As if that could be summed up in a half minute or so, Karim thought. 'Well,' he said slowly, 'it can be difficult for people like us.'

Hamid nodded knowingly. 'Little wonder, cousin. We've all been demonized. Arabs are good for oil, nothing else. You have my sympathy, living in a country that doesn't really want you.'

Not wishing the conversation to go on in this vein, Karim asked. 'What about you, cousin? What have you been up to?'

Hamid was happy to answer. At length. It appeared

he was now involved in some sort of development project by the Red Sea. Before Karim could make sense of Hamid's 'great opportunity', his father rose from the table and nodded in a general way that included all the men present.

It was the signal to move into the smoking room, light the *nargileh*, and talk of worldly matters while the women cleaned up. Karim had a mild dread of the shared water pipe and its sweet, mild smoke. He had gone cold turkey from a pack-a-day cigarette addiction back when Dina was pregnant with the twins, and he had no wish to be hooked again. But the *nargileh*, nicknamed the hubble-bubble, was more than a tradition in the Ahmad household: Hassan Ahmad had made a fair part of his fortune by importing tobacco, and the ritual was not to be bypassed.

I won't inhale, Karim told himself.

The smoking room was what might have been called the den in an American home. It was furnished in the old style: walls lined with banquettes covered with brightly colored hand-woven Berber fabric from Morocco. Every few feet, there was a small inlaid table, now laden with almonds and candy.

The house was a large one, as befitted the affluence and social standing of Hassan Ahmad. Set in one of the better northern suburbs of the capital, it sprawled around a large central courtyard in the traditional manner, combining Arab elements of design with such modern comforts as a well-equipped kitchen and several lavish bathrooms.

Samir and his family lived in one wing; it was their father's wish, and Samir had always been a dutiful son. Karim and the children occupied a wing that had been reserved for guests. The furniture was mixed: but the richly hand-woven carpets on the floor were traditional to the Islamic world. As was the art: gorgeous examples of Islamic glass and magnificent antique tapestries emblazoned with verses from the Qur'an hung on the walls. Karim found his parents' home comfortable in a deeply heartfelt way, yet already he had begun looking at other properties that were built in a more modern and efficient style. He had not mentioned this to his father.

The mouthpiece of the pipe was passed to him and he took a sip of the cool, tantalizing smoke. Just enough to be sociable. He realized that his father was addressing him.

'My grandson,' said Hassan. 'My oldest grandson, I mean. Jordan.' He spoke the name with a wry twist of the mouth, as if there were a private joke in it. 'If he were here, he would be old enough to share this pipe. Did you say when he would be coming, son?'

'No,' said Karim. 'I mean, it's not certain, *Abbi*. He's in school. Almost ready for college. University. It's important for him to finish his studies.'

Samir, who knew more of the truth, looked off into the middle distance. Hassan merely nodded. 'Yes, of course. But I would like to see him all the same.' He smoked from the pipe and his face was sad. For the first time in his life Karim thought of his father as an old man.

An hour later, Karim and Samir walked together in the courtyard. They were alone for the moment. The party was winding down.

'I wonder,' said Samir, 'about Jordan. This episode you told me about – this kind of thing happens all the time. It doesn't necessarily mean anything. Do you remember the big fuss that was made years ago, when cousin Sharif was doing . . . well, the same kind of thing?'

Karim nodded tentatively, not certain of where Samir was going.

'Well, now Sharif is a married man with three sons. And no one cares what he did when he was a young boy.'

Karim said nothing.

'But you know,' his brother continued, 'I wonder about sending him off to that kind of school, prep school, whatever you call it. I saw this kind of thing in England.' Samir, like many well-off young Arabs of his generation, had survived a gloriously brief period of higher education in Great Britain. 'It seems to me that it might . . . aggravate the problem. Not to tell you how to manage it, but of course he's my nephew, too.'

'You don't understand,' said Karim.

'No? Probably not. But I just wonder . . . why not bring him here? Is it Dina who stands in the way?'

It would have made things easier to say yes. Karim's family had never warmed to Dina. Especially after it was made clear to them that Karim's bride had no interest in coming to live in Jordan. Not then. Not ever. They had thawed just a little after Jordan had been born. But that had been a temporary condition; after all, they only saw Jordan, and later the twins, once – occasionally twice – a year. And for such brief periods, not for the long family visits many of their acquaintances enjoyed with children who lived abroad. For that, they blamed Dina. Because they knew in their hearts that Karim would not deprive his parents of their greatest pleasure, the company of their children and grandchildren.

Now Karim had abandoned Dina and taken their children with him, but he still couldn't make himself betray her in this small way. 'You don't understand,' he told his brother. 'You can't understand. America is . . . it's not like here. Nothing like here. It's why I came back. But I can't do anything about Jordy. Take my word for it.'

'It's all right,' said Samir. 'It's OK. We'll talk about it later. Any time you want.' And suddenly he gripped Karim by the back of his neck and kissed him on the forehead. 'My brother,' he said quietly, a world of meaning in two small words.

Karim nodded, brushed a tear from his eye, and knew he was home.

CHAPTER TWELVE

Sarah didn't want to make the phone call. She avoided talking to Ari as much as possible – in fact, she rarely spoke to him at all unless the subject was their daughter Rachel. Yet now she was punching in his number, about to ask him for a favor – when she had asked him for nothing at all during the three years since the divorce. Nothing, that is, except the *get*, which he had steadfastly refused to give.

He answered on the third ring. She heard the melodious strains of Rimsky-Korsakov's *Scheherazade* and wondered if he might be entertaining a woman. Ari had played this music for her when they were courting.

'Sarah,' he said heartily, 'how nice of you to call.' As if she were an old friend.

'Ari,' she began carefully, 'I'm sorry to disturb you, but there's something I need to ask you. It means a great deal to me, and I—'

'Sarah, please,' he cut in, 'not that again. I've told you—'

'No, Ari, it isn't *that*. Will you let me explain? Please?' This last word came out weak, almost whiny. Funny, she thought, on Dina's behalf, she was willing

97

to coax and wheedle, though she'd never beg Ari on her own behalf. Not even for the *get*.

'All right, all right, Sarah, what is it then?'

She hesitated. If Ari had a woman with him, perhaps this wasn't the time to get into Dina's problem. 'Is this a good time?' she asked. 'If you're busy, I can call—'

'Of course it's a good time,' he boomed. 'I always have time for my family, Sarah, you should know that.'

Yeah, right, she thought. If there is a woman in the apartment, he's just giving her the needle. Like he used to do with me. Letting her know there was someone in the background, a friendly ex-wife who wanted him still. 'Well,' she said, 'my friend Dina has a big problem—'

'Oh. Her.'

'Ari, please . . . are you going to let me speak?'

'I'm sorry. Go on.'

Sarah explained what Karim had done.

Ari made a sound. Almost like a chuckle. 'What a bastard,' he said. 'I guess I must seem like a prince compared to him. At least I never took Rachel from you.'

Sarah let that pass. She knew very well Ari had no interest in raising a daughter.

'Well, what can I do about it, Sarah? You want me to get on a plane and chase the guy down? Last I heard Israel isn't at war with Jordan.'

Very funny, she thought. She said, 'What I thought . . . what I was hoping . . . Ari, I know that you know a lot of people in Israel. People who can . . . do things. Would you be willing to ask if . . . if someone could help get Dina's twins back?'

Silence.

'Ari? It would mean a great deal to me, it really would.'

'I'm thinking, Sarah, I'm thinking.'

'Oh, I'm sorry . . .'

'Look,' he said finally, 'I won't make any promises – because quite frankly, helping Dina Ahmad is not a big priority to me. But since you're asking, I'll make some inquiries—'

'Thank you, Ari—'

'Mind you,' he cut in, 'I'm certainly not going to ask for any big favors from anyone on your friend's behalf. But if someone knows someone who can put some pressure to bear, well, we'll see.'

'Thank you for whatever you can do.'

'It could be nothing.'

She sighed. 'Well, that's where we are right now, isn't it?' She hung up, wondering if she heard the sound of a woman's laughter over the sound of the music.

CHAPTER THIRTEEN

Dina knew the news would not be good. David Kallas had phoned and asked her to come to his office. It was just like the calls doctors made after you had a test. If all went well, they'd tell you on the telephone that everything was fine. If they had bad news, they invited you to come in. Why? she wondered. Wasn't it easier just to get it over with, without the added torture of imagining every possible bad scenario?

And now she and her friends were once again seated in David Kallas's small reception area, watching his cousin Rebecca work at her computer. Once again waiting.

When David came out of his office, he smiled at the three women, but the smile didn't quite make it to his eyes. 'Good morning, Mrs Ahmad, Mrs Gelman, Ms LeBlanc.' He hesitated a moment. 'Mrs Ahmad, I know you said that you wanted your friends present at our discussions, but I'd like you to step into my office alone for just a moment.'

Dina looked at her friends. Emmeline shrugged. Sarah said, 'Go ahead, Dina, we'll wait right here.'

Dina followed Kallas into his office and sat down. 'I wish I had something positive to tell you,' the lawyer said gently, 'but here's where we are: I've spoken to your husband's attorney in Amman. He's made it clear that Mr Ahmad's position is not flexible and that there can be no negotiation in the matter of the children. Mr Ahmad feels he's been generous as regards your finances: he's left you the marital home as well as some joint assets. The attorney also informed me that he's been instructed to make regular monthly transfers to your account. But as for custody of the twins,' here David sighed, 'your husband's position is that they are to live with him in Jordan. And that you're free to visit them there at any time.'

Dina bit her lip to keep from crying out. She had expected something like this, yet she had hoped, prayed, for something better.

'We could, of course, sue for divorce,' David continued, 'and then for custody and a formal order for child support.' He paused.

'Yes,' she said eagerly, 'we could do that. Then the courts would force Karim to bring the twins back, wouldn't they?'

Kallas shook his head. 'Doubtful. I've done some research and found a number of cases like yours. One father snatched his children and took them to Uzbekistan. The American courts ruled for the mother, ordered him to return the kids. But the order was basically unenforceable.'

Dina pressed on. This couldn't be all, it couldn't. 'Are you telling me that no mothers ever get their children back?'

'Well,' David said slowly, 'there was one case, involving a Chinese father and an American mother. Her children were returned after a large cash payment was made to the father. From what I can see here, that wouldn't work with your husband.'

'No,' Dina said, 'it wouldn't. So there's no point in trying any kind of legal action?'

David shook his head again. 'The only ones who would gain from that would be me and the attorney in Jordan. We might prevail in an American court, but as I've said, an American court's rulings will not be enforceable in another country. In these troubled times, I sincerely doubt that our government would be willing to press the Jordanian government over an issue like child custody.'

'Then there's nothing I can do?' Dina implored. 'Nothing? I want my children back. I would walk through hell if necessary to get them.'

David sighed again. And when he spoke, it was reluctantly. 'I know. That's why I asked you to come in here alone.'

Dina straightened up in her chair. He was going to give her something, she could feel it.

'You didn't hear this from me,' he said carefully. 'I never said it. But there are ways . . . outside the legal system. I can give you the name of a man who specializes in this kind of . . . activity. But again, you never heard it from me.'

'What are you talking about?'

As David explained in purposely cloudy terms, she gradually understood. Stealing the children back. Kidnapping.

'There are experts in this kind of work,' he said. 'Professionals.'

'And you know some of these professionals?' she asked eagerly. It sounded crazy, but it was *something*.

David nodded. 'I might know of one. But I've heard

that he's very expensive. That's understandable, since the work is dangerous. And illegal.'

Dangerous. Illegal. In normal times, such words would have frightened her off immediately. But these were not normal times.

'. . . and that's why I'm not even suggesting such a step to you. In fact, if you were to ask, I would advise against it.' As he spoke, David slid a business card across the desk. *Gregory Einhorn, Private Missions*. 'You didn't get this from me,' he said.

'I understand.' And she did.

'Good luck,' said David, 'I hope . . . well, I hope you get your children back, Mrs Ahmad.'

Dina believed him. She rose and offered her hand. He squeezed it lightly. As he walked her to the reception area, Sarah and Emmeline got up quickly. Dina could see they were full of questions. She shook her head, then turned to David. 'Thank you,' she said softly.

'I didn't do anything,' he said quickly. 'I wish I had been able to help. Truly. In fact, if there's anything else I can do for you, I hope you won't hesitate to ask.'

Sarah looked quickly from her friend to the lawyer, as if she sensed something hidden. Then she spoke. 'Mr Kallas . . . I wonder if I might come in to see you about a problem of mine.'

David looked startled, then pleased. He smiled at Sarah. 'Of course,' he said. 'Just give me a call and we'll set up an appointment.'

Sarah and Em peppered Dina with questions. What was she talking about in there? What was so hush-hush that they couldn't hear?

Dina wasn't ready to tell them about the possibility

that David had raised, of taking the kind of action he had hinted at. She didn't want to hear that it was crazy and dangerous. Not yet. If this was the only hope she had, then she wanted to hang onto it a little longer. So she doled out whatever information she could. David had made inquiries, she said, had contacted Karim's lawyer in Jordan, but nothing good had come of it. 'He told me I could file for divorce, but he doesn't think that will help me get the children back.'

'And?' Em demanded.

'And . . . I don't know,' Dina said. 'Maybe I'll just go home and think for a while. Maybe there's something I haven't thought of . . .' She trailed off.

Em and Sarah looked at each other, then at Dina. 'Girl, are you sure that's all you talked about in there?' Em asked. 'You're acting kinda funny.'

Dina attempted a smile. 'I guess I am. Look, I'm sorry I dragged you here for nothing. But really, I think I'd better just get home. OK if I call you both tomorrow?'

Reluctantly, her friends put Dina in a cab and then went their separate ways.

Dina felt guilty about deceiving her friends, but she really did need to think. On her own. Should she even consider doing something that was not only illegal but terribly risky in other ways? If it failed, would she ever see the twins again? And if she did decide to go ahead, was it fair to involve Sarah and Em?

CHAPTER FOURTEEN

The trees that surrounded Samuel Phillips Hall, affectionately known as 'Sam Phil', were dappled with sunshine, the lawn was lush and green, the entire scene spread before her was like a picture postcard. But as Dina strolled the Phillips Academy campus with her son, she was oblivious to the beauty of her surroundings. All she could think of was the task that lay ahead: telling Jordy that his father had taken the twins, and that he intended never to return.

At first she'd had a glimmer of hope that she could somehow avoid telling Jordy, that she might get the twins back before the need for truth became pressing, but it had soon become clear that there would be no such miracle.

Get it over with, she told herself. Jordy will realize something's wrong, so it's better if you break it to him in your own way. But what was her own way? During the drive up to Massachusetts, she had tried to formulate a speech that would inform Jordy without allowing him to blame himself. She was still trying.

'We have a few hours before our dinner reservation, sweetheart,' she heard herself saying. 'Is there anything you'd like to do?'

'Well . . . I need to pick up some stuff at the Andover Bookstore. Do you want to walk over with me?'

Dina looped her arm into Jordy's, pulled him close. How she loved this beautiful boy with his thick dark hair, his smooth olive skin, and his soulful dark eyes, so heartbreakingly like his father's. She had no heart for sightseeing today – or for anything that parents normally did when they visited children at school. But Jordy had been denied the normalcy of his father's love, and the least she could do was make their time together pleasant – at least until she broke the news. That's why she had invited two of his friends – Brian and Kevin – to join them for dinner. Because isn't that what visiting parents normally did? And why she was now smiling as she ruffled Jordy's hair when she felt like crying?

The Andover Bookstore had been a school institution since 1800; it was located in a restored barn with three floors and a fireplace. In better times, Dina would have enjoyed spending a leisurely hour or so here, but now she wandered aimlessly among the books while Jordy looked for the texts he needed.

Her eyes swam over titles, not lingering – and then suddenly stopped, captured by words that pierced her apathy: *Prayers for Bobby: A Mother's Coming to Terms with the Suicide of her Gay Son*. Oh God, she thought, oh God, did you show me this as a warning? Or as a reminder that there are worse things than having your children taken by their father? She touched the book, wanted to buy it. But she didn't dare. Not now, not when Jordy could see. As she glanced around, she realized that there were other, related books nearby. *Remembering Brad: On the Loss of a Son to AIDS*. She almost gasped aloud at the horror implied by that title. Her eyes moved quickly away to *Sudden Strangers: The Story of a Gay Son and His Father*. It was as if the books were speaking to her, warning her to protect Jordy, now more than ever. She would buy them all, she resolved. But not here. When she got home.

From the corner of her eye, she saw Jordy approaching. She moved towards the next display, picked up a volume without reading the title, began to turn the pages, unseeing. She looked up: 'Do you have what you need?' she asked brightly. Jordy said he did. She paid for his books and they walked out into the bright sunshine.

'We haven't done anything fun for you, Mom. Do you want to go over to the museum?'

Dina was about to say 'no', but quickly reconsidered. When was the last time they had gone to a museum? A movie? Something pleasant they could share? 'What a good idea,' she said.

As they walked towards Chapel Avenue, she remembered the first time they had come to this campus, she and Karim. Without Jordy. He was not to be consulted. He was the problem and he was to have no say in the solution. Karim had pointed out the academy's merits: foreign languages taught, foreign students from many countries. 'My father made my decisions until I went away to college,' Karim said adamantly when Dina suggested that Jordy should have a say in which school he attended. 'And even then, he was always consulted on matters of importance.'

Dina had protested that America was not Jordan and that American children could not be expected to behave as he had. Karim had looked at her, almost pityingly, as if to say: Don't you understand – that's what I'm trying to change? She sighed now – and Jordy looked at her with those same dark eyes, but his were loving and tender. 'Something wrong, Mom?'

'No, sweetheart. I was just thinking what a beautiful campus this is.' Liar, said a voice in her head. Coward. Later, she pleaded, I'll tell him later. And the 600-acre campus was beautiful. She had tried to take comfort in that – and the school's distinguished pedigree, which Karim had detailed at length when he'd selected the place of Jordy's exile. It had been founded during the American Revolution. John Hancock had signed the academy's act of incorporation, and George Washington had addressed the students. Since then, the school had turned out many distinguished alumni, including President George W. Bush, his father, and his brother 'Jeb'. Samuel Morse and Oliver Wendell Holmes had been Phillips graduates, as was Dr Benjamin Spock.

All that would have been fine with Dina – if Jordy hadn't been banished to the academy as a punishment for simply being who he was.

On their way to the museum, they passed some fine boutiques and antique shops on Chapel Avenue, and Dina made a note to buy Jordy a gift before she left. She had come bearing a carton full of his favorite snacks – Mallomars and cheese crackers and pastries from Grace's – but she wanted to leave him with something tangible, something that said, 'I love you, no matter what.'

When they arrived at the Addison Gallery of American Art, Dina conceded that the museum was yet another strong point in the school's favor. Not many high schools, public or private, had a major art museum on campus, as well as an archeological museum. Not to mention a $500-million endowment.

Dina and Jordy spent a quiet hour admiring paintings by Winslow Homer, Mary Cassatt, John Singer Sargent, and the other American artists that made up the permanent collection. Jordy was especially drawn to the section of the museum devoted to the photography of Margaret Bourke-White. He mentioned that he had been taking pictures himself, of the many historic buildings on campus and in the town of Andover. 'Maybe you'd like a new camera,' Dina offered. 'If you're serious about this hobby, you could probably use—'

'Relax, Mom,' he cut in, with a knowing smile. 'My old Canon is fine. I'm not that good yet. And you don't have to buy me stuff to make things OK for me. I'm fine. Honest.'

Now, Dina thought, now is the time. But the moment passed. And soon it was five o'clock, the museum's closing time. Jordy went back to his dorm to pick up his friends, and Dina went back to the Andover Inn. It was a pleasant place, European in atmosphere, with comfortable accommodation and good service. But the inn's principal attraction was that it was a short walk to Jordy's dorm.

She stripped off the slacks and sweater she'd been wearing, lay down on the bed, and closed her eyes. She was so very tired these days. Sleep had been difficult, some nights impossible. Maybe she'd ask Sarah for some pills. She knew she couldn't go on like this – whatever 'this' was. She would have to get through the days and the nights ahead. She would have to survive somehow until her babies came home. Please God, she prayed silently, please help me find a way to bring them home.

She must have fallen asleep because the next thing she heard was the ringing of the telephone. The wake-up call from the front desk. She showered quickly and dressed carefully, in one of her better business suits. It wouldn't do to look less than her best when she met Jordy's friends. She was so glad he'd made some. Were they all gay? she wondered. Or were they . . . ? Were they what? Normal? Heterosexual? Straight? The opposite of Jordy? She hated herself for such thoughts, but here they were.

Maybe if she read all those books she'd seen, maybe she could make herself a better mother to a gay son. Because she needed to be, God only knew she wanted to be.

At seven o'clock, she went into the dining room. The three boys were already there. Shiny and clean and well turned out in their almost identical blue blazers and khaki pants. Dina greeted them all, gave Jordy a light kiss on the cheek, not wanting to overdo the display of parental affection in front of his friends. She smiled at the other boys and murmured a hello.

'Mom, I think you met Brian the last time you were here. And this is my friend, Kevin Doolan.' The two guests shook her hand and waited until she was seated to resume their own seats. She had chosen the inn for dinner because they offered a Dutch Indonesian *Rijsttafel* on Sunday evenings. She thought the boys would enjoy the kind of meal where you could take what you liked and as much as you liked. The dining room was pretty, the tables set with flowers and candles, and light classical music played in the background.

'Jordy mentioned that you've all eaten here before,'

Dina said to her guests. 'You'll have to tell me what's good.'

'It's all pretty good,' said Kevin. After a moment's hesitation, he added: 'The beverage of choice with *Rijsttafel* is beer. They have a good selection here. That's what my dad and I had when we came last month.'

'Nice try,' said Dina, smiling at the boy. 'I'm afraid your beverage selection this evening will be limited to soft drinks, juice or mineral water.'

The trio accepted her statement with grace, as if they hadn't expected anything else. Jordy helped Dina select cold marinated vegetables, roast chicken on sticks with peanut sauce, shrimp with vegetables, and seasoned ground beef. 'Here's how you do it, Mom,' he said, arranging her plate. 'You put the rice in the middle and you make sure not to mix the side dishes or you lose the taste. Kevin's dad had it in Amsterdam, so he knows how you're supposed to eat it.'

Dina followed her son's directions, and though she had no appetite, she made a good show of enjoying her dinner. Thanks to Jordy's friends, conversation moved along. Brian mentioned his new girlfriend at the Abbot Academy, the girls' school that had merged with Phillips in 1973. So that answered one of Dina's questions: Brian wasn't gay. And Kevin? She couldn't say. He talked about college. 'Some of the schools send recruiters here . . . they run open houses, you know, telling us why we should apply. What I'm hoping for is Harvard or Columbia. Because those are the law schools I'm after later. They're the best,' he said authoritatively. 'But if I don't make them, I can probably get into Yale. My dad went there and he gives them a lot of money.'

111

Kevin turned to Jordy. 'Where are you applying? You never said.'

'Don't know,' Jordy mumbled. 'It's still early.'

Of course, Dina thought, he doesn't know his father's gone. He thinks he won't have any say about college either. 'There's plenty of time,' Dina said. 'By the time you're juniors, you may have a change of heart.'

'Not me,' said Kevin. 'I've known what I want to do since ninth grade.'

'That's good,' Dina said, hoping for a change of subject. Brian obliged with a story about a priest from his parish who had been arrested for embezzling. 'My mother won't believe it. She thinks the papers made it all up.'

'That's terrible,' Dina said, 'the embezzling, I mean.'

'Yeah. Well, at least he wasn't molesting kids like some of the other guys.'

Dina shouldn't have been shocked – the scandal of priests molesting children had been front-page material for so long – but hearing it now and in such a casual, almost cynical way, made her sad. She recalled her own favorite priest at St Catherine's in Spring Lake and the trust she'd always had in him. She'd enjoyed a sheltered life during her summers in New Jersey – and even during the rest of the year, in the city. She thought, not for the first time, how different her children's world was from the one she'd grown up in.

Though the boys ate heartily, they were still up for dessert, so they all had fried bananas sprinkled with palm sugar and Indonesian cinnamon layer cake.

After Dina signed for the bill, she asked Jordy if he'd visit with her for a while before he returned to his dorm. This is it, she thought. I'm leaving tomorrow, so this is my last chance. They said good night to his friends, and they thanked her politely for dinner.

Dina and Jordy returned to her suite. She took the bottles of water she'd ordered earlier from room service, offered some to Jordy. Finally she sat down beside him on the chintz-covered sofa. 'So,' she said, touching his arm, 'how are things at school? Really.' The question wasn't simply routine. In spite of the school's ethnic diversity, having an Arab name during such troubled times was not the same as being of Italian or German or Japanese descent.

'I told you the last time, Mom, it's fine, really.'

'And no one is . . . you know, bothering you about . . . being Arab?'

Jordy's smile was beautiful to behold. How could Karim have hardened his heart against this child?

'Not the way you mean, Mom. I mean, sometimes people say sh . . . stuff. And sometimes I end up feeling I have to defend the whole Arab world when the only place I've ever seen is Jordan. But I'm handling it. In fact, I bet I get an A in History this term . . . I've had a lot to say in class.'

'You have? I mean what do you talk about?'

'About terrorism. About the Palestinian problem. The demonstrations in Jordan and Egypt and all the other Arab countries.'

Now it was Dina's turn to smile. In New York, Jordy had seemed not at all interested in politics, whether American or foreign. Odd, she thought. Given Karim's rejection, she might have expected him to turn completely away from anything Arab, but now it seemed the opposite had happened.

'I've been in the middle of some pretty fierce

113

arguments. And not always with the Jewish kids, which surprised me. But I've only had one real fight.'

'Oh, Jordy . . .'

'It's OK, Mom. I had to – or it would have been really bad for me. All I got was a bloody nose.' He added: 'I gave as good as I got.'

Dina was thinking of what to say when Jordy asked: 'How's Rachel?' It was so unexpected that she was startled. Sarah's daughter? If Jordy had not been . . . gay, she would have started thinking like a matchmaker. But as it was . . . 'She's fine,' Dina said tentatively. 'Why do you ask?'

Jordy looked as if he were debating what to answer. 'We've been writing for a while,' he said cautiously.

Dina's eyebrows lifted.

Jordy tried to joke. 'Two maladjusted kids who used to have fathers. We have a lot in common.'

The flippancy made her ache. She squeezed his hand. Then, panic. Had Rachel mentioned anything about Karim taking the twins? She couldn't have or Jordy wouldn't be so calm. So she had better do it herself, right now.

'Jordy, there's something I need to tell you, sweetheart.'

'I knew it,' he said. 'I knew there was something. You sounded so funny when we talked on the phone.'

Dina nodded. She had tried hard to maintain a normal demeanor. But when he had asked to talk to Suzanne and Ali, she had made up a story that sounded odd even to her.

'It's about your father . . .'

'What's he done now?' Jordy asked bitterly.

She told the story, simply and with as little emotion as she could manage.

114

'That bastard! That lousy bastard!'

She reached for him, held him close.

Suddenly he pulled away. 'It's my fault, isn't it? It's my fault he left you.'

'No, Jordy, no! It's not your fault.'

'Yeah, it is. Everything was fine before . . . before I told him I was gay. It's me he hates, not you. I bet he wishes I were dead instead of being gay.'

'Don't say that, sweetheart, don't even think it!'

'Yeah,' he said, 'sure, don't say it. But I know it's true.'

'It's not,' Dina protested.

'I remember how he looked at me that day. He looked like he wanted to kill me. You acted like he was just, you know, being a dad. Like when a kid racks up the family car and the dad gets really mad. But this was worse, and you know it. And now he's gone.'

Dina sighed. She reached for her son again. 'It isn't that simple, Jordy. OK, your father went a little crazy that day. But things weren't all right before then. There were problems.'

He looked skeptical. 'Like what? What kind of problems?'

She sighed again. She didn't want to be having this discussion with Jordy, but there was no way to avoid it. Not if she was to convince her son that he wasn't the cause of his family's breakup. At least not the only cause. 'There were differences, sweetheart. Maybe they didn't seem so bad . . .' No, they didn't, she thought. I didn't even realize how bad they were. 'But your father seems to feel they were insurmountable.'

'Like what? You're not telling me anything.'

'Oh . . . like the fact that I wanted to work and your father wanted me to stay at home.'

'That's it? That's the big difference?'

'No . . . but he wanted us to be more like his family at home, not so . . . American.'

Jordy looked puzzled now.

'You mean he decided all of a sudden that he didn't like us because we were American.'

She shook her head. 'Not all of a sudden. I think this has been going on inside his head for a long time.'

Jordy waited for more.

She plunged in. 'I think September Eleventh brought it to a head. You know, his culture against the American culture. He chose his.'

'Christ,' Jordy muttered, 'that really sucks.'

She smiled in spite of herself. 'Yes,' she said, 'yes, it does.'

CHAPTER FIFTEEN

Gregory Einhorn's office was on Third Avenue in the 40s, in a building occupied by a cross-section of typical Manhattan enterprises: accountants, computer and internet firms, a major publisher of textbooks, talent agents and lawyers. Einhorn shared the thirtieth floor with a graphic design company and a travel agency. The door said simply 'Einhorn Associates'. No elaboration.

Dina arrived a few minutes early. A fiftyish receptionist in a gray silk button-up blouse took her name and said that Mr Einhorn would be only a moment. British accent: Dina thought of Moneypenny in the Bond movies. The office's quiet, almost austere, appointments bespoke efficiency, competence and discretion.

Einhorn himself came out to greet her. 'Mrs Ahmad?'

Dina wasn't sure what she had expected – Bogart? Connery? – but Gregory Einhorn wasn't it. Thirty-five or so, blond, crew-cut, square-jawed, all-American, he looked as if he had exchanged a Green Beret captain's uniform for an expensively tailored suit.

His office looked out toward the East River.

'Coffee? A cold drink? Something else?'

'No, thank you.'

A jet was rising from LaGuardia or Kennedy, Dina could never keep their locations straight. Einhorn gestured toward a chair and she sat. He leaned comfortably against a dark cherrywood desk that had a look of extreme order, the few papers on it precisely aligned. A small matte-black tape recorder. A laptop, closed, to one side. A high-tech-looking phone. On a wall a photo bore out Dina's impression about a military background: a very young Einhorn in uniform was shaking hands with the elder President Bush. The picture was surrounded by many smaller ones – family snapshots of some kind, they appeared to be.

Einhorn opened a manila folder and inspected its contents briefly, a doctor checking a patient's chart. She had stated the basics of her situation when making the appointment.

'So, Mrs Ahmad—'

'Please, just Dina.'

'Dina.' A quick smile, a switch turned on, then off again. 'And I'm Gregory.'

'Gregory.' Not Greg.

'So your husband has taken your two children, twins, to Jordan. Eight years old.' He checked the folder again. 'Two weeks ago.'

'Yes. Two of our three children. I also have a teenaged son.'

'Yes. Any new developments? Since you first contacted us?' His speech was as accentless and generically American as his looks.

'He's called several times. Allowed me to speak to the children. But otherwise, no developments.'

118

'I'm going to record our conversation, if you don't mind.'

'No. I mean, fine.'

He turned on the recorder, spoke her name, the date, and the time, and said, 'Tell me everything you can.'

She did. He listened intently, breaking in often with questions: where precisely were Karim and the children? What kind of house? What kind of neighborhood? Who else was in the house? When were the children separate from their father? Did they go to school, he to work? To many of his questions Dina had to answer that she didn't know. 'I feel as if I haven't been much help,' she apologized when she had told him all she could think of.

He waved it off. 'No matter. We'll find out all these things and a lot more before we start. We'll know everything we need to know. Which brings me to the most important question.' He moved behind the desk and sat. 'In your opinion is there any chance of a resolution of this matter through normal channels?'

'I'm not sure what you mean.'

Einhorn nodded as if he had expected precisely these words. 'I mean is there any chance, in your opinion, that this might eventually be worked out between you and your husband? That you might reconcile? Or, failing that, that he might return the children for other reasons?'

'I . . . I don't think so.' She was surprised that she couldn't be more definite.

Einhorn studied her. 'It's early yet. I like for my clients to be sure.'

'You want a yes or no?'

'No, that's not necessary. It's for your peace of

119

mind. And to save you some money, if other solutions are available. Quite a bit of money. But it's your call. We can carry out the mission regardless of other possible scenarios.'

The mission. 'Mr Einhorn – Gregory – can you get my children back?'

'Yes.' Absolute confidence. Dina felt a surge of elation touched with fear.

'How would you do it?'

He shrugged. 'Depends entirely on the specifics of the situation. Best case? Sometimes a well-placed bribe is all you need: a teacher takes her eyes off the school-yard for a critical few minutes, for example. Or sometimes there's a resource on the other side: a girl-friend, say, who's found out that caring for someone else's kids isn't quite as rewarding as she expected.' He glanced quickly at Dina. She'd already told him she didn't think there was another woman. Not yet, anyway.

'But sometimes there are no easy vulnerabilities,' Einhorn went on, like a young professor warming to the subject of his lecture. 'In that case the best approach is usually the simplest: a quick removal by competent force, followed by a fast withdrawal.'

'What kind of force?' The word made Dina uncomfortable. They were talking about her children.

Again the on-off smile. 'Don't worry. We're not going to war here. Our people are very, very good. The best. Nobody gets hurt. That's rule one.'

'Have you ever had a . . . case like this one? In a foreign country?'

'Something like forty per cent of our operations are foreign. It's a specialty, really. Very few outfits have the resources that we do.'

It suddenly struck Dina that the whole situation was almost surreal. She was talking with a man whose profession, at which he was apparently very successful, included taking children from one parent and giving them to another.

'Is two children a problem?' she asked. 'More difficult?'

'Not really. Multiples are fairly common. You can see several right here.' He gestured toward the photos on the wall. Dina looked more closely and saw that they *were* family pictures, but not of the kind she had imagined. They all showed a happy parent and child, sometimes two children. In most the parent was a woman, but there were a few men as well. One or two appeared to have been taken at the actual moment of reunion, in an airport lounge or similar setting. Most were more domestic; one had a Christmas tree in the background.

One photo caught her eye, possibly because both the woman in it and her pretty, kindergarten-age daughter looked so radiantly happy.

'Can you tell me about any of these?' she asked Einhorn.

'In a general way, sure.'

'This one?'

'Belgium,' he said immediately. 'The father was a dual citizen. Divorced. Weekend custody, the usual kind of thing. An outing to McDonald's, then to the airport. Brussels. Weekdays the little girl was in the care of the grandparents. A townhouse – the European sense, a house, not some condo. Wealthy neighborhood, these were well-off people. There was a nice open park practically across the street. Our man – British – got in with some story about following the

121

footsteps of his own dad back during the Second World War. We had two more men on the ground, he let them in. The granddad wanted to resist, actually grabbed the fireplace poker' – Einhorn seemed amused remembering this – 'but that was no problem. Nobody hurt. I told you we use only the best. Landed a chopper right in the park. An hour later they and the kid were in Germany, where Mom was waiting. A half-hour after that she and the girl were on a flight to the States.'

The story disturbed Dina, as much as she'd like to have something similar happen with the twins. It was the business about the grandfather. What if he'd had some other weapon? What if he had been younger, stronger? What if something else had happened – someone had alerted the police, for instance? 'Competent force' – it still sounded dangerous. With her children in the middle. Still . . .

'I suppose I need to know how much you charge.'

Einhorn leaned forward, flashed the smile, was instantly serious. 'Every job is different. For example, Jordan isn't Belgium. The neighboring countries aren't Germany. But we won't ask you for a blank check. Part of our service is a solid estimate up front. I'll have some basic research done, no charge, take just a couple of days. Unless of course you'd rather not go forward based on what you've already heard.'

'I guess what I need is a general idea of the cost. I'm not . . . my resources aren't unlimited.'

'All right. I can tell you that our minimum for a foreign mission is a hundred thousand. Beyond that it's a question of what needs to be done. The situation you've described, I have to tell you, sounds as if quite a bit will need to be done. As I said, we'll work up a firm estimate. But I think the max would be two hundred and fifty thousand. Unless there are very unusual expenses.'

The sum took Dina's breath away. Where could she possibly get that kind of money? But she said only, 'When can you give me the estimate?'

'Give us three days. Is that OK for you?'

'Yes, of course.'

'Miss Easterly will set up an appointment.'

'Do you need anything now? Any payment?'

'No. But we do ask that you make half the minimum payment at the time you engage us for the mission.'

'Fifty thousand.'

'Yes.'

'I see. Of course I'll need to think about this.'

'Of course.' There seemed little more to say. Dina rose and Einhorn stood as well.

'I know it's a difficult time for you, Dina,' he said. 'Remember what I said: it's early. Be sure. We'll be here whenever you need us. No rush.'

She thanked him and he walked her out to the comfortably daunting Miss Easterly to make an appointment.

On the way back to her empty home, Dina considered that she didn't much like Gregory Einhorn. At the same time, she realized, she had not for a second doubted one thing: his ability to do exactly what he said he would do.

CHAPTER SIXTEEN

'A quarter of a million dollars!' Emmeline couldn't believe it. 'And you went to see that . . . that mercenary all alone?'

'He isn't a mercenary. Not exactly. He's a . . . kind of specialist. Very professional, very businesslike. And the quarter of a million . . . well, that's the maximum. Unless there are very unusual expenses. It might be less.'

'I wouldn't count on that,' said Sarah. 'In fact, I'd count on the unusual expenses.'

The three were meeting in a SoHo restaurant they remembered from the playschool days. It had changed its name, ownership, and decor and seemed to attract a young crowd. As young as they had been when they first met.

'Do you have it?' asked Emmeline.

'Not on hand. Just the deposit or whatever it is, fifty thousand, would tap me out.' The money Karim had left in their account. Some jewelry she could sell. Maybe she could get a second mortgage on the townhouse. No, on her modest income, a bank wouldn't give a second. Maybe her Roth IRA . . . she had a good chunk salted away there. But not enough.

'We could raise the money,' Sarah said.

'How?'

'Any number of ways.'

Sarah could probably write a check for the balance. That was the last thing Dina wanted. 'I'm not dragging either of you into this,' she said.

'Don't be an idiot,' Sarah answered.

'We *are* in it,' Emmeline seconded. 'And I have a fair amount vegetating in money market funds. Nice and liquid.'

Another last thing Dina wanted.

The conversation paused while a waitress assimilated their orders of various salads and drinks – white wine for Em and Dina, a martini for Sarah. When she was gone Dina said, 'Look, I know you're with me. I thank you. I love you both. But I don't want you putting money into my problem. I can't have that, won't have it.'

'Can't. Won't. Tell me you wouldn't do the same if it was one of us.' Emmeline might have been correcting a child for some sandbox misbehavior. Dina felt tears in her eyes.

'We can get the money,' said Sarah flatly. 'That's not the issue – although we'll need to make sure it's well spent. The question is whether you want to go through with this. Whether you think it's the best way to go.'

'Right now I . . . What other way is there?'

'Do you trust this Einhorn guy?' Emmeline wanted to know.

'Yes. He seems like he knows exactly what he's doing.'

'Do you *trust* him?'

'Yes.'

'Then let's find out exactly what he has in mind and how much he wants for it,' said Sarah.

'Yeah,' said Em. 'And then let's do it.'

A night, a day, a night, a day, another night with no further word from Karim, meaning no word from or about the twins. The only contact with Jordan was with her son Jordan. Unfortunately his call of commiseration was mainly a bitterly sarcastic diatribe against his father, which, however much Dina might secretly agree with much of it, provided little in the way of comfort. There were Em and Sarah, of course. Em was like a cheerleader. Sarah discussed finances. A bank loan made more sense than simply pooling their assets. Sarah could arrange for it and would be signatory if necessary. There were even ways to write it off against taxes, she assured Dina, who understood none of it.

All along, her hopes hung on Gregory Einhorn. By the morning of their meeting she was bursting with a strange mixture of anxiety and anticipation.

Miss Easterly greeted her again in the quiet, austere reception area. She seemed, if anything, more properly British than before. Dina wondered if this reflected her status as a likely, rather than a merely possible, client.

From the second Gregory Einhorn appeared she knew that something was wrong. He flicked the same here-then-gone smile, ushered her into his office as before, made the same perfunctory offer of coffee or cold drink, but something was different.

He came to the point as soon as she was seated. 'Mrs Ahmad' – she noted the reversion to formality – 'I've looked into your situation as I promised. And

I'm afraid I'm going to have to pass on this one.'

'What are you talking about? Why? You said you'd do it.'

'I said I'd look into it. And what I found isn't good. Not from my viewpoint, at least.'

'In what way?'

'Mrs Ahmad, I'm not sure you were completely forthcoming with me. Your husband is very well connected back in his homeland.'

'I told you he was.'

'You didn't tell me he was part of a very important family with powerful connections. That changes things. Changes them very much.'

Dina was confused. 'But . . . I thought I'd explained. Yes, he has connections, his family too, but that's how it is in the Arab world. I thought you understood that.'

The smile was very brief, patronizing. She wondered if she had somehow offended him. She glanced at the photo on the wall, the one of the smiling woman whose daughter had been brought back from Brussels.

If Einhorn was offended, his voice remained cordial, even soothing. 'I pay people to understand these things for me, Mrs Ahmad. In my business there's no substitute for accurate information. Believe me, my caution is for the benefit of my clients as much as myself.'

'So you're saying . . . you won't take this job? My children?'

'I'm afraid not. The risk factor is too great. For everyone.'

It was as if the floor were sliding away beneath her to reveal the thirty-story drop. For three days she had thought of little except the tough, competent, experienced Gregory Einhorn commanding a 'mission' to bring back her children. And now he was turning her down flat.

'I really didn't understand. I can see that it might be more complicated than I thought.' She could hear the thin desperation in her voice. 'I could pay more. Not much, but more than you said.'

'Mrs Ahmad, I take chances for a living. But I'm not a gambler. The reward must be proportionate to the risk. Not only for me, but for my people. I couldn't take this case for less than two million dollars.'

'I can't pay that much.'

'I'm sorry. Truly very sorry. I can't do it.'

And that was that. Dina thought that Miss Easterly gave her a look of sympathy on the way out, but she couldn't be sure. She didn't let herself cry until she was in the elevator.

Chapter Seventeen

I can't believe I'm doing this, Sarah thought as she checked her make-up in the compact mirror for the second time. I can't believe I actually asked the man for a date.

In truth she hadn't done all the asking and it wasn't exactly a date. But here she was, nevertheless, waiting for David Kallas to join her for dinner. All because she had called for an appointment and found he was booked during her few free hours. And because he had suggested an after-hours meeting. 'Perhaps a drink, if you like,' he'd added. 'Then we could talk without either one of us rushing off to the next appointment.'

'How about the Harvard Club,' she volunteered. 'It's near your office.'

A pause. 'We could even have dinner,' he said, 'if you have time. We both have to eat.'

So actually he had made the dinner invitation. And now she was waiting nervously in the elegant wood-paneled Grill Room, a place that had been a source of pleasure and pride for years.

And now David was coming toward her, smiling. She rose, said hello, extended her hand and smiled back.

'What a good idea this was,' he said, as if to allay

any embarrassment on her part. 'When I'm as busy as I have been lately, I sometimes end up making do with a stale bagel or half of an old corned-beef sandwich.'

'And your Jewish mother allows that?' she teased, rather boldly, she thought, for such brief acquaintance.

He laughed. 'If she knew about it, she wouldn't allow it. I guess that's one of the reasons I moved out of the house as soon as I finished law school. Now at least once a week, I hear that my room, in my mother's splendid brownstone – so conveniently located near Ocean Parkway – is still there for me.'

'I know what you mean. I grew up in Brooklyn, too. Near Eastern Parkway. I had to get married to leave home. I just didn't see any other way of getting out of the house.'

'That's terrible.'

'I'm joking. But just a little. And that's what I wanted to talk to you about. My marriage.'

A waiter arrived to take their orders. A wine spritzer with lime for Sarah, red wine for David. The drinks came quickly, and as Sarah started to sip hers, she realized that this was the first time in years she was with a man in something other than a hospital setting.

'So this meeting isn't about your friend, Dina? I thought . . . I guess I thought you wanted to voice your concerns about some issue connected with her problem. Though you know I couldn't tell you anything about what we discussed privately.'

'No. Well, of course I'm very concerned about Dina. Em and I both are. In fact, Dina's situation is one reason that I had a conversation with my ex.'

'Your ex-husband? How do you think he might be able to help.'

'I'll tell you in a minute. But would you mind if we

went into the dining room now?' Sarah asked. 'So we can get something to eat before it gets too late.'

The club's main dining room had oak-paneled walls and an ornate forty-foot ceiling. The tables were set with fresh flowers and candles; a pianist was rendering a sophisticated take on a Broadway show tune. Soon after they were seated, a waiter took their orders. Sarah resumed the conversation.

'Ari carries two passports . . . American and Israeli. He does a lot of business in Israel and he knows a lot of people. Some of them operate through what you might call back channels. I asked him if he could do anything to help get Dina's children back. He said he would make some inquiries.'

'It couldn't hurt, I suppose,' he said. Then he considered the possibility that Dina might employ the professional whose name was on the card he'd given her. And the possibility that outside interference of any kind could jeopardize a professional operation. 'But you know,' he added, 'if your ex-husband were actually to get involved, there's always the chance that something like that would backfire.'

Sarah shook her head, smiling at the thought of Ari attempting a rescue mission on Dina's behalf. 'No, I'm sure Ari wouldn't go that far. Not for me and certainly not for Dina. What he might do, though, is ask around – and maybe he'll come up with something Dina could use.'

'Well, that would be all right,' David said, then added quickly, 'and I didn't mean to discourage your efforts. I think it's wonderful that you and Ms LeBlanc want to help your friend. It's just that we have to consider the time we live in. So much hatred, so much bloodshed in that part of the world.'

Sarah nodded. 'That's another reason I think Karim is crazy to take those kids to Jordan. They're as American as . . .'

'. . . apple pie?' he finished with a smile.

'Yes.' He's handsome when he smiles, she thought, less intense. 'The twins talk and act like American kids. Jordy, though, he's the image of his father.'

'Jordy . . . that would be the older son, the one who was left behind.'

'Because he's gay. His father has rejected him completely.'

'Mrs Ahmad told me a little about that. It's very sad. I can't imagine how the boy must feel.'

They were quiet a moment, contemplating Dina's situation. Then Sarah spoke. 'What I wanted to see you about was my divorce.'

'A divorce? I thought you just said "ex-husband".'

'I did. And he is. We were divorced three years ago. But he refused to give me a *get*. And he still refuses whenever I bring it up.'

'You want a *get*?' David was obviously surprised.

Sarah understood his reaction. No doubt he was wondering why a woman like her – by all appearances a thoroughly modern woman rather than an observant one – wanted a religious divorce in addition to the civil one. 'I'm not sure I can explain,' she said slowly. 'I don't go to *schul* regularly. I do observe the Sabbath unless a patient really needs me. I observe the holy days, but I don't keep a kosher kitchen . . .' Here she smiled at the memory of her mother who did keep kosher – but who insisted on her regular 'fix' of Lobster Cantonese once a week.

'I am a Jew in my heart and my soul even if I don't look the way some people think I should, or follow all the rules. But I believe marriage is one of the most important things we do. I want to end mine the right way. Does that make any sense to you?'

David thought for a moment. 'I suppose. My cousin Arlene paid her husband, Morris, a great deal of money to give her a *get*. I know that's not the spirit of the *get* – husband and wife are supposed to consent freely. But she wanted to marry again and have children, and if she didn't have a *get*, any children from a second marriage would be illegitimate. So . . .' He shrugged as if to convey the way of the world. 'She gave him what he wanted. I'm sure you know that spouses sometimes withhold consent as a bargaining chip in the distribution of marital assets.'

'Ari doesn't need any more money. He has plenty for two lifetimes. Maybe three.'

'Then what? Why do you think he refuses you?'

'I'm not sure. I think it's about control.'

'Ah. Well, that makes a certain kind of perverse sense. Maybe he feels he can keep you from starting another family.'

'I'm not planning to have any more children.'

'But you haven't ruled out remarriage.'

'No,' she said. 'I haven't ruled it out.' She smiled ruefully. 'I just don't see it happening, given the hours I sometimes keep – and the fact that I don't meet anyone except doctors. Don't smile – they're generally married or much too young.'

'OK, no smiling. So what is it that you'd like me to do for you, Mrs Gelman.'

'Sarah, please.'

'Sarah, then.'

'I'd like you to research ways of putting pressure on Ari.'

133

'Wouldn't that be better accomplished if you appealed to a rabbinical court?'

'I've thought about that. But I just . . . well, I don't think I could prevail. Ari is a very good actor. I'm afraid that if we went before a court of rabbis, he'd come across as the good spouse, hoping against hope for a reconciliation. And I'd be the bad wife who doesn't even make *schul* regularly.'

'I see. But then why did you think I could help?'

'I'm not sure. I guess the idea just popped into my head. It was after you spoke about your mother. Your aunt. And your cousin. You seemed like someone who cared about such things. About people. Not the kind of lawyer people make bad jokes about. I just hoped . . .'

David seemed thoughtful, as if he were absorbing what she said. Then a broad smile lit his face. 'I believe that's the nicest thing anyone ever said to me.'

'. . . and my friend Dina said you seemed like a nice man.'

The smile exploded into laughter. 'With a recommendation like that, I guess I have to try to come up with a solution to your problem.'

By the time their dinners arrived – lamb chops for Sarah and salmon for David – they were chatting comfortably about their respective Brooklyn childhoods, comparing the quirks of their families, debating the merits of egg creams versus cream soda.

David was a good listener, an intelligent listener. I suppose good lawyers are like that, Sarah thought. It doesn't mean there's anything personal going on, she cautioned herself. After all, this isn't a date. And then she blurted out: 'You never married?' Because he had referred to himself as an old bachelor.

'No.' A touch of sadness there. 'And don't think that hasn't been a source of *tsuris* to my family. In my community, kids marry young, and almost always within the community. It's not unusual for them to have a couple of babies before they're twenty-five.'

'But you didn't do any of that.'

He sighed. 'It wasn't for lack of trying, believe me. My mother, my aunts, they worked overtime looking for women. I just never met anyone I wanted to spend my entire life with. My cousin Ikey once asked me if I was gay.'

Sarah laughed, then stopped herself. Was he gay?

'I told him I wasn't. I said I had just seen too much in my line of work to jump into marriage.'

'A good answer.'

'Ikey had a better one. He said that at forty – this was a few years ago – I wasn't exactly at a jumping age. Not when everyone around me was married by twenty or twenty-five.'

'And you said?' Now Sarah was amused and intrigued.

'I said I was looking for the kind of woman who didn't want a boy in his twenties.'

'Ah.'

A brief conversational lull followed, but it wasn't uncomfortable. They ordered coffee and agreed to share a flourless chocolate cake for dessert.

'Your friend Dina's husband – what did you think of him, before this . . . this unfortunate business?'

Sarah had to think. Her opinion of Karim was colored so much by the heinous thing he had done recently, and it was hard to shift her perspective. 'I don't think I ever liked him,' she said slowly. 'But maybe that was because I knew he didn't like me.'

'Why ever not?'

'I'm pretty sure it was because I was Jewish, though he never said anything. Neither did Dina. And, of course, Ari was from Israel. I don't think Karim liked Em, either. Not because she was black – I think that's a non-issue where he's from – but because she's so, you know, free: bigger than life, speaks her mind, never defers to men or women.' She paused. 'But I also didn't like that Karim made Dina feel as if he'd done her a big favor by allowing her to work. At least Ari never did that.' No, actually Ari always wanted her to do something more high profile. He had been furious when she turned down a prestigious affiliation with Columbia University in favor of working at a hospital clinic. She had teased him about wanting a trophy wife, but he hadn't laughed. 'To be fair,' she added, 'Ari didn't much like my friendship with Dina. And that was definitely because Karim was an Arab.'

'But neither of you gave up your friends.'

'Hell, no!' she said emphatically.

'That's good. How was Mr Ahmad with the children?'

'Good,' she said grudgingly. 'Before the thing with Jordy, I would have said you couldn't find a better father. He really doted on those kids. Why do you ask?'

'Just to put my own mind at ease. Sometimes . . . well, sometimes parents take children just to cause pain to their spouses.'

'No,' she said, still grudgingly. 'I'm sure that's not Karim. He may be wrongheaded and a louse, but he took those kids because he wants them.'

Their time together seemed to go quickly and when Sarah looked at her watch, it was past ten. 'Oh, gosh,' she said, 'I'd better get going. Early day tomorrow. Very early day.'

David called for the check and insisted on paying, even though Sarah pointed out that it was her club and by rights she should take the bill.

'Next time,' he said. She was pleased by the remark, even while she told herself it was simply a polite rejoinder that meant nothing. She was even more pleased a few minutes later, when, as they walked out into the street, he said, 'This was fun, Sarah. I'd like to do it again. If you're interested.'

She agreed readily, noticing that while they were standing side by side, he was but a few inches taller than she was. Why, she thought, we practically see eye-to-eye.

CHAPTER EIGHTEEN

'It can be done,' said Sarah. 'Barely. I think.'

'No. I absolutely refuse to put you at that kind of risk.' Dina meant it. She would chance anything to bring back her children. But she couldn't allow her friends to take ultimate gambles.

Huddled over coffee and sandwiches in the hospital cafeteria – Sarah had only half an hour – they were a council of war suddenly without a plan, without troops, without ammunition.

'Maybe we're going too fast,' said Sarah. It was clear that even she was daunted by the sound of two million dollars. 'These things can take . . . months.' She had started to say years. 'Maybe we should try harder to come up with other options,' she finished lamely.

'Or maybe we should just go find a wise guy,' said Emmeline, suddenly bitter. 'They say you can hire a hit man for a thousand bucks. Less. How much could a kidnapper be?' It wasn't entirely clear that she wasn't serious.

'I could call Danielle Egan at the State Department again,' suggested Dina. 'She said she'd try to make contact with someone in Jordan. Maybe if I pressure her, make myself a nuisance . . . maybe she'll actually do something.'

'Couldn't hurt,' said Sarah without enthusiasm. 'And maybe Ari will come through with something that will help,' she added without conviction.

Em brightened marginally. 'Who's that woman at *The Times*, the one who's always writing about the problems that Muslim women face in some Arab countries? Maybe she'd take a look at this. A different angle to the story, sort of.'

Dina wasn't sure that publicity was a good idea. What good would it do to paint Karim as a bastard if there was no way to reach him? No way to make him give back the children? But maybe if he were to be embarrassed in print, maybe that would put some pressure on him. 'Do you know her – the writer?' Dina asked.

'Can't remember her name,' Em admitted, looking a bit sheepish. 'Well, hell,' she added quickly, 'we're both part of the great liberal media conspiracy. If I put my mind to it, I'm sure I can get her to talk to me.'

Of that Dina had no doubt. But would it do any good? Would anything within Dina's power do any good?

'All right,' said Sarah, in charge if for no other reason than that they were in her hospital and she was a doctor. 'You bug Danielle What's-her-name. Em goes after this writer. I'll see if David has any new ideas.'

'I'm not gonna touch that one,' said Em. It was the closest any of them had come to a laugh, though both Em and Dina had teased Sarah unmercifully about her dinner with the attorney and her reluctant admission that they would probably see each other again. On that note they ended the impromptu meeting, Sarah back to her patients, Em heading for the studio. Dina cabbed to *Mosaic* – she could no longer bear just sitting at home, waiting for something to happen. She would go through the motions of designing a floral theme for an upcoming AIDS benefit, leaving most of the real work to her capable assistant – and then return to her very empty house.

Two days passed with nothing very hopeful.

Emmeline reported that *The Times* writer had shown mild interest in the story, but only in a general way, as something she might look into if she could find another case or two like Dina's. She had taken Dina's name. That was all.

Sarah had met with David – another dinner date. Another pleasant evening, better than pleasant, actually. He had spoken of Sarah's situation to a cousin who was a rabbi, but for Dina, he had little new to offer. It was his opinion that unless something changed in the situation, there was nothing that he or any lawyer could do except run up useless hours.

Dina had hounded Danielle Egan, cajoled her secretary, invoked her father's service once, and had been rewarded with a five-minute conversation that was similar to the one they'd had before. The bureaucrat, although cordial and compassionate, had essentially said that the State Department had other and more important issues in the Middle East. Dina had the distinct feeling that there was a memo on the woman's desk with the words: *Delicate situation. Do nothing.*

And now, Saturday night, she was alone. She flipped aimlessly through TV channels but everything seemed totally vapid, even PBS. If only she were a sports fan, she could perhaps lose herself for three hours in the fortunes of the Mets or Yankees or Knicks. Maybe some music. But everything she thought of seemed either depressing or frivolous. And she couldn't concentrate on reading.

The phone rang. She had already spoken with Em, Sarah, her mother. It had to be Karim.

'Mrs Ahmad?' A man's voice, husky, unfamiliar.

'Yes.'

'My name is John Constantine. I sometimes work with Gregory Einhorn. He gave me your name. He tells me you have a case he can't take on.'

Dina was suspicious. 'He told you about me?'

'Only what I just said. And that I might want to take a look at the . . . problem. Assuming you're interested. Feel free to check this out with him.'

'You're a detective? You work for Gregory Einhorn?'

'*With* him. Sometimes.'

There was something in the voice besides the huskiness and a New York accent. A solidity. Dina took the leap. 'Yes, I'm interested. Interested in discussing it with you, I mean.'

'Sure. When's good for you?'

'Any time.'

'Well, if you mean that literally, we could meet in an hour. Tonight. I know that sounds a little odd – Saturday, you probably have plans – but in my business I don't keep very regular hours.'

Something in the voice. In for a penny, in for a pound, thought Dina. 'I'm free. Yes, let's meet somewhere.'

'Wherever you prefer.'

She named a coffee shop on a corner three blocks away.

141

'I'll see you in an hour,' he said. 'How do I recognize you?'

For the first time in days Dina felt as if she were leaning on something solid enough to make a joke. 'You're the detective,' she said. 'You figure it out.'

Forty-five minutes later she walked into the coffee shop. The place was nearly empty and she saw no one who fit her mental picture of a detective. She took a table and sat. Ordered coffee and sat some more. Ordered a refill and checked her watch. An hour and fifteen minutes. Not a good sign. If the man couldn't even be on time, how was he going to manage something as difficult as getting her children back.

Finally a tall man with an olive complexion and craggy, faintly Mediterranean features came into the coffee shop, glanced in her direction, then walked over to her and nodded. 'Mrs Ahmad?'

'Yes,' she said, trying to keep annoyance out of her voice. He didn't look like a detective even though he was wearing a rumpled trench coat. He didn't apologize for being late, which annoyed Dina even more. This wasn't a good beginning.

'Do you want something to eat?' he asked.

'No.'

'Well, I'm starved. Forgot to stop for lunch today.'

Oh, great, she thought, he can't keep time and he forgets to eat.

After ordering a burger deluxe, Constantine went straight to the point. 'Einhorn didn't tell me much, but there are only two reasons he'd turn down a case: it's too dangerous or he priced himself too high. Or both. I figure both. They go together.'

'So what about you?' Dina wanted to know. 'You're the second string? Cut-rate kidnapping?' She knew the

142

questions were rude, but she had to get them out. When it came to her children, she wasn't interested in anything second-rate.

He smiled, showing even white teeth – and a sense of humor. 'We work differently. Maybe our priorities are different. I work small. I don't turn every job into D-Day. And if I take the job, I take the risk. Do you want to tell me what the job is?'

She did. When she had finished, he said simply, 'I get five hundred a day plus expenses. This case, the expenses will be mainly for travel. If you hire me.'

'And what do I get for that?'

'Your children back.'

Well. That took her breath away. But was it real or empty bravado? She should call Sarah and Emmeline. Or her mother. Or David Kallas. Or all of them. Yet what other choices were being offered?

And so she said, 'When can you start?'

CHAPTER NINETEEN

Dina's first on-the-clock session with John Constantine took place at her home two mornings after their coffee-shop introduction. The location had been a matter of some discussion.

'You can come to my office,' he had said, 'but I have to tell you it's not much: part of an old loft off lower Broadway. A phone, a mailbox, some records. No secretary.'

'Hmm.' Doubt flared up – and Dina had to remind herself that while Gregory Einhorn had all the trappings of success, he would not help her.

For a big man Constantine had an odd little smile. Just the corners of the mouth. But something in her expression must have conveyed the New Yorker's conviction that serious professionals should have professional premises, because he added: 'I told you, I don't work like Greg Einhorn. I'm not out to get rich, which is good, since I'm not getting there, trying to or not. I bought this loft years ago, back when you didn't need to be a millionaire. I rent the rest of the space, except the office, to a photographer. He does fashion shoots, needs lots of room.'

The notion of John Constantine as a landlord struck

Dina as incongruous, but she murmured a polite: 'Sounds interesting.'

'The photographer?' He shrugged. 'Yeah, it's interesting. I thought I knew something about appearances – being deceiving and all that. There are mornings I get on the elevator with some gawky teenaged kid looks like she overslept for high-school volleyball practice. Couple of hours later I see her heading out in her make-up and she's a supermodel.'

'I always wonder,' said Dina, 'whatever happened to just plain models. Why are there only supermodels now?' She wondered why she was making meaningless small talk when she cared nothing about models, plain or super.

Constantine did his little smile again, then got back to business. 'Look, I'm going to need to see your place anyway.' To her questioning look: 'No special reason. I just like to get some idea, a feel for the kids. Your husband. You.' He paused to study her for a moment. 'It doesn't have to be,' he said, 'if you're not comfortable . . .'

'No. That's good.'

And so here he was, filling the door of the apartment. Charcoal sports coat over a black turtleneck and gray slacks. When she offered coffee he followed her into the kitchen.

'This is great,' he said, taking in the spacious room and easing into a chair at the refectory table. 'Like living in the country.' It was the only comment he made on the house.

While she brewed the coffee – Jamaican, her personal favorite – he brought out a reporter-style notebook and fiddled with a small tape recorder.

'Anything new from Karim?' he asked. The use of

the first name surprised her, but she saw that it made sense. They couldn't go through this referring to him as 'Mr Ahmad' or 'your husband'.

'Not since you and I talked.'

'Do you call him?'

'I've called several times trying to talk with Suzanne and Ali. But whenever I make the call, I always get some excuse: they're with their tutor, they're asleep, they're out with their grandfather. It's as if I'm only allowed to talk with my children when Karim makes the call.'

'Who answers the phone when you call?'

'Usually Soraya, my sister-in-law. Sometimes Samir, my brother-in-law.' She made a face. Expressing distaste.

Constantine had the notebook open; he wrote a few words in it.

She poured the coffee. He disappointed her by shoveling three heaped spoons of sugar into it, turning it into designer syrup.

He turned on the recorder and said, 'OK. Tell me what happened. Start with the day Karim took the children. Then give me the background.'

She told him everything she could, holding back nothing. He listened intently but without looking directly at her, as if he were following some important news story on the radio. From time to time he jotted something in the notebook, but he said nothing until she had finished. Then he asked to see the children's room. She showed him. He glanced around, picked up a toy or two, opened the closet and glanced at the remaining clothes, but made no notes. They went back down to the kitchen.

'Twins,' he said. 'Is one of them the leader? The dominant one?'

'The dominant one?' Dina had never thought of it quite that way.

'I've never worked with twins before. But with all kids, brother and brother, brother and sister, sister and sister, one is the leader. I'm betting that's true even of twins. So I'm asking which one follows the other's lead.'

'Suzanne's a little more mature. Girls are at that age.'

'So her brother would probably go along with her in any . . . unusual situation?'

'I think either one would go along with the other, if it seemed important to both of them.'

He nodded and slipped a new cassette in the recorder. 'All right, tell me all you can about where they are now. You've been there, I gather.'

'You mean Jordan?'

'Not so much the country. The house. The people in it. Their lives. Their routine. Whatever you can.'

Now, while she talked, he broke in often with questions and took notes steadily despite the tape recorder. He showed particular interest in Samir and Soraya. What did Dina think of them? What did they think of *her*? All she could tell him was that Samir actively disliked her – maybe disapproved of her was a better word – while Soraya seemed more sympathetic. Not that they were the best of friends – they didn't know each other really well; it was just that sometimes she felt as if she and Soraya had something in common. Maybe nothing more than that they were the wives of brothers, or women in a man's world. But something.

Dozens of questions. What was the neighborhood like? The arrangement of the house itself? Were there other children in it? Other adults? Servants? If the children were in school, where would that be? Different schools for the boy and the girl? Where was grocery shopping done? When? By whom? Were the Ahmads strongly religious? What was the family's actual relationship with the power structure in Jordan?

She answered everything to which she had an answer. Described the large and rambling house, built in the old style, around a courtyard. She mentioned the servants that had been in attendance during her last visit: a housekeeper, a laundress who came in once a week – and the miserable Fatma, of course. She recalled that Samir and his family lived with her in-laws; and that the house was always filled with company – neighbors, other relatives, friends. Shopping was done by the women, by her mother-in-law and the housekeeper: once a week, then. The family was religious, but not intensely so. And while she couldn't describe the exact nature of their connections, they did know a great many important people, including the royal family. 'In case he didn't tell you, that's the part that seemed to throw your friend, Einhorn,' she said.

Constantine nodded, as if Karim's connections were of no great concern to him. Dina began to feel a little better about this man. He seemed to be even more thorough than Einhorn. Not to mention involved.

Finally he closed the notebook and clicked off the tape recorder.

'I'm going to do a little work here,' he said. 'Research, talk to some people. Lay a little ground-work. A few days at most. Then I'm going to have to go over there, take a look for myself. I assume you know that. I'm telling you because it's on your ticket.'

'I understand. All right.'

'I won't be there long, and I won't be living high on the hog. Business-class air, but otherwise I try to keep expenses down.'

'OK.' She didn't know what else to say.

'Give me a week, maybe two, overall. I'll be in touch daily while I'm here, when possible when I'm there. I'll probably have more questions for you. Once I've seen the layout, done a few other things, we'll decide on a plan.'

'Any idea what . . . the nature of the plan will be?'

He shrugged. 'Not yet.' He had started to rise but eased back into the chair. 'Every job is different. You never know.' He was silent for a moment as if reflecting on missions past. 'The best job is the one that doesn't happen,' he told her. 'The one where the two parents work it out together.'

'That doesn't seem likely, I'm afraid.'

Again he shrugged. 'It happens sometimes.'

Another silence. It occurred to her that she was literally putting her hopes in this man's hands, yet she knew almost nothing about him. 'How did you get into this work?' she asked.

The corners-of-the-mouth smile. 'By accident. Someone had a problem, a friend of a friend. Asked me if I could do anything. I looked into it. Things worked out. Next thing I knew, someone else was asking me for the same kind of help. I found out that I was good at it and I liked it. Decided I might as well try to scratch out a living at it.'

'You were with the police?'

'At one time. You're asking about my background.

149

My qualifications.' The smile. 'When I was a kid I made the mistake of joining the Marines. Mainly to tweak my old man – I was going to Columbia at the time. Anyway, it was such a dumb decision that naturally I ended up in so-called Naval Intelligence.'

'Vietnam.'

'No, that was over by then. But I saw some of Southeast Asia, yeah. I re-upped a couple of times, might have been a lifer if I could stand the system. But I couldn't. Then I was with the NYPD for a few years. And now and then I did something for the old outfit – on a freelance basis, you might say. They called me back for the Gulf War. Which is lucky for us.'

'You know Jordan?' Dina asked.

'Not really. But I happened to work with a couple of Jordanians. Very closely. Did a pretty big favor for one of them. So we won't be exactly alone on the ground over there.'

'That's good news.' It was. *Very* good, Dina thought.

Constantine seemed disinclined to continue his story, so she prodded: 'And after the war?'

'After the war was a strange time. I found I didn't like being a cop any more. Too much . . . too much garbage that had nothing to do with the job. Hard to explain. The war sort of emphasized that for me. I guess I was drifting. And, like I told you, I drifted into . . . what I do now. I got jobs on my own, and Greg Einhorn was just kicking into high gear about that time. He heard about me and threw a lot of work my way.' Another smile. 'The rest is history.'

'But you like it.'

He nodded to himself. 'Yeah. I do. The jobs I take, they're – well, they're like yours. I feel like I'm on the

150

right side, you know? Doing some actual good for someone. The kids.'

'And the mothers?'

'It's not always mothers, you know,' he said seriously. 'But yeah, usually. And some of the things . . . not that it applies here, not with Karim, but I've actually seen people hurt their kids, physical harm, the worst, just to hurt the other parent.'

'No, thank God, Karim wouldn't do that,' Dina said. It was a direction she didn't want to take. There were other kinds of harm than physical. 'Tell me about one of your jobs,' Dina said impulsively.

He looked at her quizzically.

'I don't mean the confidential details. Just . . . what happened. How things turned out.' She remembered Einhorn's description of the dramatic helicopter rescue in Belgium. Did Constantine have similar tales of derring-do? Mainly, she wanted to know what to expect.

Constantine thought it over. 'Mexico, last year. Guy out in Oregon, well off, cleaned out the accounts, took the kid – a boy, six years old, put him in the Mercedes and headed off for an early retirement in Margaritaville. An American, not Mexican – lots of Americans down around Oaxaca.' He took a last sip of coffee, waved off her gesture to refill the cup.

'I went down there thinking it would be pretty easy. The guy wasn't all that security conscious, and with any luck we could whisk the boy away to a private plane almost before anyone knew about it. But it turned out to be even easier than that.'

He obviously remembered the job with pleasure. 'I had a couple of contacts down there, one thing led to another, I found out that this guy wasn't at all popular with the locals. Including the cops. He was a cheapskate, in a place where if you've got money, you're supposed to spread it around a little. He never spread it around anywhere, except with some of the women. One of whom happened to be a big favorite of a police captain.'

Constantine shook his head at the man's folly. 'They probably would have bounced on him sooner or later anyway, but it fit right into my needs, my client's needs. So I went straight to this Mexican cop. We hit it off. What I paid him was probably just a small fraction of what it would have taken if he hadn't had a personal grudge. Or maybe he wouldn't have done it at all – he's a good enough man, it's the system that's lousy. But as it was, I flew my client down from Portland, and that very night they busted the dad right there in his villa. Drug raid. And who's right there to take custody of the kid but the mom, all the papers ready and waiting and a good Mexican lawyer at her side. And so farewell.'

'What happened to the dad?' Dina asked.

'They found enough cocaine that he'll probably be in a Mexican prison until the kid's grown.'

'He was a drug dealer?'

'I said they found it. I don't know how it got there.' He seemed to brood over this. 'I didn't like that part, but something along those lines was probably going to happen anyway.'

It was about as far from the grab-and-run helicopter escape as possible. Dina found herself oddly comforted by that fact.

As if reading her thoughts, Constantine warned: 'Don't count on your situation being that easy. It probably won't.' He rose, gathering his recorder and notebook. 'By the way, the other night you mentioned your friends, Sarah and . . . Emily?'

'Emmeline. Em.'

'Right. Mind if I talk with them, too? They might have a different angle on something. Probably not, but you never know.'

'Well . . . sure.'

'Give me their numbers.'

She wrote them in his notebook.

'Call me right away if there's anything new,' he said at the door. 'Anything from Karim, anything at all.'

She nodded.

'And look. Your two friends know about this. You and I know about it. But it's got to stop right there. Nobody else. Not your mom, not your dad, not your other son.'

'I understand.'

'Good. It's important.' He softened this message with one last smile. 'Thanks for the coffee. Talk with you soon.'

And he was gone.

CHAPTER TWENTY

When the phone rang at seven in the morning, Dina knew it was Karim. Did he check the clock as often as she did? Dina wondered.

He greeted her pleasantly and began to give her news of the twins. He had hired a tutor, he said, and once they were acclimatized, there would be a school for Ali and a girls' school for Suzanne. 'They've really taken to the Arabic lessons,' he said enthusiastically. 'The tutor says he's never had such bright pupils.'

Silence. Did he have any idea what torture this was for her?

'They'll be starting school in a couple of months. I'm sure they'll be able to keep up well.' Apparently he thought that Dina would find this information reassuring.

'The children belong with me,' she said stiffly, knowing it would do no good. 'With their mother. Do you really think I won't fight you on this?' Stupid, she thought, after she'd spoken. She wasn't supposed to let him know she was planning to fight in any way.

'I'm sorry, Dina,' he replied gently, sounding as if he meant it, 'but I've made up my mind. I'm doing what's best for them. You can fight all you want, but it won't change anything. Ask your lawyer. He'll tell you.'

And then he hung up.

Always after Karim's calls, there were tears. The only difference this time was that she knew she had taken a step towards getting her children back.

CHAPTER TWENTY-ONE

A taxi could be one of two things for Emmeline: an extension of her office, a place where she worked her cell phone and checked her notes for show ideas, or an island of relative peace, a small mobile sanctuary in which she could relax and let her mind drift between busy destinations. Tonight she opted for the peaceful island. She had already made all her mandatory calls, and for once there was nothing pressing.

Dina seemed to be holding up, in spite of the disappointment with that rescue specialist or whatever he was. She had assured Emmeline that there was no need to come over tonight. Even so, Em would check in with her again in the morning, just to make sure she was OK.

Sean had called to offer a quiet night at home, dinner cooked by him, and that sounded good. He did only a few simple dishes, mainly Italian, but he did those few very nicely.

Even before she reached the apartment door she smelled the bacon and onions and tomatoes and knew that it was pasta *putanesca*. An open bottle of Barolo on the table in the dining alcove confirmed it. In the kitchen Sean was tasting the sauce – the 'gravy' as he called it – with a large spoon. When he saw Em he did a quick impression of a master chef savoring a masterpiece, then smiled: 'Hello, beauty!' and gave her his best good-mood-greeting kiss.

'Hi, stranger,' she said. 'Whatcha burning here?'

'Half-hour,' he said. 'If you can wait, that is. Or I can start the pasta now, if you're starving.'

'I can wait, if I can get a drink in this trattoria.'

'Wine, or a real drink?'

'Wine.'

He filled two glasses and they took them into the living room. The thudding pulse of a bass line from whatever it was that teenagers thought of as music these days issued from Michael's room, the door closed. Em gave Sean a questioning look.

'Joy and Josh are here,' he explained. 'They're all on the computer. As always.'

Joy Nguyen and Josh Whiteside were classmates of Michael's at Stuyvesant High. What the tiny Vietnamese girl, the lanky WASP boy and Michael had in common besides brains and a love of computers was anybody's guess, but they were inseparable.

'What do you think they're doing, hacking the Stock Exchange?' Em asked.

'Let's hope so,' said Sean. 'Maybe they can support us in our old age. But you're not supposed to call it hacking.'

Michael had already explained that he and Joy and Josh were *crackers*, not hackers. Hackers, it developed, were benighted and ignorant persons who did things like write computer viruses and deface Web sites – like, for instance, the site for the Pentagon or the White House. Crackers regarded this sort of exploit as child's play and mindless vandalism. The way Michael

157

described it, crackers were like martial-arts black belts, forever perfecting their arcane skills but never employing them for evil.

Em was secretly proud of and hopeful about her son's computer skills. Maybe someday he would be Bill Gates 2.1, the upgrade version, without all the glitches. Certainly he was devoted enough to the work. And ambitious enough. He was aimed like an arrow at college and career. It was almost as if he had inherited all of her drive and none of Gabriel's easy, footloose let-the-good-times-roll. Or as if he had consciously decided against his father's approach to life.

'Tough day?' asked Sean, interrupting Em's mini-analysis of her only child.

'A slogger. But it all worked out in the end.'

Sean had positioned himself to give her a neck rub. He was good at it, knew what to do with his strong, beautiful hands. 'How about your day?' she asked.

He grimaced. 'I was up for a Tidy-Bowl this morning.' He meant an audition for a commercial. 'The experience gave new meaning to the phrase "My career's in the toilet." '

She laughed, but she couldn't miss the touch of bitterness in his joke, the hint of tiredness in his self-mocking grin. She didn't ask how the audition had gone; if he'd gotten a call-back, he would have said so.

Sean could have used the job. As it was, his bartending gig barely covered his living expenses and his share of the rent-controlled walkup he shared with another actor. Anything else – restaurant meals, weekend getaways, theater tickets, et cetera – Em took care of. Sean's pride was slowly eroding, and Em had to admit that she was old-fashioned enough to want her man to stand on his own feet. Especially after her failed marriage to Gabe.

'What's new with Ms Dina and her personal mercenary?' he asked, transparently changing the subject.

'Didn't work out. He decided the job was too risky.' Em had purposely omitted any mention of Einhorn's fees when she mentioned him to Sean; she didn't want to underscore the fact that she and her friends could lay their hands on substantial sums of money, whereas he had virtually nothing in reserve.

Sean took a sip of wine and gave her a look she loved. 'You're beautiful, Em,' he said. 'Really beautiful.'

It was the ultimate switch of subject.

'Hungry, too,' she said. They both knew that there was nowhere else to go with this line of thought, given the presence of Michael, Joy and Josh in the next room.

'Right,' he said with a rueful smile. 'Let me get on it.'

'In fact, I'm famished,' she added, keeping the mood light.

'Five minutes.'

She went with him to the kitchen and sipped her wine while he worked, tossing a garden salad while the garlic bread warmed and the pasta approached *al dente*. She enjoyed watching him cook. For a man who had scars on his knuckles from youthful brawls, he could be as nervously fussy as a new bride over the stove.

They were finishing their salads when the thumping bass beat from Michael's room abruptly stopped and the three young people came tumbling out like a lost fragment of some rugby scrum.

'We're outta here, Mom,' Michael announced. 'Going to Josh's.'

'Whoa. How late?'

'Not early,' said Michael.

'Josh just got some serious bandwidth,' Joy explained, if it was an explanation – Em couldn't tell. Joy was maybe four feet ten and couldn't weigh ninety pounds. According to Michael she had an IQ over 160 and was as good as in MIT on a full scholarship.

'Yeah, so don't wait up,' Michael said.

'Anyway, *y'all* enjoy your dinner,' Michael advised, taking a smiling shot at his mom's leftover southernism. 'And then you can just chill – you've got the place to yourselves.'

Then they were gone, with a certain amount of giggly laughter beyond the closing door.

'Ah, youth,' said Sean with a theatrical sigh.

'I guess they must see us as pretty much ready for assisted living.' Actually, she thought she had detected a quick conspiratorial glance between Michael and Sean. Two men of the world.

'The trouble with assisted living,' said Sean, 'is that it's wasted on the old.' He lit two candles on the table, turned out the lights, and served the pasta. Instant trattoria.

'Spaghetti, working-girl style,' he said. 'Don't be shy. There's nothing for dessert.'

'I might have some ideas for that,' Em told him.

'Ah.'

'Ah.'

CHAPTER TWENTY-TWO

Dina stood for a long moment gazing at the gold letters on the window: *Mosaic*. And in smaller letters: *Floral Designs by Dina*. The sight of her business usually gave her a small *frisson* of pride, but now she wondered if that pride had somehow cost too much.

Yes, she knew that was unreasonable. Certainly no one expected a man to give his all to his home and family; so why should it be expected of a woman? But that was logic, and people who made emotional decisions rarely resorted to logic.

If Karim had been thinking logically, wouldn't he have considered that something in his own genetic background might have made Jordy gay? Just the way that it was his genetic make-up that gave Jordy his dark hair and dark eyes?

But no, it was so much easier to blame her. To blame American culture, for God's sake!

Dina turned the key and went into her shop. It was not a large space, just a few hundred square feet in all, but it was all she needed. *Mosaic* was officially closed – today was Sunday – which gave Dina exactly what she wanted: a little time alone in the place where she had spent the hours away from her family.

Here were the sketches for her newer designs. And here were the gorgeous color photographs of some of her most beautiful creations. Karim had taken a few of those pictures, back in the days when their marriage had seemed to be sound; a professional photographer had taken the rest. Here were the magnificent pieces she had designed for one of Donald Trump's spectacular parties. And there was the stunning cascade of Hawaiian blooms she'd made for the third wedding of a society columnist and a gay man some fifteen years her junior.

Above Dina's desk was a dramatic photo of her signature piece, the one that had been in such demand ever since she had made it for the awards banquet following the New York Marathon. She had taken her inspiration from the speech former mayor David Dinkins had made some years ago, when he'd described New York as a gorgeous mosaic. She had loved that sentiment, the concept of people of all races and nationalities bringing the richness of their diversity here, to this one place. Like her marriage, she'd once believed. She had fashioned a mosaic of flowers, gorgeous bright blooms intricately woven together in a kaleidoscope of colors and complementary fragrances.

Once upon a time, Karim appeared to be proud of her ability to design beautiful things. Why, after a business trip to Paris, he had traveled south to Gras and commissioned, at great expense, a perfume blended especially for her. He had called it MOSAIC, had even suggested she market it, but she had been so moved by the gift that she demurred. 'I want it to be just for me, Karim. It's too special to share.' They had made love then, with the same passionate intensity they'd brought to the early days of their marriage. 'Darling,

Dina,' Karim had murmured, 'there's no one in the world like you.' How long ago that time seemed. And how painful to remember.

And yet . . . had their marriage really been a mosaic even back then, with all the pieces fitting perfectly? How many times had Karim talked about how things were done 'back home'. And how many times had she reminded him that the children were only half Jordanian? She believed that she had tried to compromise, to blend – but had she really? Was a gorgeous mosaic possible within a marriage?

As always, the fragrance of flowers permeated the air of the small shop. She was so accustomed to the scents that sometimes she was scarcely aware of what she was smelling. But today she noticed the heady sweetness of the jasmine she kept near her desk, the perfume of the single rose in her bud vase.

She breathed deeply and willed herself to be strong. She wanted her children to feel her presence, to know she was thinking of them in between their brief moments on the telephone. Perhaps a letter . . . but could she be sure that it would reach the children? Would Karim keep it from them? Fatma certainly would. And probably her in-laws, too. She sighed; the sound came out a groan. But she had to try.

On impulse, she picked up her sketch pad, reached for her colored pencils. Quickly she began to draw. Tore off the first attempt, crumpled it and started over. Sketched furiously and began to smile. When she was finished, she had drawn a pair of conjoined hearts made of pink and blue flowers. Not at all original, perhaps even trite – but her audience wouldn't care. She wrote Ali's name, then Suzanne's within the hearts; below, she wrote: 'I love you.' She put the

163

sketch into a DHL envelope and wrote her in-laws' address on the airbill.

She spent the next two hours reviewing her books. Eileen was doing a good job running the business. Dina had enough designs in inventory so that she could keep her regular clients happy for a while. Until she found a way to get her twins back, she could work mostly at home and fax her sketches to the shop, where an expert European florist would bring her designs to life. She wondered why she hadn't considered working like this before . . . before Karim had left. Was it because that would have seemed a concession to Karim? Had they reached a stage where pleasing him would have seemed a kind of surrender?

She didn't know. Couldn't know. And what did it matter now?

She locked up the shop and dropped the DHL envelope off at a box on the next corner.

She thought about going back to the apartment, dismissed it. When Jordy returned home, things would be different, but for now there would be nothing to do but worry and brood. Instead, she took a taxi down to the Village, to her parents' apartment.

'Your father's much better today,' her mother said in response to Dina's question. Dina wanted to believe her.

Joseph Hilmi was stretched out on a lounger on the terrace. Though the day was warm, her mother had laid a light blanket over his legs. A glass of water with lime was at his side. Dina kissed his head, detecting a sharp, faintly sour smell. Was it the chemo? Or the smell of illness? Either way, it was a reminder that he was fragile and not to be upset.

164

So when he asked, 'What's wrong, *elbe*?' the tenderness in his voice startled her. The endearment – 'my heart' – she hadn't heard it for years, since she'd been a little girl.

'Nothing's wrong, Daddy. I'm fine.'

He shook his head impatiently. 'The children are fine? Why didn't you bring them?'

It took all her self-control not to break. Gone were the days when she could throw herself into her father's arms and ask him to make everything right. 'Oh,' she said, striving for a casual tone, 'didn't Mom tell you? Karim took them to Jordan to visit his family. Maha isn't well, and he thought a visit with the children might cheer her up.'

Her father's expression didn't change. Her answer had apparently not satisfied him. 'Are things all right between you and Karim, Dina? Is he treating you the way he should? Because if he's not . . .'

Where is this coming from? she wondered. Had her mother let something slip, something to do with Karim?

She thought for a minute, then decided a half-truth would be easier to sustain than a lie. 'We are having some problems,' she admitted.

'I thought so,' he said grimly.

'Really? Why?' Dina believed that she and Karim had always presented a good face to her parents. Her father's good opinion had, in fact, always matters to Karim.

'Something,' her father said. 'Something . . . I'll put my finger on it in a moment.'

'We have our differences,' she offered helpfully.

'Of course. What couple doesn't?'

'Karim would like me to behave in more traditional

165

ways. Give up the business. Stay home with the children. Dress more conservatively. You know.' She waved a hand. Her father, after all, though he was a Christian and a dedicated New Yorker now, shared a culture with Karim.

Joseph nodded. 'Yes, I see.'

'What do you see, Daddy? Please tell me.'

He reached over and squeezed her hand. His pale gray eyes flickered. Was he in pain? 'Are you all right, Daddy?' she asked, trying not to let voice reflect her alarm.

He smiled. A wan smile. 'Yes, my Dina, I'm fine.' A pause. Then he spoke slowly, as if choosing each word carefully. 'When Karim began courting you . . .' Dina smiled at the quaint usage, 'he seemed a well-balanced fellow. Well-educated, somewhat worldly, which I counted a good thing for a Muslim. Or a Christian, for that matter. Because I must tell you, Dina, that I have always mistrusted people who are one hundred per cent anything. Or profess to be. It was people like that who destroyed my beloved Lebanon. My beautiful Lebanon . . .' His tone grew dreamy, his eyes misted, as if he were seeing the majestic mountains, the beautiful beaches and grand boulevards that had made Beirut the jewel of the Middle East.

'In any event,' he said, brisk again, 'I've seen Karim change over the years. Or perhaps the face he showed me was like a suit of clothes he'd acquired in the West and which no longer fit him . . .'

Dina listened intently. 'But why didn't you say anything?'

'Say what? That your Jordanian husband is perhaps becoming more like his father?' Joseph shrugged, as if

166

to say, What would have been the use of such a conversation?

So. Was it her fault after all for not seeing what others had seen? But what could she have done? Stolen the children away herself and run away? To where? She sighed, then caught herself. This wasn't the time to burden her father any more. 'I don't want you to worry, Daddy. We'll work all this out, I promise.'

He looked at her. Said nothing. And the moment passed.

CHAPTER TWENTY-THREE

By now he should be over Newfoundland, Dina thought, as she studied the luminous dials on her bedroom clock. And tomorrow he'll be in Amman. And then . . . and then. She couldn't finish the thought. She trusted John Constantine, she wanted to have confidence in him, but dear God, so many things could go wrong.

She fluffed her pillow and thought about sleep, but she knew there would be little sleep tonight. She felt as if she had to be awake, had to be aware of Constantine's journey, as if she were somehow helping him on his way. Answering questions. Giving support. Praying.

The phone rang. Constantine! No, it couldn't be. His flight would be in the air – and besides, he couldn't have anything new to report.

It was Jordy. His voice was ragged and nasal, and Dina guessed that he had a bad cold. Or perhaps he'd been crying.

'Mom.'

'Yes, sweetheart.' Waiting.

'I want to come home.'

'Of course. I'll send you a train ticket. We can have a nice weekend, and—'

'No, Mom!' The voice firmer now. 'Not for the weekend. I want to come home to stay. With you.'

'But why, Jordy? Is there a problem at school?'

'School is fine. I just want to be with you. You shouldn't be alone.'

Sweet, loving boy, she thought. How could his father have turned on such a good person? 'I would love to have you with me, if that's what you really want,' she said. 'But we need to wait until the term is over. It's only a couple of weeks. Take your exams, finish the year – and we'll see about finding you a school in the city.'

'And I want to choose it, Mom.'

A pause. Karim had allowed Jordy no choice in his own education. But Karim wasn't coming back, so it didn't matter what he wanted. Still, she couldn't just say 'yes' to this without knowing what her son had in mind. 'We'll talk about that later, Jordy. OK?'

'OK.'

'And Jordy . . .'

'Yeah?'

'I love you.'

'I love you, too, Mom.'

Dina hung up, sighed, looked at the dials on the clock again. It seemed as if they'd hardly moved at all. Her longing for her children was almost physical, she was so hungry for the sight of them, the smell, the touch – it was an ache that grew rather than diminished. She could live without Karim. Yes, she could definitely live without Karim. And how strange that seemed now. If he'd been killed in an accident, she would have been devastated. If he'd been on an ordinary business trip, she'd be missing him, waiting for his familiar form to come through the door, anticipating his embrace, his . . . When was the last time they had made love? It was the night before he left. And it had been good. The way it hadn't been for a while. Now she loathed him for that. Taking the memory of her body as a souvenir, something to remember her by. Another in a string of betrayals, big and small. Yes, she could live without him for the rest of her life. But not her children. She had to have them back, she could not conceive of a life without them.

The phone rang again.

She picked it up. 'Jordy, you have to get some rest. We'll—'

'It's me, Dina.'

Karim.

A shudder of fear shook her body. A call from Karim even while Constantine was on his way. Was it a bad sign, an omen?

'Dina? I hope I didn't wake you.'

'No,' she said. 'I don't sleep much these days.'

Silence. You don't have an answer to that, do you? she thought.

'Dina, I just wanted to let you know the children are fine . . . I didn't want you to worry. If you watch the news, you'll probably see stories about a big demonstration in Amman. I wanted you to know that it was at some distance from the house. And that I kept the children indoors, in any case.'

Now she was silent. 'And you expect me to be assured by that? To appreciate your thoughtfulness

170

and sensitivity? What is it that you expect from me, Karim? To accept that you've taken my children to a place where they'll be hated because they've been brought up in America? Because they have the accents to prove it?'

'No!' he said fiercely. 'That will never happen. I will see to it.'

'Oh, that's good. Because you've already damaged one child. So with only two to go, you'd better be careful,' Dina heard the bitterness in her voice, the raw anger. Careful, she told herself, you can't let it all spill out. Not until you have the twins back. But she couldn't seem to help herself. 'Unless you've already picked out wife number two – and then you can have more children. That's an idea, Karim. If you have more children with someone else, then you can give mine back to me.' Her voice sounded shrill, almost hysterical. Stop, she told herself, stop.

'Dina, don't. I don't want another wife. I never wanted another wife. I only wanted you . . . I still—'

'Don't!' she spat. 'Don't you dare say it.'

'All right.' Now his tone hardened. 'As I explained, all I wanted to do was assure you that the children are fine. I'll have them call you tomorrow. Goodnight, Dina.' And then the connection broke and she was alone again with her anger and her fear.

Oh God, oh God, oh God.

She turned on her television set with the remote control, punched in the numbers for CNN. Watched. Within a few minutes she heard what she couldn't wait until tomorrow to hear: more violence in Israel, anti-American demonstrations in Manama and Cairo and Amman.

171

Oh God. She tried to imagine what, if anything, her children might be aware of? Would her in-laws be watching on Al-Jazeera, the CNN of the Middle East? Would they give any thought to her? Her fear, her worry? For a moment – a very brief moment – she thought about Karim, living in New York in the aftermath of September Eleventh, during months of undeclared war between Israel and the Palestinians. She recalled the anti-Arab sentiments in the American media. It's not the same, she told herself fiercely. But how is it different? the voice in her head asked, the voice that always tried to be fair, to stand in someone else's shoes before making a judgment. She didn't want to hear that voice now. All she wanted was to wrap herself in her righteous anger and hope it would see her through the night.

When, many hours later, the call she'd been waiting for finally came, Dina was exhausted. She'd slept an hour or so at a time, waking at regular intervals as if by an inner alarm – and trying to imagine where in this world John Constantine was.

By two in the afternoon, he was in Amman. He was using a phone card and a public telephone in the lobby of the Inter-Continental Jordan. 'I'm here,' he said simply. 'I just wanted to let you know that I've made contact with the friend I mentioned to you.' Dina knew this meant the local man who owed him a favor. 'After I grab a few hours of sleep, I'll meet him and we'll go from there.'

'Karim called. He said there had been demonstrations . . . I saw it on CNN. You'll have to be careful.'

'I will. I've been in places where worse things were happening.'

Was that supposed to be reassuring? she wondered. Yes, she thought, it was. 'Be careful anyway. And please keep in touch.'

'Sure.'

And that was all. She hated to hang up the phone, to break the connection between her and the man who was going to make her life whole.

Chapter Twenty-Four

'All right,' said Sarah, taking charge of a discussion that threatened to become a quarrel. 'You hired the man without discussing it with anyone?'

'Yes.' Dina glared at her friends across her kitchen table, daring them to give her grief at a time like this.

Em ignored the look. 'What do we know about this guy?' she demanded.

Dina recited the brief résumé Constantine had given her. 'He was in the military when he was young. Post Vietnam. And for a while he was a cop. Here in New York. He left – he didn't tell me why – I think he's just too much of a maverick to follow the rules. Then he did some security consulting. He was called back to duty during Desert Storm. I got the idea it was some kind of intelligence work. Then he went into . . . this line of work.'

'Sounds like a cowboy,' said Em.

'Maybe a cowboy is what I need.'

'Have you talked with David about this?' Sarah asked.

'I haven't talked with anyone. You two are the first to know.'

'Hmmph,' Em commented, clearly miffed at being

left out of the decision-making process.

'And he's in Jordan right now?' Sarah asked.

'Yes. He arrived earlier today.'

'But not to get the kids.'

'No! Not unless they walk into his hotel room and ask for a ride to the airport. He's checking things out. The "set up", I guess you'd call it.'

'Hmmph,' said Em, still not won over – and still miffed.

'So what's he like?' Sarah asked, taking a different tack.

'I just told you.'

'I mean what's he like? As a man.'

'Attractive, I guess. He's a big tough guy who seems to know what he's doing. That's why I hired him.'

'Married?'

'I didn't ask.' No ring, she remembered. 'Divorced maybe. Who cares?' Now Dina was annoyed. 'Am I supposed to be shopping for a new man now, just because my husband left me a minute and a half ago?'

Sarah flushed. 'I'm sorry, Dina . . . I didn't mean that. I just . . .' She shrugged, not sure what she meant. Was she turning into Esther Pearlstein, inveterate matchmaker?

'It's OK,' Dina said, regretting her outburst. Sometimes she felt she had to let some anger out or explode. But not at her friends. 'I'm sorry, too.'

Sarah reached over the kitchen table and squeezed Dina's hand. 'I understand.' She got up from the table. 'Be right back,' she said.

'Dina, have you heard anything new from Karim?' Em asked, her tone gentler now. 'If you don't want to talk about it, just say so . . .'

'No, it's OK. He called last night to tell me the kids

were fine and that I shouldn't worry. Even though there were crowds of people in the streets of Amman screaming anti-American slogans.'

Em's magnificent eyebrows lifted. 'Not worry? That bastard.'

'That's pretty much what I said.'

'And you were right, Dina honey, you were right.'

There was a long silence. Em was not one for small talk at times like this. Times like this, she thought, called for action. But what? What could she do for her friend that would matter. 'Dina . . .' she began tentatively, 'do you think it's a good idea for you to be sitting in this house all alone while . . . while all this is going on? I mean, maybe you need to get out more. A mental health day, just—'

Dina shook her head. 'I feel like I should be here. For the phone calls . . . all of them. Karim's. Constantine's. Anything.'

'Well, then, how about I spend the night with you tonight? Michael can manage just fine without me . . . maybe I'll ask Sean to stay over, keep an eye on things.'

Dina started to protest that she didn't need a babysitter, then stopped herself. Her days were bad enough, but the night were even worse. 'I'd like that. If you're sure . . .'

'I'm sure. We'll have an old-fashioned girls' pajama party. We'll eat junk food and popcorn and just hang out.'

'Who's eating junk food and popcorn?' Sarah asked as she came back into the room and resumed her seat at the table. 'What did I miss?'

'Nothing. I'm just spending the night with Dina, that's all. Maybe we'll have a pizza party. On second thoughts, maybe I'll make some of that jambalaya I used to make back home in Grosse Tête.'

'Can I come, too?' Sarah asked, sounding like a kid.

'Nope. You can come over tomorrow. If Dina won't leave this damn house, then we'll just have to keep her company.'

'OK. Oh – I just called David. He says this Constantine is good. He said he would have recommended him in the first place, but he thought the guy worked for Greg Einhorn.'

'You told David about this?' Dina asked. 'What, you just called him up and discussed it?'

Sarah flushed. 'Well, he asked me to keep in touch. He said—'

'And when did he say all that?' Em probed.

'Last night,' Sarah replied, dropping her eyes and poking at an imaginary crumb on the table.

'I see,' said Em, infusing the words with a rainbow of meaning.

'Oh, yes, I see, too,' Dina joined in, glad of the diversion, glad to escape for a moment into the teasing that was firmly rooted in affection.

Sarah's color ripened into a deep pink. 'It was just dinner.'

'Just dinner, umm-hmm,' Em went on. 'And how long had *this* been going on?'

'*This* is just a couple of dinners,' Sarah protested, but weakly.

'That's what you say today, sugar. But who knows where a couple of dinners might lead?'

'Nowhere,' said Sarah firmly. 'They're leading nowhere.'

*   *   *

Later that night, after a splendid dinner of Em's jambalaya and a dessert of homemade bread pudding, the women changed into soft, comfortable sweats and perched on Dina's king-size bed.

'Thanks,' Dina said.

'For what, *cher*?'

'For everything. For dinner. For being my friend.'

'You're welcome. Now tell me the truth. How are you holding up?'

Dina shrugged. 'I'm not going to lie and say I'm fine – but I'm not after a pity party, either.'

'Fair enough. So what should we talk about? Or would you rather just watch a video or two?'

Dina thought for a moment. 'Let's talk about you. How's it going with Sean? You haven't said much about him lately?'

'There's not a lot to say. We have fun, but longer term than that . . . I don't know.'

'Is that because of what happened with Gabe? I mean, I never really understood what happened with Gabe. All you've ever said was that he was Billy Dee Williams and Peter Pan all rolled into one. And that he left soon after you had Michael.'

Em smiled. 'Yeah, that's Gabe all right. Beautiful man. But a musician,' she said, making that sound like a very bad thing.

Dina waited.

'He's doing OK now. Sends cards from different places. Sends a check now and then and asks me to buy something nice for Michael. Hasn't seen our son in I don't know how many years.'

'And he never asked?'

'Once. When he was in Toronto. He sent concert tickets and a plane ticket. Said if Michael wanted to see him play, he'd love to have him.'

'And what happened.'

'Michael was just ten. I sure as hell wasn't going to put him on a plane all by himself just to see his father perform. And then have him dumped all over again. I told Gabe that if he wanted to see his son, he could come and pick him up. Do the right thing for once. He hasn't asked again since.'

Dina thought about that, about her own situation. 'But at least you have Michael. He's yours – and Gabe has never tried to take him from you.'

'Yeah. Guess I never appreciated Gabe's lack of interest in his son.' She looked at Dina's face. 'I'm sorry, *cher*, that wasn't funny.'

'Nothing is funny when marriages get broken, when kids are in the middle of the mess. At the beginning, you never believe your relationship can get so messy, so . . . cruel.'

Em closed her eyes; her face took on a dreamy expression. 'At the beginning, it was just pure magic with Gabe and me. The way it can only be when you're young. There I was, the best cook in Grosse Tête, and, *cher*, this was a place where *everyone* could cook. But folks came from miles around for my sweet potato pie, my pickled okra, my red beans and rice, my chicken and sausage gumbo . . . um, um, I'm making myself hungry again just talking about it.'

'You're making me hungry again, too.'

'Well, anyway, there I was, little Emmeline Fontenot – and there was Gabriel LeBlanc. Looking like Billy Dee Williams and playing zydeco like it had never been played before. Let me tell you, we made some fine music together.'

Dina smiled, wondering if Em knew how her face

changed when she talked about those happy times.

'Funny, I didn't mind working hard then,' she continued. 'Supporting Gabe. And then we got lucky. Or so we thought. Gabe's band made a record, and Lord, it was a hit. Played all over, not just Grosse Tête or New Orleans, but all over the south.'

'That must have been great.' But Dina knew the 'great' hadn't lasted long.

'Well, *cher*, it might have been just fine if we'd stayed where we were. But Gabe *would* go to New York. I told him New York was a different kind of place. But he would not listen, the man would not listen. He acted like I was trying to cheat him of his big chance. So we came.' She sighed deeply. 'Only one good thing happened in New York.'

Dina waited.

'We made Michael.'

Dina smiled again. There was so much tenderness in her friend's voice when she spoke her son's name.

'The rest is . . . not so great. Well, Gabe was playing weddings and small clubs and he's barely making enough to pay the band's expenses. And his big-city success never came. Meanwhile, I was working like a dog, right up until the time I delivered Michael.'

Dina shook her head, recalling her own first pampered pregnancy. The way Karim had fussed and doted and spoiled her.

'It got worse later, after Michael was born. We never had enough of anything. Then one day Gabe just left. We didn't have a big fight or anything like that. He just left. Took eleven hundred dollars that we had in the bank. And he was gone. I didn't hear from him for almost a year. Then he sent back the money. No note. Just eleven hundred dollars.' Em paused, sighed.

'I guess he did me a favor, though I sure didn't see it that way then.'

Dina knew the next part of the story. Em had gotten a job in a popular Louisiana-style restaurant in Manhattan, started as a sous-chef, took over the kitchen when the chef left to open his own place. Luck brought a noted critic to the place, but it was Em's culinary skills that earned a glowing review. The rest, as they say, was history.

Food critics came, proclaimed her a rising star. And later, with the backing of investors, she opened a restaurant of her own. A book of hometown recipes followed. Em did it all: dabbled in interior design, but in a casual, unstudied way. She created comfortable, folksy environments. Then put it all together in what she modestly referred to as a 'little' cable show – though, in fact, the show had brilliant ratings. So good that when contract-renewal time came, Em had been offered more than any other performer on that cable network had ever been paid. She sold the restaurant and then made some excellent investments.

Now her agent was flogging her show for prime time – and there was even talk of a product line of cajun spices and other specialty items.

Dina wondered if Em was happy. Though it was easy to see when Em was angry or frustrated, it was hard to tell if she had found contentment in the life she'd made for herself and Michael. Dina was very aware of the differences between her background and Em's; sometimes she was ashamed that there had been so little struggle in her life. But before this happened, Dina more or less had the life she wanted. A husband, beautiful children, and a modest but pleasing career.

'You're kinda quiet over there,' Em said. 'You about ready to pack it in tonight?'

'Not really.' A pause. 'Em . . . did you ever see Gabe again after he left?'

'You sure are full of questions tonight.'

'Sorry.'

'I'm just teasing, sugar. Yes, I did see Gabe once. When Michael was three, I took him back home to Grosse Tête, to see his grandparents. Well, you know how a small-town telegraph works . . . long story short, Gabe heard that we were coming. And he just turned up one day, smiling that smile, just as if he'd been part of our lives all along. Asked if he could see his son.'

Em retreated into that memory, recalled how she'd turned the full force of her anger onto Gabe. 'Your son? So he's your son now after you turned your back on him for three years? This is not a petting zoo, Gabriel LeBlanc! You don't just show up, say "hi, y'all" and then run out on him for another three years.'

'You're a tough woman, Emmeline Fontenot,' Gabriel had said, his smile dimming just a little. But he hadn't denied the truth of her words.

'Need to be when folks you love let you down.'

'So what did you do?' Dina asked, cutting into the flow of memories.

'Well, he promised to do better if I'd let him see Michael. So I did. Michael was shy at first, but he warmed up to Gabe. Most people do. It's hard not to like him,' Em continued. 'Anyway, Gabe sort of kept his promise. Like I told you, he sends checks for Michael – and postcards from the towns on the Texas–California zydeco circuit. I knew Gabe's career picked up after a while because the cards started coming from cities in Canada and France. Once in a while, he'll call . . . sometimes Michael will take the call, sometimes he won't.'

'What does Michael say about Gabe?'

Em shook her head. 'He's hurt and angry . . . I don't blame him. Maybe postcards are better than some kids get, but Michael knows that's not the way it's supposed to be. Still, I try to get hold of my own anger, for my son's sake. I don't want him to poison himself with bad feelings. So I tell him: "One daddy is all you get, honey. I'm sorry you don't have the one you deserve – because Lord knows you deserve the best. But Gabriel LeBlanc is what he is. I believe he loves you in his way, even if it isn't nearly enough. Best you make peace with what is – if you don't want to grow up to be an angry man." '

'And what does he say?' Dina asked.

'He says, "Humph," ' Em replied with a smile, knowing how much her son sounded like her.

They talked a little longer, but eventually Dina drifted off to sleep, and Em followed soon after.

CHAPTER TWENTY-FIVE

'So who is this guy?' Rachel demanded, as she watched Sarah get ready for another dinner with David. Hands on hips, with attitude to spare, she was a formidable interrogator, albeit a striking one, with her mass of curly red hair and her pale green eyes.

Sarah knew she shouldn't take a wheedling tone with her daughter, that 'please accept what I'm doing' tone, but she couldn't seem to help herself. 'I told you. His name is David Kallas. He's a lawyer. We met when Dina consulted him about getting her children back.'

'So why are you going out with him again? This is the fourth time, you know. Don't think I'm not counting.'

Oh, Sarah thought, it's really too bad that spanking is out these days. She couldn't imagine taking such an imperious tone with her mother, not without risking a smack in the mouth. But times had changed. She sighed. 'It's not your place to count, Rachel. I'm an adult. I'm single, and I'm—'

'No, you're not! You keep saying that you're not divorced. Not really divorced.'

Damn, Sarah thought, trust Rachel to bring that up. 'I'm divorced enough to date,' she said crisply, hoping that would be the end of it. 'And clearly your father feels the same way.' She didn't know why she threw that in. She knew Rachel wouldn't let it slide – and she was right.

'What Daddy does has nothing to do with this. You're just evading the issue.'

'And what is the issue?' Sarah hated the way she sounded when she argued with her daughter: like a teenager herself instead of a parent.

'The issue is: I want to know what you're doing. And what it means.'

Now Sarah almost laughed aloud. 'You're asking what my intentions are?'

'Yes,' said Rachel, with an upward tilt of her chin. And in spite of her frustration, Sarah thought: How beautiful she is.

'I don't know. My intentions are to go out with David as long as I please. To enjoy his company. And if my intentions change, I will let you know.'

Rachel looked as if she were about to launch a fresh salvo, but Sarah cut her off. 'And I expect you to be civil to David – just as I expect you to be civil to anyone I see.'

Rachel's lovely mouth twisted and she stomped off to her room. Not for the first time, Sarah thought: Boys must be easier. I'm sure boys are easier.

When David arrived to pick her up, Sarah wasn't quite ready, so she invited him to wait in the living room – and hoped Rachel would stay in her room. Yet David had thus far seemed unperturbed by Rachel's reactions to him, which had ranged from cool disdain to outright rudeness. Did he have a legion of difficult nieces? Sarah wondered. Or was it just the fact that Rachel wasn't his problem?

When she heard Rachel stomp back into the living room, Sarah held her breath, bracing herself for a fresh onslaught of rudeness. She could chase after Rachel, cut her off – but she decided to be a grown-up, to wait and see what happened. Would David's aplomb hold, regardless of what Rachel threw at him? She eavesdropped – and was quickly impressed by what she heard.

'I have only good intentions toward your mother,' David said earnestly.

Rachel made no reply.

'I'm sure you know that she loves you more than any other human being on this earth. I wouldn't think of interfering with that. All I hope for from you is that you'll understand that your mother needs some adult companionship.' He paused. 'Someone who will care for her when you leave home.'

There was still nothing from Rachel. And though Sarah couldn't see her daughter, she could picture her: arms folded across her chest, her full, pouty lips compressed into a tight little knot. David was apparently undeterred because he continued to speak in a soft, pleasant voice. 'Maybe you haven't given much thought yet to leaving home, Rachel, but you will – and sooner than you imagine.

'One day you'll have a life of your own, perhaps a family of your own. So think of this: what if you deny your mother the kind of companionship I'm talking about? What if she says to me: "Look, David Kallas, you're a good man" – and I am a good man, Rachel, just ask my mother – "but my daughter is unhappy that I'm seeing you, so I'm giving up my relationship with you to make her happy." What if your mother were to do that, Rachel?'

Sarah heard a rustle – Rachel shifting but still not speaking. Where was David going with this?

'Well, perhaps that would please you, at least for now, not because you're a bad person but because it's natural for children – and some parents, too – to want what's most comfortable for them. So let's fast-forward a bit, say twenty or twenty-five years. You have a career – I think your mom said you were interested in graphic arts? – and maybe you have a family, too. There's not enough time in the day to do all the things you need to do. But here's your mom . . . her own career is slowing down, her nest is empty. She's often lonely.

'Do you want her phoning you two or three times a week complaining of the sacrifices she made for you? Suggesting that you should drop everything and see to her needs? Showering you with guilt if you can't – or don't want to – put her needs first?'

Rachel made a sound. Was it a giggle?

Encouraged, David pressed on. 'These possibilities hadn't occurred to you? How could you be a nice Jewish girl and not know about the kind of guilt only a parent can inflict?'

Now Rachel laughed. Of course she would know. She had overheard many of Sarah's calls to her own mother. The excuses for trips to Florida not made. The promises to call more often, to stay in touch with half-forgotten relatives scattered all over the country.

Very interesting, Sarah thought, how David had

made his point without criticizing Rachel's point of view, but by simply appealing to her self-interest. She had heard enough. She made her appearance.

David said, 'You look very lovely tonight.'

'Thank you.'

Rachel said nothing. But she did take a long look at her mother. As they left the apartment, David made a point of saying good night to Rachel and wishing her a pleasant evening. As they waited for the elevator, he said to Sarah: 'Rachel and I are going to be friends.'

'You sound very confident.'

'Well,' he smiled, 'part of being a good lawyer is visualizing a positive result. That's the first step to making it happen. That and having a good case. Which I do.'

The evening turned out to be the best yet. An over-priced dinner and dancing at the Rainbow Room. Sarah loved the romantic ambiance of the place, though she'd only been there once, at a hospital fund-raiser. And she loved dancing, which she hadn't done in years, and which David did surprisingly well. She thought about the folk wisdom that said a man who danced well was also a skilled lover. But she didn't mention that, and tried not to think of it either. Too soon, she told herself. Much too soon.

When he brought her home, he kissed her at the door. Once, then a second time, longer and deeper, in a way that reminded her sweetly of high school, of breathless moments stolen away from the sight of parents. 'I guess that's all for tonight,' he said. 'Wouldn't want Rachel to catch us necking in the hall.'

'No,' said Sarah, laughing, though the prospect wasn't at all funny.

'So maybe one of these days we'll have dinner at my place?'

Sarah heard the question behind the question. Yes, she thought, it was reasonable, expected, kind of hoped for – and yet dreaded.

She said yes.

Chapter Twenty-Six

Dina listlessly pushed the vacuum cleaner around the living room, knocked a vase off a side table, then shut the damn machine off. Cleaning the house had seemed like a good idea; getting rid of the city dust that filmed everything would be therapeutic, she thought. But it wasn't. It was just busy work and it didn't take her mind off the things that really mattered. Like wondering what Constantine was doing now. Was it going to be good news when he returned? Or another crushing disappointment?

She re-started the vacuum cleaner and moved to the carpeted stairs. She had no household help now; she had discharged the twice-weekly cleaning woman because Karim had hired her. She didn't want anyone connected with him in her house; after Fatma's betrayal it seemed dangerous to bring a stranger, possibly a spying stranger, into her home. Maybe her feelings would change in time, but right now, she would go it alone.

'When the house gets filthy, I'll call a cleaning service,' she'd assured her mother, who worried aloud about Dina taking on too much. 'Mom, I'm not doing much of anything these days,' she said. 'As long as I fax in my sketches, Eileen does a great job of running the shop. The only appointment I have all week is to talk to someone at the new Craft Museum . . . the one on Columbus Circle? I'm hoping to put my proposals in early, before construction is even completed.'

'Good for you, sweetheart! You deserve every success. You're talented and original.'

Dear Mom. She would say that even if Dina's designs were dreadful and trite. That's the kind of thing that mothers did. That's what she used to do – would do again – for her own daughter. She yearned for her Suzy, ached for the sound of her voice, the touch of her skin, the sweet fragrance of her hair.

Forcing herself to push on, Dina moved to Jordy's room. It was neat, painfully so, as if her son had to prove that he was no trouble at all, that he was worthy of love. As she ran a dustcloth over his desk, she noticed an envelope stuck under the lamp. It bore Sarah's return address. She picked the envelope up. It had already been opened. She held it for a long moment, debating.

She had never been a nosy parent; she believed wholeheartedly that a child's privacy deserved respect. And yet. Now her life, like the world around her, was different. She was much more aware that all kinds of unexpected and awful things could happen. For Jordy's sake, she thought, she needed to know what was going on with him. She slid her fingers into the envelope, extracted a newspaper clipping. The story was about gay Muslim men and the difficulties they faced in a society that abhorred – and often killed

– them. The piece quoted several young men who believed that the Prophet had never intended to punish and exclude any believers. An imam who refused to be identified speculated that perhaps homosexual behavior in Muslim countries had historically always been clandestine – not because of any specific animosity towards homosexuality, but because of Islam's insistence on discretion in sexual matters in general.

The article also mentioned a support organization based in Washington, with a chapter in New York. This line was highlighted in yellow. Also in the envelope was a piece of notepaper with Rachel Gelman's name printed on top. 'Dear Jordy,' the note began, 'I think the whole situation sucks. I thought that even before your father did this really shitty thing to you and your mom. I thought it when he sent you away, but I didn't want to say too much because I didn't want you to get any more bummed out than you already were. So I talked about what a good school Phillips was and how you could network with all kinds of kids and how you could probably get into a great college. I figured when you were ready to be a great journalist, somebody in your class who was really rich and connected could help you get a great job on a really important newspaper. Like *The New York Times*. Anyway, for now, I saw this in the paper and I thought maybe it would help you a little to read it . . .'

A great journalist? Dina thought. When did Jordy ever say he was interested in journalism? He had not. At least not to her, though he had mentioned something about taking pictures.

She wondered why he had not spoken to her of his

ambition, if indeed that's what it was. They had always been close, or so she'd believed.

She had protested when Karim had sent him away, but she had done nothing to stop it. Had Jordy seen that as a betrayal? He seemed perfectly 'normal' with her, but now she resolved to ask him how he'd felt when she'd gone along with Karim's sentence of exile.

'. . . and here is something I thought you'd find interesting,' the note continued. 'I actually met a kid in school whose brother belongs to this group. So – if you're interested, let me know and I'll give you the kid's number. His name is Riyad and he's a really good person.'

Dina looked at the clipping again. Gay Muslims. Support groups. Why hadn't she thought of that? Probably because she never really thought of Jordy as Muslim, though by definition the son of a Muslim father is Muslim. She had bought the books she'd seen when she'd visited Jordy at Andover. But she had scarcely made a dent in the first one. Had she been ashamed, too? Not of Jordy but of the situation he had precipitated? Splitting the family. Creating yet another divisive issue for an angry Karim who was all too ready to assign blame? A Karim who now seemed to believe that the only hope for the future was Ali?

And all along, Jordy had been alone. Thank God for Rachel, she thought. Thank God there had been someone he'd been able to talk to about his parents.

Yes, she had written. Sent packages filled with homemade cookies and cakes, the kinds of things he could share with his classmates. His new friends. Yes, she had visited regularly – but always with some guilt, some anxiety about whether the visits might somehow provoke an argument with Karim. As if she were going to see a lover instead of her own son. And so she had tried to make her visits when Karim was away on business. How clever, how non-confrontational she believed she'd been. No doubt the treacherous Fatma had reported every visit, every contact she'd had with Jordy. And no doubt these visits had figured prominently in the catalog of offenses Karim had compiled.

I hate this, she thought bitterly. I hate this and I wish Karim would die. The thought startled her. Did she mean it?

Yes, she answered herself. Yes, I do. But not before I get Suzanne and Ali back.

Later that night, she called Sarah. After a minute or so of small talk, she asked: 'Did you know that Jordy and Rachel have kept in touch while he was away?'

A hesitation. 'Yes,' Sarah replied. 'I knew that. Is something wrong?'

Dina bit her lip. 'With me, I guess. I didn't realize they were close.'

'Well,' Sarah said, 'if I were to guess, I'd say it's because they're familiar and safe. No pressure. Sexual or otherwise. They've known each other since they were kids, and even though they're in different schools, it's almost as if they're related somehow.'

Dina considered this, 'Yeah,' she said. 'And since we're friends, they can dish their parents to one another.'

'That would be a big plus for them. Look, I don't mean to change the subject, Dina, but how are you doing? Do you want to go out tonight? A movie? Or dinner?'

'Thanks, Sarah, but no . . . I want to spend the evening writing to Jordy. And Sarah . . . if you don't think it would be too mushy, tell Rachel I think she's a good person.'

Sarah laughed, though not exactly with delight. 'I'm afraid I'm not the person to pass on that message right now.'

'Why? Is something wrong?'

'Rachel seems to think I'm a regular Jezebel because I'm seeing David.'

'Oh, Sarah—'

'No, I understand. I feel like smacking her, but I do understand. On some level, I know it's about her, rather than me. She likes the way things are, just the two of us. She doesn't want to deal with a strange man getting in the middle and maybe changing things. She—'

'Changing things? That sounds serious, Sarah. Is it?'

Sarah gave a snort of exasperation. 'How the heck do I know if it's serious yet? I haven't really had a chance to find out, have I?'

'I'm sorry, Sar . . . I don't mean to be nosy.'

'You're not. Not you, Dina. I guess I'm a little edgy because I know it ain't going to be easy. Seeing David, I mean. And just to make it more interesting, I think Rachel's been giving her father an earful. About her wicked mother. I'll bet you a year's worth of Haagen Daaz that he's been egging her on.'

'Bastard.'

'Yeah, well. Sticks and stones might hurt Ari, but if name-calling would do it, that guy would be pulverized by now.'

'I'm sorry, I—'

'Don't be. Your problems are a heck of a lot bigger than mine. So give Jordy my best when you write – and tell him that I think he's a very good person.'

'I will,' Dina promised. 'Because he is. And I'm going to make sure he knows I feel that way with all my heart.'

CHAPTER TWENTY-SEVEN

Constantine looked tired. And, of course, he'd brought no children. But Dina had hurried to 'their' meeting place like a starving woman, hungry for whatever crumb of information he did bring.

The place was a classic Paris bistro transplanted to Greenwich Village. From the exchange of good-humored insults between Constantine and the bartender, Dina gathered that they were old acquaintances. He ordered a substantial glass of 'the usual', which turned out to be Black Bush Irish whiskey for him. A glass of white wine for her. And then came the report.

It was not encouraging.

'The kids are in the house almost all the time,' he said. 'I only saw them twice. Both times in cars. Once with their father and once with the sister-in-law and a woman about my age – probably the nanny.'

'Fatma.'

'Probably. I couldn't do my best street stakeout. I can pass for a European in Amman, but not for a local. Most of the time I was using binoculars from a little hotel a quarter mile up a hill. The only really good thing: I didn't see any serious security. But the house is busy. People there, coming and going all the time.'

'Karim has lots of relatives,' Dina said. 'It's a typical Arab family. They're all very close.'

Constantine nodded. 'That's a problem. The only good time to get the kids would be when they're outside the house. Without so many people around. From what I saw, that doesn't happen very often.'

'Maybe Karim is being extra careful, until he's sure I won't do anything.' She paused. 'Your friend Einhorn told me about getting into a house.'

'I think I mentioned we work differently. A house intrusion – there's too much risk of people getting hurt.'

Dina's shoulders slumped. 'So what can we do?'

'We need some help from someone in the household. We need to learn the routine.'

'Who? Do you mean a family member?'

'Maybe your sister-in-law? You said she wasn't unfriendly toward you.' He paused. 'But actually I was thinking of you. You've got permission to visit the twins. Maybe we should use it.'

And that became the beginning of a plan. It was sketchy at first – and Constantine cautioned Dina that it might take more than one visit to get what they needed. On the other hand, opportunity could arise at any time. They would need to be prepared to move quickly.

'What we're doing is serious, Dina,' he cautioned. 'Your husband has resources that we don't. He hasn't needed to use them so far. But don't imagine for a minute that he won't use his connections. So you'll need to be careful. I bought you a secure cell phone to use when you get to Amman. You won't call me directly. We'll make contact through the friend I mentioned . . . we'll call him the Major. And if I need to, I can hire one or two good men I've worked with before.'

Could she do it? Dina wondered. Could she face Karim and pretend that she had accepted what he'd done, that she'd be content to be an occasional visitor in the twins' lives? Could she face her in-laws who had never been that fond of her to begin with? And most important, would she be able to get whatever information Constantine needed to bring her children home?

Chapter Twenty-Eight

Em and Sarah came to Dina's house bearing gifts – and warnings. Em brought a special sunscreen that was guaranteed to protect Dina's fair skin from the Jordanian sun. Sarah handed Dina a Ziploc bag filled with medications to deal with various infections and maladies, including travelers' tummy.

Now they were sitting in Dina's kitchen sipping tea.

'So,' said Sarah, 'this is it. You're actually going through with this crazy scheme.'

'Yep,' said Dina.

'I've already told you how I feel about it,' Sarah said, 'so I'll say it just once more. I don't like it. I don't like it at all.'

'Of course you don't like it,' Em put in. 'You think *Dina* likes it? Nobody *likes* it. Liking it's not the point.' The truth was that Em wished she could go along, to protect Dina, just in case that Constantine fellow fell down on the job.

'I'm open to a better plan if anyone has one,' Dina said, a little defensively. She had plenty of misgivings about the whole thing herself, but she felt that this was the time for wholehearted support, not doubts, from her best friends.

'That's just it,' said Sarah, disregarding the coolness in Dina's voice. '*What* plan? I mean, it sounds to me like you're both winging it, you and this detective or whatever he is. Go over there and see if anything comes up, is what it sounds like.'

'Well, that's what is *is*. We can't *make* a plan until I get there and see the lay of the land.'

'That's the whole idea,' Em said loyally.

Sarah shook her head. 'I'm just not sure you're taking into account how dangerous this might be. *David* says' – Em and Dina exchanged a look – 'David says that you could end up in a lot of trouble. Even in prison. I mean, we're talking about the *Middle East* here.'

'Oh, come on, Sarah. Jordan isn't Af*ghan*istan or someplace like that.'

'Dina's *from* the Middle East,' Em pointed out. 'Her dad is, is what I mean,' she added quickly when Dina gave her a stare. 'And besides, she's been to Jordan before . . .'

'Yeah, with her husband,' Sarah pointed out.

Dina and Em both glared at her.

Sarah threw up her hands. 'OK, OK, you're gonna do it, I know. We know. I just wanted to . . . sound a little note of caution.'

'I appreciate that,' Dina said, meaning it. 'Look, I'm not some kid going off on a lark here. I'm a little scared, if you want to know the truth.' More than a little, she thought. Getting on that plane the day after tomorrow was going to be like stepping off a cliff in the dark.

'Well, being scared is good,' said Sarah, mollified. 'Scared can keep you from taking crazy chances.'

Now it was Em's turn to raise the caution flag. 'John

Constantine doesn't sound like someone who's scared,' she said. 'I just hope to hell and gone he knows what he's doing.'

'He's a professional,' Dina said simply. 'I trust his judgment.' And she did. She had come to see that while his image might be a bit rough around the edges, Constantine was careful when it came to the important things. Like her welfare and that of her children.

'Well, OK, then,' said Sarah. 'So the main thing is what *we* can do.' Meaning she and Em.

'We can order in some food,' said Dina, looking towards the stack of take-out menus on the counter.

'I'm serious,' Sarah insisted, and Em leaned forward to show that she was with Sarah on this. 'Money, something. I mean, this is going to cost a bundle, and—'

'Look,' Dina cut in, 'let's just see how it goes. If it goes well, great. If not . . . well, I might need both of you more than any of us want to think about. If something goes wrong, I might need money. I might need someone like David. And if things go *really* wrong, I might need somebody to look out for Jordy.' That could be either one of her friends, she thought. Jordy and Michael had been pals in childhood, and though they hadn't been close for a while, Dina felt she could trust Michael to be a pal again, if necessary. Rachel was still a friend, one who had been there for Jordy in ways his own mother had failed to understand. That kind of friendship was real, the kind she had with Sarah and Em.

'Don't you dare talk like that,' Em said. 'Don't you dare. You know we'd do anything for you – or your kids. But I don't want any more of that "if anything happens to me" kind of talk, you hear?'

202

'I hear. Anyway,' Dina added breezily, to break the somber moment, 'you're both on standby. You're my lifeline. Remember the time difference when you get a call from me at three in the morning.'

'No problem,' said Sarah. Em nodded. Dina thanked God for her two friends.

Food was ordered and consumed. Dina looked at her watch and said it was time to call it a night. She had calls to make, to her parents and to Jordy. Tomorrow she would meet with Constantine to make sure everything was in order.

'All right, guys,' she said, as she saw her friends to the door. 'This is it. I'm off. Wish me luck.'

'Luck,' said Sarah.

'Break a leg,' said Em, who clearly had spent too much time around actors.

Suddenly they were all hugging. There were tears. Last minute warnings. Promises to take care. *Goodbye. See you soon. See you and Ali and Suzy soon. Absolutely. Goodbye. Goodbye. You call the instant you need anything, you hear? I will. Goodbye.*

Then her friends were gone and Dina was alone. Her trip seemed both very near and a million years in the future.

Oh God, she wondered, *what's going to happen to me? Am I really going to get my babies back?*

Chapter Twenty-Nine

The final meeting with Constantine – at their usual place – was brief and to the point. 'I'll be flying out with you, just to make sure we both get to Amman at the same time. But I don't want you to talk to me on the plane. I don't want you even to look at me.

'When you arrive, remember that you're playing a part. Your husband has the upper hand; he has your children. All you want is to spend some time with them. And to keep that possibility open in the future, you have to stay on good terms with him. Remember that when you're tempted to belt him one in the chops.'

Dina smiled. 'I'll try to remember.'

Constantine did not smile back. Dina supposed he was in his 'mission' mode now, totally focused on the work ahead. Good, she thought, that's very good. He passed her a piece of paper. 'This is the number of the contact we'll be using. As I told you before, we'll call him the Major. He's a good man and completely trustworthy. You'll call him if you need to communicate anything. And if there's any kind of . . . opportunity . . . something where we can reasonably expect to take the children without any trouble, get in touch immediately. Or as soon as you can. Can you do that?'

'I've already told you, I can do anything . . . anything at all to get my children back.'

He nodded, then passed her another piece of paper. 'This is the number of the pager I'll be using over there. For emergency use only, please.'

'I understand.'

'Good. Now, do you have any last-minute questions?'

She started to shake her head, then stopped. 'I just want to know . . . do you think we have a chance? A good chance?'

'If I didn't, we wouldn't be getting on that plane tomorrow.' He reached over and squeezed her hand, gave one of those tiny corner-of-the-mouth smiles, but his eyes were still serious.

It wasn't the answer she had hoped for – she had wanted him to assure her, to promise somehow, some way, he'd get Suzy and Ali back – but it would have to do.

CHAPTER THIRTY

As the jet descended from the northwest, Dina had a
travelogue view of Amman, the capital of Jordan, that
was both modern and ancient. The white city, as it
was called, for the low-lying white stone houses that
sprawled over nineteen hills. When she'd seen it for
the first time, on her way to her wedding, she'd felt as
if she were flying into a fairytale. She remembered
pictures of Grace Kelly, who had sailed into the
harbor of Monaco to marry her prince – and thought
that her own journey was at least as romantic. She
was coming to Lawrence of Arabia country, to a place
where history reached back for centuries, and where
she would see the remains of ancient cultures and
civilizations.

Though American convention called for the bride's
family to give the wedding, Karim and his parents had
wanted it to be held in Jordan, where all their friends
and all the people who had watched Karim grow up
could easily attend. Dina had persuaded her parents it
was what she wanted, too. Back then, she *had* wanted
to make him happy, and in the end, she had loved her
wedding, which had been a spectacular affair. Karim's
family had hosted all of Dina's friends at Amman's

best hotels. There had been parties for an entire week, and extravagant gifts from Karim. 'It's an old tradition, gifts to the bride,' he said, presenting Dina with one magnificent piece of gem-studded, handmade gold jewelry after another: a necklace fit for a queen, a half-dozen bracelets and an equal number of earrings. 'These things were supposed to make up the bride's trousseau. Her personal wealth.'

The gifts took Dina's breath away – especially as Karim had already made a down payment on a splendid Manhattan townhouse. 'Well, it's a lovely tradition,' Dina laughed, thinking: Wait till my friends see all this. Her pals from college were already envious of her gorgeous three-carat-diamond engagement ring and the big house she would live in; most of them were barely able to afford tiny studio apartments.

The wedding ceremony was performed by a Muslim sheikh at the Ahmad home, with both fathers as witnesses, as was the custom. Dina had readily consented to this, since they had already been legally married in the state of New York by a superior court judge. The reception, which went on for a full twelve hours, was held in two enormous tents erected on her in-laws' property, one for dining, the other for entertainment. The menu was as international as the guest list, which included, in addition to relatives and friends, a troop of foreign diplomats and members of the Jordanian royal family. On tables set with the finest china, crystal and silver, guests could dine on anything from entire roasted lambs reclining on beds of rice to the best Iranian caviar. To drink, there was fine French champagne and Lebanese *arak*, as well as fruit juices for the observant. The music was international, too. In addition to a well-known western orchestra, there was Bedouin music, a belly dancer, and two popular Egyptian singers, one male and one female.

The fairytale continued in the weeks ahead. The lazy days and dreamy nights aboard Karim's yacht. The long drives to explore the country he loved so much, the country he wanted to share with her. She'd had no sense of compromise then, no sense of 'giving in' by doing what made Karim happy. She had been happy, too. No one could have asked for a more romantic honeymoon. Karim had been an adoring lover, passionate and tender, wooing her every time they made love.

Yet when things changed between them, he seemed to want things that did not make her happy, that were very different from what she wanted. When she'd noted every compromise she'd made, kept score. And now she understood very well that Karim had been keeping a scorecard of his own. She sighed deeply and covered her eyes.

'We'll be landing soon,' said the woman next to her, clearly mistaking Dina's sadness for apprehension.

'Yes,' Dina said, smiling at her seatmate. She looked out the window again. Somewhere down there were Suzanne and Ali.

Moments later the airliner landed with a reassuring thump of tires on tarmac at Queen Alia Airport. As it taxied to the gate, Dina took deep breaths and slowly let them out. Be calm. She hoped she looked a little less flightworn than she felt. The crowd at the terminal was an international one, much the same as she might see at most airports, with travelers in western clothes mixing with robed Arabs from the Gulf and women wearing the headscarfs and long dresses of conservative Muslims.

Karim was waiting when she cleared customs. He was alone. He had told her that he would not be bringing the children to the airport, but still it was a disappointment.

He looked no different. She wondered if she did. There was an awkward moment when it seemed as if he might want to embrace her in greeting, but if he did, he thought better of it. In the end they simply said hello.

Jet lag had been setting in for hours, so she was happy to follow Karim, happy to let him carry her two suitcases. Just another married couple.

Outside the temperature was in the seventies, the sky perfectly clear.

'A beautiful day for it,' said Karim.

'Yes.'

That was the extent of their conversation until, in the car, Karim asked: 'Where are you staying?'

'The Hyatt.'

He nodded. 'Downtown. I could have found you a place a little closer.'

Then why didn't you? she thought. But that wasn't fair. She hadn't asked him for help or advice. She had chosen the hotel for its familiar name and because Constantine had said that a large, anonymous, American-style place would be best. She wasn't here as a tourist. All she cared about were her children.

'I'll drop you there,' Karim was saying. 'You can rest a while, freshen up, then I'll come and get you, bring you out to see the children.'

'I thought we'd go straight there.'

'It's better this way. You've got to be tired. And they're with their tutor until afternoon.'

Letting her know who was in charge. All right. No need for a battle. She *was* tired.

'You don't have to pick me up. I can take a cab.'

'Expensive.'

'It's all right.'

'It's no trouble to drive you.' Not much protest.

'No, I'll get a cab. Once I get my bearings I might rent a car.'

He shrugged. 'Whatever you want. But really it's no trouble.'

They rode in silence for some minutes, the city reaching out to meet them along the roadway. Amman was a city of contrasts, its ancient roots still visible through its modern façade. Roman ruins overlooked the bustling downtown; gleaming white contemporary buildings and smart new villas coexisted with turn-of-the-century stone houses; chic boutiques competed with old markets and *souks*. The city had grown since Dina had first come here. The last time she'd been here with Karim, he'd informed her proudly that the population was 1.5 million. It seemed now to be still growing, as Karim made his way past buses and cars and service taxis.

Americans who asked Dina about Amman often assumed a place of crumbling ancient buildings lining narrow, twisting streets. And while it was true that tourist sites like the ruins of the Temple of Hercules and the Roman amphitheater recalled Jordan's distant past, by far the greater part of Amman dated to the past few decades. It was in fact considerably newer than New York. Not to mention much cleaner.

Karim drove as he always did, carefully and a little

stiffly. Dina had the oddest sensation of being in a dream. They had ridden like this a thousand times together. Now they were doing the same thing, but they were not together.

He tapped a finger nervously on the steering wheel. 'One thing I wanted to talk about, since we have this opportunity.'

Just one? Dina thought, but said nothing.

'I really haven't told my family the whole story,' Karim went on. 'About Jordy, for example. Or even about us.'

She waited.

'I mean, I told them we've separated, that we had some problems. I've come home with the twins. Nothing more definite than that, really.'

'You're saying they think we're trying to work things out? Something like that?'

He shifted uneasily in his seat. 'Let's just say I've been a little vague. Purposely. I think it's best for everyone, including Ali and Suzanne. I don't want them to think this is a war or something.'

Dina fought back anger. 'In other words, you want me to go along with this little charade,' she said coldly. 'Pretend that everything's just fine, just fine except we have these little *problems*, just fine except that you took two of my children.'

'*Our* children, Dina. But that is not the point. I just think it's best for the kids not to think we're at each other's throats. And we're *not* at each other's throats.'

'If you're so worried about the children, maybe you should have left them in their home. No, what you're worried about is what Daddy and Mommy and Little Brother and all the uncles and cousins might think, God forbid they should think their darling firstborn

211

son left his wife and kidnapped his own children.'

Karim's jaw tightened. He started to speak, then stopped, let out a breath. 'Look, I know you're angry, you're right to be angry. I wish things had worked out better too, but . . . all I'm saying is I've done what I think is best for the children. I'm going to keep doing that. You see it your way. I understand that. But I won't have it spilling over in front of the kids. My family has nothing to do with it. They would support me no matter what.'

When Dina made no answer, he seemed to think that he had gained a point.

'All I'm asking is that we don't go into all the unpleasant details. Don't you agree that's best? Because if you don't . . .' He sighed. 'Because if you don't, then I'd really rather you didn't see the children. Even now.' He waved a hand to indicate her journey, her presence here.

She knew him well enough to know that he was sincere in what he said, that he believed it and meant it. Nothing she could say or do, neither tears nor anger, would change his mind. And he held the two trump cards. For now, at least.

'Don't worry,' she told him grimly. 'I'll be the perfect little separated Stepford Wife. Just get me to the hotel and tell me when I can see the twins.'

Relief showed in his face. 'Sure. Rest is the main thing; that trip is a killer. You can come for dinner if you like. Or after. Either one would be fine.'

'After, I guess.' She had a vague notion of eating something at the hotel, although food was the farthest thing from her mind at the moment. Mainly she felt uncomfortable at the thought of sitting around the dinner table with all the Ahmads eyeing her.

'Fine.'

The Hyatt could have been in Los Angeles, palm trees and all. Karim tipped the porter who took her bags. She didn't protest; she wouldn't have known what the proper amount was; Karim had always taken care of such things when they'd traveled here together. He found a sheet of paper and, using the hood of the car as a desk, wrote directions to the house. He showed no intention of entering the hotel with her, and they said goodbye at the door.

The lobby was a vast expanse of marble and steel that made her wish for just a moment that she had chosen a smaller and more picturesque place of lodging. But at least she was here. If the clerk had any doubts about registering a woman traveling alone, she didn't detect them. This is Jordan, she reminded herself. Women have rights here, they run businesses, they even hold political office. The room had a few Arab touches in its furnishings and decoration but otherwise resembled any decent hotel room in New York. She tipped the bellhop the same amount she had seen Karim give the porter and then was alone.

The window overlooked the hotel's swimming pool and beyond that a sweeping view of the city. In the near distance a blue dome marked the King Abdullah Mosque. Tourists assumed that it dated to the early days of Islam, but in fact it had only been completed a dozen or so years ago – Dina could remember seeing it under construction. She closed the drapes and sat on the bed.

What am I doing here? she thought. Of course she had come to see the children. To get the children, if possible. But that wasn't the question. *How did I end up this way? How did it come to this?*

She glanced at the phone. The message light was dark. She doubted that Constantine would be so indiscreet as to leave a message here in enemy territory. So it was now up to her to make contact with the man he'd called the Major. And then . . . and then, what?

Suddenly it all seemed absurd and impossible, like being trapped in some bad television show. She was too weary, too angry, too lost to cry. She lay back on the bed and closed her eyes.

CHAPTER THIRTY-ONE

At the sight of her children, Dina felt as if her heart would burst. 'Mommy, Mommy!' the twins shouted in unison, throwing their arms around her and smothering her with hugs and kisses. How beautiful they were, Dina thought. Their chubby faces lightly tanned; their dark eyes glowing with health and energy.

'Come and see the jungle gym,' Ali insisted, fairly dragging her to the garden.

'Daddy and Uncle Samir just finished putting it up,' Suzy said proudly. 'Daddy hurt his finger and he said bad words and *Jiddo* heard and yelled at him!'

Dina smiled in spite of herself at the thought of Karim being scolded by his father and hugged Suzy again. She hated the new installation; it spoke to her of permanence.

Without asking, Soraya brought her a cool and welcome lemonade. Dina took it gratefully. She smiled tentatively at her sister-in-law, offered her hand. Soraya took it, then moved in for a hug. 'Welcome, Dina. *Ahlan wa sahlan.*' The gesture warmed her. Maybe this wouldn't be so difficult. Her other in-laws greeted her stiffly, but correctly. No doubt Karim had arranged for that. But Karim obviously couldn't erase the sour expression from his own mother's face or the body language that told Dina she was about as welcome as a case of plague.

Karim was the soul of graciousness, polite to a fault. Showing her what a reasonable man he was, no doubt. How civilized they all were here. But as the evening progressed, Dina saw something beyond the show, something real. Karim was happy here, she realized. And to her great dismay, so, too, were her children. They'd missed her, of course, but it was clear that they had a full and fun-filled life here: picnics in the beautiful gardens surrounding the Ahmad home, pony rides, cousins to play with, a big, extended family – and more attention than they'd ever had.

'It's better here than it is in New York, Mommy,' Ali declared. 'Are you going to stay with us now?'

'For a while,' she replied evasively, watching Maha's lips tighten. What else could she say, surrounded by Karim's family? And what answer would make sense to the twins? They were happy. They had clearly been happy even in her absence.

As she watched them climb the jungle gym, she felt off balance, a little disoriented. She had come to slay dragons, to fight the villains. But there didn't seem to be any dragons here. What she saw was the kind of life Karim had always wanted: there was always time for a visit with neighbors, always time for children and family, for news and gossip over the never-ending cup of dark, sweet coffee. For a fleeting and painful moment, she thought: Maybe I'm the one who has been wrong all along. No, she told herself, I can't afford to think like that. I want my children back and I will do anything to get them.

She smiled non-committally and held her babies.

When she glanced up, Karim was smiling too, his expression tender and loving. 'It's a beautiful picture, Dina . . . you and our children. It's the way things should be,' he said softly. 'It's the way I always hoped we would be.'

She wanted to be angry; she wanted to be furious. How dare he! But when she attempted an icy stare, she saw not the monster who stole her children but the man she had fallen in love with a long time ago. His smile was warm and genuine and a little sad. How did we come to this? she wondered, not for the first time.

And now it was time to say good night to her children, to leave them and return to her cool, impersonal hotel room. She kissed her twins, hugged them so hard that Suzy cried out. And then there were tears in her own eyes.

'Dina.' Karim's voice was low, gentle. 'Let me drive you back to the hotel. You don't want to be waiting for a taxi now.'

Startled, Dina looked at her husband. Was he that sensitive to her feelings?

'Yes, all right,' she said. 'Thank you.'

He guided her to his car, a large Mercedes that she didn't remember from previous trips. She wondered, but only briefly, if he'd acquired it recently, to reflect his new distinguished resident status.

She closed her eyes and pressed her head against the soft leather of the headrest, uncomfortable with the silence, yet too weary to make conversation.

'Dina . . .'

'Yes?'

'Dina, I know this is difficult for you, but really wouldn't you rather spend all your time here with the children, rather than traveling back and forth?'

217

'What are you saying?' she asked, knowing the answer.

'I'm saying that it would make sense for you to stay at the house. There's plenty of room and you could then see Suzy and Ali all day long.'

Stay under the same roof with the enemy Fatma and the in-laws who probably couldn't wait until Karim got himself a new wife? And yet . . . what better way to look for opportunities? It might be difficult to communicate with Constantine's friend, the Major, without being overheard, but she could always step out into the garden and pretend to be calling New York. Yes, she thought, she would do it.

'Yes,' she said, after an appropriate pause that would show her reluctance. 'Yes,' she repeated. 'I don't want to waste precious time away from my children. Thank you, Karim,' she forced out, 'that's a very considerate offer.'

In the darkness of the automobile, she couldn't read his expression. She hoped she had said nothing that would arouse his suspicion. And hoped even more that she was closer now to accomplishing what she had come for.

CHAPTER THIRTY-TWO

The Major was not what she expected. With his silver hair and matching handlebar mustache, he looked like someone's jolly old uncle – or even grandfather – not someone who had ever been in Constantine's line of work, whatever that had been. Yet Constantine had hinted that they had, over the course of years, exchanged favors. And now, after a few cryptic phone calls, here was the Major, seated across the table from her, at a tiny café about a mile from the hotel.

'Be sure to walk,' he had instructed, 'and not in a straight line. Glance behind you from time to time, but be casual about it. If you see anyone who appears to be following you, return to the hotel. If I don't see you here within the hour, I'll call to make another appointment.'

When she was seated, he said, 'So – you are the brave lady who has been separated from her children.' Dina had done what she'd been told. And she had not been followed, she was reasonably sure of that. There had been no introductions. When he'd spotted Dina, the Major had stood up and held a chair for her.

Startled to hear herself described as 'brave', Dina blushed. 'I . . . I suppose that would be me.'

The Major smiled broadly. 'And modest, as well. I can see why our friend admires you.'

Another surprise. Constantine admired her? But why?

'So – tell me what has happened since you arrived.'

'Well, I'm staying at the Hyatt – but I'm sure you know that.'

The Major nodded. 'I've been to the house. To see the children. My . . . the children's father invited me to stay at the house. So I could have more time with them.'

Now she had the Major's full attention.

'And you accepted?'

'Yes.'

'Brava. That was excellent. Now you will be able to give our friend the information he needs. But,' he added quickly, 'you must be careful. If you arouse suspicion, that will make his task more difficult.'

'I understand.' How could she not be careful if she was preparing to sleep in the house of the enemy?

'Do you have any questions?'

She shook her head.

'Is there anything I can do for you, dear lady? Anything that will help you?'

She thought for a long moment. 'Pray for me,' she said simply. 'Pray that I will somehow get my children back.'

He smiled sweetly, tenderly. 'That I will do, dear lady, and with all my heart.'

CHAPTER THIRTY-THREE

This evening was going to be different, Sarah thought, as she climbed the steps to David's brownstone building on West Eleventh Street. She knew that he would want to make love, but she didn't know exactly what she wanted. The thought of sex filled her with anticipation and also with anxiety. Maybe it would be different with him, she thought.

She rang his bell and he buzzed her in instantly. That pleased her; he must have been waiting. He opened the door, kissed her lightly on the lips, invited her to come in and look around while he saw to their dinner. The apartment was redolent with aromas that made her mouth water. It was on the parlor floor and had sixteen-foot ceilings, ornate moldings, a well-used fireplace – and an impressive cook's kitchen. A warm and inviting home with floor-to-ceiling shelves crammed with books.

The sound of a Bix Beiderbecke recording came from an excellent sound system. To one side of the living room, a small round table was set with candles and flowers, crystal wine goblets, and delicate white china. It was not at all what she expected from a self-proclaimed 'old bachelor' – in fact, it was more elegant than what she might have put together after a long and demanding day at the hospital.

'Something smells very, very good,' she said.

'It's my Aunt Sadie's *dja'jeh b'kamuneh* – chicken with cumin.'

'I'm impressed,' Sarah said, and she was. 'No, make that *dazzled*.'

'Let's see if you like it first.'

Sarah did. It was the first time in recent memory that someone other than Em or Dina had made her a meal, and she loved it. The way David served the food and awaited her verdict, the way he filled her wineglass and waited anxiously as she tasted the Pinot Grigio he'd chosen.

'It's wonderful,' she said, 'all of it. Now what else is in this chicken? I taste scallions . . . and garlic, I think.'

'Right on both counts. I also used what we call Aleppo pepper . . . it's kin to paprika. The chicken was browned in olive oil,' he added, 'in case you're really interested.'

'I am. I want the recipe. And the rice . . . it's delicious.'

'We call it Syrian rice.'

'I call it yummy. I'll take that recipe, too.'

After dinner, Sarah attempted to help clear the table.

'Leave it,' David said, taking her hand and leading her to the center of the room. He flicked the control for his music system and Beiderbecke gave way to Artie Shaw's 'I Only Have Eyes for You'. He took her in his arms and moved slowly around the room. Sarah felt weightless, carefree. How long had it been since she'd enjoyed such a feeling?

222

After a while he moved her towards his sofa. 'Sit,' he invited, 'and I'll bring in dessert.' He served coffee – excellent Kona from Hawaii – and store-bought black-and-white cookies, for which he apologized. Sarah pronounced them delicious. And then she began to tense up. She thought she was doing a good job of hiding her nervousness, laughing heartily at a story David told about a particularly difficult client, then telling one of her own about an eccentric hospital administrator. David put his coffee cup down, took hers as well, and held her hand. 'What's wrong, Sarah?' he asked gently. 'I know you were having a good time. And then . . .' he gestured, 'it was like a switch was thrown and you were suddenly doing something else.'

She smiled nervously. 'You must be a very good lawyer . . . the way you read body language.'

'Not always. Only with people I care about.'

She took a deep breath and decided to go with the truth. 'I'm so embarrassed, I don't know if I can look at you and talk . . .'

'Do you want me to put out the light?'

'No!' The word was so loud, they both burst out laughing.

'Sarah, I get it that you're nervous – and I get it that you're nervous about something we might or might not do. But why? When I kissed you the other night, I thought you might be ready to take our relationship a step further. But if I made a mistake and you're not, it's no big deal. We'll have our coffee, we'll talk a while – and we'll say goodnight.'

She shook her head. 'You didn't make a mistake. Not exactly. The thing is . . .' She took a deep breath. 'The thing is, I just don't know if I can . . .'

He looked at her quizzically. 'Sarah . . . are you maybe nervous because you haven't been with anyone since you and your husband separated?'

'No . . . well, not exactly . . . though I haven't been.'

He nodded encouragingly.

'The truth is, I wasn't . . . I just wasn't very good at it when I was married.'

David looked at her quizzically. 'Wherever did you get that idea?'

She flushed a deep red and soldiered on. Now that she'd started, she might as well see this through. 'Ari . . . my husband . . . he said I was frigid.'

David's expression froze. 'And you believed him? Sarah, you're a doctor, you know there's no such—'

'But I was,' she cut in, 'I knew I wasn't very . . . responsive.'

David took her hand. 'Sarah, if you didn't respond to your husband, maybe he wasn't—'

She shook her head vigorously. 'I'm sure it was me, David. Ari had a lot of girlfriends before we got married. I . . . well, I had never had sex with anyone else.'

'And you think Ari's so-called experience made him a good lover?'

Sarah nodded.

David sighed. 'I think maybe he wasn't such a good lover for you.'

Sarah said nothing, remembering how often Ari had criticized her sexually. When that happened, she'd had no defense save resentment. Ari may have been unkind, she thought, but he was, she believed, right. Perhaps that was why she tolerated his infidelities for so long – a mistake, she understood later, for it seemed to make her husband feel she was indifferent to the physical side of their marriage. To him.

224

'Sarah, sweet Sarah,' he murmured, stroking her hair.

'I've tried, David, I just—'

He placed a finger on her lips. 'Hush,' he said. 'Maybe trying too hard was part of the problem. You don't have to do that any more. When you're ready, and not a minute before, we'll make love. And I promise you, whatever it takes, we'll make it all right.'

'I wish I could believe that,' she said wistfully.

'I'll settle for something less: if you suspend disbelief and just let us make up our own story as we go along. Can you do that?'

She attempted a smile.

'I'll tell you something else,' he said. 'However all this started, I'm certain your husband made it worse. How could anyone enjoy sex if their partner is critical and judgmental?'

'But—'

'No buts, Sarah. Maybe you're determined to blame yourself for the fact that the physical side of your marriage wasn't so good. Well, I'm equally determined to convince you that it takes two.' He held out a hand to ward off any interruption. 'Have I made my case?'

'Maybe.' She was not yet convinced.

He leaned over and kissed her, smoothed her hair, then whispered in her ear. 'Sarah Gelman, you are a woman worth waiting for.'

Without thinking, she kissed him, long and hard. Gratitude or passion, it didn't matter, it felt good.

'Thank you,' he said when they finally drew apart. 'Now let's have another dance.'

CHAPTER THIRTY-FOUR

Dina closed her eyes and let the stillness settle over her. The cool breeze from the garden carried the scent of jacaranda and night-blooming jasmine. The quiet eased her tension, and she began to drift. To remember when she had slept in this house, in this very room with Karim. No, not the last visit . . . things had not been great between them then . . . she had been eager to get back to New York. Whereas Karim acted as if he never wanted to leave.

What she remembered were the early days of married life: cruising in Karim's small yacht, diving in the Gulf of Aqaba, eating freshly caught fish and fresh produce from local markets, making love under the stars.

Because *Lawrence of Arabia* was one of Dina's favorite films, Karim had taken her to Wadi Rum, where the real Lawrence spent much of his time during the Arab revolt, and where many scenes from the movie were shot. Dina had been overwhelmed by the spectacular desert scenery, by the bizarre, soaring rock formations known as *jebels*. There were no hotels in the area, just the goat-hair tents of the nomadic Bedouins and a few houses and shops. When Dina enthused that she loved the place, Karim had taken her on an overnight desert expedition, with camels as their 'ships of the desert'. She had slathered herself with sunscreen and donned a *kaffiyeh* to shield her face from blowing sand. 'You're a proper Arab,' Karim had declared as he took her photograph. The picture, showing her shielding her eyes and staring into the vast desert vista, had always been one of her favorites. Was it because during that trip Karim had told her how much he loved her – and how glad he was that she was adopting his country as her own? How sad that all seemed now.

Later, they traveled by car to some of the historic sites Dina had read about but never seen. Taking great pleasure in the role of guide to his young wife, Karim had taken her around the amphitheaters and temples of Jerash, which had been known as the Pompeii of the east. Karim pointed out the tracks of chariot wheels on the paving stones. 'This was a great city once . . . it was the Corinthian capital, so naturally there were shops filled with ivory and gold, wine and spices and silk, all brought from the Orient by camel caravan.'

If she had been impressed by Jerash, she had been stunned by the beautiful rose city of Petra, had felt like an explorer of old when she and Karim had ridden donkeys into the narrow canyon. She had gasped with pleasure at the glorious city the ancient Nabateans had carved out of rock. 'This was the capital of the Nabatean trading empire in 300 B.C.,' Karim informed her. 'It was considered the eighth wonder of the world.

'In Petra, what is unique is not just architecture cut from living rock, but the degree of articulation on a site of this size, with facets of such monumental

227

magnitude. Look, at the classical use of columns, Dina, the pilasters, friezes and pediment elements.'

She had looked. And she had been proud then that her husband was not only handsome and charming, but also knowledgeable about things that mattered. His country, his work.

Karim, of course, had seen all the places he showed her, and more than once, so it had been natural that he had taken the role of teacher. It had delighted him then, for she had been an attentive and admiring pupil. Now she could reflect that it had been a role he needed to hold onto – and one that must have seemed increasingly difficult the more she involved herself in a life of her own.

Had the distance that had grown between them been inevitable? she wondered. Or was it something that might have been prevented? Was it, as Sarah had once said, cynically, that: 'Life happens. And then everything is ruined.'

Dina found that hard to accept. After all, her parents were still happy together, in spite of the terrible illness that might soon separate them forever. As for Karim's parents . . . well, Dina never could say whether or not they were happy. Karim's mother was always busy, always bustling about doing something for her family, always forcing her will on someone, whether it was the servants or her family – with the exception of her husband, Hassan, who had the contented air of a benign despot, generous with his subjects but quick to comment when the household affairs were not to his liking.

All right, what about her sister-in-law Soraya? Karim's brother had none of Karim's charm – or his good looks, for that matter. Could Soraya possibly be content? Dina had tried to ask her once – not during this visit, she didn't dare raise any questions that would upset anyone this time. But she had once inquired, very gently, whether Soraya felt any constraints upon her, whether she missed the carefree life of a college student with the relatively cloistered life she lived here. It couldn't be very pleasant living under her in-laws' roof, Dina thought, not when Karim's mother ran the household like an absolute monarch – and often a tyrannical one. But when she'd asked Soraya if she was happy, the younger woman had looked at her quizzically, then smiled indulgently, almost as a parent to a child. 'Of course. I have a good husband, a faithful husband, two beautiful children, thanks be to Allah, and a very comfortable home. When the children are older, when they are ready for college, I will perhaps teach – Samir agreed to that before we were married. So what is there to be unhappy about?'

But was it really as simple as that? And if it was, then Dina had to ask herself why she had sacrificed her marriage. And to what? It was a question that had many answers – and no answers at all.

And now as she lay comfortably settled on the feather bed, covered with starched and crisp sheets scented with rose water, she had to wonder. She heard a small noise. Her imagination. And then it came again. Tapping at her door. She got up, walked barefoot. Perhaps it was one of the children.

It was Karim. Quickly she reached for her robe – how quickly the easy intimacy of marriage had vanished, as if all those years of shared beds and shared intimacies had never happened. 'What is it?' she asked. 'Is something wrong? The twins?'

He shook his head. 'No,' he said quietly. 'I just wanted to talk. Alone. With your permission.'

'Yes . . . yes, of course,' she agreed. Could it be that he was having second thoughts about keeping the children?

He moved toward her and she stepped back hastily. Did Karim imagine that he could pretend they were still man and wife after what he'd done? He made no move to touch her, but sat down on the room's single chair and gave her the sad smile she had seen more than once since she'd arrived. She sat down on the bed, prepared to spring into action should he make a move she didn't like.

He sighed deeply. 'Dina,' he said, 'is there no hope for us?'

Was he mad? she thought. Was he living some other story than the one she was in? She wanted to give in to anger, to throw his crimes against her in his face. Instead she spoke patiently. 'How can you talk about hope for us when you took my children like a thief in the night? I believed we were going to counseling. I thought we were going to try to work out whatever differences we had. But all along, you were plotting and scheming, laughing behind my back—'

'Dina, Dina,' he cut in, 'I was never laughing. Don't you understand that it broke my heart to leave you? And as for your counseling, it's a joke. Half the people in New York are in counseling – and most of them get divorced. I knew you wouldn't listen if I told you the truth. I want our children to grow up to be decent adults with good family values. Not . . .' Here he trailed off, unwilling to even speak Jordan's name.

Dina sighed. What was the point in trying to reason with Karim? 'We're not going to settle anything now,' she said, thinking they were never going to settle their differences – and that Constantine was really her only hope. 'Please leave now. I'd really like to get some sleep. I want to make the most of my time with the children,' she added more sharply than she'd intended.

He got the point, flushed beneath his deep tan. 'Of course,' he said a little stiffly. 'I didn't mean to . . . to interfere with your rest.'

But after he left she felt as if sleep would be a long time coming. Karim's plaintive plea, his hangdog demeanor, his . . . sincerity. She could believe he did still care for her. But that made matters even worse. Because if he did indeed care – and he was still capable of this – why, then, there was no hope for anything. Except John Constantine.

CHAPTER THIRTY-FIVE

Karim had hoped to leave Dina's room unnoticed. But no sooner had he turned the corner of the courtyard than he ran into Samir.

'Why, brother, I thought you'd be asleep by now,' Samir said, a knowing smirk on his face. 'I didn't realize you'd be . . . spending time with your wife.' He managed to make the word 'wife' sound dirty.

Karim felt resentment flare. Samir had overstepped more than once since he and the twins had arrived. As the older brother, Karim was due the respect of his younger sibling. Was Samir perhaps trying to assert some sort of primacy? He had, after all, lived here during the years when Karim was in America, making only annual or semi-annual visits.

Well, if that were so, Karim would have to be patient while everyone adjusted to the new situation. He said simply, 'We had a few things to discuss. Regarding the children.'

'Of course. The children.' Again the smirk, as if humoring Karim. Or perhaps allowing him to save face. After all, what could it mean if he were seen creeping in and out of the room of a woman he had rejected? But a moment later, Samir's expression changed to concern. 'Shall we have some tea together, brother? Perhaps if you need to talk about anything.'

Karim softened. '*Shukran*, *akhi*, thank you. But not tonight. I think I will just get some sleep now.'

'As you wish, my brother. *Allah ma'ak*.'

CHAPTER THIRTY-SIX

If her first day under her in-laws' roof had been difficult, Dina's first morning was near impossible. The breakfast table was certainly inviting, laden as it was with freshly baked pita bread, cheese and olives, and the fava bean salad known as *ful muddamas* – as well as pastries from one of Amman's western bakeries.

But the atmosphere was far from inviting. After a cursory 'Good morning', Samir ignored Dina. 'I hear great things about you, brother,' he said to Karim. 'I hear that you have a great future at the ministry.'

Karim smiled and shrugged off the compliment. 'I'm simply doing the job I was brought here to do,' he said modestly. 'As for the future, only God knows what that holds.'

'You're being too modest,' Samir persisted. '*W'Allah*, I know your children will be very proud of you. As they should be.'

'Yes, indeed,' Maha chimed in. 'Anyone with any sense would know what a fine and upstanding man our Karim is. And would respect him accordingly.'

Dina flushed. It was clear that the Ahmads thought of her as gone, invisible, as of no consequence in the family's future.

234

Soraya leaned towards her. 'Dina, would you like to try one of these excellent croissants? They're very good with my homemade jam.'

Soraya earned herself a stern look from Samir and a jab in the side from Maha. Now it was her turn to flush and she fell silent.

'No. No, thank you,' Dina said softly.

'Western women don't know how to enjoy the food God gave us,' Maha declared. 'It's unnatural. A sickness.'

Soraya looked as if she'd like to say something, but it was clear she was afraid to address any remark that could be construed as friendly to Dina.

As Fatma shuffled in from the kitchen, bringing fresh coffee, she looked at Dina as she had never dared when she worked in New York: with contempt. Dina couldn't help but return the look to the traitorous and deceitful woman.

As soon as she could do so without making a scene, Dina left the table and busied herself with her children. Only they made it possible for her stay here. They were brown and healthy and full of life, eager to tell her tales of adventures with their cousins, to show gifts from *Tayta* and *Jiddo*, to describe places they'd gone and wonders they'd seen.

More than once her fortitude wavered. She wanted her children back, she would do whatever she had to do to get them back. But after that, what? What did she have to offer that could compete with the idyllic childhood that the Ahmads could provide?

It was Suzanne who, innocently enough, gave Dina her answer. Dina was brushing her daughter's hair, savoring every moment of the closeness she had once taken for granted. Then Suzy turned serious eyes on her mother and asked: 'Mommy, why did you let Jordan be unnatural?'

Dina stared with horror at her eight-year-old daughter. What kind of propaganda had they been feeding her? Before she could answer – or even think of an answer, Ali declared fervently that he would rather die than be like his older brother.

No, Dina thought, a place where they will learn to hate and despise their own brother is not a place for my children. And then an inner voice demanded: But is it better that they grow up in a country that hates and despises their father? Dina's response was quick: Maybe not, but at least they will be with me.

CHAPTER THIRTY-SEVEN

The peonies arrived at five o'clock. Em was having a cup of tea and waiting to hear from Sean, who was having a breakfast interview with a prospective agent. She hoped that a new agent might somehow change his luck, because heaven only knew, something needed changing.

Sean had gone through a couple of agents in the last few years, which was not a good thing. Em had fixed him up with this prospect, a woman she'd met during a media event. The woman was young, she was bright, and she seemed hungry. When Em told her about a good friend, a young actor who was talented and ambitious, she said she was interested.

And now here were these beautiful flowers. But had Sean remembered it was her birthday? She always kept quiet about it – but maybe Michael had reminded him.

Though Em fussed over other people's birthdays, she generally tried to ignore hers – a habit from childhood, when there wasn't much money to spend for special occasions. She'd learned it was better not to expect much; that way, she wouldn't be disappointed. And once in a while, if something nice happened, it would be all the sweeter for not being expected.

Now Em wondered if perhaps she *had* mentioned that peonies were her favorite flower. The bouquet was huge and clearly expensive. She was touched because she knew Sean couldn't afford such a lavish gift – and because there was no card, an omission that seemed sweet and somehow romantic.

He called an hour later, to say that the new agent had agreed to take him on. Then he added: 'Thanks, Em. I appreciate the introduction. I think this one's going to work out.'

'You're welcome. And Sean – the flowers are beautiful, and I thank you for them. You remembered my birthday!'

There was a long silence. 'I didn't send any flowers, Em. I wish I had. And I wish I'd remembered it was your birthday. But since I know now, I'm going to take you out tonight – someplace really nice. I'll pick you up at seven.'

When he hung up, Em contemplated her flowers again. Had Michael sent them? But when he came home from school, he, too, regretfully declined to take credit for the peonies. He did give her a beautifully wrapped antique perfume bottle to add to her growing collection. And teased her about a secret admirer. 'Bet old Sean's going to be jealous.'

To Em's annoyance, however, Sean wasn't jealous. If he really cared, he would be a little jealous, she thought. Or at least curious. Em was as curious as hell. The mysterious flowers insinuated themselves into the dinner – a special one, as Sean had promised, at *Le Cirque* – and into her thoughts when they later made love.

The following morning, Em called Dina's assistant, Eileen. 'I'm sorry to bother you, honey, I know you've got your hands full with Dina gone. But I got some flowers without a card yesterday, and I'm dying to find out where they came from. They came through the FTD network. If I give you the name of the local florist, do you think you could find out who sent them?'

Eileen could. Em had a way with her – when she wanted to use it – that made people want to help. Eileen called back an hour later. 'The flowers . . .' she said, as if reading from a card. 'They came from a Mr Gabriel LeBlanc. The order was phoned in from Texas. Houston.'

So he remembered, Em thought. After all this time, he remembered.

CHAPTER THIRTY-EIGHT

When Dina and Suzanne entered the kitchen, Soraya and Karim's mother, Maha, were there, along with a rich aroma of stewing chicken. The two women were conversing intently but stopped. Maha gave Dina a hard look, stood, and left without another word. Soraya seemed disconcerted by her mother-in-law's rudeness. In the Arab world, good manners were an ingrained part of daily life, but Soraya's words now were just formally polite, in case Maha might overhear.

'Can I get you something, Dina? Coffee?'

'A glass of water, that's all, thanks. And Suzanne was hoping for a snack.'

'Can I have a Pop Tart?' Suzanne elaborated.

'Why not?' After pouring Dina's water, Soraya rummaged in the pantry for the desired treat.

'And one for Lina too?' Suzanne pressed.

'All right. What about the boys?'

'They're playing computer games. They'll just get the mouse sticky.'

Soraya smiled and put two Pop Tarts into the toaster.

Dina was surprised to see Pop Tarts in Jordan but

decided not to mention it. It might seem patronizing. Instead she said, 'I passed a supermarket a mile or so away when I was coming in. Do you shop there?'

'Sometimes. It's—' she gave an Arabic name that Dina didn't understand. 'In America I think you call them Safeway.'

Ah. The mystery of the Pop Tarts solved. In truth Jordan was a great deal more westernized than Dina remembered.

'See you later!' bubbled Suzanne, taking her prizes with her.

There was an awkward moment between the two women now left alone together. 'They seem to get along well,' Dina said to break the silence.

'Suzanne and Lina? Oh yes. The boys, too.'

'Well, that's good, anyway.' Dina didn't know what else to say. It *was* good that the children got along with their cousins, wasn't it? But in her heart, she supposed she had hoped that they would be desperately unhappy, begging her to take them home. Instead the only question they had asked was whether *she* would be living here with them. She had told them that, no, this wasn't going to happen.

'Does that mean we'll be going on airplanes a lot?' Ali had asked. 'To visit you, then come back here and visit Dad? That's how it is with Kyle's mom and dad.'

Kyle was a school friend of Ali's whose parents were divorced – as, it seemed, were the parents of half the class. 'Not quite like that,' Dina had explained. 'Daddy and I aren't divorced.' She had started to add *yet* but caught herself. 'And anyway, we haven't got everything worked out. Right now, I'm visiting you *here*.'

To her dismay, that had seemed enough for Ali.

But of course she couldn't tell any of this to Soraya – who at the moment was asking her something she had missed.

'I'm sorry? What?'

'I said you're here for a few more days? That is what Karim said.'

'Well, another week at least.'

'Ah.' Soraya opened a large pot on the stove and stirred. The aroma of the stew freshened and thickened. She covered the pot and lowered the heat. 'The children have been begging me to take them to the zoo,' she said without turning from the stove. 'Since you are here for such a short time, maybe we could go together, sometime before you leave.'

It was said cautiously, but Dina wasn't in a position to pick and choose. 'Sure,' she answered quickly, then to cover her eagerness: 'I didn't know Amman had a zoo.'

'It's new. I haven't seen it myself, but it's supposed to be quite nice.'

Suddenly it hit Dina: a place away from the house, away from Karim and the other men. Just her and the children and Soraya. Wouldn't that be exactly the kind of situation Constantine would want?

'Well, thanks,' she said as casually as possible. 'I'd like that. Just let me know when.'

Soraya turned from the stove. 'Sunday, I suppose, when there's no school and the twins don't have their tutor. But maybe you'd rather just be alone with them, have them to yourself.'

'No, the zoo sounds like fun.'

Her sister-in-law gave her a cool, evaluating look. If she was pleased with what she saw, it didn't show. But she said, 'Let me give you some tea; you can't want only water. In fact, I want some tea myself.'

The tea was cold, flavored with lemon and rosehips and heavily sweetened with honey.

'Good,' said Dina, taking a sip.

'Why don't we have it in the courtyard? It's a pretty day and I'm tired of this kitchen.'

Was it Dina's imagination, or did Soraya glance at the door by which Maha had exited? Was the old woman eavesdropping on their conversation? In any case, maybe Dina wasn't the only Ahmad wife who had trouble with her mother-in-law.

There was a small fountain in the courtyard, with a bench beside it. Soraya gestured toward the bench and Dina sat. Soraya sat on the edge of the fountain, as if not wanting to be too close.

'Your plants are beautiful,' said Dina, hoping to find common ground. 'Is that some kind of hibiscus?'

'I really don't know. I know nothing about plants, I'm afraid. We have a man who comes once a week to take care of them.'

Soraya traced one finger in the water of the fountain, as if writing words that only she could see and that disappeared as she wrote them. Over the years, she had matured into a beautiful woman, thought Dina. She had been so young, still in her teens, when they had first met, at her wedding to Samir. A slightly chubby girl with a shy, pretty smile, who seemed awed by her dark, young husband. Now Samir was the pudgy one and Soraya was a slender, confident beauty – although Dina had yet to see her smile again.

'I remember when I first met you,' said Soraya, as if reading her mind. 'I liked you. I admired you. I thought I would like to be like you someday. Can you tell me what happened?'

243

'With what? Me and Karim?'

'Yes. Or actually, no, not unless you want to. I understand you've had trouble between you. What I can't understand is how you – how any woman – could give up her children so easily. Is this something American?'

Dina was stunned. She wanted to shout that she wasn't giving them up, easily or in any other way. But if words like that reached Karim, it might be the last time she would see Suzanne and Ali.

'It's not like that,' she said lamely. 'I'm hoping . . . hoping for the best, I guess.'

'You want to, how do you put it, fix things up?'

'I honestly don't see how that can happen,' Dina said. This was dangerous territory.

'But you would if you could?'

Dina didn't answer.

'Can you tell me, even a little, about the problems, whatever they are, between the two of you?'

'I . . . it's not what you might imagine, what people might imagine, that's all I can really say. We're not, neither of us, involved with someone else. I mean, I know I'm not, and I don't think he is.'

'So . . . what, then?'

'I really can't explain it,' Dina said miserably. 'We grew apart, I guess that's the phrase. Only I didn't realize how much. And he wanted to come back here . . . for a while. And bring the twins.'

'That's the part I don't understand,' said Soraya.

'I don't really understand it myself.'

Soraya waited.

'All I can tell you,' said Dina, 'is that it came as a shock to me. I'm not saying everything was perfect. We'd had some difficult times. But I didn't imagine there was anything so serious, so . . .' She trailed off, not knowing how to explain the situation to Soraya without breaking her promise to Karim. She added simply: 'I thought we were going to be all right.'

Soraya nodded sadly. 'I don't know Karim very well,' she said. 'Not much better than I know you. But from what he's said, I don't think he is as . . . optimistic as you.'

'No,' Dina said with a trace of bitterness, 'obviously not.'

'And I don't know what you can do about the children. Or what you want to do.'

Maybe soon you'll find out, thought Dina. But what she said was, 'They're my children. I love them. I want to be with them, of course. And them with me. I don't know what else to tell you. I'm just doing the best I can.'

Soraya said nothing for a moment.

'And what about you?' Dina asked. 'Are you happy here? With, you know . . .' She glanced pointedly at the doorway.

Soraya sighed. 'To expect a perfect life is wrong,' she said simply. 'Allah expects us to bear some burdens in life, and so we do.' She stood, then took Dina's empty tea glass. 'I'd better go check on that stew. Any minute Maha will be calling to tell me that it's boiling over – even if it's not.'

'I'm sorry to sound like such an idiot,' said Dina. 'But thanks for listening.'

Soraya waved that off. 'You're my sister-in-law,' she said, 'why wouldn't I listen to you?'

'About that zoo trip. I really would like to go. Should we make it definite?'

'Let me just check to make sure Samir doesn't have

245

something planned for Sunday. But even if he does, maybe we can do it another day.'

'Well, just let me know.' Dina stopped herself from adding *as soon as you can*. After all, she was supposed to be the woman without an agenda – guileless, harmless – just a mother visiting her children.

As soon as she could, she would find a way to be alone and she would call the Major. Then she would wait for his instructions.

CHAPTER THIRTY-NINE

A few tinny bars of Bach sounded in the middle of breakfast. Even though the music came from her handbag, it took Dina a moment to realize that it was her cell phone.

She excused herself from the table and took the phone into the next room before pressing the green button.

'Hello?'

'Dina Ahmad?'

'Yes.'

'You recognize my voice, I think.'

'Yes.' It was the Major.

'Pretend you are talking with one of your friends in New York.'

'Oh, Em! It's you. You don't sound like yourself. Must be the connection.'

'Good. Go grocery shopping today. The Safeway supermarket at the Seventh Circle. You know where it is?'

'Yes!'

'Tell me if you can do this today, the time doesn't matter, any time after noon.'

'Yes. We're just eating breakfast. My God, what time is it there?'

'Someone will contact you and give you something. If you are accompanied, try to be alone at least for a minute. It won't take longer. Do you think you can do this?'

'Oh, yes. I'm having a wonderful time, really. And the twins are just fine.'

'If you cannot, we will find another way. But it will be best if done this way.'

'Absolutely.'

'Our friend's plan is very simple. When you are at the zoo, your sister-in-law will have a fainting spell. You will cry for help. There will be many people, confusion, during which you will slip away with the twins. Our friend will be there to help.'

'Good.'

'What you will be given at the supermarket today is what will cause your sister-in-law to faint. It's very safe. She won't really faint, only become very sleepy, then sleep. You must make it look as if she has fainted. You understand?'

'Sure. I think so.' Dina was trying to process it all.

'You will be eating at the zoo, yes? Put it in whatever she is drinking. You must find a way to do this. It's very important. She will be the only one there who could raise the alarm.'

Dina could see into the dining room, where Karim was looking at her with either irritation or suspicion – or both. 'I miss you, too, kiddo. But I'll see you soon.'

'There will be a private plane waiting. There will be no difficulty boarding it. No delay. By the time your sister-in-law awakes, you will be gone.'

'Yes, I'll bring something back for you. If I have time.'

'Our friend will contact the person you pretend to be speaking to – so that she will know to say she made this call, in case anyone asks.'

'Excellent.'

'Clear the callback feature on the cell phone. And the log. Unobtrusively.'

'Sure.'

'Be at the supermarket if you possibly can. The person who gives you the package will also give you a phone number to be used in case of an emergency. Memorize it and use it only if absolutely necessary. Goodbye, Mrs Ahmad.'

'Bye. See you then.'

The connection was gone. She pretended to be mystified by the phone. As she returned to the breakfast table, she pressed buttons that seemed to remove any record of the call she had just received. 'Damn. We must have gotten cut off.'

'Who was that?' Karim asked.

'Em. Emmeline.'

He nodded curtly. Emmeline had never been one of his favorite people. 'What did she want?'

'Oh, she and Sean were out celebrating. He got a commercial or something. A big deal for him.'

Karim regarded her closely, then shrugged. 'I suppose a commercial is cause for celebration in some circles.' He rose and actually smiled. 'I have to get to the office. I hope you all enjoy yourselves while I'm working for the greater benefit of our country.'

'How lucky we women are,' said Soraya, 'that we never have to work.' She looked at Dina and winked.

Dina waited till one o'clock before mentioning casually that she wanted to go to the Safeway.

'What for?' Soraya asked. 'We have enough for an army here already.'

'Just some American junk-food type stuff for the kids. For when I'm gone.' She felt deeply ashamed at lying to Soraya like this. Not to mention planning, if she understood it correctly, to slip her some sort of drug less than twenty-four hours from now. Soraya had done nothing to deserve this. But Dina saw no way around it. 'And a couple of little things for the picnic,' she added brightly. 'Surprises, you know?'

'How will you get there? I have to go out, I told you.'

Soraya had indeed mentioned that she had a meeting of one of her charity groups at two. That was why Dina had waited this long.

'Oh, I'll just call a cab.'

'Don't be silly. Samir will drive you.'

Samir had been hanging about unhappily all day. There was some story about him not being needed at work, but Dina suspected he had been assigned to keep an eye on her.

'Don't *you* be silly. I'll take a cab.'

'I won't hear of it. It would be inhospitable. You'll drive her, won't you, Samir?'

Samir grunted an assent, clearly wishing he were somewhere else.

There was no way out of it without making everyone wonder what she was objecting to. 'Thank you,' she said to Samir.

A half-hour later they pulled into the lot of the Safeway. It was like a piece of home; save for a few details, it could have been in the middle of New Jersey.

'I'll only be a few minutes,' Dina told Samir.

'I'll come with you.'

'Oh, there's no need for that.'

'I will help you carry.'

'There won't be much. Nothing I can't handle.'

'I come with you,' he insisted.

The last thing she wanted was Samir lumbering a few paces behind her through the Safeway while she waited for contact with some unknown person carrying God knew what. She thought fast. 'Maybe you're right. I only have a few things, but I want to get some Maxi-Pads, and the box is bulky. You can help with that?'

'Maxi-Pads? This is what?'

'You know. For women. For their time of the month.' She gestured in a suggestive direction.

Samir visibly paled. Clearly he did not carry such things for Soraya – or even discuss them with her. 'If you say it's easy, OK,' he said hastily, 'I wait here.'

'No problem,' Dina smiled sweetly. 'It's just, you know, a woman thing.'

Inside, the supermarket looked little different from its American counterparts. She headed for the candy aisle and put M&Ms, Fruit Loops and several packets of Kool-Aid in her basket. No contact from anyone. No one appeared even to notice her. She took her time selecting several apples that looked as if they had been on a tree in Washington State the day before. That would do for the picnic surprise. She became aware of a man who was carefully squeezing avocados for ripeness. He was in his forties, wearing a business suit, and studying her more than the avocados. She paused, waiting. He smiled at her but did not approach. She moved slowly out of the produce section, expecting him to follow. He did, casually and at a distance.

Was he the contact, or just some horny local she had inadvertently encouraged? Damn. Almost forgot the Maxi-Pads. Contact or no contact, she was going to have to buy them in case Samir actually looked. She roamed until she found the aisle. The man was still trailing her, half the length of the aisle away. If he was going to pass her some mysterious package, he needed to get on with it.

'You. Tell me this.'

Dina stepped back, startled. She was confronted by a late-middle-aged woman in very conservative dress and a headscarf. She looked disapprovingly at Dina's western attire. The woman brandished a box of Pampers. 'You. Tell me. Is this the thing they use now for babies. My granddaughter asks me to buy this for my great-grandson.'

'Yes,' Dina stammered. 'Yes, they're for babies. You know.'

'Unh.' The woman stared disapprovingly past Dina down the aisle. Dina turned in time to see the man in the suit beat a retreat.

'I'm Alia,' the woman said in a near whisper. 'I am here because a man asks me to do this thing. If he does not ask, or if another man asks, I say no, let Americans take care of Americans.'

Dina stared. This was her contact, then?

The woman grasped her hand and, in a normal voice, said, 'Thank you, daughter, for your help.' Dina felt a small, hard object pressed into her palm. Alia's voice dropped again. 'Don't look. Put it away without attention. Now look at this.'

She held up the Pampers. Stuck to the package was

a small Post-it with what appeared to be a phone number written on it.

'Memorize it – now,' said the woman who called herself Alia. Dina stared at the number, trying to engrave it on her mind.

'Call it only in the last circumstance. If you cannot do the thing you wish to do.'

'I understand.'

Alia looked at her as if true understanding was quite beyond the capacities of such a neophyte, and an American to boot. 'You have the number?'

'I think so. Yes.'

Alia wadded the Post-it into a tiny ball. 'Use all of the medicine. It is harmless, just quite strong. It will cause sleep in five minutes. No more than ten.'

'It's safe?'

'Do you listen at all? One more thing: sunglasses. Wear sunglasses. On your eyes. The person you are meeting will wear them as well. If either of you suspect something is wrong, you will push the glasses up on your head. That will cancel the action.'

Alia touched her lips, and Dina realized that she had eaten the Post-it. 'Thank you, daughter, once again. May God give you great-grandchildren as well.'

With that, she turned and was gone.

Dina went to the corner of the aisle, checked to see that no one was watching, put the thing she had been given under the waist of her skirt. As she did so, she saw that it was a small glass vial filled with clear liquid. She paid for her purchases and went back outside. But when she reached the Land Rover, it was empty. Oh, God, where was Samir? He was supposed to be here. He should have been here. She had tried to be so careful – but had he somehow managed to follow her after all? Had he seen the exchange between her and Alia?

The door was unlocked so she put her packages into the vehicle and climbed in. She tried to compose herself. Where was he? Should she call the Major and tell him that something might have gone wrong? Then she saw Samir coming towards her. There was something in his hand. What was it? When he got closer, she saw that he was carrying an ice cream sandwich. She forced a smile onto her face and said brightly, 'All ready to go?'

He grunted and stared at her, taking a bite of his ice cream.

'Did you get that from the supermarket?' she asked. 'I didn't see you there.'

He stared a moment longer, then started the car. They rode back to the house in silence.

As soon as she could arrange a moment of privacy, Dina called the Major and quickly told him what had happened.

'I will contact our friend,' he said. 'When he decides what he will do, I will call you back.'

Dina tried to go on as if everything were normal. She even offered to help Maha with dinner, but her mother-in-law looked at her as if she were proposing to poison the family. 'No,' she said. 'You go outside. Wait for Karim.'

As Dina left the kitchen, she ran into Soraya, who was just returning from her meeting. 'Did you find everything you needed at the market?' she asked.

'Yes. Yes, I did, thank you.'

'What's wrong?' Soraya asked. 'You look a bit upset.'

'Do I?' It wouldn't do to show how nervous she

was. 'Oh, it's just our dear mother-in-law,' she improvised. 'I offered to help and she threw me out of the kitchen.'

Soraya made a face, then smiled sympathetically and squeezed Dina's hand. 'Never mind,' she said. 'Why don't you relax for a while and I'll go in and help our *dear* mother-in-law.'

Dina smiled back, grateful to have this little bit of support.

The call from the Major came just as the family was sitting down to dinner. When Dina's phone began to chirp, all eyes turned toward her. 'I'm sorry,' she said, getting up to leave the table. 'I'm terribly sorry, but I have to take this. It . . . it might be about my business.' She hurried to the garden, pressed the green button and said, 'Hello?'

'Our friend says he will proceed as planned. He will be cautious and so should you be. You will both use the sunglasses if necessary.'

'He's sure?'

'He said, dear lady, that he did not wish to waste this opportunity and that there would be no risk to you or the children.'

No risk to us, she thought as she ended the call. But what about him?

When she returned to the table, all eyes were once again directed at Dina.

'We do not use the telephone during meals,' Hassan declared.

'I know,' she said, 'and I'm so sorry. But this *was* important.'

'Another commercial for Sean?' Karim asked sarcastically.

'No,' she said, thinking quickly, 'it was . . . about Jordy. He . . . he had the flu when I left and I asked Sarah to keep in touch with him – and with me. She just called to let me know he was completely recovered.'

'*Nushkorallah*, thanks be to God,' Hassan said fervently. He loved Jordy almost as much as Karim had once done. 'I hope he will come to see us as soon as he finishes with school.'

Dina looked at Karim who had gone strangely still.

'Well,' she said sweetly, 'if that's what Karim wishes, I'm sure it can be arranged.'

'Excellent, excellent.'

Karim had little else to say during the meal, and for the bit of discomfort she had caused him, she was glad.

CHAPTER FORTY

Sarah put the key into her door, turned it and stepped inside. The apartment was empty. Quiet. There was a note on the kitchen table: Rachel was having dinner with one of her friends. She would be home 'later' – whatever that meant.

Sarah checked the stack of take-out menus she kept in a kitchen drawer, decided on a greasy cheeseburger with French fries from the nearby Greek diner, called the order in – and sat down to wait. She would eat the burger on a tray in her bedroom, watching whichever of the hundred-plus channels she could tolerate until she was tired enough to sleep. Not very healthy – and not much fun. So that would be her life soon. When Rachel went to college, all of her nights and weekends would belong to her. It was not a thrilling prospect.

She couldn't be sure where the relationship with David was going. But so far, everything she knew, she liked very, very much. And wanted to know more. But she still had to be careful where Rachel was concerned.

The last time she'd gone out with David, she'd put

257

on her special-occasion black suit. Rachel had noticed, of course – and she'd looked decidedly sullen when Sarah announced 'dinner with David' while adding make-up and jewelry.

Sarah was no psychologist, but she understood that her limited social life over the past couple of years had made Rachel very comfortable. Rachel had no reason to welcome a third party into their snug little routine. The occasional dinner for two at neighborhood restaurants. The rented video – and bowl of popcorn – evenings. Sunday mornings at the Chelsea flea market, with Rachel looking for vintage clothes and Sarah on the prowl for antique linens.

Rachel, of course, had friends of her own, including Jordy Ahmad. She had parties and dances and phone calls galore, not to mention the e-mails that kept Rachel online for hours at a time.

Sarah knew that Rachel had seen firsthand the problems some of her friends had with step-parents or near-step-parents. Yet knowing all that – and more – didn't make dealing with Rachel any easier.

Give it time, she thought, we all need time to make adjustments. Hadn't she been a wreck after her separation from Ari? Even though she was the one who'd wanted the divorce? Time. That's what they needed. She and David. She and Rachel.

When the phone rang, she thought it might be David. It was not.

'Sarah?' Ari's voice, commanding rather than questioning.

'Yes, Ari.'

'I've made some inquiries about your friend's problem.'

'Yes?' Now he had her full attention. 'What did you find out?'

'No small talk? No "how have you been, Ari?" Just get right down to business, is that it?'

Sarah sighed. 'Please, Ari. It's been a long day and I'm very tired.'

'All right, all right,' he said, sounding aggrieved. 'As I said, I made some inquiries, just as I promised I would. My people know who Karim is . . . they say his position is solid. So unless you go in with a couple of commandos and snatch the kids, your friend Dina's out of luck.' He sounded pleased with his report.

So his inquiries came to nothing. She began to doubt that he'd even made them. It didn't matter any more. Dina and her mercenary were already in place, so Ari's help or lack of it – was irrelevant. 'Well, thanks,' she said – meaning thanks for nothing. 'If that's all, I really have to—'

'That isn't all,' Ari cut in. 'I've been wanting to talk with you about your social life, Sarah.'

She sat up straighter, alert to possible trouble. 'My social life? What does that mean?'

'It means that man you've been seeing,' he replied, with an edge in his voice.

'And this is your business – exactly how?' Trying to hold on to her temper, thinking: You've got a damn nerve even mentioning my social life when you live like a tomcat.

He sighed. Ponderously, she thought. 'It's my business when it affects my daughter,' he said.

Anger flared quick and hot. So Rachel had been tattling to her father, just as she suspected. She willed herself to keep calm.

Ari took her silence to mean she was paying attention. 'Rachel doesn't like the man. A Sephardic, she tells me,' implying that was beneath contempt. 'Surely you could do better than that.' This said in a pitying way, as if to imply that Sarah had, in fact, fallen so low that she couldn't do better.

She wanted to shout, He's light years better than what I did before, but she held back. She didn't want to fight with Ari, so she said simply: 'It's not Rachel's place – or yours – to tell me who I may or may not date.'

'Be careful, Sarah, you want that *get*, you should be more careful.'

She laughed, an ugly laugh for an ugly situation. 'Go ahead, Ari, pretend you were going to be a nice guy and give it to me. Pretend that if I just do exactly what you say now, you *would* give it to me.'

Before Ari could answer, the doorman buzzed the apartment. It was the delivery man from the Greek diner. 'I really have to go,' she said firmly. 'I have a delivery coming up.'

Before she could hang up, he delivered his parting shot: 'Be careful, Sarah,' he warned, 'unless you've gotten some serious help, you won't be any happier with this guy than you were with me.'

Bastard, she thought, you rotten bastard, you're doing it again. I will be happier with David, she vowed to herself, a lot happier.

And now what? she asked herself after Ari had finally hung up. Her appetite diminished, she nibbled at the cheeseburger, then left it. Good thing Rachel isn't home, Sarah thought, or I'd confront her now for sure. And no good would come of that.

She's just a kid, Sarah reminded herself. She's frustrating and aggravating and she gives me *agida*, but she's still a child. And I love her, even when I want to spank her. It has to get better, she thought, otherwise no one could survive raising kids these days.

CHAPTER FORTY-ONE

Sunday morning dawned clear and bright. Dina could hardly choke down her breakfast, so anxious was she about the hours ahead. The plan had been made. It could work. It had to work. Now all she could do was keep up appearances – a smiling, normal demeanor – and pray that all went well.

After breakfast Soraya went outside; when she returned, she was frowning. 'It's going to be very hot today – and the sun is going to be very strong. Perhaps we should put off the zoo for another day—'

'No!' The word shot out before Dina could stop it. Quickly, she added. 'The children will be so disappointed if we don't go. We've all been looking forward to this time together. On our own.'

Soraya looked at her, long and hard. 'Well,' she said finally, 'I guess it will be all right if we don't overdo.'

Dina's heart began to thump rapidly. This is it, this it, this is it.

'If we're going to go, let's prepare a little picnic lunch,' Soraya said. 'If I know those children, they'll want something to eat as soon as we arrive.'

Dina agreed, glad for the chance of something practical to do. The two women prepared peanut butter and jelly sandwiches and packed fruit, cookies and drinks in a large cooler. Soon it was time to go. The children were fairly bursting with excitement as they all piled into Samir's Land Rover.

The zoo in East Amman was clearly still partly under construction, but what had been completed was first-rate. The star animals appeared to be the big cats, especially lions and tigers. Soraya explained that the facility had a special interest in breeding hybrids of these animals, but no such hybrids were on display. It didn't matter to the children: ordinary lions and tigers were more than enough.

As they passed among the well-designed and pro-fessionally maintained habitats, Dina looked more at the human beings than at the animals. She saw no sign of Constantine in the streams of zoo-goers. She felt almost as if she didn't want to see him. His presence would mean that the 'mission' was finally real, that they were actually going to attempt it. Up until now, it had always been something in the future, something only planned, something that could happen.

She was nervous. No, she was terrified. Maybe this was all wrong. Maybe there was a better way to do it. A less dangerous way.

She fought to calm herself, to contain the fear. If she truly couldn't cope, she could always abort the action simply by putting her sunglasses atop her head. Once she almost did just that. She forced her hand to stay at her side. *No gain without pain*, she told herself. What an idiotic thing to think. It was something Jordy's coach had preached, the one year he tried to make the track team at school. Jordy had hated the man.

They had seen the oryxes, gazelles, other indigenous

and exotic animals – less interesting to the twins and Nasser and Lina than the fiercer species. The day was warming toward noon. Soraya suggested that it was time for their picnic. The children chorused enthusiastic assent. Dina could not imagine swallowing even a morsel of food.

With Soraya leading, they made their way to the zoo's little park/playground. There were slides and other children's rides. Green grass and picnic tables. Women unpacking baskets. There seemed to be a rather large proportion of men with their children. In New York that would mean they were divorced or at least separated and this was their custodial day with the kids. It meant something different here, where men often took time to be with their children.

Soraya spread a cloth on a tree-shaded table. Lina helped. Ali and Suzanne ran to join two or three other children spinning on a small whirligig or roundabout. Lina and Nasser asked if they could play too. Soraya assented. Dina opened the picnic basket. She barely trusted herself to set out the plates. The pleasant little park felt like a battleground to her, the table like a bunker. This was where it was going to happen. And if it happened, it was going to happen soon. She felt to make sure the vial was still in her pocket.

She looked once more for Constantine, didn't see him. Then she did. She realized that he must have been there for at least some minutes, but she hadn't noticed him. Or had noticed him but not recognized him.

It took her a moment to understand why. It wasn't that he was disguised, exactly, unless you counted the designer sunglasses, but he *did* seem different – his dark hair oiled sleekly straight back, a lightweight sports coat that appeared to be silk, the collar of an expensive shirt open to reveal gold jewelry on his chest. A compact, high-tech-looking video camera carried casually in one hand. The first impression was of a successful generic-Mediterranean businessman whose enterprises might perhaps be something less than perfectly licit. But that wasn't what had caused Dina to overlook him. What had done that was the boy who was with him. Twelve or thirteen, in an Oakland Raiders jacket and Nike shoes, he looked enough like Constantine to be his son. And that was how Dina had seen them, if she had seen them at all – as just another father and son on an outing to the zoo. She wondered who the boy was. A relative of the Major's? Some street kid bribed with the jacket and shoes to play a part for an hour?

She was so caught up in the surprise – and in a surge of admiration for Constantine's resourcefulness – that it took another moment for the realization to hit her: this was it. This was the moment. The thing they had planned for, hoped for, crossed the ocean for. It was here. Here and now.

Her hands were ice and she felt lightheaded. Hyperventilating. Oh, God, don't faint *now*, Dina. Breathe slow and deep.

She looked to Constantine for – what? Guidance? A signal? It didn't matter. He was talking with the boy, not even looking in her direction.

His sunglasses were in place. It was a go.

Hardly knowing what she was doing, as if she were on some kind of autopilot, Dina drew the little vial from her pocket. 'Would you like a drink, Soraya?' she heard herself ask as if from across a room.

Soraya was opening containers of food. 'Yes, I'm dying of thirst. A Diet Coke.'

'Sure.' The soft drinks were in a small cooler pack. Dina set it on the table's bench to open it. The move concealed her hands. She would pop the cap first, she decided, then quickly open the vial and pour it into the Coke.

She looked for a last time. Constantine was showing the boy something about the camera. The boy looked in the viewfinder and panned around the playground. Constantine followed the direction of the lens as if to see what the boy was seeing. Then he laughed and clapped the boy on the shoulder. Father and son. He took back the camera and adjusted something on it, pushing his sunglasses up onto his forehead to see the controls better. Then he said something to the boy and they both turned and casually walked away.

It didn't register on Dina for a moment. She had the vial in one hand and Soraya's Diet Coke in the other. It was the crucial moment and Constantine appeared to be abandoning her. Was it a ploy? Did he mean for her to go forward?

The sunglasses! The signal! Something had gone wrong.

What?

She forced herself to be casual. To look around smilingly as if savoring the balmy day. She turned in the direction the boy had aimed the camera. Perhaps fifty yards away she saw him – one of the men from the car perpetually parked in front of the house. He was wearing sunglasses himself but she knew instantly that he was watching her. A few yards beyond him stood the other man from the car. He was looking in the direction Constantine and the boy had taken.

266

Did they realize what had been about to happen – or were they just watching her and anyone who might approach her?

'Where are you, Dina?' said Soraya with a laugh, waving her hand as if to interrupt a trance. 'Don't tell me an American doesn't know what to do with a Coke.'

Dina smiled distractedly and handed her sister-in-law the can. She should empty the vial onto the ground, she thought. What was an empty bottle? An empty bottle in these circumstances was a lot. The words *chemical traces* came into her mind. But there was no alternative. She started to unscrew the top.

She would have recognized the cry anywhere in the world: Ali! She spun and saw him, howling, fallen beside the roundabout, clutching his arm. She rushed to him. Suzanne was wailing too, not hurt herself, merely in empathy with her twin. There was a nasty scrape, with a deeper cut in the middle of it, on Ali's hand. Blood oozed.

Christ! Now the first man was coming this way. Had he seen what she was doing? She thought he must have. A belated instinct made her push her own sunglasses to the top of her head, even though she knew that it was foolish, pointless, that Constantine was no longer watching.

The vial was still in her hand. Damning evidence. She didn't dare put it in her pocket with the bodyguard walking straight for her, now forty yards, thirty-five yards away, his eyes fixed on her. And now the other one was heading this way too.

Soraya was right behind her. 'Is this bad?' she asked, her English suffering from fear.

'No. No, just a scrape, I think.' At this moment

Dina remembered her other difficulty. She was holding Ali's arm with her free hand and cuddling Suzanne with the hand that held the vial. A gaggle of children and parents had gathered, their attention focused on Ali's injury. They formed a screen that would last only for a few more seconds.

With a quick flip of her wrist behind Suzanne's back, Dina tossed the pharmacist's vial under the roundabout.

'He's all right, Mrs Ahmad?' someone said in Arabic. It was the first man. He addressed Soraya but he was staring at Dina. The second man was close behind him. If either of them had seen her . . . She moved her newly empty hand into plain view.

'Yes, it looks all right,' Soraya said, then focused on the man. 'What are you doing here, Khalid?'

Khalid shuffled his feet and looked into the distance before answering. 'Mr Ahmad – Mr Karim asked us to see if you needed anything.'

Soraya snorted and gave Dina a quick, pained look. 'What we need right now is a bandage and some antibiotic ointment for Ali's scrape. But I don't suppose you have anything like that, do you? So I think we'll go back to the house. Your services won't be needed, thank merciful God.'

Khalid stared at Dina a moment longer – she glared right back – and then shrugged. 'Whatever you say, Mrs Ahmad. We only do what Mr Ahmad asks.' He and the other man exchanged a glance. Then they turned and walked away together.

Dina decided to play it innocent. 'Aren't those the two guys, you know, the ones that watch the house?'

Soraya looked her in the eye, a challenge. 'You know they are. What I want to know is why your husba – why Karim had them follow us here. Why, Dina? Do you know?'

Dina resisted the temptation to drop her gaze. 'I don't know,' she said. 'I think it's crazy.' It was as close to an honest answer as she could come. In fact, it occurred to her, it was perfectly honest.

Soraya looked into her eyes for a moment longer, then shrugged and stood. 'The day is spoiled. Let's get this little man home. Bring us a napkin to wrap his hand, Lina.' The little girl, who had been watching it all in silent awe, hurried to comply.

Ali had stopped snuffling. He and Suzanne were examining his wound as if it were some unusual bug encountered in Central Park. Dina parted them long enough to wash out the cut with Evian water from the cooler and wrap the hand in the fresh napkin. Then, gathering what was left of the picnic, the six of them beat a slow retreat from the playground. Just before they reached the Land Rover, Dina thought she caught a glimpse of an Oakland Raiders jacket turning a corner in the distance. But she couldn't be sure. All she was sure of was that there would be no plane bound for New York with her and her children on it. Not today. Maybe not ever.

When they returned to the house, the children were tired and cranky. Though Ali was behaving like a brave soldier, Suzy was whining on his behalf. Dina coaxed her into taking a nap while she tended to Ali's cut and scrape. She promised them both a special treat later – she'd have to think of one – and tried to think of when she could safely call the Major.

When she left the children, she walked through the courtyard garden and towards the kitchen, where she thought Soraya might be. Instead she found Samir, blocking her way.

'You will have to leave the house today, Dina,' he said, his tone and expression reflecting his pleasure.

'What? What are you saying?'

'I'm saying you will have to leave. Pack your things and I will call you a taxi.'

'But why?' she demanded, knowing she had to play the innocent. 'Karim invited me to stay. He—'

'I've spoken already to Karim. He wishes you to go.' She debated the wisdom of arguing further but knew it would be no use. So, she thought, now it's really all over.

CHAPTER FORTY-TWO

At the hotel Dina immediately called the Major. No answer.

What had gone wrong? What had made Karim suspicious enough to send the bodyguards to the zoo? Was it the calls on her cell phone? Had Samir alerted him after the trip to the supermarket? Or had he simply mistrusted her from Day One?

She fidgeted. Flicked the TV on, then off. Should she call Constantine's pager? She was supposed to use the number only in an emergency. He had been very definite about that. Was this an emergency?

She decided against it. Constantine was the expert. She was in his hands. She'd follow his instructions.

She tried the Major again. No answer.

She couldn't sit still. Every few minutes she dialed again and listened to eight, nine, ten rings.

It was past noon when, just as she hung up the phone for the twentieth or thirtieth time, it rang.

'You're all right?' It was the Major.

'Yes.'

'Alone?'

'Yes.'

'I called twice before. Your phone was busy.'

'I was trying to reach you. Something went wrong—'

'You can tell me all about it later. You've had a difficult morning. You must be hungry, yes?'

'I hadn't even thought about it. What I could really use is a cigarette.'

'Surely they sell them at your hotel, yes?'

'I quit twenty years ago.'

'Ah.' The Major laughed. 'But you must eat. I know a good place. Very few tourists. Will you join me?'

It finally dawned on her that his insistence on food was more than avuncular concern.

'Oh. OK. Sure. Where?'

He named an intersection in the Eastern Heights section. No address, just the cross streets.

'When?'

'Why don't you catch a cab in fifteen minutes or so? It's not a long distance.'

'All right.'

'I look forward to seeing you again, dear lady.' And then he hung up.

Dina went to the window and looked out at Amman. It didn't seem real. What was she doing here? She was accomplishing nothing.

If the plan had worked, if everything had happened as Constantine had set it up, she'd be on a plane right now, she and Suzanne and Ali. Or if something had gone wrong – what? Jail? Probably. Deportation at the least – with all hope lost of getting her children back.

But that hope seemed lost anyway.

She freshened her make-up – keeping it light – and put on the large sunglasses. Downstairs, she let the doorman summon a cab.

The driver, an overweight but rather elegant man

about her own age, flirted with her in the subtle Jordanian manner she no longer found very attractive, but otherwise seemed uninterested in her or her destination, which turned out to be a reasonably busy but unremarkable street corner in one of the city's better neighborhoods. No one appeared to be waiting for her, and she felt conspicuous after the cab pulled away, passers-by giving her curious glances. But less than a minute later another cab pulled up.

'You the American lady?' said the cabby. It wasn't really a question. 'The Major sent me. Please to get in.'

'The Major?'

'Yes.' He was a handsome, smiling young man. For half a second Dina hesitated. Should she trust him? She decided she could not afford to be paranoid.

A few minutes later they were passing through what Dina recognized as the University of Jordan campus. The cabby pulled over. The Major was waiting on the curb. He exchanged a few words with the young man and paid him much more than the fare would have been.

'Hello, dear lady. A disappointing day, yes?' He jerked his head at the departing cab. 'My good friend Nouri says you weren't followed from the hotel. Except by him, of course.'

'Good,' said Dina, not knowing what else to say. It was nice to know that the Major was taking precautions on her behalf, but she wondered – not for the first time – how necessary all this care was. Especially since the opportunity to take the children had been lost. Maybe it's just the way he always is, she thought, in his line of work.

They walked down a tree-lined street among university buildings. The campus was pleasant – modern, well-maintained, in a hilly setting. Except for the fact that most of the faces were Middle Eastern, it might have been any college in, say, northern California.

'What happened?' the Major asked, smiling as if they were discussing the pleasant weather.

'I don't know. Karim must have suspected something. Or maybe he just doesn't trust me around the children. Our friend was there, and it seemed like he was all ready to . . . you know. And then suddenly he backed away. I saw the two bodyguards. Then Ali fell and it was all over. I realized that Karim had the men follow us from the house.'

The Major nodded. 'Our friend thought something like this must be the case. He saw two men at the park. They were watching. Not there to enjoy themselves. Our friend says they stood out like two sore thumbs. He has these sayings, yes?'

'Yes.'

'Describe these men, these bodyguards.'

She did.

'Maybe these were the men at the park. Maybe not. No matter. Obviously your husband suspects that you are not here simply to visit your children.'

'I think that perhaps he had me followed when I went to the supermarket. I told you that his brother drove me, didn't I? And then after I . . . after I finished my errands, he wasn't in the car. I . . . I had no idea if he was in the market or not. And there was something else.'

'Yes?'

'There was a man in the supermarket. I should have told you before. He seemed to be following me. I thought at first he might be someone I was supposed to meet. Then I decided he was just, you know, flirting with me.' She blushed and the Major smiled encouragingly, as if to say, Of course, that would be a natural assumption. 'But now,' she paused, 'now I wonder if he was one of Karim's people. If Samir might have sent him to keep an eye on me.'

The Major shrugged affably. 'Who knows? Things can go wrong sometimes. And sometimes we don't know exactly why. It happens.'

I hope it wasn't because I was careless, Dina thought. And then realized how ridiculous that was. What difference does it make? Over is over. The Major gestured toward a building they were approaching. 'This is the university restaurant. The food is only what one would expect, but the surrounding is . . . congenial.'

The restaurant was several steps above a collegiate student union in the States, but there was something of the same atmosphere. Dina realized that the campus was an ideal place for their meeting. Like most major universities, it was relaxed and cosmopolitan. Men and women, both students and faculty, sat and talked together freely. There were a number of westerners. To anyone noticing her, she would be just another visiting academic.

She ordered coffee and allowed the Major to persuade her to take a salad as well. He had only tea.

'Tell me again all that happened this morning,' he said when they were seated. 'All details.'

Once more she recited the morning's events as best she could remember them. Now and then he interjected a question. 'And nothing before today?' he asked when she had finished. 'Nothing to show any problem?'

'No. Not really. Well,' she reconsidered, 'it's hard

to say because Karim's family have acted cold and kind of suspicious since the day I arrived.'

The Major nodded thoughtfully but said nothing.

'What do we do now?' Dina finally said.

The Major turned his hand in a fatalistic gesture. 'That is not for me to say. I will tell our friend what you have told me. Beyond that, it is for the two of you to decide.'

'I haven't even talked with him since I've been in Jordan. How can we decide anything?'

'Again, I will tell him what you say. It's possible that he will want to meet with you. I, too, think it would be OK if precautions are taken. But it's not my operation.'

Two young men who had the look of graduate students took the table next to them.

'Did you enjoy the salad?' the Major asked Dina with studied casualness. 'Would you like something more? More coffee?'

'No, I'm fine. It was very good.'

'The food is only adequate, I'm afraid, but it's convenient.' He glanced at his watch. 'But we really should go.'

Outside, a taxi was waiting. Dina recognized the same young driver who had brought her. The Major obviously was a man for details.

'You are here for only a short time longer?' he said, holding the door.

She nodded.

'Yes. Then perhaps this is the last time I see you. Depending on what our friend says.'

Dina hadn't considered this. 'I'll be sorry if it is,' she said, meaning it. 'Just knowing you were here . . .'

'I, too, will regret it. When our friend contacted me, I did not know what to expect. I acted out of loyalty to him. But in our small time together, I've come to . . . to how you say it, root for you.'

'Thank you.' The Major's words touched Dina. It was the tiniest of comforts to know that someone in Jordan was on her side.

'Nouri here' – the Major indicated the cab driver – 'will be at your service. He will take you where you wish to go, when you wish. He's worked for me before. He's very dependable.'

'Oh.' Dina felt that she was being handed off. 'Well, thank you again.'

'If I don't see you again, dear lady, I . . . I will continue to pray that you get your children back. *Insh'allah*, it will happen soon.'

On the ride back to the hotel, Nouri smiled in the mirror and handed her a card. 'My numbers. Bottom is the pager. When you remember them, you will throw away the card, OK?'

'All right.' Dina had to wonder what kind of other jobs the Major and Nouri worked on together.

'Call any time. The colonel is a good man. He says take care of you, I take care of you.'

It took Dina a second to realize that 'the colonel' was the Major.

'But I take good care of you anyway,' Nouri went on. 'I like Americans. I live there two years myself. At University of Florida. I study to be engineer. Chemical engineer. I like to go back there.' The smile disappeared for the first time. 'Not so easy now, though. Very difficult.'

Suddenly Dina found herself sobbing.

'Hey, I say something wrong?' Nouri asked.

'No. Nothing. It's just . . . just that the world is such a . . . such a terrible *mess*.'

The young cab driver nodded solemnly. But solemnity didn't sit very long with him. 'But not so bad sometimes, yes?'

His smile was infectious. Dina wiped her eyes. 'Sometimes,' she agreed. 'Whenever that is.'

CHAPTER FORTY-THREE

Back in the room she felt like a prisoner under luxurious house arrest, chained to the telephone. She expected to hear from either the Major or Constantine any minute. Two hours passed. Three. Her despair was turning steadily to anger. Everything had gone wrong, and what was Constantine doing? Didn't he realize how much she needed to talk with him?

She debated calling his pager, decided against it. To hell with him and his spy games. She had problems of her own to deal with. Damage control. She had been trying to work up her courage to call the house. Now her anger pushed her to do it.

Fatma answered. Bad luck.

'Put Ali or Suzanne on, please.'

'They're not here. They are . . . they are at the movies.'

'When will they be back.'

'I don't know. Later. Late.'

'Then let me speak with Soraya.'

'She's not in.'

'What about my husband.'

'Not home.'

She was lying, Dina knew it. She tried to control her growing rage.

'When they get back – any of them – I expect a call. You pass that message along.'

There was an interruption on the other end, hurried mumbles.

'You don't call here.' It was Maha. 'You are not good for Karim and not good for children. You go to New York and stay with all the bad people.'

'What? Listen, old woman—' But Maha had hung up.

Dina calmly put down the phone. Then she ripped the bedside lamp from the wall and threw it across the room.

They were going to stonewall her. She had feared that they wouldn't allow her back to the house. She hadn't imagined they would stop her from speaking to her own children.

'Damn, damn, damn!'

Calm down, Dina. This is accomplishing nothing. Right, as Em was so fond of saying: Tomorrow *is* anothah da-ay.

My God, it had all gone to pieces. Bitterly she remembered the excited, hopeful version of herself who had gotten off the plane barely a week ago. How naïve she had been. What a fool.

She wanted desperately to hear a friendly voice. Em or Sarah. Or both. She reached for the phone, remembered the time difference. What could she tell them, anyway?

There was only one thing to do under the circumstances. She ran a deep, hot bath, complete with scented oils from the array of complimentary toiletries on the counter. She poured herself a brandy from the room's well-stocked minibar and let the soothing water and the merciful alcohol soak away her frustration, her disappoint, her defeat.

She must have dozed in the tub, because at some point she realized the water was tepid. The brandy glass was empty. She dried and slipped into the soft terry robe the hotel provided.

Maybe she'd order a room-service dinner. Turn in early.

It was deep dusk outside, the lights of the city coming on like evening stars.

She gasped and backed toward the door. A man was sitting on the couch, silhouetted against the twilit window.

He stood quickly. Light from the bathroom fell on his face.

'Son of a bitch,' Dina said. 'You scared me to death.'

'Sorry,' said John Constantine.

Dina flicked on the lights. Constantine had a touch of sunburn on his dark skin. From his morning in the zoo, she supposed. It looked good on him. She had never been so happy to see someone in her life. And so furious at the same time.

'What are you doing here? How did you get in?'

'Old Indian trick,' he said vaguely. Sunburn or no, he looked tired. 'You were dozing. Had to be a tough day. So I waited. Must've dozed off myself.'

Dina felt herself blushing. If he had seen her 'dozing' . . . well, she was damned if she was going to acknowledge it. 'You know, the phones work in this country,' she said.

'Yeah. Maybe they work too well. Something put Karim's guard up, anyway.'

'You think—'

281

'Who knows? Maybe that phone I got you isn't as secure as my source told me it would be. If it isn't . . . well, if it isn't, then a good scanner would pick up what you're saying.'

'God. That would mean we never had a chance.'

Constantine shrugged. 'I don't know that. It could have been any of the things you told the Major about. The guy in the market. Samir. Whatever. All I'm sure of is that he's spooked. He's got two men sitting in a car in front of the house. Same two I saw at the zoo. At least one of them looks like he's carrying.'

'You mean a gun?'

Constantine only nodded. 'As far as I can see,' he said thoughtfully, 'his whole security effort is defensive. I don't think he's got anybody on you right now. I checked the street for an hour and the lobby for another hour. *Nada*. The room's not bugged. I checked that while you were napping.'

She felt her cheeks warm again. 'So what do we do now?' she asked.

He sat wearily on the couch. 'Nothing. Call it off. We didn't plan for this and we don't have the resources to handle it.'

'Just give up, then?' Her own words seemed distant to her, as if someone else were speaking them. *Just give up my children* was what they meant.

'Not give up. Go home and . . . regroup. Come up with a better plan. You'll visit again, and from what you've told me about the guy, I don't think he'll try to stop you. He's angry now, but when he cools down, he'll figure out a way to let the kids see their mom – and guard them from anything you might try. Sooner or later, maybe in a few months or so, we'll get our chance. Or maybe it'll work out some other way . . .'

His voice trailed off. He looked beaten, like a pitcher who had lost the final game of the World Series. Dina hadn't realized until that moment how much this mission – this mission for *her* – had meant to John Constantine. She wanted to touch him, comfort him. She moved across the room and put her hand on his shoulder.

'It's all right,' she said.

'Nah,' he said. 'It's not all right. It sucks.' He gave her hand a quick squeeze. That was all. His hand completely covered hers. Then it was at his side.

'So what do we do?' she repeated. 'While we're still here, I mean.'

He looked as if he hadn't really considered it. 'I guess you try to see the kids. I stay out of the way. You've still got the Saturday flight, right?'

'Yes.'

'I'll stick around till then, make sure you get off OK.'

She shook her head. 'No need for that. Go tomorrow if you want.' She didn't know why she was saying it. She didn't mean it.

'Might as well stick around,' he said. 'See the sights, have a drink by the pool. But it's on my dime from now on, not yours.'

'I wonder,' she said, relieved that he would be nearby, 'if he'll even let me see Suzy and Ali again. They're giving me a hard time out there.' She told him about her call to the house.

'He'll let you see them,' Constantine said with certainty. 'At least to say goodbye. Anyway, you need to play it out. If you back off now, that would just confirm his suspicions.'

'I guess so.' She hadn't thought of this angle at all.

The only thing she wanted now was to see and touch and hold Ali and Suzanne again.

There was a short silence. Constantine broke it. 'Mind if I have a drink?'

'Oh! Where are my manners? Of course.'

He moved to the mini-bar. 'What would you like?'

'Oh, I don't know. Just some sparkling water.'

He poured a water for her and made a scotch and soda for himself. Light on the soda, heavy on the scotch, she noticed.

'To better luck next time,' he said, touching glasses.

'Better luck next time.' The words sounded hollow, almost pathetic.

They sipped their drinks.

'I'd like to know what set him off,' said Constantine.

'I wish I knew,' Dina said. 'I wish I knew none of this was my fault.' Then, 'Next time we'll do it better,' she said without much assurance. Toasts and wishes couldn't work magic. In all probability there wouldn't be a next time. Just a long useless drag through the courts.

Constantine finished his drink. 'I should go,' he said. 'I think it's OK, but no sense in taking chances. And I've got to grab a bite somewhere. I haven't eaten since this morning.'

'I could order room service.'

'No. I mean fine, for you, but the last thing we need is some room-service waiter bringing dinner for the two of us.'

'Oh. I guess you're right. Maybe a little paranoid, but . . .'

'Paranoid is good sometimes.'

He stood and so did she. Suddenly she didn't want him to leave. The night ahead, in a lonely room in a strange city, seemed to stretch into endless empty darkness. But more than that, she realized now how much she needed and trusted John Constantine. Trust was something she hadn't believed she could feel again. At least not where a man was concerned. And yet here she was, leaning hard on this strong man with the gentle eyes.

'I could order for one,' she said, 'and you could have it. I'm not really hungry.'

'That's all right,' he said. 'It's been a long day. I'll get a sandwich or something on the way to my place.'

'Don't leave just yet,' she said softly.

He looked at her inquiringly.

'Hold me for a second,' she said. 'Just for a second. I . . . just—'

He didn't wait for her to finish the thought. His strong arms went around her, drew her close. His hand went to her hair, her cheek. His touch felt so good, so right. She felt weak in the knees and she knew that if she let go, he would not let her fall. Stay, she thought, more than a second. Stay.

He pulled back to look at her. There was sadness in his dark eyes. And longing. He wanted her, she knew. But did she want him? Here? Now? In the middle of this awful, awful mess?

The phone rang.

It was the front desk. 'You have a visitor, Mrs Ahmad. A Mrs Soraya Ahmad. Shall I send her up?'

'Soraya? Well . . . yes, of course, send her up.'

Constantine raised a questioning eyebrow.

'My sister-in-law. I have no idea what she's doing here.'

He nodded. 'I'm history.' He scooped up his glass,

put it back in the mini-bar, and moved quickly to the door.

'Call me tomorrow?' She didn't know what else to say.

'I'll be in touch one way or another.' And he was gone.

A minute later Dina opened the door to Soraya's knock.

Before coming in, the younger woman looked down the hall both ways, as if fearful of being observed. She was dressed as if for some important business appointment.

'I was just on my way home,' she said, eyes darting around the room, 'from a meeting . . . a charity for the Queen Alia Center. I'm on the board.'

'Come in, sit down. It's a pleasant surprise.'

Soraya sat but didn't remove her light coat. 'I can't stay but a minute. I just wanted to say . . . I'm sorry about this morning. About how Samir spoke to you. I don't know what happened. Men, you know.'

'Yes. I know.'

'This is a nice hotel. You're comfortable here?'

'Oh yes. Listen, about this morning, it's OK. I don't want to cause trouble for you. But I need to see my children.'

'I understand. It's only . . . well . . .'

Dina decided to take a chance. 'Soraya, if I tell you something, will you promise not to say anything to anyone else? Not Samir, especially not Maha or Hassan.'

Soraya hesitated. She had already taken a chance by coming here. No doubt she feared that there might be consequences to keeping Dina's secret.

'It's nothing bad,' Dina assured her. 'It's just that

286

Karim doesn't want me to tell his family . . . ?'

'What?' Soraya asked. Apparently curiosity – and perhaps some affection for Dina – had won over caution.

'Soraya, I never gave up my children. Karim took them away while I was at work. I came home thinking it was a normal day – and all I found was a note saying he was gone. That he had the children and wasn't going to give them back. Ever.' She paused, allowing the impact of her revelation to sink in.

Soraya looked stunned. 'My God,' she said. 'What a thing. What a thing to happen.'

Maybe she realizes it could happen to her, Dina thought. Maybe she's saying to herself, If it could happen to an American woman, with kinds of rights and privileges, it could certainly happen to her.

'Soraya, I need to see my children,' she said, pressing now. 'Do you think I can drop by tomorrow? I called this afternoon and Maha gave me a hard time.'

Soraya grimaced. 'That woman.' She thought for a moment, then appeared to have gathered some resolve: 'Come anyway, I'll let you in.'

'I don't want to cause you trouble,' Dina said again.

'Well . . . maybe you should call Karim. At work, you know? He won't keep you away. It would make him look bad, how do you say, lose face.'

'That's an idea.'

Soraya stood abruptly. 'Well,' she said, 'I think I will have to go now. Maha will begin to wonder if I stay out too long. And then she'll say something to Samir.' She walked to the door, then stopped. 'So perhaps I'll see you tomorrow.'

'I hope so.'

'It's a shame about this morning. The children

would have loved to spend more time at the zoo. Mine and yours. They get along so well, don't you think?'

She put her hand on the doorknob, then stopped again. 'There's something you should know,' she said. 'Something I want you to know.'

'What?'

'If Karim will allow it, there's a chance you might see the children tomorrow. But on Friday they will be gone. Karim is taking them to Aqaba. He has a boat there. At the Royal Palms Marina. The twins are very excited about the trip.'

'They went on the boat once – we all went on it – when they were small. A few years ago.'

'Yes, that's right, I remember. But not since then.'

'No.'

Soraya gave her a searching look. 'Do you see what I am telling you?'

'That I won't be able to see the children after Friday?'

'No. Not just that. They will go Friday and stay at a hotel and take the boat out on Saturday. Then they will come back Sunday. It will be just the three of them. Or maybe just one other man, to help with the boat. No one else, out there on the sea.'

Then Dina *did* understand. She saw her understanding register on Soraya, who nodded as if confirming an idea she had held all along.

Soraya turned the doorknob and spoke more to it than to Dina. 'I don't know why I'm telling you this, I honestly don't. It's just . . . the children, you know.'

She was gone before Dina could find words to thank her.

CHAPTER FORTY-FOUR

'What's with the shoes?' Celia interrupted her shutting-down-the-office routine to nod at Emmeline's new Nikes. 'Don't tell me you're taking up jogging.'

'Walking,' Em told her. 'I've got to get some exercise.'

'How long has this been going on?'

'I just started. A couple of days.'

'I give it maybe a week.'

Em laughed but told herself that her secretary was a cynic. Once she got into the routine, she might even walk both ways. It was damn time-consuming, but so was her health club. And at least on a walk you might see something interesting, maybe even stumble on something that would make a good show, while in the health club, all you ever saw were other people's flabby thighs or washboard abs.

Celia jangled her keys. 'Want me to lock up? Or you want to do it?'

'You can do it. I'm outta here.'

'Walk carefully.'

'See you tomorrow.'

On the street, Em headed downtown at a brisk, if not exactly Olympic, pace. It had been a good day, spent not actually on the set, but discussing, booking and prepping prospective guests. One pairing looked especially promising: a mystery writer whose heroine was a forensic anthropologist, matched with a real-life forensic anthropologist.

In the middle of it all her accountant had called. Not with some tax problem but with a line on a Fire Island beach house, right on the water. Another of his clients needed to rent it out and was talking an extremely good price. Right away she had thought it might be just the thing. A little weekend getaway now and then. A place to take Michael, maybe even his friends. And Dina, of course, when she got back. She and her kids would need a place where they could relax and get back to normal.

Yep, all in all a very good day. Except that somewhere she had come up with a nagging headache. What with carbon monoxide and bus fumes, maybe walking wasn't all it was cracked up to be – at least in rush-hour New York. Or maybe she needed glasses? Wouldn't that be great? First the body was going, now the eyes. She was too young for this, damn it.

A Pakistani – or maybe he was Indian – was lowering the steel shutter of a small electronics shop. He wore a white skullcap. It looked like an Islamic kind of thing, and that made Em think immediately of Dina again. In truth Dina had been in the back of her thoughts, and often in the front of them, ever since she had gone to Jordan. What in the name of sweet Jesus was happening over there? Not a word of news. Oh, a call when she arrived safely and one more passing the time of day. John Constantine seemed to know what he was doing, but he had been a pain about phone security. Keep the calls to a minimum and don't say anything substantive, nada, zero, nought.

If anything was going to happen, it would probably be soon. Dina was supposed to be returning home in a few days. Em said a silent prayer for her friend and the twins. If she'd been near a Catholic church, she would have gone in and lit a candle for Dina's success. To have them all back safely. And wouldn't that make a great show: Dina and the kids, Constantine – she could picture it. But Dina would probably veto the idea. Dina hated all the so-called 'reality' shows – and it didn't get any realer than having your children kidnapped and then getting them back.

At Fourteenth Street she detoured to her favorite Mexican food store. She loved the sweet, peppery smell of the place and usually spent half an hour browsing and stocking up on hard-to-find-elsewhere items. But the headache was still nagging – she'd take a couple of aspirin when she got home – and so she settled for a pound of ground anchos and a bag of *masa harina*. Staples for the cabinet. She wasn't going to cook Mexican or anything else tonight. What she'd really like . . . what she'd really like, she guessed, was for Sean to be at the loft and in his best mood. They'd order pizza, maybe rent a movie, or a half-dozen early *Sopranos* episodes. Normal stuff. Kick back, make plans for the weekend. Chill.

Turning into her street she bumped into Perry Wiltz, an upstairs neighbor, going the other way. They chatted briefly about the ratty carpeting on the hallway stairs. Would a letter from the tenants motivate the landlord finally to replace it? Or did they need to talk to a lawyer? Or maybe a Mott Street hitman.

Musing on this, and hurrying a little toward her appointment with a couple of aspirins, she almost failed to notice the man crossing the street toward her. She registered only that someone was intruding on her projected path. Acquired New York instinct clicked on: she avoided eye contact and balanced her posture, firmed up her stride – a tall, confident woman not to be messed with.

'Em? Emmeline?'

A fan? But that voice. She stopped and faced him. Oh sweet Jesus and Mary! Surprise of surprises. 'Gabe?'

He laughed. The old Gabriel laugh. The melt-your-insides laugh. 'Yeah, me. And you're you, I see.'

'What . . . what are you doing here?' It sounded incredibly trite.

'Oh, I'm in town for a couple of days. I just, you know, thought I'd drop by and say hello.' He actually shrugged.

'Uh-huh.' She was recovering from the shock. 'You get this craving, what, every fifteen years? Like clock-work?'

'I know, I know.' He looked down and then away, a six-foot-two, thirty-seven-year-old little boy caught with his hand in the cookie jar.

'And you were just going to come up and knock on the door? Not even a phone call?'

He raised his hands in a gesture of helpless inno-cence. 'I was in the neighborhood, you know?'

She stared at him. She had often wondered what he looked like as time went by, how he had weathered the passing years – or how they had weathered him. He looked good. She remembered him as a tall, rail-thin young man with features so perfect they bordered on pretty, rather than handsome. He had filled out now, broadening in the chest and shoulders. Nice sports coat, she noticed, looked like fine imported wool. His jawline was stronger, and the two little dimples she had once loved had deepened. She realized that she had known him as a boy; now he was a man.

'So this is where you live, huh?' he said, using the old south Louisiana accent that he could turn on and off at will, He nodded toward the limestone building.

For a split second she thought of denying it. But obviously he knew where she lived or he wouldn't be here. 'Not the whole building,' she said sardonically. 'Just an apartment. A loft, actually.'

Gabriel nodded. 'So I guess you're not going to invite me in,' he said after a moment.

She hadn't even thought of it, but now that he mentioned it, it seemed like a very bad idea. She wasn't about to spring Michael's father on him in this manner – or on Sean, either, if he was here. 'No, I'm not,' she said.

He nodded resignedly. 'Didn't figure.'

'I hope you didn't figure, Gabe. I hope you didn't figure you could just waltz out of my life for fifteen years and then just waltz back into it. You want to talk to me, you want to talk to your son, you get on the phone. Write a letter. Send a goddamn e-mail. But don't you dare come bouncing up to my door like you just went out for a pack of cigarettes.'

He hung his head with the guilty-little-boy smile. 'Well, I quit smoking.'

'Good for you.'

He traced a pattern on the sidewalk with his toe. Nice new Italian loafers. She had a flash of him making the same nervous gesture with his ratty old running shoe on a gravel parking lot in Grosse Tête.

293

'You know,' he said quietly, 'I don't think there's been a day that passed, not a one, without I thought about you one way or another.'

She didn't want to hear it. Or maybe, deep down, she did. But so what. It was history. Gabriel LeBlanc was history. It was almost surreal that he was standing here. She crossed her arms and shrugged with elaborate disdain.

'Don't take me wrong,' said Gabriel. 'You know, I just—'

'Don't take you wrong! What on earth gives you the crazy idea that I would take you wrong, just because you show up on my doorstep with some line of bullshit after fifteen years? Fifteen years, Gabriel. That's how long ago you dropped the ball. And guess what, baby? The game is over. It's been over for a long, long time. Over and done and forgotten.'

'I know that,' he said so softly that she almost didn't hear him. 'I just . . .' He trailed off. He'd never been very good with words, she remembered, unless he was singing them.

She waited. Finally he said, 'Well, it's good to see you, Em. You look great.'

'Thanks. You look like you're doing OK yourself. So is that pretty much it? Why you dropped by, I mean? Because right now I've got a life to take care of.'

He said nothing but didn't move. Eyes still on the ground.

'Well, nice to see you, Gabe. Let's do it again in another fifteen years.' Christ, what a bitch, she thought even as she spoke. But wasn't she entitled? She turned toward her door.

'Em, wait.'

She stopped.

'Look, Em, *cher*, coming here like this was dumb, I see that, me, yeah. But you know, it's not . . . I didn't just drop by, like you say. I been walking up and down this street, this block, two hours, maybe more. Surprised somebody didn't call the cops. Every time I get to one end, I say, "Forget it. Go away, go home. You got no business here." But then I think I'll do one more time up and down. Maybe you'll come out your house, or to the window, or round the corner. Or maybe the boy will. I wonder, would I know him?'

She said nothing.

'You know, *cher*, I wanted to see you. But I wanted to ask, to . . . to ask . . .' He looked at her searchingly, then averted his eyes again. 'People do change, *cher*. Time changes 'em, if nothing else does. What you say is true. I dropped the ball and that game is over. For me, anyway. But the boy, Michael, he's got his own game, and it's just starting.'

Em listened. It was the longest speech she'd ever heard him make without a few beers in him.

'What I'm saying, *cher*, I know I can't be a father, not like a real one, to the boy. That ball, I dropped that one too, me. But what I want . . . what I'm asking . . . what I'm hoping, is maybe I can be something for him. What you think, *cher*? You think it's too late for that, too?'

Oddly, Em remembered a show she had done once, on birth mothers' reunions with children they had given up for adoption. One of the mothers had said almost exactly the same thing – minus the accent, of course.

'I don't know,' she said honestly. 'I guess you'd have to talk with Michael about that.'

He brightened so obviously it almost hurt to watch.

'You think I could? Talk with him. Not now, no, I don't mean that. I know you're busy, I know I'm interrupting. But sometime?'

Suddenly Em was crying. 'God damn you, Gabriel, what are you doing here? Why are you pulling this . . . this number?'

He looked as if he wasn't really sure himself. 'I don't know, *cher*. Maybe just, for once, you know, I'm trying to do the right thing.'

'Great. Doing the right thing. I don't need this shit, Gabriel. Why don't you . . . just go? Go back to Grosse Tête or wherever.'

'I'm sorry, Em,' he said simply.

He still didn't move, so she turned away, fumbling with her keys. Oh, damn it to hell. She turned back to him. 'All right,' she said, 'all right, I'll think about this. No promises.'

'That's all I'm asking . . . thanks.'

'Don't thank me. I haven't done anything and I might not do anything.'

'That's more than I got coming. I leave it up to you. Whatever you think is best.'

'No. Whatever Michael and I think is best. Assuming I decide to tell him about it.'

'Right.'

'What, you want to talk with him, meet with him?'

'Like I said, whatever he wants. Yeah, if he wants to.'

'You said you were here for a couple of days.'

'Right. This time. But I can be in town more often, I really can. I was . . . kind of planning on it, if things work out.'

Em digested this. The concept of Gabriel LeBlanc 'planning on' anything was foreign to her experience.

296

'All right. Like I said, I'm going to think about this.'

'You want me to call? Tomorrow, maybe?'

'No. Where are you staying?'

'Just up at the Holiday Inn. I'm in and out, some appointments, but you can get me there in the evening.'

'All right. I'll call you.'

'I appreciate it, Em, I really do.'

'One thing: whatever happens, Michael is not going to get hurt any more than he has been already. You understand?'

'I understand.'

'I'm not making any guarantees.'

'I know.'

'OK then.'

For the first time Gabe smiled. He had always had one of the better smiles on earth. 'Thanks, *cher*. I mean it. And I meant it too when I said it was good to see you. You look just as good as I remembered.'

'*Lache pas*,' she told him – *Lache pas la patate*: don't drop the potato. Stay cool.

He watched until she got the door open and went inside.

The apartment was empty. A note from Michael: studying at his pal Brendan's. Sure. Nothing from Sean. No message on the machine. She needed a glass of wine. No, a real drink. There was something she was forgetting. What was it? Oh, aspirin.

But for some reason her headache was gone.

CHAPTER FORTY-FIVE

I can't believe I'm doing this, Sarah thought – and then smiled as she realized she'd had this same thought any number of times since she'd started seeing David. Sure, she was halfway to crazy about him. But she wasn't one thousand per cent sure things were going to work out, was she? So there was no reason to be meeting his relatives, was there?

And yet now here she was, seated beside him in the bright red TT Roadster he called his summer car, driving on the Garden State Parkway towards the summer home of his cousin, Simon the Designer. That was how David referred to his relatives: Simon the Designer; Harry the Doctor; Herb the Accountant.

Though Sarah had what she believed was a solid work ethic, David had somehow convinced her that even a dedicated and hard-working physician was entitled to escape the city for more than a few days, and that it would be fine if Rachel stayed with her father for those days.

And now she was having fun, sort of, but she was also trying to figure out what it all meant – and how things had moved ahead so quickly. Was she falling in love? She couldn't remember how it had been with Ari, in the early days – it must have been good or she wouldn't have married him, right? Well, never mind that for now, she thought, she was happy to be here and she was going to have a great time.

That question settled, she turned to David. 'So how do you manage to have a summer car and a winter car in the city? Most people can't even manage one. The only reason I have no problems is because I have MD plates – and a bargain garage.'

'It's not easy, believe me,' David replied. 'When I was a kid, I always wanted a classic 1957 Thunderbird. Then, when I was able to afford it many years later, I didn't want the T-Bird any more. And that seemed somehow sad. So – now I try to indulge my teenage desires as they come up.' He turned a mock leer in her direction and made her laugh.

From Exit 105, he drove down Route 35 to Deal Road. Moments later, she felt the air temperature drop, inhaled the sweetness of new-mown grass, began to see big houses surrounded by lush banks of flowers. Apparently this was one of the Jersey Shore towns that employed legions of gardeners. As they turned onto Ocean Avenue, she oohed and aahed over the grand houses.

'There are lots of McMansions here,' he said, 'but actually, the borough was much prettier when I was a kid. We had gorgeous Victorians, magnificent Mediterraneans. Many were torn down, and now some of these newer places are just . . . big.'

'And your cousin's house?'

'It's one of the good ones.'

And it was. Simon Kallas's summer place was not an old house but a splendid new one, a bold modern statement in gleaming white and glass. Perched on a gentle slope overlooking the ocean, it offered sweeping vistas to forever. On the ocean side of the house was a pool with a retracting glass roof; in back, a tennis court.

Cousin Simon's greeting was a whirlwind of hugs and kisses and overblown compliments. 'So petite, so slim, so chic,' he burbled at Sarah. Sarah could think of nothing to say but 'hello'.

'Don't let him overwhelm you,' said David. 'He loves to bowl people over. That's how he's been getting his way since we were kids.'

Sarah smiled. She could see why.

Cousin Simon appeared to be about David's age – and perhaps even more boyish. What was it about the men in this family? she wondered. The Peter Pan thing? He was also slim, dressed in a white silk T-shirt and a pair of immaculate white linen shorts with just the appropriate natural fiber wrinkles. A crimson tie held back his artfully highlighted brown ponytail. Sarah looked into the startling green eyes – they had to be contact lenses – and murmured her thanks for his hospitality.

He brushed them away. 'I love filling my home with people,' he said, 'and David is one of my favorite cousins. Any friend of his, yada, yada, yada.' His effervescence stopped as abruptly as it had begun. 'You'll have to excuse me,' he said, 'I have phone calls to make, people to abuse, so why don't I let David show you the guest room and you can freshen up.' And with that, he disappeared in the direction of what might have been the kitchen.

David took her bag along with his and guided her up a staircase that Scarlett O'Hara would have been proud to ascend. And to a guest room that would have

300

impressed Martha Stewart. The decor might have been described as shabby chic, but it wasn't really shabby. The antique furniture was painted white and decorated with canna lilies. The sprawling king-size bed had a headboard of ornate white wicker and was flanked by matching nightstands. An old kilim area rug adorned the pickled wood floors and gave the room a muted touch of color. 'I guess Cousin Simon likes white? Not that I'm complaining,' she added quickly. 'This is much nicer than my own bedroom at home.'

'It's always nice at Cousin Simon's,' David said. 'And yes, right now, he likes white. Before it was some kind of green – celadon, I think he said, and before that, I think it was taupe or sand or something like that. Anyway, I'm glad you like it. Do you want to freshen up, then meet me downstairs in an hour or so?'

Sarah gazed longingly into the bathroom, where an oversize tub beckoned. But she agreed to the one-hour break. She quickly emptied her suitcase, noting with appreciation the dresser drawers that were lined with lavender-scented paper, the closet that was carefully fitted with racks and shelves and cubbyholes. It all seemed much too grand for the few things she'd brought – but still, it was fun to see her clothes put away in such a luxurious environment.

As for the bathroom, Sarah thought she could easily spend the entire visit enjoying it. In addition to the deep Jacuzzi, there was a wonderful marble pedestal sink, big wicker baskets filled with fragrant toiletries, shampoos and bath salts, and big fat candles to light while she bathed. Later, she thought, resisting the temptation to indulge herself immediately. Instead, she washed her face and reapplied her tinted moisturizer with sunscreen, a bit of blush and fresh lipstick. She changed from her wrinkled slacks and shirt into a pair of white shorts and a sleeveless linen blouse.

When she met David at the appointed time, he looked even younger, as if he had shed some years along with his city clothes. Now he wore tan slacks and a matching golf shirt. He looked relaxed, content – and seeing him, she felt that way, too. Simon was nowhere in sight. 'Are we the only guests?' Sarah asked.

David laughed. 'Wait,' he said, 'by dinner time, the place will be full. Meanwhile, let's take advantage of the quiet . . . I'll show you around. It's a good excuse to drive my car.'

Sarah agreed. David took her through the neighboring towns. In Elberon, he pointed out the spot where President Garfield had died. 'Poor Garfield was shot in Washington, but they brought him up here by train in the hopes that the sea air might help him recover. He died anyway.'

'Poor man.'

'Now we're in Long Branch,' he said, a short time later. 'Seven presidents summered here . . . it used to be a grand resort with grand hotels. Now it's just another Jersey Shore bedroom community.'

They continued along Ocean Avenue through the towns of Monmouth Beach and Sea Bright, then through Sandy Hook – seven picturesque miles of beaches, salt marshes, nature trails and dunes.

'This is all so pretty,' Sarah said. 'I didn't think there were so many pretty places in New Jersey.'

David laughed. 'You and a few million other people. Everybody thinks it's only chemical plants, industrial waste, and *The Sopranos*. I'll show you more tomorrow. We'll drive south and I'll take you through some areas that will knock your socks off.'

The promise of 'tomorrow' pleased Sarah. She also liked the idea of getting her socks knocked off.

That almost happened at dinner, when Cousin Simon's mother, Effie, arrived from Brooklyn. Though to say she arrived was an understatement, as if to say a hurricane or a tornado arrived. While Simon was no slouch in the drama department, Effie raised him one, as she complained loudly and passionately – about traffic, about the doubtful quality of the bread she had picked up from Shlomo the baker, as well as the cheese, the phyllo dough, and just about everything else. In short, she was absolutely certain her dinner would be a disaster.

David signaled Sarah just to listen and let Effie run down. Which she did eventually. And then she turned her attention to Sarah. 'So, sweetheart, you like our David?'

Well, that was right to the point. Sarah nodded. 'David's n . . .' – she almost said 'nice'. 'David's terrific,' she amended.

'Of course,' Effie said, as if Sarah was being slow. 'And you, sweetheart, are you SY? I don't know your family, do I?'

Sarah looked baffled. David intervened. 'No, Aunt Effie, Sarah's Jewish, but not SY – that means Syrian, in case you didn't guess. Her family lived near Eastern Parkway.'

'Ah,' Effie intoned, infusing the single word with layers of meaning. 'Well,' she perked up a moment later, 'at least she's Jewish.'

Sarah might have taken offense from someone else, but Effie was . . . well, she was . . . a force of Nature. She began unwrapping food. Boxes and plastic containers disgorged their contents, until every available surface in the kitchen was covered and there appeared enough food for the proverbial army.

'She carried all that from Brooklyn?' Sarah asked in a whisper.

'Aunt Effie's very particular about her food. She has her designated butcher, her designated baker, and so on. And they're all in Brooklyn. So – she brings Brooklyn with her, whenever she travels.'

Sarah professed her amazement.

'You ain't seen nothin' yet. Effie pulls out all the stops when she's in Deal.'

Effie's dinner was nothing short of spectacular. And it was clearly appreciated by the throng of assorted relatives and friends who showed up to partake of the *hummus* and *tabbouleh*, the *kibbeh* and meat pies, the broiled fish and the chicken with lemon and olives. For dessert, Effie brought forth two overfilled platters, one bearing *sabeyeh b'lebeh*, ricotta filled triangles made of phyllo dough sweetened with rose water syrup, the other, laden with *baklawa*, layered phyllo dough stuffed with pistachios, and also sweetened with rose water syrup.

Sarah liked the food as much as she liked this loud and boisterous family, their easy laughter and the pleasure they took in Effie's dinner. Now she thought she could see why David was such a sweet and caring man.

David picked at his dessert and whispered again to Sarah. 'Let's leave now,' he said. 'I always go for ice cream when I'm here.'

Sarah was incredulous. 'You haven't had enough to eat?'

'I haven't had my pistachio ice cream fix.'

304

And so they went. Excuses apparently were not necessary – people seemed to be coming and going as they pleased at Cousin Simon's house.

David and Sarah drove to Hoffman's in Spring Lake Heights – and joined the snaking line of people who had similar cravings. David ordered a large sundae made with pistachio ice cream. Sarah stared.

David smiled sheepishly. 'What can I say? I always get like this at the Shore. It's an excuse to indulge.'

Sarah joined him with a pistachio cone and found to her great surprise that she finished every finger-licking bite.

David sighed contentedly.

He's adorable, she thought, like a little boy after a treat. She reached out and wiped some errant ice cream from the corner of his mouth with her fingers. He took the fingers and kissed them. For a long moment they looked at each other. Then David asked: 'Do you want to go somewhere to listen to some music? The Stone Pony if you're in the mood for rock and roll. Or maybe . . .'

She shook her head. 'I'm content to just . . . be,' she said. 'I'm always running around doing things in the city. It's nice to just have nothing to do.'

'Then nothing it is.'

They drove back to Cousin Simon's house and sat on the back patio. A sliver of moon hung over the cobalt ocean, laying down a silver sheen over the water. Now it was Sarah who sighed contentedly.

David took her hand. 'I've made some inquiries about your *get*,' he said, 'but before I go any further, I want to get your permission.'

'For what?'

'Well, I think we should do a little investigation in

305

Israel. My cousin, Abe the Rabbi, has many connections there. He said he'd be willing to make some inquiries on your behalf.'

Sarah looked doubtful.

'You said Ari does a fair amount of business in Israel. Abe and I thought we might find something there, someone who would have some influence on Ari. At this point, it would seem your best bet is to apply pressure. Or to negotiate using something he wants.'

'Do you really think that will do some good?' Sarah's expression brightened.

'I think it's our best chance. I'll do everything I can, Sarah, I promise.' He drew her close and kissed her, gently at first, then deeply.

Sarah kissed him back so enthusiastically that it was David who drew away. 'Well,' he said, laughing shakily, 'this time it's my relatives who could catch us making out.' He inclined his head toward the sounds of laughter and conversation that emanated from the house. Sarah understood. This wasn't the place, they both agreed. She suggested a walk on the beach.

Fifteen minutes later, after the most perfunctory of walks, they were necking feverishly on the sand, as heated as a pair of teenagers. 'Sarah,' David said hoarsely, 'this isn't what I pictured for us.'

'I know.' She kissed him again, pressing her body against him with an urgency that was unmistakable.

'Sarah . . .' he began again, then stopped. When he slipped his hand under her linen top, she made a small sound that was part whimper, part sigh. His touch was gentle but sure and to her great surprise, her body responded.

Like teenagers, they fumbled with buttons and

zippers. Sarah's skin felt hot against the cool sand. This is crazy, a voice in her head protested weakly. Crazy it might be, but Sarah felt good. It felt good to be touched and held and kissed and caressed. It felt good to hear the sound of her voice saying yes, oh yes, when David parted her legs and began to stroke her.

And when he was inside her, she sighed again, as if she had been waiting a very long time for this. He did not move at once, but continued to caress her with his fingers, as if he knew instinctively what would please her.

But how, when she hadn't known herself? Was it the waiting, the knowledge that nothing had been expected that had freed her to respond to David? Was it the forbidden pleasure of making love on a beach? She didn't care, she simply gave in to it. To the orgasm that began as a gentle ripple and built to a climax that shuddered through her entire body, leaving her weak and senseless. And laughing.

At first David was startled. Then he started to laugh, too.

'Well,' he said finally, 'I guess we'd better stay out here for a while, until everyone either leaves or goes to sleep. Because if they see us now, they will definitely know what we've been doing.'

'Yes,' she said, laughing again, 'yes, they will.'

CHAPTER FORTY-SIX

Constantine called back two minutes after Dina rang his pager.

'Something?'

'Yes, something. Maybe. We need to talk. Can you come to the hotel?'

'Maybe not a good idea. But if something's up . . .'

Dina thought of the moment they'd shared before the call from the front desk had interrupted. Had it really happened the way she remembered? She could still recall how his arms felt around her, the touch of his fingers on her face. Yes, it definitely had happened.

'Should I just tell you about it?' she asked.

'Not on the phone. Can it wait till morning?'

'I . . . it's very interesting.'

'But nothing we can deal with tonight?'

Why was he being so casual? Had she done something wrong? Maybe he was just tired – he sounded exhausted. 'No, I guess not. But it can't wait long. Not long at all.'

'First thing tomorrow. Why don't you take a nice morning walk?'

'Anywhere in particular?'

'Just a walk.'

'All right.'

'Anything else I need to know?'

'No. I don't think so.'

'See you tomorrow.'

To her surprise, the night was not the misery she had feared only an hour ago. She ordered a room-service meal and found herself drifting pleasantly toward drowsiness even before she had finished her dinner. As she settled comfortably between the linen sheets of the soft bed, the sleepy thought came to her that what was different was hope. Where she had been utterly defeated, now suddenly there was one last chance that she would win her children back after all. And in the warm darkness cradling her to dreams came a final conscious image: John Constantine's soulful dark eyes looking into hers.

The sun was well up when she woke. She nearly panicked with the thought that she might have over-slept whatever contact Constantine had in mind. She threw on her jogging clothes, brought on this trip for the outdoor activities that had never materialized – the big sunglasses, and Mets cap.

Downstairs she waved off the doorman's offer to get her a cab. 'Exercise! Walking!' The man looked almost alarmed. Perhaps she had been too emphatic.

It was a beautiful day, crystal clear and cool enough that she was glad of the long sleeves on her warm-up jersey. She went down the long crescent drive of the hotel and out along the avenue at a good power-walking pace. Three blocks later she became aware that a car was prowling along behind her just off the curb. A little chill of fear touched her.

It was broad daylight on a busy thoroughfare. She turned to confront the follower.

'American lady!'

Nouri in his cab.

'We don't go far,' he said when she was ensconced in the back seat. 'I like you cap!'

She took it off. 'It's yours.'

'You kidding!'

He was still thanking her for the cap when he pulled up at the Roman amphitheater.

'Busy today,' he observed. Tourists were already swarming the site.

'This is where we're going?' Dina asked.

'Up above there,' said Nouri, 'is a nice overlook. You enjoy the view. I wait.'

She got out and climbed through the amphitheater. The tourists appeared to be mostly Germans. None gave her a second glance.

On the heights, there was a little overlook with coin-operated telescopes. A man was looking through one of them. Constantine. She edged up beside him.

'Need change for the machine?' he asked. He fed a couple of coins into the slot. 'Take a look, and tell me what's up.'

She looked through the telescope and told him what Soraya had said.

'That's it?' he said when she had finished.

'That's it. What do you think? Is there a chance?'

He looked disappointingly unenthusiastic. 'A boat,' he said. Then came the questions: How big a boat? Twenty-eight feet, she told him. Was Karim an experienced sailor or an amateur? Capable, as far as she could tell, but no America's Cupper. Who was this other man who might help? She didn't know. Did

Karim keep any weapons on board? She didn't think so. Well, a flare gun.

'What the hell, it doesn't matter, if this guy's a bodyguard, they might bring a piece or two along for this trip. Let's walk.'

They strolled through the amphitheater site, to all appearances just a couple of western tourists enjoying the brush with a civilization far more ancient than their own. Constantine had even brought a camera.

'Maybe I'm just dreaming,' Dina said. 'Maybe this is crazy.' His less-than-enthusiastic attitude had dampened her own spirits. And the questions about weapons had reminded her that there was very real danger – with Ali and Suzanne in the middle of it. How had she managed to forget that?

Constantine said nothing. He had a glowering look. Maybe she had angered him, Dina thought, dragging him out here for what must seem to him like a desperate fantasy. But no, now he was nodding at her. 'I can picture ways of doing it,' he said at last. 'I'm not wild about it, and I need to think it through. I also need to get down to Aqaba and take a look at this marina. Meanwhile, you need to go see the kids. If you don't, you'll look guilty as hell. Act normal, like nothing's happened. Deny that you've done anything. Learn whatever you can, but for God's sake, don't ask any questions. Nothing, you understand?'

'I'm not even sure they'll let me in the house.'

'Find a way. Don't make a scene, but do it.'

'OK.'

'Another thing: if this is going to happen anything like I'm seeing it, it's going to take more money than we . . . than I figured. We're going to need a specialist.'

'How much money?'

'The guy I'm thinking of, probably twenty thousand. And another few thousand for other expenses.'

'Fine.' She would give all she had for a chance to salvage this rescue.

'All right. Here's what happens. You see the kids and I go to Aqaba and check things out. If it looks do–able, I call my guy, and we take it from there. One way or another, you're on that plane Saturday. You're not here when it goes down. If it goes down.'

'Wait a minute. You're not thinking of keeping me in the dark about this? How am I going to know what's happening?'

'I'll be back tomorrow, maybe late. We'll meet. For one thing, you'll need to have the money for me. The guy I'm talking about, he won't get paid till it's over, but the other stuff, I'll need ready cash. Get it wired, let's say seventy-five hundred bucks. Any luck, we won't need it all, but we have to have it available if it is needed.'

'We'll meet where?'

'I'll let you know.'

He was in his brusque, cool, efficient mode. She supposed that was what she had hired him for. The moment of near-intimacy was nowhere to be seen.

They had come to the edge of the amphitheater site. Dina spotted Nouri's taxi.

'I'm worried,' she said. 'This scares me. It's so sudden. Like we're rushing into something, making it up as we go along.'

He nodded. 'I don't like it either. I'd like a month to set it up. Even longer. But sometimes things happen fast.'

'Whatever happens, I don't want Ali and Suzanne to be in danger. Any danger.'

'Dina,' he said softly, his look tender, 'that's been understood from day one, hasn't it? Look, I'm gonna check this thing out to the best of my ability, then I'll give you my evaluation. Whatever I come up with will be minimal risk. And it's your call anyway. Or,' he paused, 'we can forget it right now. Go home and regroup, like I said. Just tell me what you want.'

It couldn't hurt to have more information, Dina decided. 'Go to Aqaba.'

'OK. Good. I'll see you tomorrow.'

'Good.'

He turned to go, stopped, took her hand. 'It'll be all right, Dina, I promise. Whatever happens, we're not gonna run some Einhorn-style operation. Enjoy your kids and don't worry.'

He melted into a gaggle of Germans spilling from a bus.

CHAPTER FORTY-SEVEN

The phone was ringing when Em came in the door. She got to it before the machine did.

It was Sarah with news. Something was happening in Amman. Dina had asked David to transfer money.

'So what's it for?' Em asked.

'Do I know?'

They worried and guessed about it together. Was the money for bribes? Lawyers? Something more sinister?

The only thing that was clear was that some action was under way, or about to be under way, to take back the twins – and that this action might well be dangerous.

By the time they hung up, with an agreement to let each other know the minute either had news, Dina's mission had taken on a new reality for Em. Until now, except for her very real horror and disgust at Karim's abduction of the children, all the plotting and planning had felt almost like a game, an intellectual exercise that might never produce any result. Now the thing was actually happening, and Em felt the helpless anxiety of the caring but distant spectator. At this very moment, Jordanian police might be dragging Dina out into the night.

For God's sake, girl, look on the bright side, she told herself. After all, the whole thing might go off as smooth as cream.

The apartment was quiet. It was Sean's acting-class night, and he'd be out late with his classmates and other acting pals afterward – too late for an early riser like her. There was the usual note on the fridge from Michael: he was at Brendan's. Of course. She wondered if she needed to talk with him again about Gabe's reappearance. It was strange how Michael had taken the news that his father was back. After, digesting Em's account, he had asked simply, 'Do you want me to see him, Mom?'

When she told him it was totally his decision, he nodded and said he'd think about it. That was all. Until he asked for Gabe's phone number. And then closed the door to his room while he made a call. Em hadn't asked how it went, and Michael had volunteered just one bit of information – that he'd agreed to meet his father.

Now she took a baggie of homemade marinara sauce out of the freezer. Some mushrooms and pasta would make a cozy little feast. She would prop her feet up and watch TV, maybe read a book, try not to worry about Dina. Call Sarah again later.

She was putting water on to boil when the phone rang.

It was Sean. 'Hello, beauty. Feel like a night on the town?'

'What happened to your class?'

'Nothing. I just decided to blow it off. I have something to tell you. Thought we might go to the Orchid.'

The Orchid was a little Italian restaurant on the Lower East Side. It had been their special place when

315

they first knew each other. They hadn't gone there for months now.

'I don't know. It's been a long day. I just want to chill.'

'Come on. I'll pick you up. Twenty minutes?'

She had meant it about wanting to chill, but Sean insisted. Finally, out of curiosity more than anything else, she gave in. Had he finally landed the big part he was forever expecting? That would be nice. She would be happy for him. For him, she realized – not for us.

A dreadful thought occurred to her: surely he hadn't suddenly decided to pop the question. He hadn't sounded as if he'd been drinking.

In the cab he still wouldn't tell her the big secret. He was at his most charming, but she thought she detected little lines of anxiety in his professional actor's smile. It made him look just a little bit older.

The Orchid was the same neighborhood place it had been since, probably, about 1970: candles, checked tablecloths, a faded mural of Venice on the wall.

Sean ordered a scotch and soda for himself and a white wine for Em.

'So what's the big news?' she asked when the waiter went to get the drinks.

'In good time, beauty.'

The drinks arrived.

'A toast,' Sean said. 'To us.'

Uh-oh. Em took a sip of the wine. The Orchid's wines had never been the best. 'I like a drawn-out story as much as anybody, Sean, but this is getting silly.'

He laughed. The little lines were still there. 'OK. So here it is. You know how we've been talking about me moving in . . . you know, the two of us living together?'

Actually, no, she knew nothing of the kind. The

316

only times the subject had arisen, she had gently dismissed it. She didn't want a live-in man in the house, certainly not with Michael still there.

'Let's do it,' Sean went on, sincere and serious now. 'It's time for that commitment, don't you think? I do.'

'That's it?' Em said. 'That's what you wanted to tell me?'

Sean's face fell, but he recovered quickly. 'Well, it's pretty big, isn't it? I mean, I thought it's something you wanted, too. It just seems like the logical next step for us. The right step, you know?'

Would she want Sean living in her house even without her son's presence? The answer came to her undeniably: no. Not really. It was pleasant to have his company a few days a week, to go to bed with him now and then, but it was clear to her in that moment – if it hadn't been for months now – that Sean wasn't the man she wanted in her life for ever.

She couldn't tell him that, though. Not in so many words. His expectancy and anxiety were so obvious. She couldn't just shoot him down.

But then something else clicked.

'Sean, tell me the truth. This isn't about the lease, is it?' For weeks Sean had been complaining that his lease was coming up for renewal and the landlord was bumping the rent to the max. Sean and his roommate, Dean Crosser, another struggling thirty-something actor, could handle it, but it was the principle of the thing. It was rent gouging.

'The lease? Hell no.' Sean's expressive features went from mystification to mildly offended to innocence. 'I hadn't even thought about it. But since you mention it, yeah, it would be logical. Otherwise I'm locked in for another two years. Why not make a clean break?'

So it was about the lease – at least partly. Em was beginning to get angry.

'Sean! Hey, dog, what's happening?'

It was a friend of Sean's, yet another actor; Em remembered his name only as Brad. He was with a pretty, if vacuous-looking, blonde.

'Bradley, what brings you here, my man?'

'Well, it's a restaurant. Got to eat, no? Hey, how about our boy Deno?'

'Yeah, something, huh? So how's it going? Introduce us to this beautiful lady.'

Em realized that Sean was trying to change the subject. She could swear he was sending eye signals to Brad to talk about something else.

'Deno?' she said to Brad. 'Dean? What about him?'

Brad either missed Sean's signals or ignored them. 'You didn't hear? Our boy here didn't tell you? Maybe he's jealous. Deno hit the jackpot – they cast him for the FBI agent in Ron Howard's next movie. Off to La-La Land.'

'Dean's going to LA?'

'Gone already, right, Sean? Who wouldn't?'

'Who indeed,' said Em. So that was the whole story.

She waited until Brad and his date had left them before she picked up her purse.

'This is for the wine. And don't bother coming around tomorrow.'

'Aw, come on, Em. You've got this wrong. I was going to tell you about Dean, but it's no big deal. I mean, it's great for him, but it doesn't affect me. I can handle the rent myself.'

He couldn't even have handled the old rent without a roommate. And while Em didn't mind giving Sean a

318

helping hand now and then, she wasn't about to take him on as a dependent.

'Don't call either. You've got some stuff in my closet. I'll have one of the guys from the studio bring it to you. Goodbye, Sean.'

She walked out. He followed her, pleading for her to listen.

'Leave me alone or I'll make a scene, Sean. I mean it.'

Providentially, a cab appeared; they were rare in this neighborhood.

She didn't cry until she was home.

CHAPTER FORTY-EIGHT

'The children are not here. 'They have a special language class. For foreigners.'

Fatma was lying. Dina was sure she had heard Ali's voice in the background, and no one had ever mentioned any special classes.

'When will they be back?'

'I don't know. Much later. Late.'

Bitch, Dina thought, and hung up.

All right, she thought, enough was enough. She'd endured enough lies and evasions for the past two days, and she was not about to put up with any more. She sizzled for a few minutes, then found Karim's office number in her address book. A secretary answered and asked who was calling Mr Ahmad.

'Mrs Ahmad.'

'Hold on, please.' A full minute passed. 'Mr Ahmad is out of the office. May I take a message.'

Dina had had enough. 'Mr Ahmad is new there, isn't he? Why don't you ask him the company policy on employees' wives who come to the office and raise holy hell? Because that's exactly what I'm going to do if you don't put him on this phone.'

There was a longer hold this time.

'Dina,' her husband said coldly, 'this is totally uncalled for.'

'Don't give me "uncalled for", Karim. I came all the way to Jordan to visit my children, and I'm damned if I'm going to spend my time watching television in the Hyatt. You call the house right now and tell that bitch Fatma or whoever is guarding the door that I'm coming over and the door better open, unless you want to continue this conversation right there in your office.'

She could almost hear him wondering if she were bluffing. 'All right,' he said. 'I'll accommodate your wishes once again.'

'Thank you.'

'But the children are not to leave the house with you. Or anyone else.'

'Why not?'

'I think you know very well why not.'

'No, Karim, I don't know. Why don't you tell me?'

There was a pause. He didn't want to say how he'd been checking on her, monitoring her movements. All right, that was good for her.

'Well?'

'Suzy and Ali are my children too, Dina, and it's my house, and those are the rules. I'll go this far. No further.'

'All right. Thank you,' Dina said formally. There was no sense in pushing harder. She had what she wanted.

She went to the house after lunch. The two men Constantine had mentioned were parked out front. Dina recognized them as the bodyguards from the zoo. They watched without expression as she alighted from Nouri's cab.

She spent the afternoon just being with her children.

321

Touching them often. Talking. Listening. Watching as they played with their cousins. Loving them with all her heart and soul. Hating their father for putting her through this. Soraya, distant and coolly polite, made sweet tea and sandwiches. Dina didn't press her sister-in-law for more; she didn't want to cause her any problems, not after what she had done. Neither of the other two women appeared at all. Dina wondered where they were hiding.

'We're going on Daddy's boat,' Suzanne said at one point. 'Saturday. Can you come too?'

Dina and Soraya exchanged a glance across the table. 'No, Suze, I can't. I'm going home, back to New York on Saturday – remember?'

Suzanne pulled a long face. 'I wish you weren't going back.'

'I have to. You know that.'

'When will you be back?'

'I don't know. But soon. I promise.'

The afternoon went too quickly. Dina had just called Nouri when Karim came in. It was early for him to be home.

'Oh, Dina,' he said. 'I'm glad I caught you. Can we talk a minute?'

'Why not?'

He drew her into the living room. 'I'm taking the children on a holiday.'

'Suzy told me. Saturday. The boat.'

He seemed taken aback for a moment. Had he really expected that the children wouldn't mention such a thing?

'Yes.'

'So I can't expect to say goodbye to them at the airport.'

322

'Well, actually, we'll leave on Friday. So tomorrow is the last day that you'll see them.'

'That's not fair, Karim! You could take them another time, when I'm not here, damn it!' That should be sufficient cover for the fact that she already knew his plans.

'Please don't use that language in my parents' home, Dina. No, this is the only time I can take off. I'm sorry, but that's the way it is.'

'I don't believe you. You're doing it on purpose.'

'Believe as you wish. Listen, let's don't make this more unpleasant than it has to be. Come tomorrow, spend the day. Then we'll have dinner together, just the four of us. You'll have the whole day with them. I'm sorry, but it's the best I can do.'

Dina pretended to consider it. She dreaded returning to the home of the enemy. But he had said 'just the four of us', so perhaps it would be manageable. 'You don't give me much choice,' she finally said.

He smiled. 'Tomorrow, then. I look forward to it.' He looked out the window. 'Your cab is here.'

The two men in the car were still watching as she left.

At the hotel Dina used the computer room to email David Kallas. She asked him to call and confirm – discreetly – that the transfer of money had taken place. He had been instructed to transfer $7,500 to the account Constantine had set up at an Amman bank for exactly this kind of eventuality. Dina needed to be sure that the money would be available the next morning. The day after that would be Friday and the banks would be closed.

She calculated the time difference. It was the lunch

hour in New York. The few lawyers she knew were fond of high-end restaurants and not averse to a martini or two with their meals, all billable somehow to the client. From what Sarah said, David wasn't that type. Was he one of those workaholics who grabbed a bite of deli at his desk? She had a sudden craving for a corned beef on rye with lots of mustard. Or a Nathan's hot dog smothered in sauerkraut. It was odd because she rarely ate either of these things in New York. She realized that what she really wanted was to be home. With her children.

Still, she was hungry. And not for yet another Jordanian version of lamb stew.

In the hotel restaurant she thought she caught the slightest hint of disapprobation from the *maître d'*. A woman dining alone. In most local restaurants, this wouldn't be allowed; she'd be relegated to the so-called 'Family Dining Room'. But in a place that catered to foreigners, she was seated without comment. She shrugged it off. She was in a let-them-all-go-to-hell mood. There was no corned beef on rye to be had, but she ordered something she rarely had at home: a steak that was the most expensive item on the menu, and a pricey half-bottle of French burgundy to accompany it. She gave no thought to the damage to her credit card, as she had just moved a large sum of money into a foreign bank for disposal in God knew what manner.

She wondered what Constantine was doing. Was he checking things out in Aqaba? She pictured a water-front bar, something out of an old Bogart movie, Constantine talking in guarded phrases with dark, villainous-looking men. She supposed he must actually do that sort of thing. Must put himself in danger. Must have done it many times. Perhaps enjoyed it. She remembered the lost moment they had shared, the long looks and personal remarks, the pleasure she took from his touch. No, she thought, not now, this isn't the time for it.

She ate her salad, poked at her baked potato, attempted a bite or two that barely dented the huge slab of steak. She did better with the wine. Relaxed her a bit. Trying not to think about the children. Thinking about the children. Watching them play a computer game against their cousins. The cousins, even though they were older, never stood a chance. Ali and Suzanne were a team. And they were Americans – they had practically been born playing with computers. Dina remembered the first one Karim had brought home, a 486 it had been. For Jordy. A dinosaur now. She shut off the memory.

'Very much food,' said the waiter with a proud smile as he cleared the table. He asked if she wanted the leftovers boxed. She told him no.

'A sweet perhaps? Or some coffee?'

'Nothing, thanks.'

Why couldn't she just walk in, say 'Suzanne and Ali, get your things, we're leaving,' and hop into Nouri's cab for the ride to the airport?

She paid for the meal, adding a nice tip for the friendly waiter.

In the room the phone message light was winking red. There was one call: David Kallas.

'Hello, Dina. The transaction you mentioned has been taken care of.' A little pause, as if he were trying to think of something uncompromising to say. 'Hope your visit is going well. Look forward to seeing you again in New York.'

That was all.

She would go to the bank as soon as it opened in the morning. But what was she supposed to do with $7,500 in cash? Carry it around in her purse? In a money belt? She didn't even know if it would be American currency or Jordanian. Did it matter? She supposed not but wished she knew. She debated paging Constantine, decided against it. She had no idea if his pager would even function in Aqaba. She'd never understood how those things worked. Besides, if he was meeting with unsavory types in some dark corner on the waterfront, a buzzing pager might not be welcome.

She had never felt so alone. She thought of calling Sarah or Em, but both would be at work. In the end she called her mother. The familiar voice brought a comfort, but the words themselves were all too familiar. Soothing assurances that somehow everything would work out. Of course, her mother knew only that she was here to see the children, nothing more. So it was understandable that she might still hold out hope for a meeting of the minds, perhaps even a reconciliation. 'Remember, Dina, remember what I told you . . . things weren't always perfect between your father and me. Maybe Karim will come to his senses . . .'

It was a little disconcerting, like trying to watch two different movies at once, since Dina could say nothing about the real state of things. She asked about her father. 'The same,' her mother said quietly. 'He asked about you today.'

'Give him my love,' Dina said, 'and tell him I'll be home as soon as I can.' Her father didn't know that Dina was in Jordan – that would have complicated the lie he'd been told. Instead, Dina and her mother had concocted a cover story: Dina was in Los Angeles, meeting with the planners of a record industry awards banquet that would be held in New York. It was a flimsy and unlikely scenario, but it was the best Dina could come up with. God, it was hard to sustain a story built on lies. How did Karim manage to live a lie all those weeks and months he'd been planning to steal her children?

Presently Dina said goodbye to her mother, pleading the cost of the call.

She tried the television, watched the king greet some visiting foreign dignitaries, gave it up. She read a couple of chapters of the not-very-suspenseful suspense novel she'd bought in the airport in New York to read on the plane and never finished, then took a pill for sleep. Tomorrow was going to be a very long day.

CHAPTER FORTY-NINE

'Good news, Sarah. I have some good news for you.'

'What? What are you talking about?' At a little past seven on her day off, Sarah was still groggy from sleep and caffeine deprivation. If David's call hadn't awakened her, she'd be burrowed under the covers and pretending she lived in a world where there were no such things as schedules and emergencies. But the promise of good news was almost as good as coffee and Sarah pushed herself up on her pillow.

'I'm talking about my Cousin Abe the Rabbi. He found some information that could help you.'

Now she was fully awake. 'Help me how? What information?'

'Information about Ari's . . . activities in Israel?'

'Activities? Illegal activities?' Sarah was both fearful and excited. She didn't want anything really bad to happen to Rachel's father – but wouldn't it be great if he was to get some of the same kind of *tsuris* he'd been giving her?

'No, no, nothing like that. Look, let's meet for breakfast and I'll tell you in person. Then you can decide how you want to proceed.'

Sarah agreed, and an hour later, she and David were

seated at a booth in the Greek diner that delivered so many of her meals-on-the-run.

'Tell,' she demanded. 'Tell me everything.'

'May I say that you look beautiful this morning,' he said with a smile.

'No, you may not. You don't get me out of bed on my day off to pay me compliments.'

He looked wounded. 'I find that a good way to start the morning.'

'Stop teasing,' she demanded.

'Well,' he said, drawing the word out, 'it turns out that Ari has been leading a kind of double life. It seems he's engaged – not formally – but the woman in question believes it is. She's very well connected politically and socially and she's been a great help to Ari in his business dealings.'

Sarah shook her head. Just the kind of woman he had always wanted, someone prominent and useful.

'She wants to get married.'

'And?'

'From what we could find out from certain friends of hers, Ari told her that he was having difficulties getting a divorce. A difficult wife who wouldn't let go . . .'

Sarah began to laugh, almost hysterically. 'He's kept me tied up all this time – and he tells some other woman that I've been hanging on to him, is that it?'

David nodded. 'That's it.'

She leaned over the table and kissed David soundly on the mouth. 'I love you, I love your Cousin Abe the Rabbi, and I love the woman in Israel, whoever she is. Now let's figure out how we're going to tell Ari he isn't going to screw around with me any more.'

David smiled. 'I thought you'd never ask.'

CHAPTER FIFTY

Dina called Nouri on Thursday morning. He was waiting in his cab ten minutes later. She gave him the name of the bank. 'I don't want to be followed,' she added, feeling like a total fool. But the young Jordanian merely said, 'Of course,' and took her on a tour of side streets until he could assure her: 'No one following.'

At the bank she took the money in American hundreds. It still made a substantial chunk, too bulky to hide in a money belt. She pushed it deep in her purse. The bank officer had offered to convert it to traveler's checks and had seemed surprised when she declined. She would just have to be cautious, she decided. If Constantine needed to hire pirates or whatever, they might not accept American Express.

She didn't intend to go to the house until after lunch, since it was clear that her presence was not welcome. That left the rest of the morning empty. If she were on vacation, she would use the time to buy little gifts for Em and Sarah and the girls in the shop. All things considered, she didn't feel like bringing anyone a remembrance of Jordan or this trip, but she decided to do it anyway. Nouri took her to places that he swore offered the best bargains in Amman, as long as she wasn't the kind of silly American who thought the price quoted was the real one.

In the end nothing appealed to her. Everything seemed either too tacky or too expensive or impossible to fit into her luggage. She finally bought a few scarves, more to satisfy Nouri than anything else.

He took her to an early lunch at a small neighborhood restaurant and insisted on paying. He recommended the stuffed grape leaves with yogurt and cucumbers. The food was very good, the restaurant not a tourist hangout. Nouri seemed to know everyone at the little tables around them and introduced Dina as a friend from America. The fact that she could speak a few words of Arabic made her a center of attention. This appeared to her to fit poorly with Constantine's ideas about security, but she enjoyed it like a child freed from detention hall. It occurred to her that between the poisonous ambiance of Karim's house and the claustrophobic confines of the hotel room, she was beginning to go a little stir crazy.

She drank cup after cup of very sweet tea and chatted chaotically and happily until she suddenly realized that Constantine might be calling her from Aqaba that very moment. No, she told herself, he'd never do that – never risk letting someone know he was at the scene of the planned . . . the planned what? Abduction? Kidnapping? Boat invasion? Rescue, she decided. Although that was not what the police would call it.

But he might not be in Aqaba. Maybe somewhere on the road back by now. Would he stop and call?

He didn't believe in cell phones. He wasn't even sure that hers was a secure line, and he certainly wouldn't want her to use it unless there was an emergency.

That kind of caution had made sense then. Now it seemed paranoid and an annoyance. But there was no getting around it. She could almost hear the phone ringing back in her room, the message light burning red. With many attestations of mutual esteem, she managed to disengage from the Jordanians.

At the hotel, thinking of the lunch Nouri had bought, she tipped him far too heavily. His black eyes hardened. She had forgotten about male Arab pride. She quickly explained that she needed him to pick her up in two hours, and this was payment in advance. The smile reappeared instantly, but he still handed back the money. 'If I drive you more, you pay when we finish.'

In the room the message light was dark. Nor did the phone ring during the next two hours. She didn't know why she hadn't gone to the house earlier. This might be her last day with the twins until . . . well, maybe until sometime next week in New York. Or maybe, if something went wrong . . . she would not think about that. For the hundredth time she derided herself as an idiot for being in this insane position. For the hundredth time she reminded herself that Karim, not she, had walked out of their marriage and boarded a jet with two of their children. Why? Could it really be all about Jordy? Nothing else? Was all that talk about 'moral values' and 'providing a solid foundation' only a screen for God knew what fears and inadequacies in Karim himself?

Another woman? Or the hope of one? Of course she had thought of that. But there was no sign, nothing at all. Would Soraya have told her, at least dropped a hint? She didn't know. When she tried to imagine Karim with someone else, she felt no jealousy, only a blinding anger that the 'someone else' would try to co-opt her children.

It had been hot outside when she came in from lunch. It would be hotter. She would like to have dressed in the lightest of clothes. A sundress. Better not. If Maha should be home, her lip would curl in a sneer that said 'loose woman', just as clearly as if they were in Saudi Arabia, not Jordan.

'Dinner together, just the four of us.' What did that mean? Did Karim really envision a cozy little domestic scene, something out of *Father Knows Best*. She almost laughed thinking of it, but in truth she dreaded the whole thing. God, let him not try to make it romantic – candlelight or some such madness.

She chose a short-sleeved green linen blouse, a matching skirt, and her most sensible shoes.

Nouri was waiting, his Mets cap turned stylishly backward. He drove nonchalantly, chatting exuberantly. No side streets, sudden turns or frequent glances in the rearview mirror.

'Not being followed?' she prompted.

He laughed. 'Doesn't matter. We are going where they are. Why care if they follow?'

Well, yes, she might have thought of that. On the other hand, how did Nouri know that 'we are going where they are'? Had the Major told him that all this caution was really all about her children?

'They have moved,' Nouri said as they pulled up in front of the house.

'Who?' A little *frisson* of alarm.

'Those two men. Those who were here yesterday. Now they are farther down the street. You should not look.'

But she had already looked. The car was, perhaps a

hundred yards away, the figures in it little more than indistinct shapes.

'You have good eyes,' she said.

'Yes, always. What time you want I pick you up?'

'I don't know.'

He lifted his cell phone from the seat. 'Any time. You call.'

Soraya, obviously the family member designated to deal with Dina, opened the door looking both uncomfortable and relieved. Was she to join them for dinner, then? 'I'm glad you're here,' she said.

'Is something wrong?'

'No. Not really. Just that Suzanne and Ali have been . . . at odds.' Mother to mother.

'Over what?'

'Who knows? The heat. Excitement about the boat.' She paused for an instant and added, 'Maybe you leaving.'

'Oh.'

Suzanne was at the kitchen table, staring gloomily at a book. Harry Potter, Dina noticed. She looked up and brightened as if someone had flipped a switch. 'Mommy!' She flew to Dina and they hugged fiercely.

'Sweetheart. Where's your brother?'

The switch was flipped off. 'I don't know.'

Through the kitchen window Dina could see Ali in the garden. He was alone, doing nothing, half lying on a bench, and looking as down in the mouth as Suzanne had.

She knocked on the glass. His reaction on recognizing her was decidedly different from Suzanne's: he frowned, then reluctantly undraped himself from the bench and lounged with an elaborate lack of enthusiasm into the house.

'What's up, tiger?'

'Nothing.'

'I hear you two aren't getting along. What's the trouble?'

'Nothing,' they said together. They might be at odds with each other, but that was none of the outside world's business. It still surprised Dina a little to realize that she was part of that outside world to the twins – closer than anyone else, certainly, but still just beyond the circle that enclosed only the two of them.

'Well, then. Tell me what's happened since yesterday.'

Apparently nothing had happened – nothing they wanted to mention, at least – so she told them about her morning instead. She made a funny story, with her as the bumbling tourist, of her haggling with the shop-keeper over the price of the scarves. Suzanne laughed. Ali still was out of sorts but took enough interest to offer advice. 'You have to act mad when they tell you how much it costs. Aunt Soraya does it really well.'

'Do you, Soraya? Show us. Show me, I mean.'

Soraya did, with Ali playing the shopkeeper and Suzanne correcting his errors in the role, and the ice was broken. The rest of the afternoon was not much different from old times in the apartment back in New York. Something still hung in the air between the twins, but they obviously had made a tacit truce for the duration of this visit.

At one point Hassan came in from his study and joined the talk, telling a story about a hunting trip he'd once taken with the old king. It was not a topic of great interest to the women – although Ali ate it up – but Dina could have kissed the old man for simply acting like a grandfather.

335

Maha did not appear. Fatma did. Ignoring Dina completely, she set to work preparing the table for the evening meal. Soraya joined her, dividing her attention between the job at hand and the conversation. The cousins bounced in, raising the energy level by half.

Late-afternoon shadows had covered the garden when Karim arrived, bluff, smiling, hugs to the twins, compliments to Dina and Soraya. He had brought a selection of frozen fruit juices and rushed them into the freezer: dessert.

The dinner, of course, did not turn out to be 'just the four of them' – that was impossible in an extended-family household in Jordan, and Dina couldn't understand how she had ever imagined otherwise. Everyone was there except Maha, who was 'not feeling well', and Samir, who was 'working late'.

It was all so warm and homey, Dina thought, that no one would ever have guessed the true situation hidden beneath the smiles and laughter.

It started to fall apart with Hassan's little speech. It was just a few words about how good it was to have seen Dina again, and how he hoped it would not be much longer before she would be able to rejoin her family. There was some sort of disjunction here, Dina thought: could the old man really be that clueless? Had no one, not even his sour-faced wife, filled him in on what was truly going on? Or was this some *pro forma* exercise in courtesy? But Soraya and Karim, and even the cousins, were nodding as if Hassan were expressing not only their fondest wishes, but an imminent reality.

Not Suzanne. She was staring straight ahead, looking so miserable that Dina leaned over and whispered to her, 'Something wrong, Suze?' The child only shook her head.

Karim noticed and tried to smooth it over. 'I know you're already missing Mommy, precious, but she'll be back soon. And meanwhile, we're going to Aqaba tomorrow.'

That was when it happened. Suzanne slammed her small hands on the table so hard that her dish rattled. 'No! I don't want to go to stupid Aqaba! I don't want to go on some sucky boat! I want to go home!'

She had started with a shout and ended with a wail, tears rolling down her cheeks. For a moment everyone sat frozen in surprise. This was not a country where children spoke in this fashion to their elders. The cousins stared. Dina realized that they had probably never seen such an outburst from another child, certainly not from a girl.

Karim flushed with embarrassment and anger. 'Be ashamed! Be ashamed, Suzanne! Go to your room this instant!'

Dina turned on him. 'No! You heard her!' She looked fiercely around the table. 'You all heard her!'

'She's upset because of you. God knows what you've been telling her.'

'I haven't told her anything. I haven't told her how you took her and Ali without a word to me! I haven't told—'

'Shut up, Dina! Just shut up! You're a guest here.'

'A guest? You jerk, I'm her mother!'

'A mother talks like this in front of her children? You're a—'

'Enough!' It was Hassan, his voice like thunder. 'Enough! We do not do this at table!'

Even though his hawklike glare was directly on his son, Dina felt like a scolded child herself. The old patriarch had the power of unquestioned authority.

'We eat in peace,' he declared with finality. As if to make his point, he went back to his food.

No one else seemed hungry. Karim took a bite or two as if to placate his father. The cousins picked at what was in front of them. Suzanne sat with her hands in her lap. Ali pushed a piece of eggplant around his plate.

Dina was seething. The veil of pretense had fallen for a moment, and the moment had felt good. But she forced herself to stay silent. Two more days, she reminded herself. Two more days and all this might be only a bad memory. She mustn't go too far, mustn't do anything that might cause Karim to cancel his planned outing.

'Don't forget we have ices!' Soraya said too brightly, trying to salvage the occasion. She met with silence from the adults and unenthusiastic murmurs from the children.

Hassan pushed his plate away and stood. The meal was over. Karim followed him from the room without a word. The cousins melted away. To Dina's surprise, Ali went with them. Soraya mechanically began to clear the table. Dina just as mechanically helped. Suzanne, as if making a decision, pitched in as well.

Dina set down a stack of plates and hugged her daughter. 'It's OK, Suze. You'll be home someday soon. I promise.'

Suzanne hugged her back. 'I know, Mommy.' She managed a smile. 'But do you know when? Daddy won't tell me . . . you know how he is.'

'Yes,' said Dina. She had thought she knew, at least.

Just then Karim came back in. Either the storm had passed or he was making a heroic effort to ignore it; only the smallest cloud still hung in his dark eyes.

338

'I'm sorry for the . . . scene, Dina. I wanted this to be . . . different.'

She shrugged. 'It's a difficult situation.'

'Yes, well . . . It's getting late. Almost the children's bedtime. A long day tomorrow.'

'Oh, please,' Suzanne began.

'No,' Karim said, raising his hands placatingly, 'I'm not saying you have to go to sleep just yet. But get ready for bed. Your mother and I need to talk. Then she can come and tell you good night.'

'Go ahead, Suze,' said Dina. 'I won't be long.'

'Aauugh,' Suzanne groaned. But she went.

'Tell your brother,' Karim called after her. Then he turned to Dina. 'In the garden? It's a beautiful night.'

'All right.'

He was right: it was a beautiful night – balmy, almost cool, with a silver moon skimming the treetops. Dina realized that she had hardly been out at night since she had been here. And as she thought that, she was once again struck by the unreality of it all. How had she ended up in this place, doing what she was doing? Walking in this garden with this man who was still her husband. Waiting to tell her children goodbye. Wondering what another man, somewhere out in the same night in this same city, was planning in order to steal those children back.

'What are you doing here?' Karim asked abruptly. 'I mean, what are you *really* doing here?'

It was a little scary, as if he had read her mind. 'I don't understand. I'm visiting the children. Our children. And talking with you.'

He shook his head. 'Don't lie, Dina. You're here to take the children.'

'What are you talking about?'

'You know what I'm talking about.'

'I know that your imagination is running wild.'

'Don't insult my intelligence, Dina. I know what I know.'

'What, that you think I'm going to grab the kids and make a run for the border?'

'Actually, I do think something like that.'

Deny everything, Constantine had said, and indeed she would never admit anything. 'You want to talk about insulting someone's intelligence, Karim? Think about it: if I was planning "something like that" ' – she laced his words with sarcasm – 'do you think I'd tell you? So why bother with this . . . this cross-examination?'

'This is so like you, Dina. So like you.'

'Another thing: even if I was planning to take the children, isn't that exactly what you did?'

His anger went from cold to hot. 'No, damn it, it isn't exactly what I did. Do you think I wanted to do this for no reason?'

'If you didn't want to do it, who forced you?' She hated this, it was ugly, it was futile. But she was damned if she was going to back down.

'You'd know more about that than I, Dina. You—' He stopped. 'My God,' he said. He seemed genuinely contrite. 'Is this what we've come to, Dina: fighting like two hyenas on this beautiful night?'

Again his words echoed her thoughts, staunched the rush of anger. But what else had he expected? Still, for just a moment, she felt like reaching out to touch him. Just his cheek. A moment, only that. An impulse, not of love – that was gone for her – but of tenderness. Of something shared more important than either of them: the children, of course, but something else besides.

340

Maybe it was only that, somehow, the universe and all their past had thrown them here together in this garden, on this night, under this moon, in this strange and bitter reality.

'Out of all the gin joints in all the cities in all the world,' she said.

Karim actually laughed. It had been their favorite movie. 'I've only done what I thought was best,' he said softly. 'For Ali, most of all.'

She said nothing. She didn't want to begin the argument again. The silence stretched between them. When Karim finally spoke it was very quietly. 'I've been thinking: what if we were to compromise? For now, anyway. What if you were to take Suzanne back to New York?'

She could not believe what she was hearing. 'And leave Ali here?' It was the only thing she could think of to say.

'I think it will be better for him to be with me. I think it might be better for Suzy to be with you.'

Was this some kind of trick? A trap? 'You want to split them, the children, the twins? Divide them up, here's your share, here's mine?'

'I don't think of it that way. I'm trying to reach a solution that's best for everyone.' He turned to face her directly and his voice became harder. 'You should think about it too. I can tell you that whatever ideas you might have about taking them both aren't going to work. I won't let you, and this is my country.'

'Don't threaten me, Karim. You're just . . . springing all this on me.'

'I know it seems sudden.' He had softened again. 'Look, the way we've done this visit was a mistake. It doesn't have to be . . . a war. I don't want for us to be

341

like those people who poison their children with their hatred of each other, when the other one is always the villain. I don't hate you. I hope you don't hate me. I'll make it easier for you to visit Ali. Maybe we could even meet in Lebanon, with your father's people. You'd have to promise, though, just a visit . . .'

A promise would be an admission of guilt. Dina ignored it. 'You're serious, Karim? You want me to take Suzanne home?'

'Yes, I'm serious.' He sighed. 'She's not happy here. At first she seemed fine. She seemed to be adjusting beautifully. But she misses you, Dina. You saw that for yourself.'

'What about Ali?'

'He has no problems, he likes it here. You can ask him yourself. I think he and Suzanne argue about it. More since you're here.'

So that was the conflict between them, Dina thought.

'Do you want to do this, Dina? Take Suzanne with you?'

Of course she did. But it wasn't that simple. First, what would it do to Ali and Suzanne? They were twins, for God's sake. She had never seen children so inseparable. And Karim was proposing that she aid and abet him in separating them. If that were not enough, there was her secret knowledge that, two days hence, she might have them both together. 'I can't decide now,' she told Karim. 'Not this . . . spur of the moment. I need to think about it.'

'I know you're leaving Saturday. Maybe you can delay for a few days. But if not, I need to know soon. I've promised the kids this boat trip. I don't want to call it off. Can you tell me by tomorrow morning?'

342

'God, I guess I'll have to. I'd hate to interrupt your outing.'

'Don't be like that, Dina.'

'By the way, what happens if I say yes? Do you and Ali still go off sailing?'

'I don't know.' He seemed genuinely unsure. 'He might not want to go. Or maybe he will. Maybe Samir and his boy will come with us, make it an all-male thing. Forget our sorrows.'

What were Karim's sorrows? Dina wondered. He certainly didn't seem to be missing her. 'I'll say good-night to them,' she told him. 'I'll call in the morning, one way or another.'

'Thank you,' he said simply.

In the house she called Nouri, then went to Suzanne's room. She was reading the Harry Potter again. She put the book down and Dina held her close. 'I've got to go now, sweetheart. I love you.'

'I love you, Mommy.'

'Listen. I meant what I said about you going home. But what would you think – I'm not saying it's going to happen – what would you think if you came home and Ali stayed here? For a while, anyway. Would you still want to go?'

Suzanne's eyes were very dark and deep. 'Yes,' she said.

In his room Ali had dozed off. Dina woke him with a hug. ' 'Night, Mommy,' he said sleepily.

'Ali, tell me one thing: do you want to go home? To New York?'

'Why?'

'Never mind why. Do you want to?'

He rubbed his eyes irritably. 'Sure,' he said. But then he added, 'Someday.'

343

'Not soon?'

'Not really.' He seemed to sense that his words hurt her, and tried to explain. 'I mean, I missed you, Mom, when you weren't here. But I like being with Daddy, too.'

It wasn't surprising. He was at the prime age for a boy's hero worship of his father. A father who could show him jet fighter planes and men in uniform, who could take him sailing. It wasn't surprising at all. But it broke her heart.

'Good night, sweetie,' she said.

CHAPTER FIFTY-ONE

In the cab her mind was racing. She thought of
Sophie's Choice. But she wasn't being asked to choose
one child or another. She was being offered a deal. A
'compromise'. Take it or leave it. Her mother's heart
could not bear the thought of separating Suzanne and
Ali, even for a while. But a small voice was saying, *At
least you'd have your daughter*. And what about those
visits with Ali? In Lebanon? Who could say what
might happen under those circumstances? Karim
could have any 'promise' he wanted; she would feel no
obligation whatsoever to honor it. And there was still
the boat trip – and the plan. The rescue plan. What to
do about that?

She barely heard Nouri until he repeated a question:
'This is all right with you?'

'What's all right?'

'That we see this friend of yours. At my place.'

'Friend?'

'Yes, your friend. John is all he says his name.'

'At your place?'

'Yes. My apartment. He waits there.'

'Well, yes. Yes.'

Nouri lived in a low-rise apartment building that

managed to look both new and rather worn-out at the same time. The elevator was not working – 'This happens too much,' Nouri said – so they climbed five flights of stairs. Nouri knocked an obviously agreed-upon sequence on his own door and John Constantine opened it.

He was deeply tanned – obviously he had gotten still more sun in Aqaba. His cream-colored linen shirt was open at the neck, revealing a whitened scar she had not noticed before. He looked, she thought, like a movie pirate.

'We've got to stop meeting like this,' she said, attempting a smile to lift her spirits.

He smiled back, gave her a long look that might have meant anything, but said nothing.

'I didn't know you and Nouri were acquainted.'

'Very recently.'

'The Major?'

He nodded.

'Who *is* the Major anyway? Or shouldn't I ask?'

'The Major is the Major,' said Constantine. When he went no further, Dina decided that she had intruded on some forbidden area. Or maybe that Nouri's presence dictated discretion. But then Constantine said, 'We worked together on something back during the Gulf War. We were in the same business: military intelligence.' He smiled. 'I know, it's an oxymoron. So there we were, a couple of oxymorons, from different countries but working on the same project. Which we won't go into. Anyway, we hit it off, worked well together. Then one day he landed in a bad situation and I managed to help him out.'

'You mean in the fighting? In combat?'

'No. Much more dangerous than that.'

He obviously wasn't inclined to go into detail.

'So he owes you?' prompted Dina.

'Maybe he sees it that way. To me it's more like we owe each other. It was that kind of situation.' He shook his head as if driving off thoughts of ghosts, then grinned. 'Everybody called him "the Major" even then, even though he was a captain fresh up from first lieutenant. It was because of the way he carried himself. The guy probably looked like a major on his first day of boot camp.'

Nouri's apartment was small but surprisingly modern and neat. He bustled about making coffee for them, then excused himself. 'You will want to talk. I have something I forget in the cab. I will go check.'

They sat at what might have been a coffee table in the little living room.

'So,' they both said at once, as soon as Nouri had left the apartment.

'Go ahead,' Constantine said.

'Karim offered to give me Suzy.'

'What?'

'He said I could take Suzy home. Ali stays with him.'

Constantine frowned. 'And this is OK with you?'

'No, dammit, it's not OK!' she exploded, close to tears now. 'But I don't know what to do.' She looked into his eyes, as if willing him to help her decide.

He reached out, took her hand. His touch, gentle and warm, startled Dina. 'I can't make this decision for you,' he said, his voice as gentle as his touch, 'you know that. All I can do is try to give you what you want.'

Dina bit her lip, nodded. 'What were you going to tell me?' she asked.

'OK. Well, from my point of view, the set-up for a

347

rescue looks pretty good. Eilat, in Israel, is just across the Gulf of Aqaba. We're talking a few miles, nothing in a fast boat.'

He sipped thoughtfully at his coffee. 'There are a couple of ways to go about it. One is to sabotage Karim's yacht – not sink it, nothing like that. Get aboard it in the marina the night before, fix it so the steering breaks a few miles out, something like that. That shouldn't be a problem: it's a nice boat, but it's not the *QE II*. Mess up the radio, too, of course. I've got a man on hold for the job. A good man. A real pro. He's a diver, among other things. He's in the Gulf, but he can be here on a few hours' notice.'

He waited for a comment, but Dina had none. 'So the boat's dead in the water, but happy day, here's a nice fella right there to offer a tow: me. And my friend. One-two-three, we grab the kids, head for Eilat. We need somebody on the ground there to deal with the local authorities – the Israelis aren't famous for letting unidentified boats run up on their beaches. I'm thinking David Kallas could help us there. He has contacts. And he's Jewish.'

Finally Dina spoke. 'And where would I be?'

'You'd be on a plane for New York. If you agreed to the deal Karim offered, you'd have Suzy with you. We'd want everything to look normal to Karim, in case he's still on the alert.'

'What was the other way? You said there were a couple.'

Constantine frowned. 'The other way would be to have my man aboard from the get-go. I assume they'll be sleeping on the boat tomorrow night, before they go out Saturday?'

Dina shrugged. 'Probably. *If* they go out.'

348

He raised an eyebrow. 'If?'

'I'll tell you in a minute.'

'OK, *if* they sleep on board, my guy does his frogman thing and gets on right before daylight. He hides if possible. If not, he takes control.'

'What does that mean?'

Constantine sighed. 'It means he uses the threat of force. Of course, that's going to have to happen sooner or later either way. This way is just a little surer. We don't have to worry about the breakdown mechanism working, unpredictable weather, whatever.'

Dina was silent. Then she said, 'Do you think it would work? Either way?'

He hesitated. 'On paper it should be a piece of cake.'

'But it's not on paper. And you don't seem enthusiastic.'

Constantine stood up and walked to the window. He ran his fingers through his hair. He cares, Dina thought, not for the first time. He really cares about getting my children back. He cares about me. He isn't like Einhorn, in it for the money. This isn't just a job to him.

'I told you, Dina, I don't like house intrusions. I've never done a boat intrusion, but it amounts to the same thing. Except that when things go wrong at sea, they could go wrong in a big way. And there's a lot I don't know. Too much.'

'Like?'

'Like are there any weapons aboard? Anyone who'll use them? Things like that.'

Now the silence was long. Then: 'Don't do it,' Dina said suddenly.

Constantine turned and stared at her. 'Don't do it? You mean don't do it the second way?'

'No. Don't do it *any* way. Let's forget it.'

He came back and sat down again. 'It's your call,' he said quietly. 'You're the boss.'

'I'm going to do it, John. I'm going to take Suzanne.'

'Well . . .' He seemed at a loss for words. 'It's a move. It's *something*.'

'I didn't decide until this minute. When you said that however we did the rescue, it would mean using the threat of force. I guess I knew that all along, but it only just hit me what it could mean.'

He nodded. 'Well, the risk is small. But it's there. If I were in your place, I might make the same decision.'

'Another thing. Something I hadn't really thought of until the last couple of days, or maybe I thought it was a good thing: if we took the twins – or either one of them – by force, they'd be cut off from their father. I don't think he'd even come to visit them after something like that. But this way they still have him. And all our options are still open.'

'There's that.' Constantine looked closely at her. 'So you're sure about this, then?'

'Yes.' She looked back at him, saw the concern and the questions in his eyes. 'I know,' she said, 'I'll probably drive myself crazy re-thinking it. But if we did go ahead and someone – anyone – got hurt, I don't think I could live with myself.'

Constantine nodded, smiled at her. 'OK,' he said finally, 'peace is always better than war. In my book, anyway.'

'I think I've disappointed you.'

He smiled again. 'No,' he said softly, 'you haven't disappointed me. You couldn't. I just wanted to get you what we came for. Suzanne *and* Ali.' He looked down at his hands, clenched and unclenched them.

'OK,' he said, 'you'll take Suzy – and maybe we'll find another way to get Ali.'

The coded tap sounded at the door, and Nouri entered. 'All is well?' he asked. 'I can go do more things if you like.'

'Everything's fine,' said Constantine. 'The only thing I'd like you to do, if you don't mind another fare for the night, is drive us to the Hyatt. I want to buy my client a drink.'

'Is that . . . discreet?' Dina asked him. She couldn't believe this breach of security.

'Why not? We're two Americans who happened to bump into each other in Amman. As of two minutes ago we don't have a thing up our sleeves, and we're not breaking a law in the world.'

'No, I guess we're not. But I've got to call Karim. If I'm going to do this, I want my daughter out of there tomorrow.' Now that she had made her decision, she wanted desperately to affirm it, make it solid.

'There is my phone,' Nouri said.

She called the house. Karim answered. He must have been waiting. 'My answer is yes,' she said. 'I think you're right. I'll pick Suzanne up in the morning.'

Even now she half expected him to back out, to throw some sort of wrench into the works. Instead he merely sounded relieved. 'It's the best thing, Dina. You'll see.'

'You're going to Aqaba?'

'I don't know. I haven't decided.'

'Well, whatever you decide, please make sure I don't have any problems with Maha or Fatma.'

'Of course.'

There was a pause. 'So that's that, then,' Dina finally said.

Karim breathed what sounded like a sigh of relief. 'Yes. Look, Dina, I want you to know . . . I want you to know I wish things had worked out differently. Better. But—'

'I know. In case I don't see you tomorrow, goodbye, Karim.'

'Goodbye, Dina.'

She hung up. Her great Jordanian adventure, all the rescue plans, the hope of having both her children back, had come down to that: the simple, final click of the receiver into its slot.

'Let's go have that drink,' she said to John Constantine.

He put his arm around her and led her to the door. And there it was again: that lovely feeling of warmth and strength – and a little bit of something else, something she hadn't experienced with anyone but Karim.

CHAPTER FIFTY-TWO

When Dina arrived at her in-laws' home, Maha was nowhere in sight. Thank God for that; Karim must have arranged it. There were just the four of them now, seated side by side in the spacious living room. The family they had once been. Karim had dressed Suzy – perhaps Soraya had done it, but she was not around either – in a pretty yellow sundress. To Dina, this was the most beautiful sight in the world: her little girl, all suppressed energy and smiles now, eager to begin her adventure with Mommy. She doesn't understand, Dina thought, she doesn't really understand what it's going to mean. But she will soon enough. Dina looked at Ali, solemn as a grown-up, sitting close to his father, holding his hand, needing some reassurance that somehow everything was going to be all right.

Karim cleared his throat. 'Well,' he said, 'perhaps you'd like me to step outside for a moment, while you say good – I mean, while you speak to Ali?'

Dina continued to look at her son. No, she thought, she wouldn't make Ali any more miserable by forcing him to leave his father's side. She shook her head, put her arms around her little boy and kissed him. 'I love you, sweetheart, and I'll miss you very much.'

He pulled away. 'Then why are you going?' he demanded, furrowing his brow. 'And why are you taking Suzy?'

She opened her mouth to speak, but there were no easy answers to his questions. She and Karim had both spoken to him, tried to explain the arrangement they had agreed on, but he had resisted any explanation of why he and his twin were to be wrenched apart. And now he was asking the same questions he had asked before. Dina sighed and said simply: 'This is what Daddy and I decided to do, sweetheart. I'll see you soon, Ali, I promise. And you'll see Suzy, too.'

He was unmoved, and when she pulled him closer for a final hug, he was stiff and unyielding in her arms. My poor baby boy, she thought, he'll never understand why this is happening. All he knows is that it hurts.

She turned to Suzy, whose ebullience had started to fade. The little girl looked from her brother to her father. Maybe she's starting to realize what this all means, Dina thought. Karim put his arms out and Suzy ran into them. 'My princess,' he said softly, kissing her cheeks, 'my beautiful princess. You're going to have another plane ride now, and you're going to see another film, and soon . . .' here his voice broke, 'you'll be back in New York.'

Suzy squirmed in her father's arms, turned to see what Ali was doing. He was as stiff as a soldier. He appeared to be fighting tears, so Suzy began to cry, as if for both of them. Karim murmured assurances that she and Ali would see each other often and soon. He couldn't be certain that these assurances were the truth, but he couldn't bear to see his daughter's tears, and so he said what he hoped would ease her pain.

354

*   *   *

Dina refused Karim's offer of a ride to the airport the next morning. Was she afraid he would change his mind and take Suzy back? Perhaps, for all during the cab ride, she kept glancing behind, searching the road for any sign of one of the family vehicles.

The plane ride was equally painful: Suzy kept talking about the trip they had made with their father. How she and her brother had talked and played and passed the long hours they were airborne. Her narratives were punctuated with bouts of tears.

This is impossible, Dina thought. She had made the decision – there would be no daring kidnap at sea – but how could she live with it? To have Ali snatched from her was one thing, but to leave him behind was agony. She would have to think of something, something. Maybe John could help her. Yes, she thought, maybe John would help.

They arrived home in mid-afternoon. When Dina looked around, she saw that the place was neater and cleaner than when she had left it. And there were vases of fresh flowers in the hall and in the kitchen. Bless her friends, she thought.

Yet though everything looked nice, the house felt somehow wrong. There was a sense of dislocation – something had happened to the family that had lived here – and now the house, like the family, was different.

Suzy was tired and cranky, as if she, too, were feeling this something wrong. Dina took her upstairs to bed, where there were more tears and more questions about Ali. What was he doing now? Was he playing outside without her? Was Daddy tucking him into bed? Dina was patient. She could not know what Suzy was feeling, only that she was sad and upset and confused. Dina sat with her until she drifted off and then she went to check the mail and the answering machine.

The red light was blinking furiously. Dina smiled. No doubt her friends had left messages to welcome her back. She punched the 'Play' button.

'Damn you, Dina. Damn you for your lies and your tricks!' Karim's voice, hoarse and angry. 'I tried to be fair with you, but that didn't mean anything, did it? I heard you telling Ali you'd have him soon. I should have stopped you then and there. But I didn't think you'd take him. You won't get away with this, I swear! I swear I'll get him back!'

Another message followed and another. Anger and fear in Karim's disembodied voice. He was sounding as she must have sounded when she discovered that the twins were gone. But what on earth was he talking about? What did he mean about Ali? Puzzlement quickly yielded to alarm. If he thought she had Ali, then Ali was missing. Oh God! Ali was missing!

With trembling fingers, she dialed the number of her in-laws' home.

Karim answered. 'You must be very pleased with yourself,' he began, 'outsmarting the stupid man who trusted you. You—'

'Karim, stop. I didn't take Ali. I don't have him.'

'You're lying. He's—'

'Karim, don't. I swear on Suzy's life, I don't have him.'

Silence.

'My God, are you telling me he's disappeared?'

'I thought . . . I was sure you had him.'

'I'm coming back. I'll get someone to watch Suzy and I'll come back to look for him.'

'No. Stay with Suzy,' he said. 'There's nothing you can do here. I'll contact the police – and we'll start looking, too, Samir and I.'

For a desperate moment, it occurred to her that Constantine might have carried out a rescue of Ali without her permission. Somehow seen an opportunity and taken it. That would fit, wouldn't it? But surely John would have let her know if he had taken Ali. He would realize that everyone would be looking for him – and that she would be half out of her mind with worry.

She thought of the Major. Of Nouri. Yes, she would contact Constantine, ask him to get in touch with them. Perhaps they could help in the search. She agreed to stay in New York after Karim promised to call her the minute he had any news.

Dina's friends arrived an hour later. They had expected a woman who was not exactly happy, but one who had her daughter back.

Her face told a different story.

'What?' Sarah asked. 'What's wrong?'

She told them.

For once, no one had an answer.

'What can we do?'

She shook her head. 'Pray.'

CHAPTER FIFTY-THREE

Karim and Samir had been cruising the streets for hours, Samir at the wheel, Karim watching desperately for Ali. At first, every time he saw, in the distance, a boy or group of boys, his heart lifted with hope. But a hundred disappointments had drained him of that feeling.

'He can't just have disappeared,' Samir said. He had said it perhaps a dozen times. So had Karim. It was more a prayer than a diagnosis of the situation.

They had worked outward from the house, questioning everyone they saw, showing a snapshot of Ali. But as morning drew toward noon and they moved out of the quiet suburb into busier sections, this became impractical. Now they stopped only occasionally for someone who looked as if he might have been on the street for hours. Even that seemed counterproductive. In Amman there were thousands of boys who resembled Ali and wore American-style clothes. Everyone had seen one – or several.

'Do you think anyone in this neighborhood speaks English?' Karim asked his brother. They were driving through a quarter that had a distinct flavor of the laboring classes.

'Of course they do, brother,' Samir assured him. 'A little anyway. Some of them. There are people here who work in the hotels. Cleaning, things like that.'

Karim grunted noncommittally. All day he had been agonizing over the fact that his son as yet knew only a few words of Arabic. He had always thought of Amman as a place where many people spoke some English. Now it seemed to him that in fact these people were a minority.

Samir pulled over. 'Coffee,' he said. 'You want something to eat?'

'No. But coffee is good.' While he waited he called home. Hassan answered. 'Anything?' Karim asked.

'No. But they're putting his picture on the news this evening. I had to make a call or two, but it's being done.'

'Good.' They said goodbye. It had been agreed that they would not tie up the house phone, in case anyone had word of the missing boy.

The whole family had mobilized for the search. Soraya and Maha were on their cell phones, calling everyone in the neighborhood as well as nearby sweet-shops, coffee houses, anyplace a tired and hungry child might go for refuge; the hospitals too, of course. Not only Samir and Karim, but a half-dozen cousins were patrolling the streets: occasionally they crossed each other's paths. The two bodyguards had been rehired, along with a dozen of their colleagues. They too were on the streets. It had been difficult to persuade Hassan to remain home and man the phone; Karim had accomplished it by referring to the house as the 'command center'.

Of course the police were on full alert. Karim had

gone straight to the top to see that this was the case.

Surely it wouldn't be long. Any minute.

Samir returned with the coffee.

'He can't just have disappeared,' Karim said. And yet that was exactly what seemed to have happened.

CHAPTER FIFTY-FOUR

Did they have sex offenders in Jordan? Had someone taken her baby for ransom? Was his disappearance the act of someone with a grudge against Karim's family? Dina could not bear the thought of her little boy being scared or in pain, and the fear that he was kept tormenting her until she felt as if she would lose her mind.

Em and Sarah tried to reassure her: Ali would be found, nothing bad would happen to him, Karim would put all his resources into the search for his son. But words gave Dina no solace.

'I shouldn't have done it,' She sobbed. 'I shouldn't have agreed to separate the twins. It was wrong to leave Ali without his sister, it was just wrong—'

'Oh, honey,' Em said, 'how could you not take Suzy when Karim offered? It's all his fault, not yours.'

Dina shook her head. It was no comfort to blame Karim. None. She knew he'd be going crazy, too. But that was no comfort either. She was alone in this misery and it would not end until Ali was found.

All she could do was wait, her life suspended, feeling as if every breath was measured by the seconds and minutes and hours that Ali was gone. Please God, she prayed, let him be all right. I'll do anything if he's all right. I'll even leave the twins with their father, if that's Your will.

Five thousand miles away, Karim stared into the darkness of Ali's bedroom. He touched the pillow on his son's bed, the computer game Ali loved, the pajamas he had worn before he'd vanished.

How he wished now that Dina had taken Ali with her. At least he would be safe. Was this a kind of retribution for what he'd set in motion? But how could he know that things would turn out this way? For a while it had seemed as if he had indeed salvaged something of the family he had founded with such hope. At great cost and not just to Dina, for hadn't he had to leave behind the woman he had once loved passionately? Even now he still cared for her. He had wanted only good for his children – and yet it had all come to this. His darling daughter gone from him. His precious son – no, he wouldn't even think about that.

Samir came up behind him, placed his hand on Karim's shoulder. 'Get some rest, brother. Get an hour's sleep, and we'll go out again.'

Karim nodded, but there would be no sleep until Ali was found. He would lie down here, on his boy's bed, close to him. And in a little while, he and Samir would go out again, to join the army of people who were searching for his son.

CHAPTER FIFTY-FIVE

It was two hours past midnight prayer when Samir finally persuaded Karim to give up the search till morning.

'He's indoors somewhere, brother. We'll never find him, driving around like this.'

Karim shook his head, but not very vehemently. Samir was right. There was hardly anyone out now, and certainly no children.

'Someone has taken him in,' Samir said with a conviction in his voice that was not reflected in his eyes. 'We'll find him in the morning, *insh'Allah*.'

God willing, Karim repeated to himself. But right now, he could not see God anywhere in Ali's disappearance. And although he told himself that it was indeed likely that some ordinary, caring man or woman could have taken in a lost child, he could not keep darker possibilities from his thoughts. Ali would need only to speak a few words to be recognized as a foreigner, even as an American, and there were many in Jordan who had no great love for Americans. There was also the chance that this was a kidnapping. The police didn't seem to think so, especially as no ransom demand had come, but it was early yet, at least from what little he understood of these matters.

Still, driving around the empty city streets would not help. And Samir, by the strain in his features, was as weary as Karim felt himself to be.

'All right,' he told Samir. 'Home. We'll have a better chance in the morning.'

Samir nodded, let out a tired sigh, and turned at the next intersection.

At home Maha had gone to bed but Soraya was waiting with coffee and food. Hassan was dozing in his chair by the phone. A police officer drowsily manned a telephone line that had been set up in case of a ransom call. Samir and the policeman ate a little, but Karim had no appetite. He woke his father and briefly recounted to him the failure of the search. The old man was too weary to do more than nod and say, as Samir had said, 'We'll find him tomorrow, *insh'Allah*,' before going off to bed. Samir and Soraya soon followed, each giving Karim a tight hug of encouragement and commiseration.

Karim talked for a while with the policeman. The man was full of official-sounding reassurances that must have come straight from some training manual, ending with, 'Best get some sleep, sir. Don't worry, I'll wake you if anything at all happens.'

But before Karim could rest, he had to do one more thing. He called Dina, tried to make his lack of progress sound as benign as possible. Ali had wandered off somehow. It appeared that he had gotten lost. Everyone was searching for him and he was certain to be found any minute now.

'My God, Karim, he's just a little boy! And he's been

364

missing for hours! I'm coming back. As soon as I can get a flight.'

'No, please, Dina, don't. We'll find him soon. Long before you could possibly get here. And there's nothing you could do that we aren't doing, I promise you. It's better that you stay with Suzanne.'

'Karim – how did this happen? He just . . . left?'

'Yes. I know this sounds strange, but little boys do these things, and in a strange city, it's easy to get lost.' Because he knew she would be feeling as frightened as he was, Karim tried to give comfort. 'I did it once myself, in Aqaba,' he said. 'I was lost for hours. When they found me, my father didn't know whether to beat me or kiss me. In the end, he did both. Don't worry, Dina, Amman isn't New York. We'll find him. Nothing will happen to him, I promise.' But even as he spoke the words, they sounded hollow to his own ears. How could he promise anything when he had no idea where Ali might be?

Dina paced in the kitchen, feeling as if she would go mad if she didn't do *something*. She wondered if Karim was telling her the whole story. As if it weren't bad enough as it was.

In a way this was worse than when he'd taken the twins. At least then she knew they were safe. Now she felt completely helpless, just waiting for news, good or bad.

She tried Constantine: office, home, cell phone, and got his voice message on all three. She asked him to call her right away. She had no idea where he was. Could he still be in Jordan? Once again, she wondered if he could somehow have Ali. No, that couldn't be. Then where in the name of God was her son?

'What's the matter. Mommy?' Suzanne asked, tugging at her mother's skirt.

'Nothing, honey. I just have to make some calls. Tell you what, why don't you go and watch a video while I make you a snack?'

Suzanne looked at her mother suspiciously: it was past her bedtime, so why was she being offered a video and a snack? But she didn't argue.

When Dina heard the sounds of Suzy's favorite cartoon characters, she did the only thing she could think to do. She dialed the code for Amman and then the number she had memorized in the supermarket.

It rang several times before there was an answer; it was the middle of the night in Amman.

'Yes?'

'Alia?'

'You have the wrong number.'

But Dina had recognized the voice. 'Wait! Please don't hang up. It's . . . it's the woman you met in the market.'

'No. Wrong number.'

'Please!' she begged. 'I'm sorry to call so late, but my boy is missing. My son. In Amman. Could you please ask . . . the man you work with . . . if he can please help find him?'

A silence. Then: 'I know nothing of this.'

'Just tell him. And ask him.'

'Yes. Goodbye.' And Alia hung up.

Dina had no idea whether the woman would do as she had asked. But she didn't dare call again.

When she put down the phone, she saw Suzanne standing in the doorway, her dark eyes fearful. 'Mommy, what's wrong with Ali?'

Dina sat down with Suzy and tried to tell her that everything would be all right, that Ali had just gotten lost and Daddy was looking for him.

The bed was soft and warm and Karim was as exhausted as he had ever been in his life, but sleep wouldn't come. Pictures kept forming in his mind of where Ali might be sleeping. Or not sleeping. And the thought that had tormented him throughout this nightmare could not be kept at bay: this was his fault, his doing. It was not a case of God willing. He, Karim, had willed it, not directly of course, but through the actions he had chosen: dragging the children here from their home – their real home. Separating them. For his own selfish purposes. That he had believed he was acting for the best didn't matter. He was a logical man, and results, not intentions, were what mattered. The results had proved him wrong.

A hard sob tore itself from his throat. He had been a fool. And his foolishness might have cost his son's life.

The first gray light was breaking when he finally closed his eyes and sank into a dream-tormented sleep. Long before then, he had promised himself that if Ali were to be found alive and well, he would be reunited with his sister and mother in New York. Anything else would be a new mistake piled upon all those Karim had already made.

In Amman, the man known as the Major was fast asleep when the phone rang. Not his ordinary phone, but the unlisted one. More than unlisted: its number did not officially exist in the telephone company's records.

He listened to what Alia had to say.

He had seen the story about Ali Ahmad on the television news. He had assumed that Constantine was somehow behind this, in which case it would be known soon enough. If that was not the case and the boy had simply run away, he would no doubt be quickly found; the police, not to mention the Ahmad family, had more than adequate resources for this sort of thing.

But the woman Dina Ahmad had made an impression. Though he was not overly fond of Americans – John Constantine was one exception – Dina Ahmad's situation had touched him. And there were people in many walks of life in Jordan who would never deal with the police if they could possibly avoid it. Some of these people dealt with the Major on a regular basis; they tended to be highly observant individuals in possession of all kinds of information. With three or four calls, he could initiate a chain of contacts that would alert all of these people to the importance of finding a lost American boy. If it were to be reported that the boy had been seen in the company of a large man of Mediterranean appearance, then the information need go no further. If someone had seen the child on his own, then undoubtedly there would be a happy ending. On other possibilities, the Major did not waste time. He leaned over his bed and picked up the phone.

It was well past ten when Karim woke. To his horror, he appeared to be the last of the family out of bed. There were even two male cousins sipping coffee and talking seriously with Hassan and Samir. A new police officer had taken over the phone equipment.

The looks everyone gave Karim told him that there was no news.

He sat with the other men to plan the day's actions. The bodyguards were already on the streets, not only repeating the previous day's search, but also posting flyers with Ali's photo and the promise of a sizable reward for information leading to his safe return. Samir spread out a map of the city, and there was discussion of areas that might have been missed. There weren't many, at least not within a distance that a small boy could be expected to have covered on foot. They would search those, then go over the nearer and more likely places again, this time door-to-door.

From time to time the phone rang and Hassan answered. His body language, a slight slump of the shoulders, told them that it was just another well-wisher. Hassan always thanked the caller courteously but briefly and explained that they wished to keep the line open as much as possible.

Soraya reported that she had set up a phone search based on the women of her hospital charity group. It would work something like a chain letter. Each person would call three acquaintances who she thought would be unlikely to know other women of the group. These three would in turn each call three more. In that way, she explained, hundreds of women would be contacted within a few hours. Karim personally thought that there would soon be a tremendous overlap of calls – either that or the entire phone system would collapse under the weight of the traffic – and that in any case, few people with telephones in Amman could be unaware of Ali's disappearance. But he didn't discourage his sister-in-law; like everyone else – including him – she needed to feel that she was doing

369

something useful in this situation in which they were all, in reality, virtually helpless.

The phone rang again and Hassan irritably snatched it up. By now none of them paid much attention to the instrument, so a moment passed before anyone realized that something was different in the old man's voice – and that his shoulders hadn't slumped. 'Yes?' he said. 'Yes? Colonel who? Yes, of course. And you're sure of this?' He was motioning urgently for Karim.

Even as he put the receiver to his ear Karim heard his father say something to the others that was greeted with shouts of 'Thank God!' He found himself speaking with a man who introduced himself as a colonel in military intelligence. For a second, he wondered what military intelligence had to do with the search for his son, but the man's next words banished any concerns about how and why.

'We have him,' the colonel said. 'He's fine. A little tired, that's all.'

Karim was lightheaded with relief. He felt for the arm of the chair to keep his balance. 'Where is he?'

'On his way to you. I'll bring him myself. Would you like to speak with him?'

'Yes. Please.'

An instant later, Karim heard Ali's voice. 'Daddy? It's me. I . . . I got lost.'

'You're all right, Ali?'

'Yeah, I'm OK. But I'm really hungry.'

Karim felt as if he'd burst with happiness and relief. 'You won't be hungry long once you get here, I promise.' He remembered his own boyhood misadventure in Aqaba. 'Or maybe we'll let you go hungry a bit longer, while you think about all the worry you've given us all.'

'I won't do it again. Daddy,' Ali said fervently. 'I promise.'

The colonel came on again. 'A man, a laborer, found your son late yesterday, and he and his wife kept him overnight. We'll talk with him, of course, but I don't think there's any question of anything untoward. I believe this fellow was simply concerned about a lost child on his own and so he took him in.'

'Thank God. And thank you, sir. Thank you very much.'

'You are most welcome. We will see you shortly.'

'Wait. Please. This man, the one who found Ali?'

'Yes?'

'You have his name?'

'Of course.'

'You said he's a laborer. I gather that means he's poor.'

'Poor as dust. He doesn't have a television set, that's certain – or he would have known who he had under his roof. We found him through one of his neighbors.'

'If you'll give me his name and address,' Karim said, 'he won't be poor after today.'

'Then there will be two happy families in Amman.'

Karim hung up and was engulfed by the arms of his family. Hot tears coursed down his cheeks.

Any thought of punishment vanished when Ali was returned to his family. Maha pushed away Soraya and Fatma and insisted on feeding the boy herself. She spirited him into the kitchen and began to put out all the 'foreign' foods she usually scorned: breakfast cereal, candy bars, and sweet drinks.

'No, *Tayta*,' he said, 'I want some of your food.'

'Anything,' she said, clasping him to her ample

bosom, 'anything for you, Ali.' Quickly she prepared a plate of *kefta* and potatoes – and then watched him devour every last morsel.

Outside, Karim was escorting the colonel to his waiting car. He had realized some time ago that he knew the man, at least by reputation. Everyone at a certain level of society did.

'Colonel, not to pry,' he said carefully, 'but I can't help wondering how you . . . how your division . . . became involved in the search for my little boy.'

The man known to some as the Major smiled benevolently. It was a smile his enemies never saw. He hadn't expected to like this man, but he did. There was nothing wrong with him that wasn't common to the great run of the human race, and his devotion to his son, at least, was obvious. 'Oh, I didn't mention that? I saw the story on television. I thought it couldn't hurt to put some of our people on it. That's all.'

'Well, I'm very grateful.'

'Don't misunderstand. The police are very capable. I have no doubt they would have found Ali if we hadn't beat them to it.'

'All the same . . .'

They had reached the car. The colonel hesitated before getting in. 'I hope you'll forgive me, Mr Ahmad,' he said, 'it's certainly nothing that concerns me. But when we found your son, he asked if we were taking him home. I told him we were. He said: "Home to New York?" Do you know what he meant?'

Karim nodded, said nothing. In the joy of recovering Ali, he had forgotten his pre-dawn promise to himself. Now, it was as if this distinguished man had reached into his conscience to remind him of it.

Sensing that he had gone far enough, the colonel said. 'It was an honor to meet you all and to be of service to your family. God be with you and yours.'

'And with you,' Karim said. Before he reached the door of the house, he knew what he had to do.

CHAPTER FIFTY-SIX

Ali lay quietly in his bed, too tired to stay awake, yet too anxious to sleep. He had expected to be punished, but instead he'd been smothered with kisses and hugs, fed until he could eat no more, and tucked into bed by the entire family. He didn't understand this, any more than he understood why his sister had been taken away from him.

No one here seemed to think it was wrong that Suzy was gone. That's why he had known it was up to him to find her. It didn't matter what he had told Mom. Sometimes he couldn't stand being Suzy's twin, but without her he didn't want to be here any more.

His father had promised a boat trip, but Ali knew it was going to be no fun without Suzy. He had thought about the airport. That was where Suzanne had gone, with Mom. They got on a plane and went home. That was what people did at airports. He knew that there was some matter of tickets, but that seemed to happen automatically.

He had crept out of bed and dressed quietly. In the kitchen, he put a couple of leftover pita and a handful of Fruit Loops in the pocket of his windbreaker. He thought about writing a note and putting it on the refrigerator door but there wasn't anything to write on or with. It wasn't like at home. He took one of the Fruit Loops and used his finger to paint *BYE THANKS* in sticky red on the refrigerator.

He went out the front door, closing it softly. The car with the two men in it wasn't there. The street was so dark and quiet it was scary.

He had an idea of which way the airport was. It hadn't seemed very far when they came in from it. He started walking.

He was still walking hours after the bread and Fruit Loops were gone. He was tired, hungry and lost. He had been sure the airport would be easy to find, but after a very short time he realized that he must have taken the wrong street. But the airport was huge, he knew, and if he kept walking in its general direction, surely he would find it. Soon, however, he had lost any sense of general direction. He couldn't even say which way he had come from. Then some older boys had bothered him. When they learned he couldn't talk with them, they had punched him a few times and wrestled his windbreaker off him before he had been able to run away. His nose had bled for a while, but that had stopped.

His mother had always warned him not to speak with strangers, but once or twice he asked people where the airport was. They understood the word but their replies were incomprehensible. He thought of giving them his father's name. Or his grandfather's. Everyone knew his grandfather, he was sure. But if he did that he would have to go back to the house, and he would be in trouble, and Suzanne wouldn't be there.

He walked until he couldn't walk any more. He sat with his back against a building. The wall was warm from the sun, but the sun was setting now. Ali started to cry.

Two men came down the street. Ali felt them standing over him. One man spoke to him. Ali couldn't understand a word, but clearly the man was asking what was wrong. Ali told him. The man shrugged and spoke with his friend. The friend tried saying something to Ali. He couldn't understand that either. The first man motioned for him to stand, and when Ali was slow to do it the man lifted him by his arm.

If he wasn't supposed to talk with strangers, he definitely wasn't supposed to go anywhere with them. But the man held his arm and he was too tired to run. They walked down a narrow street. A small group of men nodded greetings. There was some talk that Ali knew was about him. All of the men tried speaking to him. He just shrugged.

They walked on. At a corner the second man said a few words to the first, clasped his hand, and went away down the side street. The first man towed Ali a few houses down the street and through a door. They went up some stairs and into a small, dark room. It took Ali's eyes a few seconds to adjust. Then he saw that there were other children there, two boys older than him and a younger girl. There was a woman and the smell of cooking. He realized that this was the man's home. It was hardly as large as one of the bathrooms in his grandfather's house. A radio played the music that he thought of as Jordanian and didn't like. There was no TV.

The woman asked questions and the man answered gruffly. The woman put out food. It was only bread and beans and olive oil. Ali ate it hungrily and drank water as if he were a thirsty camel. The older of the two boys spoke to him. He didn't understand. Then the boy said '*Eengleesi?*' Yes, Ali told him. English. The boy turned to his father and said, '*Eengleesi.*' But it appeared to be the only word he knew.

Bed was only a worn rug on the floor, with the two sons beside him. He was asleep almost before he put his head down.

When he awoke, he knew from the light in the single window that it was day again. He was hungry, but worse than the hunger was the loneliness. He missed his sister, his mother, his father – everyone who loved and cared for him. Though his father had told him a man should be brave, he began to cry.

Ali didn't like to remember that, the crying. But remembering what came later was good. There had been shouting from the street, and the man who had taken him from the street rushed to the room's single window. More shouting and suddenly there were people at the door. One of them Ali recognized from among the group in the street the night before. The other was an older man who appeared to be in charge of things and who was much better dressed than anyone Ali had seen since he'd gotten lost. The well-dressed man talked to the group and gestured once or twice at Ali. Ali could tell he was saying something important. After that, everything had happened quickly. The important man had taken charge of Ali, there had been a ride in a car. And then he was here, safe and comfortable. But still there was no Suzy. And though he told himself he should be brave, once again he began to cry.

CHAPTER FIFTY-SEVEN

Two days later, Karim stood outside the door of the place that had been his home for twenty years, holding his son's hand. Was he doing the right thing? he wondered for the hundredth time. He had made a promise, but what of Ali? What would become of him in this city where children murdered one another for shoes and gold chains? All right, money would insulate him from some of the dangers, but what about his identity? Would he be ashamed of his name and heritage? Lose it all in the great melting pot? Become as American as Coca-Cola? He sighed deeply. He would drive himself mad with these thoughts. He rang the bell, just as if he were a stranger.

Dina pulled open the door, cried out when she saw her son. She grabbed Ali and held him close, covering his face with kisses. Karim cleared his throat. Dina looked at him. 'Karim. Thank you.'

He nodded. He couldn't bring himself to say 'you're welcome'. This was his son, his hope for the future. He did not want to give him up, yet this seemed to be the right thing to do. For now.

Should she invite him in? Dina wondered. She didn't really want to, didn't want Karim to think that he still had a claim to their home. They stood there for a long awkward moment. 'Suzy's not here,' she said finally. 'I wasn't sure when you'd arrive, so I let her go to school.'

Karim nodded. 'Well,' he said, 'in that case, I guess I'll be going . . .'

When Dina said nothing, he reached once again for Ali, took him into his arms, felt his throat clog with tears. He couldn't linger; the pain he felt was too intense to prolong and he would not break in front of Dina. He kissed his son on both cheeks. 'Be good,' he said, his voice husky, 'and write to me. I'll call you every week. And I'll see you soon,' he promised, though he did not know when that would be.

There was a loud and enthusiastic reunion when Suzy came home from school. She showed Ali a picture of him that she had drawn and hung above her bed. 'I missed you,' she said. 'I wanted you to come home.'

'I wanted to come home,' Ali said, not quite ready to admit out loud that he'd missed his sister. 'I didn't want to leave Dad, but—'

'I know,' Suzy said. 'Me, too.'

Two hours later, by the time Dina was preparing dinner, she heard the familiar sounds of bickering coming from the second floor. She smiled and heaved a great sigh of relief. Normal, she thought, maybe one day, things will be normal again, whatever that was.

CHAPTER FIFTY-EIGHT

'Sweetheart!' Dina flung her arms around her firstborn son, hugging him so hard that he called out, 'hey, Mom, take it easy.'

'Sorry.' When she pulled away, her eyes were shiny with unshed tears. 'I'm so glad you're home, Jordy, I'm just so glad.'

'Yeah. Me too.'

She pulled him inside, then tugged at his suitcase, which felt as if it were filled with bricks.

'Jeez, Mom, don't. I'll get it.' And he did, with only a moderate effort. He seems stronger now, she thought, and not just physically.

A moment later, the twins came hurtling down the stairs. Dina had told them Jordy was coming home, had warned them not to repeat anything they'd heard about him at their grandparents' home. But now she held her breath.

'Jordy!' Suzy cried out, flinging herself into her brother's arms. He picked her up, swung her around and hugged her close. 'It's good to see you, peanut. I missed you.'

'I missed you, too, Jordy. Are you really going to stay home now? And go to school here?'

'Yup. You'll be stuck with me until I go to college.'

'Yay!' She clapped her hands, turned to Ali, perhaps thinking he would second her delight.

Ali was silent, staring hard at his older brother. Was he trying to see what was 'unnatural' about him? Dina wondered. Her eyes sought Jordy's, willing him not to be hurt by this latest manifestation of his father's rejection. He smiled, sadly, she thought, then ruffled Ali's hair. 'Good to see you, champ,' he said, then followed Dina into the kitchen.

'I'm sorry about that,' she said softly, after the twins had gone back upstairs to their games. 'I—'

'It's OK, Mom. I can only imagine the brainwashing they got while they were with . . . him.'

'I don't believe it was like that,' Dina said, surprising herself by this defense of Karim. She quickly added: 'Look, your father did a really awful thing, but I don't think he tried to "brainwash" the twins. He probably talked to his brother or his father, and the twins just overheard them.'

'Yeah, sure. Whatever.'

'Jordy,' she pressed, 'your father is one hundred per cent wrong about you. That's his problem. If you want to be fair – and there's no reason why you should – you could consider that he was the one who was brainwashed – by the culture he grew up in.'

Jordy looked hard at his mother. 'Why are you sticking up for him, Mom? Are you trying to get back together with him? After all—?'

'No! Not for a minute, Jordy. I . . . I just want you to understand certain things. For your own good, not for his.'

'Yeah, OK. But do you mind if we don't do this right now?'

'Of course, sweetheart. You must be tired. And hungry. Let me fix you something special. Anything you want, just name it.' Dina made her offer confidently, for in anticipation of Jordy's arrival, she had stocked her refrigerator and pantries to overflowing.

'Umm,' he considered. 'How about scrambled eggs and sausage? And toast – a lot of toast.'

'That's it? That's all you want?'

'Yeah. The eggs at school aren't any good. Not like when they're made fresh.'

'Then eggs it is.' Dina prepared them quickly, the way Jordy liked them, with bits of cream cheese melted in to make them smooth and creamy. The sausage was handmade, bought from the butcher yesterday. And the toast was cinnamon bread from *Flourings* in the East Village – Dina had made a special trip downtown because Jordy had once said it was the best he'd ever tasted.

She set the plate in front of her son and watched him eat – ravenously, as if he hadn't enjoyed a good meal in days. As she studied him, she reflected once again that he seemed different, changed during this past year.

'What?' he asked. 'Why are you staring at me?'

'I'm not staring. I'm . . . drinking you in. I'm so happy to have you here. To have all of my chicks back at home with me.'

When he made no reply to that, she asked: 'Jordy, did you . . . ? I mean, when your father sent you away to school . . . did you think I wanted you to go?'

He looked up from his food, thought for a long moment. 'I wasn't sure. I knew it was Dad's idea – I mean, he was pretty clear about what he felt. With you, it was . . . different. I mean, you said all the right things, but you never asked me how I felt about going to Andover. How I felt about leaving my friends, so I thought, well . . .'

'I'm sorry, Jordy, I'm so sorry.' She reached over and took his hand. 'Please forgive me, sweetheart.' The tears streamed from her eyes now as she searched her heart for the right words. 'I was wrong. I was very wrong to just let it happen. I should have fought your father if you didn't want to go. I should have—'

'Forget it, Mom. It's over now.'

'I won't forget it,' she sniffed. 'When people are wrong, they shouldn't forget it! They should try to make it better.'

'It *is* better, Mom. Honest. Maybe it was a good thing for me to go away – no, let me finish – because I didn't have anything to live down in a new place. I didn't have anything to prove.' He paused. 'And there was a counselor at school . . . a really good guy. I felt like I could talk to him, you know, really talk to him. It helped a lot.'

Dina felt the pain of her son's loneliness, his need for someone to talk to, his feeling that there had been no one except a stranger. She had to calm herself before she could speak without crying. 'I'm glad if something good came out of it, sweetheart. But if you were happy there, then maybe you want to stay?'

He shot a sharp look at her. 'Would it be easier for you if I did?' The question was crisp, even a little harsh.

Dina was stunned. 'No! Not at all, Jordy! Whatever gave you that idea?'

He shook his head – and that was all the answer he seemed prepared to give. 'Well, if you're asking what I want, it's what I told you. I want to live at home and go to school here. If that's all right with everyone.'

Again the pain. 'Jordy, sweetheart, if I did anything to make you believe it wasn't all right, I'm sorry – and I'm asking you again to forgive me.'

He nodded. 'OK.'

Dina understood that there would be no band-aids for whatever hurts Jordy was feeling. As for Suzy and Ali, Dina knew that they needed her more than ever. And that it would be a long time before the family felt whole. She made her decision at that moment: she would continue to work from home, and if her business suffered while her family healed, so be it.

CHAPTER FIFTY-NINE

Em and Sarah wanted to give a party to celebrate Dina's reunion with her children. But Dina firmly refused. Perhaps she was being superstitious, but she felt as if her newly regained family was still too fragile to celebrate. Later, maybe in a few months, she told her friends. Instead she suggested dinner at her house.

The meal was simple: grilled tenderloin and lightly steamed baby asparagus, with a tomato, basil and mozzarella salad to start. Good bread from Grace's, a nice merlot and a chocolate cake baked from scratch rounded out her menu.

After dessert and coffee had been served and the children retired to their rooms, Dina told the story of Ali's disappearance and recovery, embellishing the bare facts she'd given previously. Em and Sarah listened in uncharacteristic silence. They had lived the story on Dina's side, had witnessed her terror and her pain.

As she looked at Em and Sarah now, she thought, This is the truly gorgeous mosaic: the friendship of three women, all different, each unique in her personality, yet enriching one another's lives with their love and loyalty.

'Well, at least he finally did the right thing,' Sarah said of Karim. 'At least he finally understood that the twins belong with you.'

Dina nodded. Of course the twins belonged with her. And yet, with the nightmare behind her, she could easily imagine how bereft Karim must be, and how lonely. No matter what misery he had caused her, she had never doubted for a minute his love for Suzy and Ali. Knowing that made her sad, so she turned to Em and said brightly, 'Tell me what's been happening with you. I'm so out of touch.'

'Well.' Em thought for a moment, as if considering what kind of information to give her friend.

'Nothing bad, I hope,' Dina said, her body suddenly tense. 'Tell me you weren't keeping anything bad from me.'

'No, no, *cher*, nothing bad. What's new is that Mr Gabriel LeBlanc himself turned up while you were away. Like the proverbial bad penny.'

'Really?' Dina studied her friend. Em's tone was light, as if to say, No big deal. But her expression said something else. That she was pleased? Maybe more?

'And what does Sean say about this development?'

That answer came quickly: 'Sean's no longer in the picture.'

'Well.'

Em's expression now said Sean was not missed. Strange, Dina thought, Sean had been around on and off for a few years, yet he had not, it seemed, made a deep and lasting impression in Em's life.

'And how does Michael feel about his father's being around?'

Em smiled. 'He's more mature about it than I am. He says "we'll see". He's been out with Gabe a couple of times. It's one day at a time with him.'

'He's wise,' Dina said. Turning to Sarah, she asked: 'And you? What have you been up to while I was away?'

Sarah's smile was part Mona Lisa, part mischievous elf. 'Well, David and I are, you know, seeing each other, and—'

' "Seeing each other!" ' Em laughed. 'So that's what you call it! Don't listen to her, Dina honey, this girl is having a romance, an honest to goodness romance.'

'That's wonderful,' Dina said. 'You deserve it, Sarah, you really do.'

'I wish everyone thought so,' Sarah said wistfully.

'What do you mean?' Dina asked. 'Is Ari still giving you grief about the *get*?'

'Not hardly,' Em laughed again. 'You tell her, Sarah, tell her what David did.'

'Well,' Sarah began, the mischievous-elf smile reappearing, 'David got his cousin to check up on Ari's activities in Israel. It turns out that my ex has a *fiancée* there. And the poor woman thinks the only thing standing between her and a wedding ring is me.'

'You? But why?' Dina was genuinely puzzled.

'Me. According to Ari, I'm a clinging, neurotic wife who refuses to give him a divorce so he can marry his true love.'

Now both Dina and Em were laughing. 'Oh, that's rich,' Dina said between giggles. Then she stopped. 'But how—?'

'Let me finish,' Sarah said. 'Not only is this poor deluded woman in love with Ari, she's also very well connected, socially and politically – Ari's kind of woman. But apparently he isn't anxious to marry her. I don't know why. Anyway, once we found all this out, David's cousin reached out to Ari and asked him to give me a *get*. Ari, of course, said no, though he was very polite, since a rabbi was doing the asking. And then,' here she took a deep breath and smiled at her audience, 'then Cousin Abe let Ari know we had the goods on him, told him that maybe his fiancée might like to know that he's been free of his terrible wife for a long time. And free to marry.' She waited for Dina's reaction.

Dina clapped vigorously. 'Oh, that's wonderful, Sarah! And did he cave?'

'He caved,' Sarah said with evident satisfaction. 'Boy, did he cave. So we'll be doing the *get* next week. It only takes about two hours, you know. After waiting for years, my marriage will be officially over in just a couple of hours.'

'Now exactly how does that work, Sar?' Em asked. 'Ari says "I divorce you" three times like the Muslims do?'

'No, it's much more formal than that. We go to the rabbi's office. We each say we understand what we're doing and that we're acting freely without coercion.'

Em laughed aloud.

'What I did wasn't coercion,' Sarah protested, 'just effective persuasion. Anyway, then Ari authorizes the scribe to write the document. After it's signed by witnesses, Ari presents it to me – and we're done. Divorce final.'

'That's it?' Em asked.

'Well, except for the formalities. The rabbi issues a certificate of proof to each of us, saying that the *get* was properly drawn up, delivered and accepted – and that Ari and I are each free to remarry.'

'Great,' Dina said. 'But then what did you mean before, when you said that not everyone was happy for you?'

Em rolled her eyes. 'The demon daughter. Miss Rachel was giving her a hard time about dating David, and now she's really pissed off about the *get* business.'

'She's not a demon daughter,' Sarah said stiffly.

Em looked surprised. 'Hey, honey, I was just kidding. I'm sorry – OK?'

'OK.' Though Sarah would never allow anyone else to say anything bad about Rachel, her daughter had been more than 'pissed' when she heard about the *get*. She had burst into tears. 'I knew it,' she had sobbed. 'I knew you wanted to get rid of Daddy for good so you can marry your new boyfriend!'

Neither Sarah's reminder that she had always wanted the *get* nor her statement that marriage was not on her mind right now staunched Rachel's tirade. 'You probably want to get rid of me, too, now! But don't think you can send me to live with Daddy, because you can't! He doesn't want me either! So why did you people have me if you didn't want any children?' A torrent of sobs followed.

Sarah had been stunned. When had she given her child the message that she was unwanted? OK, she had lost her temper; OK she had often felt like smacking the kid. But if she lost her, she would die.

She had reached out and taken Rachel in her arms. 'I've always wanted you, Rache, and I love you more than my own life. This . . . whatever it is that's making us fight . . . it's temporary, but I'm your mom forever,

whether you like it or not. And we'll find a way to fix
what's wrong. I promise.'

Rachel said nothing.

Sarah sighed now, recalling that promise and
knowing that keeping it was not going to be easy.

CHAPTER SIXTY

When the phone rang at six on a Saturday morning, Dina flashed back to the calls from Karim – and, for one horrible moment, she forgot that her children were all with her now.

The voice that spoke to her now was her mother's. 'Dina, I think you'd better get over here – as soon as you can. And bring the children.'

'Daddy?' The word was half-whispered, half-sobbed.

'Yes.'

Dina dressed quickly and roused the children. Grandpa had taken a turn for the worse, she told them. And though their expressions were quizzical, the twins for once asked no questions. Jordy simply squeezed his mother's hand, as if to say, I understand.

The streets were quiet at that hour and the cab ride downtown was quick. When Charlotte opened the door, Dina could see that her mother had not slept. Her eyes were red-rimmed, her face was drawn, and she looked suddenly older. For the long months of her husband's illness, Charlotte had labored valiantly to maintain their life much as it had been, unwilling to let their days and nights be consumed by the illness. Now

Dina could see very clearly how great a toll those efforts had taken.

'He's been asking for you,' Charlotte told Dina. 'Why don't you go in to see him now, and I'll make the children something to eat.'

Her parents' bedroom had the sour smell of lingering illness in spite of Charlotte's measures to keep it fresh. A bedside lamp cast a soft light over Joseph's features. To Dina, her father looked serene and relaxed, better than he had in a while; this must be due to the powerful drugs that dripped steadily into his veins, she thought. Yet when he opened his eyes and looked at her, he smiled broadly, and for a moment she glimpsed the happy, robust man he had been.

'Daddy.' The single word, soft and tender and suffused with love.

'Dina, *elbe*, my heart, I'm glad you're here.'

She nodded, unable to acknowledge that this might be goodbye.

'I had a dream last night,' he said. 'I was at the airport – and I was so happy. I was waiting for a flight to Beirut, you see. And while I was waiting, I imagined how it would be when I landed, how my mother and father would be there, and how glad they would be to see me. I could imagine everything, Dina: the cool air of the mountains, my parents' home . . . I could even taste the food they had prepared to welcome me home. But then, when my flight was called, I realized I could not leave yet. Because I had forgotten to say goodbye to you and the children.'

He looked into Dina's eyes, touched her arm gently, as if willing her to understand. She bit her lip to keep from crying, but she could not stop the tears that trickled down her cheeks.

'I realized there was something important I had to tell you,' he continued. 'I wanted you to know that you have always been a joy and a source of pride to your mother and me. We could not have wanted a better child than you.'

'Thank you, Daddy. And you were always the best father anyone could have.' Through her tears, she added: 'All my friends were jealous that I had such a terrific father.'

He smiled at the compliment. 'It feels as if there is still so much to say. And yet,' he paused, 'it seems to me that at the end of a man's life, it should all have been said and done.'

Dina had no answer to that. She could not bear to think that her father had reached the 'end'.

'Dina . . . the children . . . they're all here?'

'Yes, Daddy, they're all here.'

'Send them in to me, would you? I'd like to see them.'

Dina sat for a moment longer. She would not say it. She would not say 'goodbye'. Instead she kissed her father on both cheeks and whispered. 'I love you. Daddy.'

He smiled again and said: '*Allah ma'ek, elbe.*' God be with you, my heart.

While the children were seeing their grandfather, Dina sat across her mother's kitchen table, gratefully sipping the strong Colombian coffee Charlotte had brewed.

'He knew,' Charlotte said. 'No matter what we

393

told him, I think he knew that you were in serious trouble.' She dried her eyes with her delicate lace handkerchief.

'He didn't believe the story I told him?'

Charlotte shook her head. 'He didn't say, but I'm sure he knew there was more to it than what you told him. I think he just held on until he knew you were all right. He wouldn't leave us until he knew you had your children. The day you brought them over, he said to me: "Now I can rest." '

A short time later, the children came into the kitchen. Their expressions were solemn. Suzy asked: 'Is Grandpa going to die?'

Dina wanted to answer; she could not. Charlotte took Suzy in her arms and said gently: 'Yes, my sweet, he is. Grandpa has been very sick and soon he won't be sick any more. But he'll always be with you, children. You'll remember how much he loved you, and that way you'll always have him . . .' Tears choked Charlotte's attempt at comfort and she began to sob into her handkerchief. Dina got up and embraced her mother and her daughter. Then she reached out for her boys and held them very close.

Joseph Hilmi died later that day, just one week after Ali had returned home.

The obituary in *The New York Times* described him as a successful businessman, a worker for peace, a husband, father and grandfather.

Dina's friends came to her at home without being asked. Sarah and Em took turns sleeping over, just as they had when the children were gone.

To Sarah's great surprise, Rachel volunteered to help take care of the twins. And to visit with Jordy.

Sarah tried not to show her surprise. 'Thank you,' she told her daughter. 'That's a very nice thing to do.'

Did Rachel's expression soften just a little bit – or was it Sarah's imagination? It was a good moment and Sarah tucked it away in her memory – to be recovered when things were not so good.

Dina debated whether or not to tell Karim about her father's death or simply to wait until he made one of his regular calls to the twins. She decided that she should: Karim had, after all, been genuinely fond of her father, right until the end.

'Is there anything I can do?' he asked when Dina phoned.

'I don't think so,' she said, 'but thank you.' She thought for a moment. 'Maybe you can talk to the twins.'

'I'll do that,' he said, then: 'Are you all right, Dina? I know how much you loved him.'

Yes, she thought, you do know. You shared my past, all that history. And now there's no one in my life who will know me as you did. 'I'll be all right,' she said. 'It's not so good now, but . . .'

'Yes,' he said softly, 'I know.'

Karim spoke to the twins for a long time. Dina heard the sound of sniffling during the conversation, but Suzy and Ali seemed to be calmer after they hung up. They need him, Dina reminded herself, they still need him in their lives, even if I don't.

The funeral was a simple one, as Joseph would have wanted. It was held at St Joseph's on lower Sixth Avenue, the church that he and Charlotte had attended for half a century. The small church was packed with mourners: friends, neighbors, business colleagues, and a few old timers from the State Department. Charlotte did not trust herself to speak a eulogy without weeping, so she asked Dina to perform that task. Though Dina prepared an entire page of notes, when she got up to speak, the words on the paper seemed dry and lifeless and not like the man she had known. So instead she talked of her father's great love for his family and his two countries – the one he had adopted and the one he had left behind. 'Before he died, my father dreamed of seeing Beirut one last time. He dreamed of being reunited with the parents who died many years ago. I pray now that his dream came true, that he rests now in their tender embrace – and that he was somehow able to see the places he loved once again.' When Dina finished her speech, there was the sound of weeping throughout the church.

The buffet lunch that Charlotte served featured her husband's favorite dishes. It had been catered by a small restaurant in Brooklyn and included a lavish *mezze*, as well as grape leaves stuffed with rice and lamb, baked *kibbeh* – stuffed squash, and trays of *baklawa* filled with pistachio nuts and dripping with syrup.

Em and Sarah stayed close to Dina, ready to step in if she needed their support. Jordy kept an eye on the twins and saw to it that they were fed and cared for. More than once, when she glanced in their direction, Dina saw Rachel hovering at Jordy's side.

Dina had no appetite for the food or the drink. When she noticed that her mother was not in sight, she went into the kitchen, then into her parents' bedroom. Charlotte was there, staring out the window.

'Oh, Dina,' she said when she saw her daughter, 'what are we going to do without him?'

'I've been asking myself that same question.'

'I still feel him here. If I can always do that, maybe it won't be so bad.' She paused. 'I didn't want him to leave me, you know. I wanted him to stay, even when he was in pain, even when he suffered. But that last day, I sat with him, and I said, "It's OK, Joe, you've done so much for all of us, you can go whenever you want." He smiled at me and said, "Thank you, my love, thank you." He thanked me, Dina – for letting him know it was all right to die.' Charlotte began to cry again, and Dina wept with her, cradling her mother's head on her shoulder.

This was something they would both endure. They would grieve together, yet separately. Dina for the man who had made her world a safe and comfortable place for so many years, who above all others had made her feel loved and cherished. And Charlotte for the man who had shared her life and her bed for half a century.

The family counseling helped a little. The therapist, a Dr Hollister, saw Dina and the children once a week as a family; she saw Dina and Jordy on their own as needed. The twins spoke of their sadness and confusion and Jordy of his isolation.

'It's going to take time for the twins to regain a sense of stability,' Dr Hollister told Dina. 'They've suffered two grievous losses. They know that their lives have changed, but they don't really understand why.' She hesitated. 'You are being careful to support their love for their father. That's very important when a marriage breaks up.'

Dina looked hard at the therapist. 'Well, I'm certainly not bad-mouthing him in their presence, if that's what you're asking. I've explained that even though Karim and I are divorcing, he will always be their father.'

Dr Hollister shook her head. 'Not the same thing, Mrs Ahmad. No, what I mean is that even at their young age, they understand that there has been a conflict between their parents. They hear about divorce in school, they seem to understand that it will happen to them. And by "happen to them", I mean exactly that.'

'So what do you suggest that I'm not doing now?'

'Make it all right for them to say what they're feeling. Try not to take it as a criticism of you. For example, if they say, they hate divorce, let them know that of course, they would hate it. Make sure they know that it's OK to miss their father, to wish that he was at home with them. From what you've told me, he was a good father – so why wouldn't they miss him?'

Dina nodded. Whatever it took, she vowed, whatever she could do, she would do.

'And don't lose heart,' the therapist added. 'When the children act out, and they will, understand that it's part of the process. They need to grieve . . . they've lost something very precious. An intact family.'

'Are you telling me they'll be permanently damaged by the divorce?'

Dr Hollister shook her head. 'I've never subscribed to the theory that children of divorce are irrevocably damaged, though some of my colleagues would disagree. Divorce is a fact of life for so many families. What happens during and after the divorce is key. I believe it's possible to rebuild and reconstruct a family that's loving and close. If you focus on that as your goal, I believe you can achieve it.'

Yes, Dina thought, yes. That is my goal and I will achieve it.

CHAPTER SIXTY-ONE

Christmas season in New York. Snow and sleet and biting cold. Red-faced tourists informed each other that if they'd known the city could be this cold and crowded, they'd have stayed in Dallas or Omaha. New Yorkers planned festive holiday parties or trips to country homes where they could celebrate in peace.

Dina had spent every Christmas for twenty years with Karim. Though it was 'her' holiday and not his, Karim had always been respectful of her wish to give the children a traditional Christmas. His absence made her realize how accustomed she had become to the seasonal routine into which they had fallen. Over those two decades they had gradually established an informal yet somewhat predictable pattern of parties, Christmas music concerts at the Met, and perhaps a long weekend in New England enjoying an old-favorite country inn. Everything, right down to the food and drinks, fit into the pattern.

Now it all felt disconcertingly, yet pleasantly free-form. Those of her social acquaintances who had been primarily Karim's friends or business associates had vanished from her personal radar screen. She decided to give a Christmas Eve dinner party. It was important, she felt, to make the holiday as festive as she could, different from the way it had been with Karim, but good all the same.

The guest list was short: Sarah and David, Em and Gabe (who was back in her life in some not-yet-defined way), one or two other couples, her manager, Eileen, and a few other singles. And John Constantine, who had become a steady and not-yet-defined presence in Dina's life. He was the last to arrive, which made her smile; apparently he saw no need for punctuality when he wasn't on a mission. He wore a dark business suit under his overcoat; it was a new look for him and the effort pleased her.

He filled the door with his broad shoulders, his arms loaded with presents. 'Merry Christmas, Dina. It's good to see you.'

'You too, John.' It was.

Her passed her the gifts. 'Suzanne, Ali, Jordan. And you.' The packages for the children were professionally wrapped. Hers looked decidedly amateurish.

'Did that one myself,' said Constantine.

'I suspected something like that,' she said. 'Let me put the packages under the tree. Say hello to everybody. The kids are . . . somewhere. Em's in the kitchen. I have no idea what Sarah's doing.'

She was still arranging the packages under the tree when he rejoined her. 'Did I hear Em right?' he said. 'The turkey is deep-fried?'

'It's a Louisiana thing. Don't worry, you'll like it.'

She pointed to a shinily wrapped gift. 'That one's for you.' Having no better idea, she had bought a bottle of his favored Black Bush.

He eyed the shape of the package. 'I have my suspicions about its contents.'

'Well, you're a professional investigator, after all.'

'Yeah, I am.' The corner-of-the-mouth smile she had come to like. 'Are we going to open the presents tonight?'

'No. You can open yours if you want. We open presents Christmas morning. Anyway, I think there's something very similar to yours in the liquor cabinet.'

He seemed in no hurry, taking in the room, the tree, and her. 'This is nice, Dina. It's been a while since I did Christmas.'

'It is nice, isn't it?' And I am lucky, she thought. To have my family, my friends. Christmas. 'I feel bad about our dinner out,' she said. The hecticness of the holiday preparations had caused her to cancel their more-or-less regular monthly 'date'.

'No problem,' he said quickly, then more slowly: 'We could make up for it on New Year's. Dinner. Bubbly. Watch the ball come down. Can't promise dancing, you'd probably be better off with a trained bear.'

'I don't know,' she said. It was true. She didn't know if she was ready for a late-night New Year's Eve with John Constantine. 'I'll probably be asleep by ten o'clock.'

He thought it over, nodded. 'OK. But I'll give you a call between now and then, in case you change your mind. It's not like I've made other plans,' he added meaningfully.

Just then Sarah bubbled up to say that they were putting the food on the table. It was, from Dina's point of view, good timing.

As he had been the last to arrive, Constantine was among the last to leave. It was the first moment he and

Dina had been alone together since their conversation early in the evening. He stood in the doorway cradling the gift-wrapped Black Bush.

'I really enjoyed tonight, Dina. I mean it.'

'So did I. I'm glad you could come.'

'Don't forget that New Year's idea.'

'I'm not sure if it's the right time,' she said.

'Sure.'

They both stood there.

'There's something I should have told you before,' she said.

'What's that?'

'Just thanks. For everything you did.'

He shook his head. 'Hey, you thanked me. And paid me. Even though I didn't really accomplish anything.'

'No, that's just it. It wouldn't have happened without you. None of it. Getting Suzanne back. Finding Ali – then getting him back too. I just want you to know how grateful I am.'

He made a think-nothing-of-it gesture, obviously uncomfortable with the praise. 'Nah. It was you. You made it happen. You just don't know how special you are.' He turned up the collar of his overcoat. 'I better go. Hope you like your present.' He grinned mischievously. 'They say it's always a mistake for a guy to buy a woman a hat, but hey, I think I know your taste.'

'A hat?'

' 'Night, Dina.' He leaned down and kissed her lightly, then whispered in her ear. 'Merry Christmas.' And with another grin, he was gone.

An hour later, with all of the guests vanished and the children asleep, she sat with a last glass of wine before turning out the lights. A hat. What could the man have been thinking? The clumsily wrapped package sat under the tree. She wasn't about to spend half the night wondering about it. She opened it.

A New York Mets cap.

The note said, 'Don't give this one to a man in Amman. Merry Christmas.'

In the soft, multicolored glow of the Christmas lights, she smiled.

Dina endured serious telephone cross-examinations from both Sarah and Em the next day, but she declined to categorize John as her 'new boyfriend'. 'It's nothing like that,' she insisted, but without much conviction. Though she wasn't ready for a 'boyfriend' and all that involved, she couldn't deny the attraction. Still, romance would have to wait until she was certain her family was whole again.

She spent a great deal of time with Suzanne and Ali. It was as if almost losing them had made her treasure them even more than before – something she wouldn't have thought possible. For a time after the Jordanian episode, they had seemed to regress to being much younger children: bad dreams, small problems at school, insecurities surfacing every time Dina had to go out and leave them with someone else.

Dr Hollister had assured Dina this was normal; the twins would have to learn to trust that Dina would always return. This was not something she could accomplish with assurances alone; she would have to prove it by being there again and again, over a very long period of time. The same was true of her relationship with Jordy. It was not enough to say she was sorry for not having the courage to stand up for him; she would have to show him in a hundred and one ways how much she loved and accepted him.

When she had told the twins that she and their father soon would no longer be married, they absorbed the news sadly but calmly, almost resignedly. Clearly they had already considered this possibility together, whether in actual words or in their seemingly extrasensory twin-to-twin communication. In fact the divorce proceedings were moving forward rapidly.

With great reluctance – for he did not like to handle divorces for friends – David Kallas had agreed to represent Dina. He was as calm and methodical as she knew he would be, and Dina knew she was in the best possible hands. Karim was not contesting the divorce itself, and under the circumstances, it was certain that Dina would be awarded physical custody of the children.

Money was not an issue either. Karim, through his lawyer, had offered an alimony and child-support package that Dina considered more than adequate. David assured her that he could get more, possibly much more, if that was what she desired, but Dina had no desire either to punish Karim or to engage him in battle. She told David to accept the offered amount if everything else was satisfactory. 'Everything else' was access to the twins. Karim's attorney was requesting visitation rights, details to be worked out, whenever Karim was in New York, plus two separate weeks per year in which the twins would travel to Jordan. David said that the latter was a non-starter, given what Karim had done. Dina agreed. Maybe in two years or three, they could look at the situation again. For now, no. That left the question of visits in New York.

'We can make a strong case for supervised visitation,' David had told her. 'And considering the history here, that's what I would recommend.'

Dina had expected him to suggest this – in fact, it was she who had raised the possibility, in one of their first conferences. But somehow, as time went by, she had grown more and more uncomfortable with the idea. The picture of Suzanne and Ali seeing a father who was being watched like some paroled felon was not appealing. It felt wrong. And some intuition told her that Karim was unlikely to repeat his mistake.

'I don't know,' she had told David. 'Do I have to decide now?'

'Not now,' he said. 'But soon.'

So that was one big item she had on her mind. Another was Jordy. The twins hero-worshiped him, and he was an indulgent and protective big brother to them. But occasionally he stayed out very late. On some of those nights he visited Rachel; they watched videos, ate pizza and talked, according to Sarah. On other nights he apparently had other friends. Or maybe just one other friend. It was difficult to talk with him about it. Any question either put him into an instant silence or elicited an all-too-facile explanation that in turn could not be questioned without bringing out anger. She wondered how she would handle it if she knew that he was seeing a girlfriend – or a woman friend – on those unexplained nights. She asked John Constantine about it.

'It's your house,' he had said. 'You make the rules. As long as he lives there, he follows the rules.'

But it wasn't that simple. Jordy wasn't a kid. He was approaching legal age and he clearly had a mind of his own. If she laid down the law, would he accept it? Or when he left for college, would he simply not come back? And what would that do to Suzanne and Ali?

She was debating exactly these questions over

coffee and the computer one morning when the phone rang.

It was Karim.

They had spoken briefly whenever he called to talk with the children. Coolly, not cordially, but not angrily either. It was as if their mutual fear over Ali had made blame and recrimination seem a little silly.

'I tried the shop,' he said. He had always referred to her business as 'the shop', as if it were some storefront establishment selling bouquets and potted plants. 'They told me you were here.'

'I work at home a lot these days. In fact I was just checking the payables and receivables.'

'Ah. Computers.'

'What's wrong?'

'Wrong? Nothing.'

'You said you tried to get me at work.'

'Ah. Well, I'm in the city.'

'New York?'

'Yes.'

She digested this information in silence.

'I wanted to let you know,' Karim said. 'And see if I could stop by sometime. I'm here for a few days.'

'Stop by?' The question sounded stupid. Maybe it was. She had no experience of this sort of thing. She felt a little stunned.

'To see the children. And you. Talk. You know.'

'The twins aren't here right now.'

'Well, later. As I said, I'm here for a few days. Where are they?'

'What do you mean?'

'You said they aren't there.'

'Classes.' A mistake – he must know that this was their school holiday, but his questions had made her nervous. He didn't need to know where Suzanne and Ali were. 'So you're here on business, or what?'

'Yes, business. It looks as if I may be here rather often. Which is one thing I wanted to talk with you about. Is there a time when I can come by? When the twins are there?'

'No. I don't think that's a good idea.'

'Why not?' He sounded genuinely mystified. Then injured: 'I mean, Dina, you don't intend to keep me from seeing my – our – children, do you?'

'My lawyer tells me that there should be no visits of any kind until visitation rights are settled.' She was lying. She and David had not discussed this specific point. But it sounded good.

'Well, I . . .' There was indignation in his voice. For a moment Dina expected his temper to erupt. But then she heard a defeated sigh. 'All right. I guess that's the way it has to be. Lawyers. God.'

'I'm sorry,' Dina said, surprised that she actually was. She didn't want to deny Karim the children. And surely he wouldn't try the same thing again. But she wasn't ready to take the chance. Not yet.

'Well, what if I come by to see you, then?' he said. 'Or we can meet somewhere. Just to talk.'

She thought it over. She wondered if she should call David first. 'All right,' she said.

'I can come over right now, if that's convenient.'

'No. I've got a meeting with a client.' That much was true. In fact, she needed to get moving. It was a major prospective account, and being late for it would not make a good impression. 'Later. Say two o'clock.' She would make arrangements for the children. Perhaps Jordy and Rachel could take them to a movie or to see the tree in Rockefeller Center.

'Well. Yes. Two o'clock. Yes, I can do that.'
'All right.'
'See you then.'
He hung up.

Karim, unusually for an Arab, had always been a stickler for punctuality. The doorbell rang at exactly two.

'Hello, Dina.'

'Hello.' A pause. 'Come in.' There was an awkwardness to it, inviting him into the house they had shared for so long.

He followed her to the living room. He looked good. He had lost a few pounds, the forty-something paunch he had begun to develop in spite of his usual exercise regimen. Maybe he was doing even more. Or maybe he had a new woman in his life. She wasn't about to mention it.

'You look good, Dina.' He meant it. She wasn't the girl he had married. Or she was, but she was also better.

'Thanks.'

'So. The kids are taking classes during their holiday?'

Another pause. 'Yes. Art classes at the museum.' That was the truth at least, though there were no classes today.

'But you said you're working at home a lot now?'

'Quite a bit. But I have to go in sometimes, and there are meetings, like this morning.'

'It went well?'

'What went well?'

'The meeting.'

'Oh. Yes. I think I got the account.'

'Ah. Well, good.'

A silence.

Karim had the strangest feeling of experiencing the past in the present. There was something about Dina that reminded him deeply of the first time he had seen her. It struck him that this thing was an aura of unattainability. He had been smitten the moment he laid eyes on her, but at the same moment he had laughed at himself for dreaming an impossible dream. She was too beautiful, too much her own creature, even for a man like him. But he felt the same desire, then as now. A physical reaction, almost as if he were that smitten young man again.

It wouldn't do, he thought. He had lost her. She was unattainable for the second time. But then, considering the first time . . . Don't be an idiot, Karim, he told himself. You'll only make her despise you. If she doesn't already. He cleared his throat. 'I think I mentioned that I might be in New York fairly often. In fact, it seems certain.' He waved vaguely. 'War on terror, politics . . . all that has affected aircraft procurement. I'll need to be here and in Washington. So – I'm looking for an apartment.'

'Really.'

'Yes.'

'*How* often?'

'It's hard to say. Maybe once a month. For a week or so. And once we work out the details of the children – I mean, we *will* work out something, of course – then it seems good for me to have a place, a settled place, not some hotel or something, where they can spend their time with me when I'm here.'

'Well, yes. That makes sense.' Dina had the odd feeling that they were really carrying on two different conversations. On one level they were divorcing parents talking about the children. On another, Karim was looking at her very much as he did that night in the garden in Amman. And on one level she liked this. And on another it left her cold as marble.

'Good. We agree on this, then.'

'Sure.'

Feelings were tumbling over Karim. He felt as if he were in an aircraft whose controls were not functioning properly. He had made a mistake, he knew, although he couldn't say that he had been wrong: he had done what he thought was best. But what he thought was best had turned out differently than he had expected. The controls snapped completely. 'I wonder, Dina, if we could see each other sometime. I mean, not just when I see the children. I'm not talking about, you know . . .' He was babbling, he realized. 'Just have dinner together or something. Talk. Maybe everything isn't . . .' He had started to say *hopeless* but caught himself just in time. 'I mean, so many things now . . . your working at home, all that, this is what I . . .' He caught himself again. He had almost said *wanted all along.*

Dina heard the words he didn't say. She felt as if she were standing at a fork in a road – she could almost see the diverging paths. One answer would unfold in one way over the years ahead, another would lead to a completely different set of circumstances. A completely different life.

'No, Karim,' she said.

He stared at her. He knew her now. Knew her better than he had ever known her before. Knew that he had lost.

'Well,' he finally said. 'I should be going. I only

411

wanted to tell you . . . you know, about my plans.'

'Well, thanks. That's good.' She stood. He did too.

'I'll let you know about the apartment. The address. Phone number. All that.'

'Good. And I'll tell the kids that you came by. That you'll see them soon.'

'Oh, yes, good. Dina, I—'

There was the sound of the front door opening and clumping shut. They both recognized the footsteps before they heard the voice. 'Hey, Mom. It's me.'

Jordan.

And then he was standing before them, his expression first surprised, then quickly blank. 'Oh,' he said. Nothing more.

Karim regarded his son. It had been nine or ten months since he had seen him last. The boy had grown. He was taller than Karim now. A strong-looking young man. Hard to believe that . . . Karim forced the thought from his mind. He knew that he had been right, morally right, right in his heart, but was it so important to be right? At this moment Jordan had his mother's expression – cool, unreachable. And yet he looked so much like Karim. People had always commented on it, and Karim saw it very clearly now; it was almost like looking at a picture of himself as a teenager.

Dina said, 'Your father was just—'

'I just dropped by to say that I would be in New York more often,' said Karim. 'I . . .' He couldn't formulate his thoughts. There were things he wanted to say, but the words weren't there. 'I know that . . .' There was so much he had lost. He didn't want to lose this one more thing, although it might be lost already.

'Look, Jordy, things . . . went wrong. A lot of things. Maybe someday, if we could . . . if you and I . . .'

Karim felt tears welling. Where were the words to tell his son what he was feeling? He swallowed hard and held out his hand.

Jordy looked directly into Karim's eyes. Man to man. He straightened up, losing the schoolboy slouch. Then he reached out, took his father's hand and shook it, his grip strong and sure.

Thank God, Karim thought, thank God for this.

MIRAGE
By Soheir Khashoggi

In this passionate, spellbinding story of one young woman's fight for freedom, Soheir Khashoggi takes us into the hidden world of the Middle Eastern aristocracy and exposes the reality of life behind the veil for women in today's harems.

Despite her fairytale childhood of extravagant wealth and royal privilege, Amira accepts that she will be sold into marriage and that she will never be able to step outside her house without being swathed in black veils. But she is not prepared for the savagery of the husband she first meets on her wedding night, or the increasingly abusive control he exerts over her. In a daring attempt to save her life and her sanity, she escapes with her baby to start a new life in the United States where she discovers true love, as well as a fulfilling career. Yet Amira must always live with the terrifying threat of her past – and her ruthless husband – catching up with her.

Mirage is a powerful story of love and revenge. It is also a moving tribute to the strength and endurance of women who defy the yoke of male dominance.

'One of those rare books on Middle Eastern women that is lively, provocative and thought-provoking'
Jean Sasson, author of *Princess*

'Stunning! I couldn't put it down! Lifts the veil of secrecy from Muslim traditions, relationships and, above all, family ties'
Judith Gould, author of *Sins*

A Bantam Paperback
0 553 50486 X

NADIA'S SONG
By Soheir Khashoggi

Brought up on his father's cotton plantation in Alexandria, Charles Austen had always led a privileged life. But when Charles falls hopelessly in love with Karima Ismail, his world is turned upside down. For although beautiful, and blessed with a magnificent singing talent, Karima is merely a servant and her forbidden love affair with Charles is destined to end in tragedy.

All too soon Karima is forced to accept a hastily arranged marriage and learns to live contentedly with her husband and daughter, Nadia, the only tangible link that remains between her and Charles. In time, she also becomes one of the most admired and successful singers of her generation – the adored 'Nightingale'.

Yet Karima's success counts for nothing when Nadia suddenly disappears. For years this traumatic event casts a shadow over Karima's life and the life of her beautiful daughter who, with a new identity and a new name, grows up thousands of miles away. It is only when an unexpected chain of events leads 'Gaby' back to Egypt, that she can begin to unravel the mystery of her past – and discover the happiness she longs for.

'Soheir Khashoggi has smoothly combined meticulous historical accuracy with intense insight into the human heart'
Jean Sasson, bestselling author of *Princess*

'Utterly enthralling . . . Khashoggi grips the imagination'
Daily Mail

A Bantam Paperback
0 553 81186 X

A SELECTED LIST OF FINE WRITING AVAILABLE FROM TRANSWORLD

99065	5	THE PAST IS MYSELF	*Christabel Bielenberg*	£7.99
99469	3	THE ROAD AHEAD	*Christabel Bielenberg*	£7.99
50650	1	BOUND FEET AND WESTERN DRESS	*Pang-Mei Natasha Chang*	£7.99
14239	5	MY FEUDAL LORD	*Tehmina Durrani*	£6.99
13928	9	DAUGHTER OF PERSIA	*Sattareh Farman Farmaian*	£6.99
60439	4	FORBIDDEN LOVE (hardback)	*Norma Khouri*	£10.99
13356	6	NOT WITHOUT MY DAUGHTER	*Betty Mahmoody*	£6.99
81302	1	LA PRISONNIERE	*Malika Oufkir*	£6.99
81195	9	SORROW MOUNTAIN	*Ani Pachen and Adelaide Donnelley*	£6.99
50486	X	MIRAGE	*Soheir Khashoggi*	£6.99
81186	X	NADIA'S SONG	*Soheir Khashoggi*	£6.99
13953	X	SOME OTHER RAINBOW	*John McCarthy & Jill Morrell*	£7.99
40805	4	DAUGHTERS OF ARABIA	*Jean P Sasson*	£6.99
40570	5	PRINCESS	*Jean P Sasson*	£6.99
81218	1	DESERT ROYAL	*Jean P Sasson*	£6.99
99988	1	BEFORE THE KNIFE: MEMORIES OF AN AFRICAN CHILDHOOD	*Carolyn Slaughter*	£6.99
81532	6	CUBA DIARIES	*Isadora Tattlin*	£6.99
50545	9	RED CHINA BLUES	*Jan Wong*	£7.99
81306	4	A LEAF IN THE BITTER WIND	*Ting-Xing Ye*	£8.99